SUNSET EMBRACE

SANDRA BROWN

WARNER BOOKS

A Time Warner Company

WARNER BOOKS EDITION

Copyright © 1985 by Sandra Brown
All rights reserved.

This Warner Books Edition is published by arrangement with the author.

Cover illustration by Max Ginsburg
Cover design by Jackie Merri Meyer
Hand lettering by Dave Gatti

Warner Books, Inc.
666 Fifth Avenue
New York, N.Y. 10103

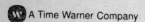 A Time Warner Company

Printed in the United States of America

First Warner Books Printing: June, 1990

10 9 8 7 6

*He knew then he was
going to kiss her and
there wasn't a damn thing
he could do about it.*

At first Ross merely touched his lips to hers.
Her fingers curled tighter into his chest. He
waited until he could deny himself no longer.
Then, tilting her head farther back to accommodate him, he rubbed his lips against hers
until they parted.

His heart was pounding erratically, but he
didn't rush. He hesitated, taking time to breathe
in the flavor of her breath.

The wake of another boat on the river caused
the ferry to wobble. They lost their balance.
Ross was on his knees, and when Lydia fell
back against a pile of bedding his body followed
hers down.

When his mouth aligned with hers again, instinct took over. He was totally lost in the kiss,
in her. She made him forget everything...

Also by Sandra Brown

Mirror Image
Best Kept Secrets
Slow Heat In Heaven*

* Published by
POPULAR LIBRARY

SUNSET EMBRACE

Chapter One

Why has God made it so painful to die? the young woman wondered.

, She gripped her distended abdomen as another pain tore through her lower body and shimmied down her thighs. When it was over, she panted laboriously, like a wounded animal, trying to garner strength for the next assault, which she knew would seize her within minutes. Undoubtedly it would come, because she didn't think she would be allowed to die before the baby was born.

She shivered convulsively. The rain was cold, each drop a tiny needle that pricked her skin, and it had soaked through the tattered dress and the few undergarments she had managed to hold together with clumsy knots. The rags clung to her like a damp shroud, a cloying weight that anchored her to the marshy ground as securely as did the relentless pain. She was chilled to the bone, but perspiration had clammily glazed her skin after endless hours of painful labor.

When had it begun? Last night just after sunset. Through the night, the ache in the lower part of her back had intensified until it crawled farther around her middle to twist her womb between angry fists. Cloud-obscured skies made it difficult to determine the time of day, but she guessed it to be midmorning by now.

She concentrated on the leafy pattern of the tree limbs against the gray sky overhead as the next contraction wrung her insides. The rainy clouds scuttled by, heedless of the woman barely twenty years old lying alone in the Tennes-

1

see wilderness, giving birth to a being she didn't want to think of as a baby, even as human.

She turned her cheek sideways into her bed of sodden, rotted leaves, remnants of last fall, and let her tears mingle with the rain. Her baby had been conceived out of shame and humiliation and deserved no happier occasion than this to be born.

"Sweet Jesus, let me die now," she prayed as she felt another abdominal upheaval rolling through her. Like the summer thunder, it rumbled inside her, gaining impetus before crashing against the walls of her body, just as the thunder seemed to collide with the mountainsides. The pain echoed through her as the thunderclap reverberated through the foothills.

Last evening she had tried to ignore the pains and had kept walking. When water had gushed between her thighs, she had been forced to lie down. She hadn't wanted to stop. Each day meant another few miles' distance between her and the body that surely had been discovered by now. She hoped it would decay and never be found, but really didn't expect such a piece of luck.

This merciless pain she was suffering now was no doubt God's punishment for being glad to see one of His creatures die. That, and her wanting no part of the life she had carried in her womb for nine months. Despite the sinfulness of it, she prayed that she would never see the life struggling so hard to be expelled from her body. She prayed that she would die first.

The next seizure was the most vicious of all and brought her to a half-sitting position. Last night, when her bloomers had been ruined by the pinkish flood, she had taken them off and cast them aside. Now she picked the garment up and mopped her rain- and sweat-soaked face with it. She trembled uncontrollably, as much out of fear as pain. She had felt herself tearing with that last rebellion of her body. Gathering the frayed hem of her dress and the cobwebby remains of her petticoat up over her raised knees, she tentatively lowered her hand between her legs and touched the spot.

"Ohhh . . ." she whimpered, and began to weep. She was open, stretched wide. Her fingertips had touched the babe's head. Her hand came away covered with blood and slime. Her mouth opened with terror, but the sound that issued out was a piercing wail of agony as her body strained and squeezed, trying to eliminate the being that had become foreign matter after being snugly harbored for nine months.

She levered herself up on her elbows, spread her thighs wide, and bore down with the pressure. Blood pounded against her eardrums and behind eyes that were squeezed shut. Her jaws ached from clenching them; her lips were peeled back into a gruesome mask. During a brief respite, she huffed precious air in and out of her lungs. Then the pain came again. And again.

She screamed, expending the last of her energy on one final thrust, funneling all her body's weight to that one narrow place that rent in two.

And then she was free of it.

She fell back exhausted, gulping air and grateful now for the raindrops that coolly bathed her face. There was no sound in the thick forest save for the bellowslike heaving of her lungs and the rain dripping heavily. The absence of sound was eerie, startling, strange. There had been no bursting cry of life from the baby she had just birthed, no movement.

Disregarding her earlier prayer, she struggled to sit up again and moved her long skirt aside. Animal sounds of grief and misery tripped over her bruised lips when she saw the infant, little more than a ball of bluish flesh, lying dead between her thighs without ever having known life. The cord that had nourished it had been its instrument of death. The ropy tissue was wound tightly around the baby's throat. Its face was pinched. It had taken a suicidal plunge into the world. The girl wondered if it had chosen to die, instinctively knowing that it would be despised even by its mother, preferring death to a life of degradation.

"At least, little one, you didn't have to suffer life," she whispered.

She fell back onto the spongy ground and stared sightlessly at the weeping sky, knowing that she was fevered and probably delirious, and that thoughts about

babies killing themselves in the womb were crazy. But it
made her feel better to think that her baby hadn't wanted to
live any more than she had wanted it to, that it had wanted
to die just as she did now.

She should pray for forgiveness at being glad for her
own infant's death, but she was too tired. Surely God would
understand. It had been He, after all, who had afflicted her
with such pain. Didn't she deserve to rest now?

Her eyes closed against the rain that poured over her
face like a healing balm. She couldn't remember a time
when she had known this kind of peace. She welcomed it.

Now she could die.

"You reckon she's dead?" the young voice croaked
hoarsely.

"I don't know," a slightly older voice whispered back.
"Poke her and see."

"I ain't a'gonna poke her. You poke her."

The tall, rangy boy knelt on bony knees next to the
prone, still figure. Carefully, as he had been taught by his
pa, he propped his rifle, barrel up, against the tree trunk.
His hands twitched nervously as he stretched them toward
the girl.

"You're scared, ain'tcha?" the younger boy challenged.

"No, I ain't scared," the older hissed back. Having to
prove it, he extended his index finger and placed it next to
the girl's upper lip, not quite touching her. "She's breathing," he said in relief. "She ain't dead."

"What do you reckon . . . godamighty, Bubba,
there's blood a'coming from under her dress."

Reflexively Bubba jumped back. His brother Luke was
right. A trickle of blood was forming a crimson pool beneath
the hem of her dress, which barely covered her knees. She
wasn't wearing stockings and the leather of her shoes was
cracked and peeling. The laces had been knotted together
after numerous breaks.

"You figure she's been gunshot or something? Maybe
we ought to look—"

"I know, I know," Bubba said impatiently. "Keep your
damn trap shut."

"I'm gonna tell Ma you're cussin' if—"

"Shut up!" Bubba whirled around to stare down his younger brother. "I'll tell her you peed in old lady Watkin's wash water after she got on to you 'bout makin' too much noise around the camp." Luke was properly cowed, and Bubba turned back to the girl. Gingerly, and disbelieving he had actually wanted to go hunting that morning, he lifted the hem of her ratty brown dress. "Hellfire," he shrieked, dropping the skirt and jumping to his feet. Unfortunately, the soiled cloth didn't fall back to cover the lifeless form lying between the girl's slender thighs. Both boys stared in horror at the dead infant. Luke made a strange sound in his throat.

"You gonna puke?" Bubba asked.

"No." Luke swallowed hard. "I don't think," he said with less assurance.

"Go get Ma. Pa, too. He'll have to carry her back to the wagon. Can you find your way back?"

"'Course," Luke said scornfully.

"Then get goin'. She could still die, ya know."

Luke cocked his head to one side and studied the young woman's pale face. "She's right fetchin' to look at. You gonna touch her any more while I'm gone?"

"Get goin'!" Bubba yelled, facing his brother with a threatening stance.

Luke thrashed his way noisily through the trees until he could safely call back a taunt. "I'll know if you look at somethin' you ain't supposed to. And I'll tell Ma."

Bubba Langston picked up a pinecone and hurled it at his brother, younger by two years. It fell short of its mark and Luke scampered away. When he was out of sight, Bubba knelt down beside the girl. He gnawed his lower lip before looking at the dead baby once again. Then, using only the tips of his index finger and thumb, he lifted the hem of her skirt and moved it to cover up the baby.

Sweat beaded his forehead, but he felt better when he couldn't see the baby anymore. "Lady," he whispered softly. "Hey, lady, can you hear me?" Fearfully he nudged her shoulder. She moaned and tossed her head to one side, then back again.

He had never seen such a head of hair on a person before. Even littered with twigs and leaves and damp with rain it was right pretty, curly and sort of wild looking. The color wasn't like any he had ever seen before either. Not quite red and not quite brown, but somewhere in between.

He took off the canteen suspended around his neck by a leather thong and uncapped it. "Lady, you want a drink?" Bravely, he pressed the metal spout to her flaccid lips and poured a small amount over them. Her tongue came out to lick up the moisture.

Bubba watched, fascinated, as her eyes fluttered open to gaze up at him vaguely. The girl saw a wide-eyed boy of about sixteen bending anxiously over her. His shock of hair was so light it was almost white. Was he an angel? Was she in heaven? If so, it was disappointingly like earth. The same sky, the same trees, the rain-laden forest. The same pain between her thighs. She wasn't dead yet! *No, no, boy, go away. I want to die.* She closed her eyes again and knew no more.

Afraid for the young woman's life, and feeling helpless, Bubba sank to the damp ground under the tree. His eyes never left her face until he heard the commotion of Ma and Pa pushing through the dense undergrowth in the full, lush bloom of early summer.

"What's all this Luke was blabbing about a girl, son?" Zeke Langston asked his eldest child.

"See, I told you, Ma, Pa," Luke said excitedly, pointing a finger. "There she be."

"Get out of my way, all of you, and let me see to this poor girl." Ma impatiently shoved the men aside and squatted down heavily beside the girl. First she brushed aside the damp hair clinging to the wan cheeks. "Right comely, ain't she? Wonder what in tarnation she's doing out here all alone."

"There's a babe, Ma."

Ma Langston looked up at Bubba, then at her husband, jerking her head in a silent signal that he distract the boys. When their backs were turned, Ma raised the dress to the girl's lap. She had seen worse, but this sight was grim enough. "Lord have mercy," she muttered. "Zeke, give me a hand here. You boys run on back to the wagon and tell Anabeth to fix a pallet up proper. Get a good fire goin' and put a kettle to boilin'."

Disappointed that they were going to miss the most interesting part of the adventure, they objected in unison. "But Ma—"

"Git, I said." Rather than incur their mother's wrath, which both had felt at the other end of a strop, they shuffled off toward the wagon train that was taking Sunday off to rest.

"She's in a bad way, ain't she?" Zeke asked, crouching down beside his wife.

"Yep. First thing is to get the afterbirth out. She may die of the poison anyway."

Silently they worked over the unconscious girl. "What should I do with this, Ma?" Zeke asked. He had wrapped nature's debris along with the dead infant in a knapsack and had bundled it tightly.

"Bury it. I doubt she'll be in any condition to visit a grave for several days. Mark the spot in case she wants to come back to see it."

"I'll put a boulder over it so the animals won't get to it," Zeke said solemnly and began to scoop out a shallow grave with the small spade he had brought with him. "How's the girl?" he asked when he was done, wiping his hands on a bandanna handkerchief.

"Still bleeding, but I've got her packed tight. We've done all we can do here. Can you carry her?"

"If you can help hoist her up."

The girl came to life and protested, flailing her arms weakly when Zeke hooked her under the knees and behind her back and lifted her to his thin chest. Then the slender limbs fell away and she went lifeless again. Her throat arched as her head fell back over his arm.

"Ain't her hair funny lookin', though," Zeke commented, not unkindly.

"Can't say I ever seen any that color before," Ma replied absently as she picked up the things they had brought with them. "We'd best hurry. It's startin' to rain again."

* * *

The place between her thighs burned. Her throat was scratchy and sore. She felt hot and achy all over. Yet there was a pervading sense of comfort surrounding her. She was dry and warm. Had she made it to heaven after all? Had the towheaded boy left her alone to die? Was that why she felt so safe and peaceful? But in heaven one wasn't supposed to know pain, and she was hurting.

She pried her eyes open. A white canvas ceiling curved above her. A lantern was burning low on a box near the pallet on which she was lying. She stretched her legs as much as the aching between them would allow, acquainting herself with the soft bed. Her feet and legs were naked, but she had been dressed in a white nightgown. Her hands moved restlessly over her body and she wondered why she felt so strange. Then she realized that her stomach was flat.

It all came back to her then in a wave of terrible memories. The fear, the pain, the horror of seeing the dead infant lying blue and cold between her legs. Tears pooled in her eyes.

"There, there, you ain't gonna start that cryin' again, are you? You been cryin' off and on in your sleep for hours."

The fingers that whisked the tears from her cheek were large, work-rough, and red in the soft glow of the lamp, but they felt good on her face. So did the voice that fell, full of gentle concern, on her ears. "Here, you ready for some of this broth? Made it from one of the rabbits the boys got this mornin' before they found you." The woman foisted a spoonful on the girl, who swallowed the rich liquid to keep from choking and discovered that it tasted good. She was hungry.

"Where am I?" she asked between swallows of the soup.

"In our wagon. Name's Ma Langston. Them was my boys that found you. You recollect any of that? You scared them half to death." She chuckled. "Luke's been tellin' the story all up and down the train. Did I mention we're with a wagon train of folks headin' to Texas?"

That was too much information to sort through at one time, so the girl concentrated on swallowing the broth. It was filling her stomach up warmly, enhancing the feeling of comfort and security. For weeks she had been fleeing, so fearful of pursuit that, except for a brief few days, she hadn't taken shelter, but had slept out in the open, eating what summer harvests she could gather in the woods.

The rawboned face that looked down at her was both stern and kind. Few would lose an argument to it, but few would know unkindness from it either. Sparse, mousy grayed brown hair was pulled back into a scraggly bun on the nape of her neck. She was a large woman with an enormous bosom that sagged to her thick waist. She was dressed in clean but faded calico. Her skin was etched with a tracery of fine lines, but, conversely, her cheeks were girlishly rosy. It was as though some benevolent god had viewed his handiwork, found it too harsh, and painted on those pink cheeks to soften the rough edges.

"Had enough?" The girl nodded. The woman set aside the tin bowl of broth. "I'd like to know your name," she said, her voice softening perceptibly, as though she sensed the forthcoming topic might not be welcomed.

"Lydia."

Jagged eyebrows arched in silent query. "That's right pretty all by itself, but don't it have nothin' to go with it? Who are your people?"

Lydia turned her head away. She envisioned her mother's face as she first remembered her from earliest childhood; beautiful and young, not the pale, vacuous face of a woman dying of despair. "Only Lydia," she said quietly. "I have no family."

Ma digested that. She took the girl's hand and shook it slightly. When the light brown eyes came back to her, she argued softly, "You birthed a babe, Lydia. Where's your man?"

"Dead."

"Ach! Ain't that a pity now."

"No. I'm glad he's dead."

Ma was perplexed but too polite and fearful for the girl's physical condition to pry further. "What were you doin' out there in the woods alone? Where were you headed?"

Lydia's narrow shoulders lifted in a negligent shrug. "Nowhere. Anywhere. I wanted to die."

"Hogwash! I ain't gonna let you die. You're too pretty to die." Ma roughly straightened the blanket over the frail body to cover the sudden emotion she felt for this strange girl.

She elicited Ma's pity. Tragedy was stamped all over the face that shone pale and haunted in the lantern light. "We, Pa and me, buried your baby boy in the woods." Lydia's eyes closed. A boy. She hadn't even noticed with that one glimpse of her child. "If you like, we can fall behind the train a few days and you can go see the grave when you feel up to it."

Furiously Lydia shook her head. "No. I don't want to see it." Tears escaped from under her eyelids.

Ma patted her hand. "I know what you're sufferin', Lydia. I've got seven young'uns, but I've buried two. It's the hardest thing a woman has to do."

No, it isn't, Lydia thought to herself. There are far worse things a woman has to do.

"You sleep some more now. I 'spect you've caught a chill lyin' out there in the woods thataway. I'll stay with you."

Lydia looked up into the compassionate face. It wasn't in her yet to smile, but her eyes softened in appreciation. "Thank you."

"You'll have plenty of time to thank me once you get well."

"I can't stay with you. I have to . . . go."

"You ain't gonna feel like goin' nowhere for a spell yet. You can stay with us as long as you can put up with us. All the way to Texas if you like."

Lydia wanted to argue. She wasn't fit to live with decent folks like this. If they knew about her, about . . . Her eyes dropped closed in sleep.

His hands were on her again, all over her. She opened her mouth to scream and his palm, salty and gritty, clamped over it. His other hand clawed at the neck of her chemise until it ripped open. Her breasts were squeezed by his hateful, clammy hand that derived pleasure from inflicting pain. She sank her teeth into the meat of his palm and was punished by a slap that left her ears ringing and her jaw throbbing.

"Don't you fight me, or I'll tell your prissy mama about us. You don't want her to know what we've been doin', now do you? I think that'd prob'ly send her right over the edge. I think she'd die if she knew I was breedin' you, don't you reckon?"

No, Lydia didn't want her mama to know. But how could she bear to let him do that to her again? Already he was grinding his hips against her thighs, forcing them to open. His fingers were poking at her painfully, probing abusively, hurtfully. And that loathsome appendage was driving into her flesh again. When she raked his face with her nails, he laughed and tried to kiss her. "I can take it rough if you can," he jeered.

She fought him. "No, no," she sobbed. "Take it out. No, no, no . . ."

"What is it, Lydia? Wake up. It's only a bad dream."

The soothing voice reached into the pit of hell where her nightmare had flung her and lifted her out. She was returned to the soft comfort of the Langstons' wagon.

It wasn't Clancey's rape that was hurting her, but the pain that had resulted from the birth of his baby. Oh, God, how could she go on living with the memory of Clancey's sexual abuse? She had had a baby by his foul seed and wasn't fit to live in the world any longer.

Ma Langston didn't think that way. As the girl gripped the sleeves of Ma's worn dress in fear of her nightmare, the older woman cradled Lydia's head against her deep bosom, murmuring soothing words. "It was only a dream. You have a touch of fever and that's given you nightmares, but nothin's gonna hurt you as long as you're here with me."

Lydia's terror subsided. Clancey was dead. She had seen him lying dead, blood pumping from his head to cover his ugly face. He couldn't touch her anymore.

Gratefully she let her head drop heavily on Ma's breast. When she was almost asleep, Ma laid her back on the lumpy pillow that felt like featherdown to Lydia. She had made her bed out of pine needles or hay during the past couple of months. Some nights she hadn't been that lucky, but had slept as well as she could propped against a tree trunk.

A sweet, black oblivion seduced her into its depths again as Ma continued to hold her hand.

Lydia awakened the next morning to the swaying of the prairie schooner. Cooking pots rattled with each rhythmic rotation of the wheels. Leather harnesses squeaked, their metal fasteners jingling merrily. Ma was calling instructions to the team of horses. She punctuated each direction with a crack of a whip. In nearly the same tone she kept up a lively dialogue with one of her offspring. Her chatter was both advisory and admonishing.

Lydia shifted uncomfortably on her bed and turned her head slightly. A white-haired girl with wide, curious blue eyes was sitting within touching distance, staring down at her.

"Ma, she's awake," she shouted. Lydia jumped at the sudden noise.

"Do as I told you," Ma called back into the wagon. "We can't stop now."

The girl looked back at the startled Lydia. "I'm Anabeth."

"I'm Lydia," she said scratchily. The back of her throat felt like a whetstone.

"I know. Ma told us that at breakfast and said not to call you 'the girl' anymore or she'd pop our jaws. Are you hungry?"

Lydia weighed her answer. "No. Thirsty."

"Ma said you'd be thirsty on account of the fever. I got a canteen of water and one of tea."

"Water first." Lydia drank deeply. She was amazed at how much energy it cost her and lay back weakly. "Maybe some tea later."

Life and all its functions were taken for granted by the Langstons. She was embarrassed when Anabeth slid a washbasin under her hips so she could relieve herself, but the girl was kind and matter-of-fact and seemed not the least bit bothered by having to empty it out the back of the wagon.

During the noon break, when the train halted for both man and beast to rest, Ma climbed into the wagon to change the pad of cloth she had secured between Lydia's thighs.

"The bleeding's not so bad. Your woman parts look like they're healin' fine, though you'll be sore for a few more days."

There was nothing crude about Ma's frankness, but it still embarrassed Lydia to have herself peered at that way. She was glad some sensibilities had remained intact considering where she had been living for the past ten years. Her mother must have ingrained some refinement in her before they had moved to the Russell farm. She knew most folks looked upon her as white trash by association. Nasty taunts had been flung in their direction whenever they went in to town, which mercifully wasn't often. Lydia hadn't understood all the words, but she learned to recognize and dread the insulting tone.

Time and again she had been embarrassed and had wanted to scream out that she and her mama weren't like the Russells. They were different. But who would have believed a dirty, ragged, barefoot girl? She had looked just as disreputable as the Russells, so she had been ridiculed too.

But apparently some people weren't so hasty to judge. The Langstons weren't. They hadn't minded her dirty, tattered clothes. They hadn't scorned her for having a baby without a husband. They had treated her like a respectable person.

She didn't feel respectable, but more than anything in the world, that's what she wanted to be. It might take years to shed the taint the Russells had smeared on her, but if she died trying, she would get rid of it.

During the day she met the Langston clan one by one. The two boys who had found her shyly ducked their heads into the wagon at their mother's introduction. "That there's my eldest, Jacob; but everybody calls him Bubba. The other one is Luke." "Thank you for helping me," Lydia said softly. No longer did she resent them for saving her life.

Things didn't seem so dismal now that she was rid of her last reminder of Clancey.

The towheaded boys blushed to the roots of their pale hair and muttered, "You're welcome."

Anabeth was a gregarious and energetic twelve-year-old. There was also Marynell, Samuel, and Atlanta, with barely a year between them. The baby, Micah, was a strapping three-year-old.

Zeke, whipping the hat off his balding head, spoke to her late that evening from the end of the wagon. "Glad to have you here, Miss . . . uh . . . Lydia." He smiled and Lydia noted that he had only two teeth in the front of his mouth.

"I'm sorry to put you to so much trouble."

"No trouble," he said dismissively.

"I'll get out of your way as soon as possible." She had no idea where she would go or what she would do, but she couldn't impose on this generous family who had so many mouths to feed already.

"Naw, now, you stop worryin' 'bout that. Git yourself fit and then we'll work somethin' out."

All the Langstons seemed to reflect that attitude. But Lydia wondered about the other members of the train. Surely there had been speculation on the girl who had been brought in after birthing a stillborn baby in the wilderness with no husband around. Ma had refused to admit even the kindest visitors who came to inquire about "the poor unfortunate girl," saying only that it looked like she was going to pull through and that they would be meeting her soon enough.

Lydia's first encounter with anyone on the wagon train other than a Langston came from a loud knocking on the slats of the wagon in the middle of the night. She sat bolt upright, clutching the sheet to her breasts, certain Clancey had risen from the dead and come after her.

"Easy, Lydia," Ma said, pressing her back down to the pillow.

"Ma Langston!" the impatient masculine voice called. A heavy fist thumped on the tailgate. "Ma, please. Are you in there?"

"Hellfire and damnation, what's all the hollerin' for?"

Lydia heard Zeke's grumble from outside the wagon. He and the boys slept in bedrolls beneath it.

"Zeke, Victoria's in labor. Could Ma come see to her?" The voice was husky, low, laced with anxiety. "She started feeling bad after supper. It's labor for sure, not just indigestion."

By this time Ma had crawled to the end of the wagon and shoved the canvas flaps aside. "Mr. Coleman? Is that you? You say your wife's in labor? I didn't think she was due—"

"I didn't either. She's . . ." Lydia heard the stark terror that vibrated in the man's voice. "She's in agony. Will you come?"

"I'm on my way." Ma turned back into the wagon and reached for her boots, pulling them on quickly. "You rest quiet now," she said to Lydia calmly and in contrast to her brisk movements. "Anabeth will be right here. She'll come flying if you need me." She lifted a crocheted shawl over her bulky shoulders. "Seems another babe is 'bout to be born."

Chapter Two

Ma hadn't returned by the time the wagons pulled out the next morning. Word filtered through the camp that Mrs. Coleman was still in labor, and that she had insisted the train not lose a day's travel on account of her. Bubba offered to drive for Mr. Coleman while Zeke drove the Langstons' wagon.

In Ma's absence, Anabeth, as eldest daughter, took over the cooking and care of the younger children. She tended Lydia with the same detached competence that her mother had. Lydia was amazed at the girl's knowledge of the birthing process.

"I'm sorry you have to do this for me," she apologized as Anabeth wadded up one of the soiled pads.

"Shoot, I done it for Ma her last two babies and I been having my monthlies since I was ten. It ain't nothin'."

When the train stopped at noon, Ma came back to inform them sadly that Mrs. Coleman had died only a half hour earlier after giving birth to a son.

"She was such a dainty little ol' thing. 'Course Mr. Coleman's acting like a madman, blamin' hisself for bringin' her on this trip. She'd told him she wouldn't be due until September, long after we reach Jefferson. It ain't his fault, but he's not takin' it too well."

"The babe?" Zeke asked around a dried, hard biscuit left over from breakfast.

"Puniest tyke you ever saw. Barely has enough in him to cry. Wouldn't surprise me none if his little soul departed this earth today." She heaved herself up into the wagon to speak to Lydia, who had overheard the family's conversation. "How're you doin', Lydia?"

"Fine, Mrs. Langston."

"Please call me Ma. Anabeth takin' care of you proper? I'm sorry I can't be here, but that little boy is in a bad way."

"Of course," Lydia murmured softly. "I'm fine. As soon as I'm able, I'll be off your hands."

"Not if I have anythin' to say about it. You sure you're feelin' all right? You look a mite flushed." She lay a calloused hand on Lydia's forehead. "Still feverish. I'll tell Anabeth to keep a cool cloth on your head this afternoon."

Lydia had a new discomfort, but didn't want to add to Ma's burdens, so she didn't mention her swelling, aching breasts. She dozed throughout the day, the train having stopped out of deference to Mr. Coleman. Anabeth fed her a hearty, if hasty, supper. Everyone was to gather after the evening meal to bury Mrs. Coleman.

The camp became quiet. Lydia lay in her bed, staring up at the canvas ceiling. She heard nothing of the gravesite ritual except the singing of "Rock of Ages." Surprising herself, she mouthed the words. How long had it been since she had been to church? Ten, twelve years? Yet she could remember the words to that hymn. That made her glad. She fell asleep smiling and didn't awaken even when the Langston clan trooped somberly back to the wagon.

The next day passed much as the previous one, but Lydia didn't feel as well. Her breasts had ballooned underneath the nightgown, and she tried to hide them whenever Anabeth tended her or brought her food or drink. They throbbed and felt full to bursting. She peeked into the nightgown and was alarmed to see that her nipples looked red and chafed. They were so sensitive, even the weight of the nightgown aggravated them.

Ma was still caring for the Coleman baby and didn't return until long after the children and Zeke had spread their sleeping rolls beneath the wagon. Anabeth, Marynell, and Atlanta were all sleeping soundly on the other side of the wagon. Lydia was awake, restless and aching. She was moaning softly when Ma climbed wearily into the wagon.

"Lord have mercy, Lydia, what's wrong? You poorly?" Ma bent over the young woman.

"I'm sorry. I . . . my bosom."

Ma wasted no time in opening the buttons of the nightgown and examining Lydia's milk-swollen breasts. "Land o' Goshen. I don't know what I've been thinkin' about. 'Course you got milk and it hurts if there's no babe—" She broke off abruptly and tilted her head to one side with the quick movement of a sparrow who has just sighted a worm.

"Come on, Lydia. You're coming with me."

"Where?" Lydia gasped as Ma pulled the covers off her and hauled her up. Her motions weren't rough, just efficient. "I don't have any clothes."

"It don't matter," Ma said, breathing laboriously as she gripped Lydia under the arms and helped her rise to a crouching position. "You got mother's milk and no babe, and there's a babe that's barely clingin' to life. He needs motherin'."

Ma planned to take her to that baby who had been crying almost ceaselessly for two days. The pitiable mewling sounds could even now be heard throughout the sleeping camp. Ma was taking her to that man with the frantic voice. She didn't want to go. She didn't want anyone gaping at her curiously and wondering why she had birthed her baby in the woods all alone. After knowing the cozy security of the Langstons' wagon, she was afraid to leave it.

But it seemed she had no choice in the matter. Ma slung a shawl over her shoulders and pushed her gently down the steps of the tailgate. "Those shoes of yours aren't much better than bare feet, so you'll just go without for the time being. Careful not to step on a rock."

The jolt when her feet hit the ground for the first time in days caused her to reel. The jostling hurt her breasts, which hung free beneath the nightgown that was her only garment save the crocheted shawl. Her hair hadn't been brushed. She knew it was a tangled, matted mess. Ma had bathed the blood and birth fluid from the insides of her thighs, but Lydia hadn't washed in days. She was so dirty.

Her heels dug into the soft, damp earth in protest. "Please, Ma, I don't want anyone to see me."

"Nonsense," Ma said resolutely, virtually dragging her by the arm toward the only wagon in the camp with a light burning inside it. "You might can save this babe's life. No one's gonna care how you look."

But they would. Lydia knew they would. She had been called white trash before. She knew just how mean people could be.

"Mr. Grayson," Ma called softly when they reached the lighted wagon. She flipped back the canvas hanging over the opening. "Give me some help here." She gave Lydia's backside a forward and upward push and the girl had no choice but to step up into the wagon. The tight skin between her thighs was stretched painfully and she winced. A pair of strong arms in blue shirt-sleeves reached out to help her inside. Ma was right behind her.

There was a moment of confusion as three strangers met face-to-face. The gray-haired man stared in wonder at the girl before him. The thin woman beside him gasped in surprise. Lydia dropped her eyes to avoid their startled stares.

"This here's Mr. Grayson, our wagonmaster," Ma said for Lydia's benefit.

Lydia kept her head bowed to stare at her dirty bare feet against the plank floor of the wagon and only nodded in acknowledgment of the introduction. "And that is Mrs. Leona Watkins." Ma was speaking in whispers out of respect for the man who was seated on a low stool, his dark head buried in his hands with his elbows propped on his knees.

It was the woman who spoke first. "Who in the world . . . and why is she gallivanting around virtually naked like that? Oh, this is the girl your boys found and brought in. I must say, I'm surprised you'd bring such a . . . a person . . . into this wagon, especially at a time like this. This is a death vigil and—"

"Maybe not," Ma snapped, her obvious dislike for the other woman evident in her voice. "Mr. Grayson, this girl had a babe day before yesterday. She's got milk. I thought that if Mr. Coleman's baby could suck—"

"Oh, my Lord," Mrs. Watkins exclaimed, distressed. From beneath her lashes, Lydia saw the woman raising a scrawny hand to a meager chest and clasping the front of her dress as though warding off an evil spirit.

Ma was undaunted by Leona Watkins's disapproval and went on addressing the wagonmaster. "The poor little babe might pull through yet if Lydia here could suckle him."

The Watkins woman interrupted before Mr. Grayson could make a comment. As a heated argument ensued, Lydia took in as much of the wagon as her peripheral vision would allow. The quilts piled in the corner were of finer fabric scraps than those she had been covered with in the Langston wagon. One had satin ribbon weaving through the quilting pattern. There was a pair of dainty high-button white kid shoes standing beside a box of china dishes.

Her eyes roamed farther afield and came to rest on a pair of black boots. Spaced now widely apart, they were knee-high boots covering long calves. The boots were scuffed, but obviously of the finest quality leather. They fit a longish, well-shaped foot. The heels were about an inch high and made of wood polished black. The man wearing those boots would be tall if the length of his shinbones was any indication.

"I tell you it's not proper." Mrs. Watkins's objections had increased in volume and intensity. A clawlike hand gripped Lydia's chin and jerked her head up. She was looking into a face which had had all the flesh and life reamed out of it. It was narrow and ridged. The bridge of the skinny nose was as sharp and drastic as a knife blade. From often being pursed in stern disapproval, the lips had a network of fine lines radiating from them. The eyes matched the voice. They were censorious and malicious.

"Just look at her. She's trash. One can tell by looking. She's probably a . . . a prostitute—may God forgive me for even speaking the word—who had a baby. She probably killed it herself to be rid of it. I doubt she ever knew who the father was."

Flabbergasted by what the woman had said, Lydia stared at her speechlessly before breathing a soft "No!"

"Mrs. Watkins, please," Mr. Grayson intervened diplomatically. He was a charitable man, though he was inclined to agree with the Watkins woman this time. The young woman did have a wild look about her. There was not one ounce of refinement either in the way she was dressed and groomed or in the shameless way she stared back at them through unusual amber eyes.

"That ain't so!" Ma denied. "But even if it was, Leona Watkins, who else on this train could nurse this baby? *You?*"

"Well, I never!"

"That's right," Ma snapped. "You prob'ly never was able to wring one drop of milk from those shriveled-up teats of—"

"Ma, please," Mr. Grayson said wearily.

Leona Watkins's eyes were flashing furiously in anger, but she kept silent, drawing herself up rigidly and pinching her nostrils together in disdain of the entire situation.

Ma ignored her. "Mr. Grayson, it's your duty to preserve each life on this wagon train, and that includes that baby over there. Listen to the poor little thing. Out of twenty families, the only other woman who has milk is nursing her twins. Lydia is that babe's only hope. Now, are you going to save his life or let him starve?"

Leona Watkins folded her arms over her chest in a gesture of contempt. She was relinquishing all responsibility for the consequences should Mr. Grayson choose to do as the busybody Ma Langston suggested. She had always thought the Langston woman was unbearably common, and now Ma was proving it.

"The only opinion that counts is Mr. Coleman's," Hal Grayson said. "Ross, what do you say to this? Do you want this girl to nurse your son on the outside chance that it might save his life?"

Lydia had turned her back on the lot of them. She didn't care what they thought of her. As soon as she was well enough, she would go somewhere where no one knew her, where she could start fresh, without a past. Unconsciously she had gravitated to the side of the wagon where the infant lay in an empty apple crate lined with flannel. She was staring down at the tiny, struggling life when she heard the shuffling motions of his father standing up.

Lydia's back was to Ross Coleman when he lifted his head, stood, and looked toward the girl who had caused such a ruckus in his wagon and interrupted his grieving over Victoria's death. He noticed first her hair, a veritable bramble bush of undisciplined curls with dried leaves and God knew what else entwined in its masses. What kind of woman goes around with her hair unbound in the first place? Only one kind Ross Colemen knew of.

From the back she looked terribly thin in the nightgown. The ankles poking out of its hem were narrow. Her feet were small. And dirty. God. He didn't need this disruption after the grievous days he had suffered.

"I don't want that girl touching my baby," he muttered in disgust. "Just all of you please leave me and my son alone. If he must die, let him die in peace."

"Thank heaven someone around here has held on to reason."

"Shut up," Ma told Leona Watkins as she shoved her aside on her way to reach Ross. "You seem to be a reasonable man, Mr. Coleman. Why won't you let Lydia feed your boy and at least try to save his life? He'll starve otherwise."

"We've tried everything," Ross said impatiently. He plowed through his thick dark hair with frustrated fingers.

"He wouldn't take cow's milk from a bottle. He wouldn't take the sugar water we spooned into him last night."

"He needs mother's milk. And that girl's nipples are oozing it."

"Oh, my Lord," Leona Watkins said.

Ross cast another glance at the girl. She stood between him and the pale lantern light, making the outline of her body visible through the thin nightgown. Her breasts did look heavy. The voluptuousness of them repelled him. Why was she traipsing around wearing only a nightgown? Even if she were sick after childbirth, no decent woman would let other people, particularly men, see her like that. His lip curled in revulsion, and he wondered what cathouse the girl had been dredged up from. Victoria would have been horrified at the sight of her.

"I won't have a slut nursing Victoria's baby," he said tightly.

"You don't know her circumstances any more than I do."

"She's trash!" he shouted. The anger he had harbored against the world since Victoria's unfair death finally erupted. The girl happened to be a convenient scapegoat. "You don't know where she came from, who she is. Only one kind of woman has a baby without a husband around to take care of her."

"Maybe once, yes, but not since the war. And not since the whole countryside is crawlin' with renegades and no-goods and Yankee carpetbaggers who think everythin' and everyone in the South now belongs to them. We don't know what she's suffered. Remember, she lost her own baby two days ago."

Lydia was mindless of the argument. Her attention had been captured by the infant boy. His skin had an unhealthy pallor. Lydia had never seen a newborn other than her own. This one was even smaller, and his meager size alarmed her. Could anything that small live?

His fingers, balled as they were into tight fists, were almost translucent. His eyes were closed as he breathed in light, shallow pants. His stomach rose and fell jumpily. His crying was jagged, as though he had to pause often to rest and collect his shrinking supply of air. But the weak crying was incessant. And it was like a Lorelei's song to Lydia. Inexorably it drew her to the child.

She felt a tugging deep inside her womb, not unlike the labor contractions but without the pain. Her heart seemed to expand, crowding her already swollen breasts. They tingled, not with the flow of rich milk, but with a need to succor, a compulsion to render maternal comfort.

She watched, unaware she was even moving, as her finger touched the baby's smooth cheek. Then her hand slid beneath his head, which she could easily cup in her palm. Moving slowly, fearful that she would hurt him, she slid her other hand under his bottom and lifted him from the crate. Staring into the wrinkled, mottled face, she sank onto a low, three-legged stool.

The baby's thin legs thrashed and his feet kicked against her stomach. She turned him sideways into the crook of her arm. The small head bobbed and the wizened face rooted against her full breast. Lydia watched, mesmerized and awed, as the birdlike mouth turned to her. It was open and seeking.

Serenely, she raised her hand to the first button on the loaned nightgown and unfastened it. Then the second. Others followed until she was able to shrug the garment from her left shoulder and peel it down over her breast. With her free hand, she lifted her breast toward the baby's face. His mouth gaped, roamed, searched until it found her nipple. The child latched onto it immediately and began sucking greedily.

The sudden cessation of the infant's cries brought an instant halt to the virulent conversation at the back of the wagon. Ross's heart rent in two. His first thought was that his son had died. He whirled around, expecting to see his son still and dead, but the sight that greeted his worried eyes stunned him even more.

The girl was holding his son on her lap. The baby was sucking gustily at her generous breast. Milky bubbles foamed on his eager mouth and around the dusky areola. She was crooning to the baby softly as she pushed her breast deeper into his mouth. Ross couldn't see her face for the unruly hair that fell across it.

"Well," Ma harrumphed in satisfaction, "guess that says all that need be said. Mr. Grayson, why don't you escort Leona back to her wagon? I'll see to things here and get Lydia settled in."

"Settled in!" Leona shrieked. "Surely she'll not stay here in Mr. Coleman's wagon. It isn't decent."

"Come along, Mrs. Watkins," Hal Grayson said. He was anxious to get back to his own bedroll. Dawn came too early these days and Mrs. Coleman's death had put a pall on the adventure of trekking to Texas. He hadn't particularly wanted the job of wagonmaster, but he had been elected, and he would see to it that those who had placed confidence in him weren't disappointed. "We'll straighten all this out in the morning. I'm sure nothing indecent is going to happen in the meantime." He practically pulled the protesting woman from the wagon.

When they were gone, Ma looked at Ross Coleman, who was staring at the girl, a hard look on his face. Ma held her breath, wondering what he was going to do. He seemed a likable sort, friendly enough, and he had treated that wife of his like she was the Queen of Sheba.

But there was a constant turbulence in his eyes that made Ma believe there was more to the man than what lay on the surface. He moved a little too quickly, his eyes were a little too sharp and shifty not to belong to a man who had seen enough of life to be wary of it. Right now he looked like a man who was fighting a battle within himself, for every one of his finely formed muscles was straining against his skin.

Ross forced his feet to move across the crowded floor of the wagon. His son was nursing hungrily. He wasn't crying anymore. This trashy girl, a stranger, was holding his son and nursing him, and he, Ross, was standing there letting it happen. What would Victoria think if she could see it?

Ross flinched as he thought of her body twisted and bloated and sweating, of her sighing her final breath even as his son had pushed his way into the world. No, no other woman, especially a woman of loose morals, was going to rear Victoria Gentry Coleman's son. It would be a sacrilege. How could he live with himself if he allowed something like that to come about? But how could he live with himself if he let his child die by standing on principle?

Torn by the decision he must make, he squatted down in front of the stool and watched his son's mouth avidly pulling on the generous breast. The only thing marring its creamy perfection was the faint blue veins rivering toward the dark nipple like lines on a map. Ross was fascinated by it and had to force his eyes upward to the girl's face.

He watched her eyelids as they lifted slowly, painstakingly slowly. The thick screen of her lashes was finally raised and then he was staring directly into her eyes. Their reactions to each other were of equal surprise and intensity, though they strove to keep them secret and silent.

Ross felt that he had sunk into a vat of femininity. It surrounded him, filled his nostrils, his throat. She personified sensuality and he found himself wallowing in it and, in light of his wife's recent death, hating it. He fought his way to the surface as a man would grope for air in a pool of quicksand. When he was able to breathe evenly again, he assessed her with forced detachment.

Her eyes were thickly fringed with brown lashes, tipped gold at the ends. The irises were the color of aged bourbon, the expensive kind that slides down a man's throat and curls around his insides in a warm embrace. They were almost the same unusual color as her reckless hair, which he guessed typified her wild nature.

Her skin was fair, but looked as though it had been recently exposed to too much sun. There was a light dusting of freckles on her nicely formed, if a bit impudent, nose. Her mouth bothered him most of all. Its full lower lip demanded attention, and a man would have to be dead not to give in to it. So he didn't try, but looked his fill, hoping to shame her for the sheer sensuality of her mouth. Instead, her tongue came out to moisten that seductive lip. Ross felt his stomach lurch again and tore his eyes back to hers.

She seemed not the least ashamed of what she was or that she was sitting there with her breasts exposed to him if he had wanted to look, which he swore to himself he didn't. Her eyes were bold as she studied him as thoroughly as he was appraising her. There was no modest fluttering of her lashes, no shy ducking of her head, no hint of demureness.

She was a whore all right. Born to be one. He had been with too many not to recognize the signs, not to see the unspoken challenge lurking in her eyes, not to sense the hot blood that flowed in her veins. She was the antithesis of his genteel, ladylike wife, Victoria. That was reason enough to despise the girl.

Lydia thought that with the least softening of the scowling expression it might be one of the nicest faces she had ever seen. It was certainly one of the most arresting. She had felt a definite shortness of breath the first time her eyes had met his, and she didn't know where such nervousness came from.

He desperately needed a shave. His jaw was shadowed with dark stubble. A thick black moustache curved over the corners of his upper lip. The lower lip was straight and stern now as he pierced her with green eyes.

The eyes. She studied them. They were rare. So very green, like none she had ever seen before. Short black lashes surrounded them. They collected in spiky clumps. She was tempted to run her finger over them to see if they were wet, as they appeared to be. His brows were brushy and intimidating.

Midnight black hair, unrelieved by any other shading or tint, lay against his head in wavy strands and curled over the tops of his ears and along the collar of his shirt.

He seemed enormous as he hunkered there in front of her, but she didn't look at his body. Male bodies frightened her, repulsed her. The hard way he looked at her did nothing to alleviate her fears. Even as she watched, his eyes narrowed threateningly, as though planning some severe punishment. For what, she couldn't imagine. Her eyes wavered for a moment before she dropped them back to the infant, who was still feeding at her breast.

"Lydia, it's time to switch sides," Ma said gently, somehow managing to wedge her bulk between Lydia and the child's father.

"What?" the girl asked huskily. The man disturbed her. Not in the way Clancey had, but he disturbed her nonetheless. When he stood and moved away from her, his immense frame seemed to shrink the size of the wagon's interior. The confines of it suddenly became stifling, and Lydia found that she was panting breathlessly as the baby had earlier.

"First one breast, then the other. That way the flow of milk will balance out." Ma lifted the infant away from her. His mouth had formed a tight seal around her nipple and, when it popped free, he began to wail again. When he was nestled in Lydia's other arm, he wasted no time in availing himself of the other breast.

Happy, spontaneous laughter filled the wagon. Lydia tossed her mane of hair back and laughed throatily. Her eyes reflected the glow of the lantern. They sparkled like whiskey with sunlight shining through it. Then they happened to lock with Ross's, and all light immediately left them. He was glowering at her with open hostility from across the wagon.

"Once the lad's done there, I'll get you settled in for the night," Ma said, beaming at the girl and the baby.

"She's not staying. Once he's done, you get her out of here." The masculine voice sliced through the atmosphere of the wagon with razor precision.

Ma turned to Ross, her fists planted in the sides of her generous hips. "Don't you think he'll get hungry again, Mr. Coleman? What do you propose to do, fetch her clean across the camp to your wagon each time he's ready for his dinner? Or are you gonna carry him over to her yourself? Seems to me that would be a lot of unnecessary steps on somebody, not to mention the hardship on the babe.

"I didn't mind takin' in Lydia and I would have taken in her own babe had it lived, but I ain't gonna shelter your babe when he'd have more room and more peace and quiet here in your own wagon," she finished huffily.

Ross drew himself up with proud dignity, but still had to duck his head and shoulders to stand upright in the wagon. "I wasn't intending to depend on your charity for my son, but the girl can't stay here."

"Her name is Lydia," Ma said. "And why can't she stay here? Who's gonna look after the boy durin' the day? You go off huntin' or scoutin'. At best you're drivin' the team. Who's gonna take care of him if he starts fussin', huh?"

The corner of Mr. Coleman's moustache was captured between his teeth and gnawed on as objections raced through his mind. "She's not even *clean*."

"No, she ain't. She birthed a babe out in the woods alone. How clean is she supposed to be? And I haven't bathed her 'cause she's been feverish and I didn't want another death on my hands. If it's her bleedin' you're referrin' to, she ain't doin' nothin' that nice and proper wife of yours wouldn't have done. It'll stop in a day or two, and Anabeth or I will come see to her until then."

Lydia kept her head bent low over the infant while her whole body went hot with embarrassment. Apparently Ma's directness rendered Mr. Coleman speechless as well, because he didn't say anything for a while. Tension was thick in the wagon. He radiated antagonism the way a stove radiates heat in the wintertime.

Finally the baby had eaten his fill. Lydia folded the nightgown closed over her breasts and followed Ma's instructions on how to burp him. He let go a gusty belch.

Ross watched the scene with mounting, impotent fury. No telling how many men the slut had entertained in her bed, and yet there she was acting like a decent woman nursing a child. His child. Victoria's child. But what choice did he have? He wanted his son to live. The child would be his only link to the woman he had loved fiercely.

He coughed unnecessarily, loudly. "All right, she can stay. Temporarily. As soon as I can find a way to feed and take care of him by myself, she'll be out. Is that understood? I'm not running a charity hospital either. Besides, I don't want a woman like her taking care of Victoria's baby. I'm sorry about her own baby, but it's probably just as well he died. She's either a prostitute as Mrs. Watkins said, or a girl who has disgraced her family, or a woman who's run away from her husband. In any event, she's not the kind of woman I want handling my son. If it weren't a matter of life and death, she wouldn't be. Now, under those terms, do you still want to stay?" he demanded of the girl cooing to his peacefully sleeping son.

She lifted her head to meet his glaring green eyes. "What's the baby's name?"

Ross was taken aback by her soft inquiry. "Uh . . . Lee. I named him Lee."

She smiled down at the infant, hugging him close. Her hand smoothed over his head, which was fuzzy with dark hair. "Lee," she murmured lovingly. Looking up at the father with a bland expression, she said, "I'll take care of Lee for as long as he needs me, Mr. Coleman." She paused for a moment before adding loftily, "Even if it means putting up with the likes of you."

Chapter Three

Putting up with the likes of you. Putting up with the likes of you.

Ross tugged mercilessly on the harness as the words reverberated in his head. Who the hell did she think she was to talk to him that way? He patted the horse's rump as if to say his anger wasn't directed toward the team that pulled the wagon.

He went back to the fire he had rekindled minutes earlier at the first pinking of the eastern sky. The coffee wasn't boiling yet. It had been his habit to start the fire each morning, to make the coffee, even to get the bacon frying so Victoria could sleep a while longer. She hadn't been accustomed to rising early, much less getting her own breakfast, and the long, arduous days on the trail had taxed her strength.

Ross stared into the crackling fire, asking himself for the hundredth time why she had lied to him. She had said she was only a few months pregnant and wouldn't be having the baby until long after they reached Texas. Because of her slight build, the lie had been believable. But after only a few weeks into their journey her burgeoning abdomen had given her away. Even when Ross remarked on how large she was getting so soon and she had meekly admitted that she was further along than she had first told him, he still hadn't realized how progressed her pregnancy had been. Lee had been born several weeks prematurely. Still, the fact remained that Victoria had lied to him in order to get her way.

He could understand why she hadn't wanted her father to know about the baby. Her father, Vance Gentry, had had a hard enough time accepting her marriage to a hired hand. But why the hell hadn't she been completely honest with him, her own husband?

Ross reached for the enamel coffeepot and poured some of the strong brew into a tin cup. On the trail he preferred that kind of utensil to the china Victoria had insisted they bring along. Sipping the scalding coffee, he let his mind wander.

No, Vance Gentry hadn't taken well to his daughter's falling in love with the man he had hired to manage his stables. Gentry had wanted a man with lineage as sterling as Victoria's to be her husband. But men of marriageable age from established Southern families were hard to come by these days. The war had seen to that. Victoria was happy with her choice and, as the months passed, everyone at the farm adjusted to the idea of Ross Coleman's being her husband. Everyone except Vance. He was never openly hostile, but his resentment toward his son-in-law couldn't be disguised.

Victoria had sensed that resentment. That's why she had waited until her father left on a horse-buying trip to Virginia to tell Ross about the baby. When he'd mentioned the land in Texas, it had been her idea that they leave before her father returned. Ross had been concerned about her pregnancy and the baby, but she had assured him they would have plenty of time to get settled before their baby was born. Well, the baby had been born. He had the baby, but no Victoria.

No Victoria. He tried to imagine what his life would be like without her. She had come into it so unexpectedly and she had left it just as abruptly. She had been a gift that had been his temporarily, before being maliciously snatched away. In his life now there would be no light, laughter, love.

He wouldn't ever see her face again, touch her hair, hear her singing. She was irrevocably lost to him, and he didn't know if he could cope with that.

For Lee he would have to. Husbands lost wives to childbirth every day, and still survived. He would too. He would make a good life for his son. Just him and Lee. Alone together. No, not quite.

Now he had that girl on his hands.

He tossed the coffee down his throat and was pouring another cup when Bubba Langston crouched down beside him.

"Mornin', Ross." Bubba had felt a sense of maturity and importance when the man, whom he considered a paragon of all a man should be, had told him to call him by his given name.

"Bubba," Ross answered laconically, his mind still on his problem.

"Think it'll rain today?"

Foreboding clouds were reflected in the green eyes that scanned them. "Maybe. Hope not. I'm sick of the rain. It's slowing us up."

Bubba cleared his throat. "I'm . . . uh . . . sorry about your wife, Ross."

Ross only nodded. "Coffee?" Without waiting for the boy to respond, he took up another cup and poured the coffee.

They drank in silence for a moment. Others in the camp were beginning to stir. Wood smoke wafted on the humid air. The rattle of harnesses and the snuffling of team horses, the soft conversations of husbands and wives before the children awoke, the clanking of metal pots and pans, filled the morning with comfortable, familiar noises. That familiarity was reassuring. Ross felt that everything in his life had suddenly become alien.

"Did you see to the horses yet?" he asked the boy.

"Sure did. Took that bag of oats to 'em just like you asked me."

"Thanks, Bubba," Ross said, smiling for the first time. He wondered how he would have turned out had he had a man in his youth to look up to. Probably no different than he had. Some people were born bad, born to scrape and claw through life. He had thought when Victoria Gentry fell in love with him and married him that he had been given a second chance. So much for good fortune among losers. "I'm lucky you were along on this train to help me look after my horses. They're all I've got to get my own herd started once we get to Texas."

The boy's white hair was tossed by a gentle morning breeze. "Shoot, Ross, even if you wasn't payin' me to look after 'em, I'd volunteer. Pa wants me to be a farmer like him. He's set on findin' a new homestead in Texas and startin' over someplace where it don't flood every year like our place on the Tennessee. I don't want to farm. I'd rather work with horses like you, Ross." He helped himself to another cup of coffee, jubilant that he had his idol's undivided attention. "How'd you get your start?"

Conversation with the boy was keeping Ross's mind off his troubles. As he talked, he sliced strips of bacon from a slab of salted pork. "Well, I was injured—"

"A war injury?" Bubba asked, wide-eyed.

Ross's eyes turned hard and cold as he stared sightlessly into the dense forest surrounding the camp. His voice was low and bitter when he answered. "No. Sort of an accident." He flipped the bacon into the hot skillet. It sizzled and popped. "An old man named John Sachs found me and took me to his cabin. It was way up in the Smokies. He was a hermit. He nursed me back to health." Ross laughed. "Mostly with the rotgut he distilled. When I was well enough to work, he suggested I go down into the valley and see a man named Vance Gentry. He operates one of the finest stud farms in Tennessee. I went to work for him and married Victoria."

"And then the old man, Sachs, he sold you the land in Texas."

Ross looked at the boy from humor-wrinkled eyes. "Have I told you this story before?"

"Sure you have, Ross. But I like hearin' it."

"Old man Sachs had fought at the Battle of San Jacinto. The Republic of Texas had awarded grants of land to the men who had fought there. But he wandered back to

Tennessee and never had the gumption to go back and claim it."

Ross had been intrigued by the thought of a section of rich east Texas land just lying there unused. He had known that he and Victoria would live forever under her father's influence if they didn't leave. Besides, Ross wanted a place of his own, a place to start his own herd of prize horses, a place where he could breathe easier when meeting strangers.

He had offered to buy the land from the old recluse. The man had laughed and simply handed over the deed sent to him by the Texas government years earlier. "I'll die here in this cabin, son," he had said. "Don't have no need for that land. I moseyed into Texas on a lark. That war meant no more to me than a big brawl and a helluva good time. You want that land, it's yours."

When he had broached the subject of relocating to Victoria, she had shown more enthusiasm than he had bargained for. He had wanted to go ahead of her, see the land, get a house started, then send for her and the baby. But she had insisted on going with him.

"Better to make a clean break while Daddy's away, Ross. Let's join up with that wagon train that's organizing down in McMinn County."

Ross had planned on doing that anyway. Traveling in numbers was safer. There was also a distinct advantage to bringing household belongings rather than trying to buy them once there. People were flocking to Texas and then finding when they arrived that homesteading supplies weren't readily available.

Victoria had seen it all as a grand adventure and wanted to keep their departure a secret. He had argued with her. He didn't want her father to return home and find them gone without a word.

"Please, Ross. He'll think up a thousand reasons for us not to go, especially if he finds out about the baby. He'll never let us leave."

Now Ross wrapped two slices of bacon in a leftover biscuit and handed the sandwich to Bubba. "I'd saved enough wages to buy the horses to start my own herd. Now I've got Lucky and five of the prettiest mares you ever saw."

"You sure do," Bubba mumbled around a mouthful.

"Thanks to the grooming you give them every night." Ross chuckled. "Lucky is crazy in love with every one of those mares."

The youth basked in Ross's approval. They were smiling at each other companionably when they heard the fussy cry of the waking infant from inside the wagon.

Bubba whipped his towhead toward the sound. Coming to them through the canvas were soft maternal murmurings. Then silence. Bubba looked inquiringly at Ross, whose expression had turned fearsomely dark as he stared at the wagon's opening.

"That . . . that girl, Lydia. Ma said she'd be stayin' in your wagon and takin' care of the baby from now on."

The lips beneath the black moustache thinned. "It appears that way, yes." Restless and angry, Ross knew he had to direct that energy elsewhere or he would explode. He rose to his feet and walked to the end of the wagon. Opening up a carpetbag, he took out a mirror, a straight-edge razor, a brush, and a shaving mug, and set them on the tailgate. Then he folded the collar of his shirt inside. He had been heating a pan of water near the fire. He dipped the shaving brush into the hot water, then into the mug, and began working up a thick, rich lather. He slapped the white foam onto his lower face and began lifting off the soap and the stubble of his beard with deft strokes of the razor. Bubba watched, envious.

"She was right poorly when me and Luke found her," he said conversationally.

"Was she?" Ross swished the razor in the water and tilted his head to one side to see better in the mirror he had hung on a nail.

"Sure was. Lyin' in the rain, pale and still as death."

The jaw being shaved tensed. "Well, she's fair to bursting with life and good health now."

Ross wished to hell he couldn't remember the way the lantern had cast light and shadow over her breasts. The unusual gold color in her eyes had bewitched him not to forget it. He commanded his body to forget. It wouldn't. Even now it responded.

His heritage was manifesting itself. It wasn't decent, his noticing the girl's body ᵃnd his wife barely cold in her grave. Damn! That's what came from being the bastard son of a whore. No matter how many respectable people you associated with, no matter how refined a lady you married, sooner or later, even when you didn't want it to, the seediness inside you took over. You couldn't outdistance your beginnings no matter how fast you ran.

All it took was one look at someone like that tart in the wagon, and he had no more control than metal shavings being drawn to a magnet. His pretense at being better than he was had been shot to hell. He had come from trash just as she had, but he had lifted himself out of it.

And by God, he would be damned before he would be sucked into that kind of life again. By her or anyone else.

The baby whimpered and Ross knew he was being transferred from one breast to another. His hand wavered. He nicked himself with the razor and cursed under his breath. Bubba shifted nervously from one foot to another, wondering what he had said to engrave that deep cleft between Ross's eyebrows. He had never seen the man so unnerved. Of course the man's wife had just died. That was probably the reason for the scowl on his face as he bent his knees to better see himself in the mirror.

"When do you reckon we'll get to the Mississippi, Ross?"

"A week, maybe."

"Ever seen the Mississippi?"

"Lots of times." Ross wiped his face with a rough towel and tossed the shaving water onto the ground. Carefully he dried the razor and packed it and the other shaving implements back into the carpetbag. The sterling silver set had been a gift from Victoria last Christmas. He tried to think on that as he studiously ignored the gentle lullaby that was being sung inside the wagon.

"Gee. I ain't never seen it," Bubba said of the river. "I can't wait."

Ross looked kindly at the boy, the muscles of his face relaxing. "It's something to see, all right."

The boy beamed. "Will you be wantin' me to drive your wagon today?"

Ross glanced quickly toward the wagon. "Yeah, I would appreciate that if you don't think your parents will need you."

"Naw. Luke can drive if Ma has something else to do."

"Then I'll saddle Lucky and go hunting. I've been eating only what others brought me since . . ." He paused, a shadow of sadness crossing his face. "I'd best find some meat today."

"I'll go tell my folks. See ya, Ross." Bubba went running across the camp toward the Langstons' wagon, where Ma could be heard issuing orders like a drill sergeant.

Ross looked up at the rear of the wagon. The flaps of canvas were closed. He had left the wagon last night when Ma had begun to tuck the girl into the bedding he had shared with Victoria. He hadn't entered it since.

He had rolled up in blankets beneath the wagon and used his saddle for a pillow. Hell, he didn't mind that. He had slept that way more of his adult life than he hadn't. What he couldn't tolerate was the thought of that girl in the bed in which he and Victoria had slept together, in the bed on which Victoria had died.

He didn't think he could bear to look at Lydia, but he would be damned before he'd let the chit and her saucy tongue drive him off his own property. With resolution and anger, he slung open the canvas flaps and climbed into the wagon.

She was sleeping. Lee was but a wad of baby flesh curled up between her protective arm and her breast. Beneath the soft cotton that covered it, her chest rose and fell rhythmically with her breathing. Her hair was fanned out behind her head in a tangle of curls.

He sure as hell wasn't going to be caught standing there gawking if she should wake up. If he was going hunting, he would need bullets. He made an inordinate amount of noise scrounging for the box of bullets when all the time he knew exactly where it was. He shook several out in his hand and dropped them into his shirt pocket.

When he turned back around, she was staring at him. She lay motionless, soundless, and it was damned irritating. It was as if he had intruded upon her and not the other way around. Angrily he yanked up a kerchief from his trunk and wound it around his neck. Still she didn't speak or move, but she watched every move he made. Why didn't she say something? She hadn't said much the night before either. Maybe she was dimwitted to boot.

When he couldn't stand that intense, silent stare any longer, he asked irritably, "Would you like some coffee?"

She nodded her head, disturbing the wisps of curls that encircled her face. "Yes."

He hated himself for asking and stamped out the back of the wagon. He hadn't wanted even to be cordial, much less wait on her like some goddamn servant. Jerking up the coffeepot, he sloshed the boiling liquid into another tin cup. Droplets splashed onto his hand and gave him a good reason to curse expansively and viciously. It felt good. He had tried hard not to curse since Victoria Gentry had first taken notice of him pitching hay in her father's stables.

Reining in a temper that was tenuous at best, he carried the cup into the wagon, stooping to accommodate his height, and extended it toward her.

She wet her lips with her tongue. "Maybe you should move Lee. I'm afraid I might spill it on him."

Ross looked first at the steaming cup of coffee, then down at the infant, then at the girl lying supine on the bed. He had never felt more awkward or helpless in his life, except maybe the time he had first taken dinner with Victoria and her father in their fancy dining room. But even then he hadn't felt that his arms had suddenly stretched out of proportion and that his hands had grown too large.

Muttering curses, he set the cup aside and leaned down on a bent knee to pick up his son. He stopped dead still, his hands extended but motionless, as he gazed down at the sleeping baby. There was no way he could pick Lee up without touching her.

She seemed to realize that at the same time, because

her eyes rose to his and clashed. Then just as quickly she lowered hers. She tried to edge away from the baby, to put space between them, but his little body only rolled against hers and molded to it again.

Goddammit! Was this what it was going to be like? Was he going to let her make him jumpy and nervous as a cat in his own home? Ross thrust his hands forward. One went to the baby's back. The other he wedged between her and Lee's small head. His knuckles sank into the lush curve of her breast. Sweat popped out on his forehead and he quickly lifted the child away and turned.

"Wait!" she called softly. Ross looked back. In his haste, he had picked up the fabric of her nightgown with Lee's blanket. The cloth was pulled tight over her breasts, outlining and detailing the large dark nipples. Ross stood mesmerized.

Reaching up, she tugged at her gown, working it free of his fingers, which couldn't lessen their grip for fear of dropping Lee. When at last the nightgown fell away, Ross moved to one of the stools and sat down. Actually, it was either sit down or fall down. His whole body was trembling.

"Hurry up and drink your coffee," he mumbled crossly, not looking at her as she raised herself to a sitting position.

Lydia winced slightly at the pinching, stretching sensation between her thighs, but the soreness lessened each day. This morning she didn't feel feverish either. Gratefully, she reached for the cup of coffee Mr. Coleman had set aside and sipped at it.

She watched the man over the brim of her cup. He was staring down at his sleeping son with an expression that softened his rugged face. "He slept all night," she said quietly.

"I didn't think I heard him until early this morning."

"He woke up hungry." There was laughter in her voice and he raised his head to look at her. Awkwardly they stared at each other, then glanced away. "He's wet, isn't he?"

Ross chuckled softly as he lifted the baby up and looked down at the spreading damp spot on his pants leg. "Yes."

"I don't know how to change him. I guess Ma can show me. Do you have any diapers?"

Ross looked perplexed for a moment. "I don't know. I'll look around. Maybe Victoria . . ." He paused on her name. "Maybe she packed some away."

Lydia sipped slowly at her coffee. "I'm sorry about your wife."

His eyes were grim and hard as he looked at her before returning his gaze to his son. He traced the baby's brow with his finger. His hand was about twice the size of the baby's face. It looked dark against the splotchy red skin.

"You're thinking why couldn't it have been me who died and your wife who lived, aren't you?"

His dark head snapped up. The motion was so sudden that the baby flinched, startled, before relaxing once again on his father's lap. Ross was ashamed that she had guessed his thought, but he couldn't apologize for it. Rather than deny it when it was so obviously apparent, he asked his own question. "What were you doing out there in the woods having a baby all alone?"

"I didn't have anywhere else to go. That just happened to be where I dropped."

Her answer vexed him. The injustice of Victoria lying cold in a grave while this woman, who wasn't worth one teaspoon of Victoria, was nursing her baby burned inside him. "Who are you running from? The law?"

"No!" she cried, shocked.

"A husband?"

She averted her eyes. "I've never had a husband."

"Hmm," he grunted smugly.

There was a flash of fire in her eyes when she turned them to him once again. How dare he sit there and judge her! How could he possibly know what she had suffered? She had been subjected to degradation by a man once before; she wasn't going to be again. "What you said last night, Mr. Coleman, about my baby being better off dying. You were right. He was better off dying. And I would have been too. I wanted to. But I didn't."

She pushed her chin up, causing her hair to ripple around her head. "Anyway, I'm here and your wife isn't.

God must have seen fit to make it happen that way. *I* didn't have any choice in it any more than you. Little Lee needs mothering and I'm going to mother him."

"You'll wet-nurse him and that's all. He had a mother."

"And she's dead!"

He bolted off the stool with a snarl curling his lip. As her experiences at Clancey's hands had taught her to do, Lydia shrank against the wagon's side and covered her head with her arms. "No, please!"

"What the hell—"

"What in tarnation is goin' on in here?" Ma demanded as she heaved herself into the wagon. "The two of you are providin' quite a show for the whole train. Leona Watkins is in a tizzy about the two of you spendin' the night together—"

"I slept outside," Ross said between his teeth. The girl had thought he was going to strike her!

"I know that," Ma snapped. "And so does everyone else by now 'cause I seen to it that they was told. Now give me that young'un. It's a wonder his neck ain't broke the way you're aholdin' him." She took Lee from his father. "And why is Lydia curled up there like she's been beat?" she demanded of the man. His mouth only hardened into a straight, stubborn line. "Lydia, what's ailin' you?" Ma asked.

Lydia, ashamed for seeming like a coward, answered quietly. "Nothing."

Ma peered at her closely, then turned to Ross and eyed him up and down in silent reproach. "Git on out of here. Anabeth and I'll take over the care of Lydia. Bubba said he's gonna drive for you today 'cause you're goin' huntin', and frankly I think that's a good idea. Gettin' away from here might clear up your head 'bout some things. Now git."

Few refused Ma's orders. Ross cast one baleful eye toward the girl, who no longer looked terrorized, but was watching him warily. Then he stamped out. Once outside, he crammed his hat on his head, hauled his saddle over one shoulder, braced his rifle over the other, and stalked toward the area where the horses had been staked for the night.

The two eldest Langston boys were watching when a

few minutes later Ross wheeled the powerful stallion away from the camp and streaked off through a meadow toward the thick woods.

"Know what I think?" Luke asked his brother.

"Naw, and I don't care, but I'm sure you're gonna tell me anyway."

"I think Mr. Coleman could be a mean sonofabitch if he was to put his mind to be."

Bubba stared pensively at the diminishing image of horse and rider. He had seen that fierce expression on his hero's face too. "You could be right, Luke," he agreed. "You could be right."

". . . and in the evenin's, after everybody had eaten supper, they'd stroll around the camp, aholdin' hands, stoppin' to chat with folks like they was out on a picnic instead of on a wagon train."

Lydia lay on the sleeping mat and listened to the cadence of Anabeth's chatter. The girl was lifting Victoria Coleman's personal belongings out of a chest of drawers and folding them into a trunk. Ma had suggested that she do that to make more room for Lydia and the baby in the wagon. Ross had grudgingly consented.

He did and said everything grudgingly, Lydia thought with a weary sigh. For the past three days she had lain in the wagon recuperating from her ordeal and nursing Lee. Anabeth stayed with her during the day. Ma checked her every morning and brought food each evening. Ross hunted for the Langstons in return for Ma's cooking for them.

He never ate inside with Lydia. She rarely saw him. He made work for himself along the train, often scouting or taking care of ailing horses for others who respected his knowledge of animals. Bubba drove the Coleman wagon. Should Ross come into the wagon, he would avoid looking at her. If he did glance in her direction, he glowered at her malevolently.

She credited most of his ill temper to grief. He was taking his wife's death hard. She must have been something, that Victoria Coleman. A real lady by Anabeth's detailed description.

"Sometimes when the sun was shining real bright, she'd sit with this lacy parasol on her shoulder as she rode on the wagon seat." Anabeth popped open the pink confection of lace and silk. Lydia had never seen anything so pretty in her life. She regretted when Anabeth closed it and placed it inside the trunk. "And they'd talk in whispers to each other, like everything they said was a big secret from the rest of the world." The girl sighed deeply. "I only wish Mr. Coleman would look at me the way he did her. I'd melt right on the spot."

Lydia couldn't imagine anything pleasant coming from the looks he cast in her direction. She couldn't imagine anything pleasant happening between men and women at all. But then every once in a while she could remember how it had been when her real papa had been alive.

They had lived in town in a big house with wide windows and crocheted curtains. Mama and Papa laughed together often. On Sundays when they visited neighbors, Papa would hold Mama's hand. She remembered that because she would break them apart and take their hands in hers. They would make a game of lifting her off the ground. Lydia guessed it was possible that men didn't always do bad, hurtful things to women.

Anabeth spoke again. "Mrs. Coleman's skin was as smooth and white as fresh cream. She was right pretty with them big brown eyes. Her hair was the color of corn silk and looked just as soft; nary a hair was ever out of place."

Lydia reached up to touch her own hair. The morning after she had come to Mr. Coleman's wagon, Ma and Anabeth had given her a bed bath. They had scrubbed her until her skin was raw and tingling. It had taken some time and effort to brush the debris out of her hair. The next day, with Anabeth fetching and carrying buckets of water, they had managed to wash it. But it wasn't ever going to resemble corn silk.

Mr. Coleman had seemed surprised to see her brushed and washed when he reached into the wagon for a fresh shirt that night, but he didn't comment on it. He had only made a grunting sound.

If he was used to hair the texture of corn silk, then

Lydia knew hers must have been a shock to him. Unreasonably, that bothered her very much.

"You gettin' tired?" Anabeth asked when she noticed that her audience's attention had wandered. "Ma said if you got tired and sleepy for me to keep my trap shut and let you rest."

Lydia laughed. She had come to enjoy all the Langstons, but particularly this girl who was so open and honest . . . and tolerant. "No. I'm not tired. I've slept enough in the past few days to last me a lifetime. But Lee's going to wake up soon and be hungry as a young bear."

She reached into the crate that they used in lieu of a cradle and patted the infant on the back. It was a miracle to her how much she loved the baby. After her mother had died, Lydia doubted that she would ever love another human being again. Maybe she loved the baby because he was totally dependent on her and couldn't hurt her. He wouldn't know any better than to love her back.

The wagons rolled to a halt just as Lee finished feeding. Lydia was rebuttoning her gown as Bubba steered the tired horses into the closing circle. No sooner had he unhitched them than Ma entered the wagon.

"How'd you like to get out of here?" she asked Lydia.

Chapter Four

"**Y**ou mean get up? Leave the wagon?" Lydia asked nervously. The only experience she had had with other members of the train was with Mr. Grayson and Mrs. Watkins. She wasn't ready to face the scrutiny and scorn of any of the others.

"Don't you feel up to it?"

"I think so," Lydia answered cautiously. "But I don't have any clothes."

"I brung some with me," Ma said, tossing down a

bundle. "They're Anabeth's and prob'ly won't fit just right, but they'll have to do unless you want to wear that bedgown from now on."

Lydia was shaky as she stood, but was soon being bathed out of a basin and dressed in well-mended stockings, bloomers, and petticoat. "You ain't no bigger than a titmouse," Ma said disparagingly, eyeing Lydia's slender hips and thighs. "How you carried a babe, I'll never know."

That didn't hold true for her breasts. The bodice of the dress wouldn't close over them. "Tarnation," Ma said, aggravated. "Well, we'll button it up as far as it will go." Lydia felt that she would burst as she was squeezed into the material, but at least she was covered.

Luke had rubbed bootblack on her shoes and replaced the strings. She sat on the stool to lace them on while Anabeth pulled a brush through her hair.

"Now, ain't you pretty," Ma said proudly, crossing her arms over her stomach as she surveyed her handiwork. "Mr. Coleman brought me some quail he flushed out today and I've got a stew already simmerin' on your fire. It'd be a treat for him to come to his wagon and see that he had a fine meal waitin' for him, now wouldn't it? He's tendin' those horses of his. Why don't you move Lee's bed over near the tailgate and sit outside for a spell? The fresh air will do you good."

Timidly Lydia let herself be led outside. She was amazed by the activity going on. Sounds she had been listening to for almost a week now were matched to actions. Women were bent over campfires and portable ovens cooking the evening meal. Men were unhitching and rubbing down horses, carrying firewood, hauling water. Children were playing and shouting, racing between the tongues of the wagons.

"Here's Luke bringin' you some spring water." Ma had things well organized. "Why don't you get a pot of coffee boiling? I'm sure Mr. Coleman would appreciate that."

"Yes, I'll do that," Lydia agreed breathlessly. She would welcome something to do. People were beginning to notice her. She was aware of the nudges, the speculative, curious glances, the hushed conversations.

"I've got to see to our dinner, but I'll be right over yonder if you need me," Ma said.

Lydia was left alone. She busied herself with stoking up the fire, with stirring the fragrant stew, with making the coffee, with unnecessarily checking on Lee. When she ran out of things to do, she sat on the stool Luke had lifted out of the wagon for her, and stared into the fire. Not for anything would she raise her eyes to meet the curious looks cast in her direction.

That's how Ross found her. He stopped dead in his tracks when he saw her sitting there minding the cooking supper. The late afternoon sun set her reddish hair afire. Her cheeks were rosy with self-consciousness and the heat of the cook fire. Her figure was much daintier than he had imagined it to be. The voluminous gown had hidden the delicate bone structure and soft curves. She could almost have been a child sitting there obeying a strict parent. Until she turned around. Then that illusion was shattered. She was a woman.

When she heard his approach, she leaped from the stool, knocking it over as she spun around. For a moment their eyes locked and held. In hers lurked wariness. His were glassy, as though he had just been dealt a stunning blow and didn't know where it had come from.

Her neck was slightly arched in order to look up at him. Her throat was long and slender and had about it a fragility that made him want to touch it. Starting at the base of it where a frantic pulse was beating, his gaze couldn't help but meander down to the deep cleft between her breasts. Calico, thread, and buttons were dangerously strained to contain her maternally lush bosom. He found it damnably hard to keep his eyes off the spot.

Her hand lifted and fluttered uneasily at the top button, which had captured his attention. "Ma thought I needed fresh air."

"Where's Lee?" He was mad as hell and his voice showed it. He was angry because she looked wholesome and not wicked as he knew damn good and well she was and because, for only a fleeting moment, he had been glad to see her waiting there for him. He wished to God he couldn't remember Lee's mouth sucking at her nipple, wished he didn't remember its color. He wished he wouldn't think of burning neat whiskey every time he looked into her eyes. Most maddening of all was the nervous habit she had of flicking her tongue at the corners of her lips each time she spoke.

"Lee's right there." She pointed toward the tailgate where the child lay sleeping in his makeshift bed. "I can hear him if he cries." She blotted her palms on the skirt of the blue calico dress and hoped he wasn't going to bawl her out where everyone could hear. Because more than likely she would yell right back and disgrace herself even more.

He stepped to the crate and peered inside. A quick smile made the corners of his moustache twitch. Lightly he patted the baby's behind, which was sticking up slightly. Lee preferred sleeping on his stomach with his knees curled up under him.

When Ross turned around, Lydia, too, was smiling fondly down on Lee. Their eyes met again, briefly this time, before both looked away. "There's coffee ready." She gestured toward the fire.

"Thanks."

He eased off the lasso that had been looped over his shoulder and hung it on a peg outside the wagon. The rifle, he braced against the wagon wheel. He unbuckled his gunbelt, untying the thong around his thigh. Lydia had never seen a man wearing a holster anchored to his leg that way. Watching him take it off his hips made her stomach feel funny.

Careful not to spill a drop, though her hands were shaking, Lydia poured a cup of coffee and handed it to him. His fingers were long and tapered, strong looking. The knuckles were sprinkled with dark hair, but it barely showed up against his tanned skin. She withdrew her hand quickly after he had taken the cup from it. Nervously she wrung it with the other hand.

"Stew smells good."

"Ma made it."

"Oh. Well, it smells good just the same."

"Yes, it does."

They didn't look at each other. He finished drinking the coffee in silence. The camp noise went on around them. They were impervious to most of it and painfully aware of each other.

"Guess I'll wash up," he said at last.

"Luke brought water from the spring. The stew will be ready by the time you're finished."

He stepped behind the wagon and poured a basin of water from the pail. Stripping off his shirt, he wondered why he was sweating so much. Again and again he doused his head and chest with the water, but his skin refused to cool.

Lydia listened to the splashing sounds until Marynell and Atlanta Langston came running up to her. In Marynell's sweaty, grimy hand was clasped a bouquet of Indian paintbrushes and buttercups. "We brung you some flowers, Lydia," Marynell said, grinning a jagged smile. Two days before, she had shown Lydia the bloody tooth Zeke had pulled the night before.

"How lovely," Lydia exclaimed, taking the damp and drooping cluster of wildflowers from the girl's extended hand.

"Smell," Marynell instructed, pushing the flowers toward Lydia's nose.

"They sure smell sweet," the more shy Atlanta piped up.

She knew what the girls were up to, but wouldn't spoil their fun. She brought one of the buttercups to her nose and pretended to take a whiff. When she lowered the bouquet, she could see the sticky yellow pollen clinging to the tip of her nose. The girls shrieked with laughter.

"We tricked you, we tricked you," they chanted.

"Oh, you! What have you done?" Lydia remembered that once she and her mother had played this game. She had never had anyone else to play with. It felt good. She rubbed at the buttery smudge on her nose.

"Them flowers would look right pretty on your dress," Marynell said. "Wouldn't they, Atlanta?" She nudged her sister's ribs.

"Sure would."

"I guess they would at that." Lydia undid the topmost button Ma had been able to pull together and fasten. She breathed easier, but was alarmed by the amount of bosom that swelled up between the fabric. By pushing the stems of the flowers into the buttonhole, the blossoms filled the space nicely and partially covered her cleavage.

If she had looked in a mirror, she would have seen what a sensual contribution the flowers made to her appearance. But then she wouldn't have recognized it as sensual or seductive. She had had a man; she had borne a child. But of romantic matters she was innocent. Mating had been something forced on her. She couldn't imagine any woman actually inviting it.

Ross, still on the other side of the wagon, was aware of the chattering, but he was distracted by his own thoughts. It had been pleasant to return to his wagon and find supper cooking and fresh coffee brewed, but the girl owed him at least that much. He had taken her in, hadn't he? When she didn't have a roof over her head, hadn't he taken her in and let her languish away her days and nights in *his* bed?

He pulled on a clean shirt. She was doing all right by Lee. He couldn't fault her for that. The boy was growing a little each day. He had filled out since she had been nursing him. He didn't look so shriveled and sickly.

Holding up his shaving mirror, Ross combed back his wet hair. When had he last combed it? He didn't remember. And for the life of him he couldn't imagine why he was bothering to now. Except that Victoria had taught him that a gentleman went to some effort to make himself presentable at dinnertime, even if he was still wearing his work clothes. It sure as hell had nothing to do with the girl who had spruced herself up. Nothing to do with her at all. Still, they might be living close together for a while. He supposed it would make life easier if they could be nicer to each other.

Ma had called to her girls from across the camp and they had skipped away. Lydia dipped a tasting spoon into the stew and sipped at it. It was delicious and almost ready.

"Evenin'."

The voice was masculine and melodious with the slow

drawl of the South. There was nothing intimidating about it. Nevertheless, Lydia's heartbeat accelerated. She didn't want anyone talking to her. Only moments before, Leona Watkins and an adolescent girl Lydia presumed to be her daughter had stalked by, their eyes forward, their noses high. The girl had risked a curious glance at Lydia. Mrs. Watkins had pinched her daughter's arm hard in remonstration. If the man who had just spoken to her meant only to ridicule her, she would just as soon he not have.

Not wanting to show her fear, Lydia raised her eyes with open challenge. The man was young, maybe a few years younger than Mr. Coleman. He swept a wide-brimmed hat from his head to reveal soft brown hair that curled snugly around his head. He was dressed in a white suit and blue vest with a gold watch chain dangling from its slit pockets. His eyes were sad, wistful, and kindly blue. His skin was pale save for his cheeks. They were stained with high color.

Lydia didn't say anything. She was surprised to find open curiosity, perhaps friendliness in his face, but no censure. "Allow me to present myself, Miss Lydia. Winston Hill at your service. And this is Moses."

He referred to a tall, stately black man standing at his side. He had on a somber black suit with a white shirt and black string tie. There were threads of white in his hair and eyebrows. But his face was unlined and eternally youthful.

Lydia was so taken by the pair and their courtly manners that she said the first thing that popped into her head. "You know my name."

Winston Hill smiled. "I apologize for the gossip that sweeps through the train, but yes, everyone has heard of you and your remarkable beauty. I'm glad to say that this time the rumors weren't exaggerated."

She blushed, never having heard such a compliment on her appearance. "Pleased to meet you," she said.

"And you. You're looking after Mr. Coleman's new son. A commendable and charitable occupation in light of your own recent loss."

She had never heard talk quite like his. It was pretty. The words dripped off his well-shaped lips slowly, like honey. "Thank you. But he isn't any trouble. He's a wonderful baby."

"I've no doubt. I admired the beauty and courage of his mother. Not to mention his father's prowess." He lifted a linen handkerchief to his mouth and coughed several times. He seemed embarrassed by it, frustrated. "Moses and I will bid you a pleasant evenin' now. If we can ever be of service, please ask."

Confused by his mannerisms, Lydia stammered, "Thank you. I will."

"I hope so." His smile was white and straight. "Oh, evenin', Mr. Coleman."

Lydia turned to see Ross standing behind her at the end of the wagon. He looked as hard and indomitable as Mr. Hill looked soft and guileless. His chin lifted a notch in greeting as he said tersely, "Mr. Hill, Moses."

"We're keepin' you from your supper. Miss Lydia." Before she knew what he was about, he leaned forward, grasped her hand, and brought it to his mouth. His lips brushed the back of it. She stared transfixed as he replaced his hat, nodded to her, and then strolled away, Moses beside him.

She looked down at the hand that had been kissed. Discomfited by the gesture, she wiped it with her opposite sleeve as she glanced over her shoulder at Mr. Coleman. His face was as dark and ominous as a thundercloud. When he wore that angry look, his bottom lip barely showed beneath his moustache.

"Supper's ready," she said with nervous huskiness. She turned back to the fire, picked up one of the china plates Ma had laid out for them, and spooned a hearty helping of the stew onto it. She was holding the plate out to him when she faced him again.

He didn't reach for it. Instead he held his arms rigid at his sides, his hands balling and stretching like he was dying to hit something. The bones in his jaw bunched up as he ground his teeth together. The sun had set and twilight had fallen. The purplish light made his face look even darker, meaner.

His green eyes shone through the dimness. Lydia saw

them slide from her face to the flowers secured between her breasts. Because she was agitated and not a little afraid of him, she was breathing irregularly. Her breasts trembled beneath the cloth and the flowers against her flesh vibrated as though they were alive. He looked at them a long, silent time, while she wished he wouldn't. If she hadn't been holding the plate, she would have covered herself from those smoldering, condemning eyes.

"You little tart," he hissed across the gathering darkness. "I don't give a good goddamn what you were or where you came from, but as long as you're under my roof and nursing my son, you'll not be drumming up customers."

Victoria would have swooned at such a speech. Lydia did not. Her eyes took on a fierce golden light and her hair seemed to bristle with indignation. She took three steps toward him until she was glaring directly up into his face. Bruisingly, she shoved the rim of the plate into his ribs. He barely had time to catch the plate of hot food before she stepped away, releasing it.

Angrily she spun away, sweeping his booted shins with the hem of her skirt. Mindless of the remnant tenderness in her lower body, she stepped up into the wagon with one swift lunge, and yanked down the canvas flaps.

Cursing and absently rubbing his throbbing ribs, Ross dropped down on the stool and began shoving the stew into his mouth. He didn't taste it, hardly chewed it, but with each bite he gnawed at his resentment like an animal worrying a sore paw.

"Damn the girl," he said as he set his plate aside and poured himself coffee. What did she mean by flouncing around in that tight dress, flirting with that highfalutin' pansy, Hill? Tomorrow she would be out. He would find a way to take care of Lee. Maybe he could get that woman with the twins to wean her own and nurse Lee. He would get rid of the girl if he had to pump cow's milk into his son's stomach.

"'Pears you ain't as bright as I gave you credit for." Ma's voice came out of the darkness to intrude on his angry musings. She walked into the firelight, a dish towel slung over her shoulders. Her hands were red from the scouring she had given a cook pot and kettle. "You done?" She nodded toward his soiled plate.

He nodded and took another sip of coffee. Ma poured water over his plate and wiped it with her cloth. "Reckon we can save that stew for tomorrow, seein' that only one of you ate."

He shifted uncomfortably on the stool. "Yep," the woman continued, "it's a pity you ain't as smart as I first figured you was."

Ross's breath rushed out from between his teeth in exasperation, but he took the bait. "Why aren't I smart?"

That gave Ma all the opportunity she needed. "You were blessed with a wet nurse for your son after your wife died. Lee would've been dead for days by now if it wasn't for that girl, who you show not the least bit of compassion or kindness for."

"Compassion!" Ross shouted, jumping to his feet and prowling the area like a caged beast. Everyone on the train was ever aware of the lack of privacy. He lowered his voice significantly. "Kindness? She was flaunting herself in front of every man on this train. Wearing that indecent dress with her . . ." He stuttered, then ended tersely, "Flaunting herself."

"If you're referrin' to Mr. Hill, I seen the whole thing. He spoke to her first, not the other way around. And she looked frightened as a rabbit even to look at him."

Ross's teeth tore at his moustache as he stalked around the fire in a furious circle.

"As for her dress, that's all we had to clothe her in. The one she was wearin' when the boys brung her in was a heap of rags."

"It couldn't have been any worse than the one she's got on. It was straining at the seams."

Ma's mouth quirked with humor, but the darkness hid it. Besides, Mr. Coleman was too wrapped up in his pacing to notice her knowing smile. "She's trash and I don't want her around me or my son."

Ma's smile disappeared. She grabbed his arm and jerked him around. She was almost as tall as he. "How do you know any such thing? She don't talk like trash, does she? Her talk is citified if you ask me. And have you ever watched the way she handles her hands? Graceful like. She eats proper. I ain't never seen no trash that walks and moves the ladylike way she does."

Ma let go of his arm, but drew herself up straighter, more piously. "You seem to put stock in a body's background and family. Never did myself. Always thought it was the person hisself and not who his ma and pa were that counted. But you'd better be careful not to judge her too harshly. She might be the daughter of somebody you might not ought to offend. So the girl got in trouble and had a baby. Lots do. I bet you and Mrs. Coleman had a few tussles in the hay in that horse stable of her pa's before you was married."

Ross's lips thinned. "Victoria wasn't like that," he said tautly.

Ma only laughed both at what he had said and at the lofty way he had said it. "Every woman's that way with the right man. And if your woman wasn't, she should have been."

"I won't listen—"

"I'm not here to speak unkindly of the dead," Ma said, softening considerably. He did look like a man going through misery and she thought she knew why. Zeke agreed with her. They had talked about it last night when they had treated themselves to sleeping in the wagon with all the children outside. "I'm just here to remind you that that young woman, whoever or whatever she is, saved your baby's life. She tried real hard tonight to pay you back for takin' her in. She wanted to have a good dinner waitin' for you." That wasn't quite the truth. The project had been Ma's idea, not Lydia's, but Ma wasn't beyond stretching the truth when she needed to. "And all you did was act as uppity and condemnin' as that dried-up Watkins woman."

She shifted her shoulders righteously. "Seems to me you ain't got no choice but to keep the girl happy to be around you. She might just hightail it away from here and leave your son to fare for hisself. If I was you, I'd make amends for my behavior tonight, Mr. Coleman." Huffily she turned and stalked away.

Ross hunched down by the fire and finished the coffee in the pot. One by one the flames of the scattered campfires were allowed to burn down to smoldering embers. Cranky children were put to bed either in the wagons or in bedrolls under them. Members of the train visiting in groups eventually drifted to their own wagons. Ross was spoken to, but he answered in desultory tones. He didn't invite conversation and, because of the recent death of his wife, people honored his need to brood alone.

The evening was still. Only a faint breeze stirred the leaves of the cottonwood, elm, oak, and sycamore that surrounded the clearing where their hired guide, Scout (which was the only name the young man went by), had suggested to Mr. Grayson that they camp for the night.

There was something to what Ma Langston had said and Ross Coleman well knew it. He just didn't want to admit it. It galled him to be harboring someone who reminded him every time he looked at her of what he had come from.

He had been running from his tainted past all his life. Victoria had made him forget it temporarily. Now this girl with the wild hair and defiant eyes and voluptuous body was making him remember things he wanted so badly to forget.

Still, what would he do with Lee if not for her? The baby scared the hell out of him, he was so small. He knew nothing about babies. All he knew was what it was like not to have a mother's love. He had grown up thinking that being neglected was a part of life. Could he deny his son a woman's care? Any woman's? And the girl did love Lee. Ross knew that.

He spat out a word he hadn't had the luxury of uttering since he met Victoria. It felt so good to say it that he repeated it. Absently he banked the fire so only a light fanning and dry kindling would get it going again in the morning. When he had run out of chores, he looked toward the wagon. The lantern inside was still lit, but turned down low. He walked to the tailgate, swallowing hard and rubbing his perspiring palms up and down his thighs.

* * *

Lydia crooned softly to Lee as he nursed. He must have been deprived of nourishment in the womb because he certainly hadn't gotten his fill since he was born. He sucked noisily, thumping her breast with his tiny fist and occasionally thrashing his legs happily.

Lydia took a spiteful pride that she was able to feed him when apparently the woman with the creamy skin and corn-silky hair hadn't been able to satisfy him. Victoria Coleman had impressed everyone as being an ideal woman. Every time she heard the woman's name spoken, Lydia's self-confidence suffered. But Lee would love *her*. Her, not his natural mother.

She wished she had the nerve to fling that fact straight into the self-righteous face of Lee's father. He had called her a shameful name. Tears sprang into her eyes, but now, as when she had first stormed into the wagon, she refused to let them fall. She wouldn't cry. She wasn't what they all thought. *She wasn't!*

She couldn't help what had happened to her, though God knows she had tried. How many times had she fought to the point of exhaustion, waking up with her body black and blue and sore as a result of her struggling? Sometimes she had won. Too many times she hadn't and . . .

She closed her eyes and shuddered with painful, degrading memories. Those times she had wanted to die. But if she had killed herself there wouldn't have been anyone to take care of Mama. So she hadn't taken her own life and had been subjected to abuse until Mama had died and she was free to run away.

How could something as sweet and innocent as Lee be born of an act so vile and violent? Stroking the baby's head, she wondered if Mr. Coleman had hurt Victoria while conceiving Lee the way Lydia had been hurt. Somehow she couldn't see him rutting and grunting the way Clancey had. She couldn't imagine him hurting Victoria, whom he had all but worshipped, if Anabeth's account of their relationship was valid.

The flaps of the canvas were flung open and she heard the heavy tread of his boot as he stepped into the wagon. She whipped her head around, sending her hair flying in every direction until it resettled on her naked back and shoulders like a fleecy mantle.

Whatever prepared speech Ross was ready to recite stuck in his throat, and his mouth opened once uselessly before slamming shut. Lydia was sitting with her back to the wagon's opening. The dress that had caused his temper to rise had been peeled off her torso and was bunched around her waist.

With his eyes he followed the softly ridged column of her spine to the place where her body was nipped in neatly to form her waist. Her eyes were wide and inquiring, her lips moist and slightly parted as she gazed at him over an apricot-colored shoulder and a clump of russet curls.

"What are you doing?" The words rasped through vocal cords which seemed to have retired from ever manufacturing another sound.

"Lee's last feeding before bedtime," she said in that low, subdued voice that irritated the hell out of him. Didn't she have a smidgen of shame? Why wasn't she shouting at him for invading her privacy, for not knocking before coming in? But then that really would have made him mad. This was *his* wagon, by God!

She must have seen the anger brewing in his eyes for she turned her head, ducked it, and looked down at the baby at her breast. Ross's body went hot all over and his vision blurred for a moment. He was blinking rapidly when she looked back up at him. "Did you want something?"

He shifted awkwardly and wished he didn't have to stoop. "I . . ." He started to say that he wanted to apologize but couldn't go quite that far. "I want to talk to you." There. That had a ring of authority to it.

She didn't say anything, which vexed him almost as much as when she spoke in that quiet voice that seemed to touch whomever it reached. Her eyes were steady on him as she kept her head turned to face him. Why in heaven's name didn't she cover herself up? Even though all he could see was her back, his imagination was running wild. Victoria would never have suckled her baby with anyone else in the room. He pushed the thought aside. If he thought about Victoria at all, he wouldn't be able to say what he had to say.

"Thank you," he said shortly.

She stared at him for a long time before responding quietly. "For what, Mr. Coleman? For not bringing men into your wagon and bedding them in front of you and Lee?"

"Goddammit." He squeezed the word past compressed lips. "I'm trying to be nice to you."

"Nice? You think it was nice to imply that I was a whore?"

"That's a helluva thing to say."

"Well, it was a helluva thing for you to think too."

"You shouldn't be using language like that."

"Neither should you! And why are you suddenly bent on being nice to me? Are you afraid I might run off with a man who'll treat me better and leave Lee to starve?"

Ross didn't speak on two accounts. First, he was too angry to. Secondly, he had been momentarily dumbfounded by seeing a firebrand's temper in such a small, delicate package.

Lydia, fearing she had gone too far and wondering why he wasn't beating her already, turned away from him and lifted the sleeping baby away from her breast. He burped almost immediately, without her even patting his back. She came off the low stool and onto her knees, placing him gently in the crate and covering him with a light blanket.

Ross watched, his throat swelling thickly as she picked up a soft piece of flannel and blotted her front. Then she pulled up the bodice of the dress, slid her arms through the sleeves, and bent her head over the buttons. When all were fastened that she could pull together, she stood and pivoted around to face him.

"What did you thank me for?"

"Thank you for saving my son's life," he said tightly.

Lydia stared up into his eyes. They were shimmering with anger, but not with insincerity. Instantly she was ashamed of herself. He didn't like her, but he loved his son. His thank-you should be accepted for what it was.

She glanced down at the baby and whispered, "In a

way he saved my life too." Raising her eyes back to the man, she said, "Because of Lee I don't want to die anymore. If I hadn't had milk, he wouldn't have lived. The way I see it, Mr. Coleman, we're even."

He would have given anything for her not to mention the milk. For as he heard the word his eyes sought out its source. The dress was still stretched over the plump globes of her breasts, pressing the nipples flat. It was an obscenely provocative yet beautiful sight, and he couldn't keep from looking any more than he could keep from breathing.

Lydia took that avid look on his face as repulsion. "I'm sorry," she said soulfully. "I know the dress doesn't look decent. I don't mean to offend you." She covered a breast with each hand as though to hide it.

Her fingers settled into the soft flesh and created ten deep tunnels. He could imagine the pebbly nipples nestled in the cushion of her palms. *Jesus!* Ross cursed silently and willed down the surge of life in his groin. He dragged his eyes away only to become entrapped by those shining eyes of hers. "Good night," he said with the desperation of a man trying to save his life.

"I'm sorry you have to sleep under the wagon. Is it too uncomfortable?"

A lot more comfortable than it would be to sleep in the wagon near her. "No," he said tersely. He was halfway out of the opening before his hurried good night reached her ears.

Minutes later, lying on his back staring up at the stars, Ross cursed the tight constriction in his loins. If he accused her of being a whore, what did that make him? How could his body betray him this way? He had loved his wife and his wife had died only a week ago.

His only justification was that since the day he had learned Victoria was going to have his baby he hadn't been with a woman. She had apologetically requested that she be relieved of her marital duties during her pregnancy. He had agreed instantly. Her sensibilities were one thing that had endeared her to him, besides her incredible aristocratic beauty. If he had suffered night after night lying close beside her, but not availing himself of her, that was part of being a gentleman. Unless one took a mistress, and Ross had loved Victoria too much even to contemplate that.

But now, after months of abstinence, his body was reacting to a flagrant display of female flesh and wanton warmth. What living, breathing man could be blamed for responding? Damn! It wasn't his fault. He couldn't control that part of his body.

Nor, it appeared, could he control his mind. For it wouldn't leave alone the thought of the girl. He kept seeing her: her hair fanning over her back, the graceful way her spine divided it into perfect halves, the gentle sloping at her waist into slender hips. With the heels of his hands, he dug into his eyesockets and tried to eradicate the image, but the sight and scent and sound of her wouldn't go away.

Most disgraceful of all was the stab of envy he felt toward Lee. His son knew what she tasted like.

Chapter Five

*T*he next morning Lydia awakened just before dawn. Lee was still sleeping. She dressed in the only garment she had, Anabeth's dress, and pulled on her worn shoes. It was no small accomplishment to gather her mass of hair into a knot, but she managed to, and secured it to the back of her head with pins pilfered from a box of cosmetics and lotions that had belonged to Victoria. She wouldn't touch any of the other things, and, had it not been a necessity, she wouldn't have taken the pins. Ma and Anabeth had packed away most of the woman's things. Lydia was glad. She needed no traces of Victoria to remind her of her inadequacies.

Glancing down at the tight dress, she sighed uncomfortably. It stood to reason that she could wear Victoria's clothes. But reason and Mr. Coleman, where his wife was concerned, came to a parting of the ways. He hadn't offered his late wife's clothes to Lydia. Even Ma, who never failed to voice her opinion on anything, hadn't dared to suggest it. She seemed to know he wouldn't take kindly to the idea.

Taking as deep a breath as the constricting calico would permit, Lydia peeled back the flaps of the canvas and stepped out of the wagon. The sun was just breaking over the treetops outlining the horizon. Ross, bending over the fire and feeding it kindling, looked up in surprise.

"Good morning," Lydia said softly. His apparent surprise at seeing her in the light of day nettled her. Did he intend to hide her in the wagon forever? Conveniently she forgot that only hours before she had been afraid to leave its safe confines. Not meeting his eyes, she stepped off the tailgate onto the ground.

"Morning."

"I'll make coffee."

He resented her cool detachment. She was acting like they did this every morning, that it was normal and nothing out of the ordinary. He looked around the campsite. At nearly every other wagon, there were couples going about their morning chores, speaking softly, personally, before the day's traveling began.

His eyes came back to her as she spooned coffee into the enamel pot. On the surface, yes, everything looked right. But dammit, they weren't a couple. He felt as awkward and callow as Luke Langston, and irrationally he blamed her complacency for making him feel that way. "Guess I'll shave now."

She straightened up to face him. His jaw was dark with a night's growth of beard. Looking at the dark moustache, she wondered what it would feel like to touch. The men she had known had had beards only because they were too lazy to shave. When the facial hair began to irritate them, they would ineffectually scrape it off. Ross's moustache was well-groomed, trimmed, and clean. Even though it was thick, the individual hairs looked silky.

"If you show me where the flour is, I can make biscuits."

While he stood at the back of the wagon shaving, she went about preparing a breakfast of fried bacon and biscuits. She even made a thick gravy with the bacon drippings. Her coffee tasted a helluva lot better than what he had been brewing for himself. He didn't want to think it, but it was better than Victoria's too. She had never made it strong enough to suit him and didn't know the difference. She had been a tea drinker.

He didn't thank Lydia or compliment her on the breakfast. They ate in tense silence. He cleaned his plate and when she filled it again without even asking, he ate all of that helping as well.

"What day is this?" Lydia asked him as she began cleaning their utensils and repacking them.

"Day? Thursday."

"Ma said the train doesn't travel on Sundays and that's when most everyone does laundry. I don't think I can wait until then to wash Lee's diapers." They had found baby clothes and diapers packed away in one of the trunks in the Colemans' wagon. Victoria had known she was going to have the baby en route.

Anabeth had been taking the fouled diapers each night and cleaning them out for Lydia, but the hamper that stored the wet ones was getting odorous. Her bleeding had stopped during the night, but she needed to rinse out the rags Anabeth and Ma hadn't gotten to. It had been hard to stay clean on the Russell place, but Mama had drilled cleanliness into her. She had been filthy when the Langstons brought her in. No one had deplored that as much as she.

"We'll heat up some water after supper. If we hang them out overnight, they'll dry."

Lydia nodded. She was placing their box of cooking utensils in the wagon when they heard Lee's hungry wail. "Right on time," she said, laughing.

"I'll douse the fire and see to the horses." Ross stalked away, hating himself for feeling so good about the coming day and for noticing the way her complexion glowed in the early sunlight.

Lydia changed Lee and leaned with relaxed contentment against the slats of the wagon while he nursed. The camp was in full operation now. Most had eaten breakfast. Women were repacking the gear and admonishing their children to get their chores done. Men were hitching up their teams. Sharp whistles punctuated the air as they moved them into place.

Lazily Lydia's eyes closed. This was a safe, comfortable world, away from the larger, more frightening one. Here she was unknown. No one would associate her with the Russells. No one knew about that body with the crushed skull. It may not even have been found. Even if it had been, no one could trace her here. She was safe, secure. She could rest.

Ross was murmuring to his team horses as he hitched them to the wagon. She liked the low, deep timbre of his voice in contrast to the pleasant jingling of the harnesses. The air was heavy with the smell of wood smoke and horses and leather. It wasn't at all a disagreeable combination. Lee wasn't finding it so either. He ate hungrily, but the tugging cadence on her breast was lulling and only contributed to the aura of peacefulness.

Her eyes opened drowsily and then flew open wide.

Mr. Coleman was standing beside the team, fastening the harnesses together. He had an unrestricted view of her under the wagon's seat and into the back where she sat feeding Lee. He was staring straight at her from the deep shadow beneath his wide-brimmed hat. His gloved hands were momentarily still as they gripped the leather thongs.

The instant she caught him looking at her, he jumped to life again, yanking his eyes away from her as brutally as he pulled on the leather strap he was securing.

A trill of sensation tickled its way up from the depths of her womanhood, spread through her breasts, and trapped her breath in her throat. Such a sensation she had never experienced before and it shocked her as much as seeing Mr. Coleman staring at her with that degree of intentness. She turned her back slightly until Lee finished, and didn't look toward the front of the wagon again.

She had just tied Lee into a fresh sacque when word came down the line that they were ready to pull out. Ma had told her that the train traveled twelve to fifteen miles a day, but that they had been drastically slowed down by spring rains. It had left the roads and meadows over which they traveled muddy and rutted and hard to negotiate. Rivers and their tributaries were swollen and flooded, making crossing them hazardous. Because of the war, the bridges that remained were in a sad state of repair and wouldn't take the weight of the wagons.

Ross was driving the wagon today and adroitly coaxed the team into line with the others. They began at a sluggish pace, but had soon accelerated to one they would try to maintain until they stopped for the noon rest.

Lydia rolled the sleeping mattress against the side of the wagon to make more room to move about. She straightened the interior of the wagon, even folding some of Mr. Coleman's shirts and deciding which ones she should wash that night along with Lee's things.

After a while she became bored. Lee was sleeping soundly in his crate. She had done all the chores she could find for herself within the wagon and dreaded another day of lying about with nothing to do. The thought of fresh air and open spaces appealed to her greatly.

Timidly she ducked her head through the front opening of the wagon and tapped Mr. Coleman on the shoulder. His body tensed as if he had been gunshot, before his head snapped around. She withdrew her hand quickly. "What is it?" he demanded.

She resented his sharp tone. Did he think she would never grow tired of the inside of the wagon? Would he be embarrassed to have her riding beside him on the outside where everyone could see her, where his beloved Victoria used to sit with her lacy parasol? "I'd like to ride outside for a while," she said tartly.

Without speaking again, he scooted over on the wide, flat seat and made room for her. The swaying of the wagon made the footwork tricky, but she held on to the canvas with one fist while she placed one foot on the seat and stepped out. She teetered there for a moment. The ground seemed a very long way down. She hadn't realized how high the seat of the wagon was. Swallowing her fear, she put the other foot on the seat.

At that unfortunate moment, the left front wheel encountered a large rock and the wagon bumped over it with a sudden jolt. Lydia lost what precarious grip she had on her balance and grabbed at air until her hand came in contact with Mr. Coleman's hat. It was knocked to the wagon seat an instant before her buttocks plopped down hard on it.

On her way down she had gained quite a bit of momentum. It propelled her against Mr. Coleman. His arm was trapped between her full breasts as she slid down its entire length from shoulder to wrist. She tried to catch herself by placing her hand on his thigh, but it slipped and plunged between his legs. When she finally stopped falling, she found herself sprawled across his lap, her arm wedged between his thighs, her cheek resting on his hip.

For a moment she leaned against him, drawing in deep breaths, battling off vertigo, and trying valiantly to pretend nothing had happened. Finally she pulled herself upright and inched away. She was still sitting on his hat!

It was when she again braced her hand on his thigh to lever herself up and extract the crumpled hat that he began muttering blasphemous curses. "I'm sorry," she apologized breathlessly, mortified by her clumsiness. "I . . . I've never been on a wagon this large before."

The eyes he turned on her were glassy, bright, and fierce. His mouth was a thin, stern line beneath the curving moustache as he said, "Please be more careful next time." Lydia noticed that his lips barely moved as he spoke and his voice sounded different. Was he in pain? Had she hurt him?

With deft movements she restored his hat to its original shape and shyly handed it to him. It seemed a shame for him to cover up that head of dark hair that shone with iridescent streaks in the sunlight. But as he pulled it low on his brow she decided the hat did him justice as well.

His clothes were serviceable work clothes but he wore them well. The dark pants fit his long legs snugly. He always wore the black knee-high boots she had first seen. His shirt was heavy blue cotton, but the black leather vest over it looked soft to touch. He had a bandanna knotted around his throat.

Afraid he might notice her close scrutiny, Lydia dropped her eyes to his hands on the reins. The edges of the black leather gloves were curled back to reveal his wrist bones, which were sprinkled with dark hair. He held the reins with seeming negligence, but one subtle flick of his wrist could direct the team. They demonstrated tremendous power, yet were capable of tenderness too. Which had he used when he touched his wife?

Such a thought made Lydia dizzy again, so she directed her musings away from the man beside her and began taking in her surroundings. There were about ten wagons in front of them. She turned her head to look behind her, but gripped the seat in fear of falling off. She couldn't see around the bulk of the wagon and she wasn't about to lean too far over the side in order to do so.

"Where are we?" she asked.

The countryside was lush and green. Wildflowers were blooming everywhere. The land rimming the meadow they were traversing was gently hilly and heavily wooded.

"Just east of Memphis." Ross had nearly recovered, but not quite. He had cursed his own susceptibility when he had accidentally seen her earlier with his son at her breast. Thank God she hadn't taken the whole top of the dress down as she had last night. Instead it had been unbuttoned to her waist, only one breast available to Lee. Ross, despite his aversion to her, had been struck by the peaceful, glowing expression on her face, the smile tilting the corners of her mouth upward. It was the kind of expression a man would love to put on a woman's face.

He shifted restlessly on the wagon seat. What in the hell had he thought of that for? He had certainly never had a woman look up at him with that kind of sublime smile. In his youth, wild and undisciplined as it had been, he had known only whores. Generally speaking, they were businesswomen who wanted him to hurry and finish so they could get on to the next customer.

And then there had been Victoria. He had never expected that kind of passion from her. Ladies of her upbringing didn't enjoy . . . that . . . and he would have been shocked if she had. She had been obliging and patient with him, even affectionate. She had never said no, but she had never initiated it either.

He would never love another woman. That was out of the question. Still, it would be nice to have one smile up at him afterward with an expression close to the one he had seen on Lydia's . . . My God! He had thought of her as Lydia.

Why the hell did she have to fall against him that way? He could still feel her hand sliding over his crotch. His arm still tingled from the contact with her breasts.

He cleared his throat loudly as though to physically throw off his thoughts. "We might be able to cross the river day after tomorrow."

"The Mississippi River?"

Was the girl dense? "Of course the Mississippi River," he said in rebuke.

"Well, you don't have to be so snippy about it," Lydia fired back. She felt like he had slapped her in the face by pointing up her ignorance. She had heard of the Mississippi River, but she had no idea where it was. She had attended only two years of primary school before she and Mama had moved to the Russell place. It wasn't by choice that she was sadly unknowledgeable.

"You're going to sunburn if you don't put a hat on," Ross muttered, looking at the tip of her nose that was already taking on a rosy cast.

"I don't have a hat," she said, staring at him in that cold, haughty way she had.

He flicked the reins over the horses' backs, venting his anger at them. Why the girl should vex him so he couldn't imagine. Maybe it had something to do with his physical discomforts.

Throughout the morning, riders on horseback passed their wagon. Most were men. Ross would grudgingly introduce her. "This is Lydia. She's taking care of Lee." The men would doff their hats politely and introduce themselves. She met their glances shyly, but though they were curious, she didn't meet with the scorn she had expected.

The only one who unnerved her was Scout. He eyed her in a leisurely way. His grin at Ross was sly. "Pleased to know you, Lydia," he said. He had long, curly, butter-colored sideburns and a wide moustache that was almost white. Lydia wouldn't trust him as far as she could throw him. Thankfully he was away from the train most of the time. Everyone seemed pleased with the job he was doing. He had mapped out a route so that they could use roads when possible and flat public lands at other times. He had promised that if all went well, they would camp near shallow running water every night. So far, he had kept that promise.

Bubba and Luke Langston rode up pell-mell when the sun had almost reached its zenith. "Chicken tonight," Luke chortled happily. They had found two scrawny roosters in the woods. He held them up by their wrung necks.

"Ma said she'd fry it up and for the two of you to share it with us."

Lydia was watching Ross as his mouth split wide in a grin appreciative of the boys' exuberance. His smile was heartstopping and, looking at it, she felt a strange fluttering in her breast. It wasn't her milk coming because she had felt that a while ago. This was an alien unsettling, as though something had stirred up her insides and everything was trying to find its proper place again. His teeth were brilliantly white against the dark moustache and tanned face.

"I reckon I could take you up on that invitation if you'll drive the wagon after the noon break and let me give one of the mares some exercise."

"I'd be glad to take a horse out for you, Ross," Bubba said excitedly. His blue eyes had nearly popped out of his head when he had seen Lydia sitting on top of the wagon with Ross where Victoria used to sit. But it was the bodice of her dress that had drawn his attention. He knew his ma would skin him alive if she caught him gawking at the girl, and he wasn't sure what Ross would do either. He found himself fairly shouting to release some of the energy surging through his body.

Ross was shaking his head. "That would leave no one to drive the wagon."

"I could drive the wagon," Luke said. He was jealous that Bubba had been asked to help take care of Mr. Coleman's horses. Ma had said Bubba was the oldest and it was only right that he be offered the job first. Still, Luke didn't want to be discounted altogether, as though he held no more rank in the family than Samuel or Micah or one of the girls.

Ross considered the suggestion while both boys waited in breathless expectation of his answer. "I guess that would be all right. I could keep an eye on you," he said to Luke. "And two horses would be exercised instead of one."

"Yippee," Luke said, whipping his own mount around and heading toward the Langstons' wagon to tell his good news.

"Only if Ma gives her approval," Ross shouted after him.

They stopped but briefly at noon. Lydia went into the wagon to nurse Lee, who had awakened a few minutes before. He had lain in his crate and fretted. Ross had curtly suggested that she not try to get back into the wagon until he pulled it to a stop.

Luke brought her a wide-brimmed straw hat when he came to take over for Ross as driver. "Mr. Coleman told Ma your nose was gettin' sunburned. This is an old hat of Bubba's, but it'll keep the sun off."

Lydia took it, looking sightlessly at it as she turned it over and over in her hands. She didn't know if she was more moved by the Langstons' generosity or by Mr. Coleman's concern.

She didn't see him for the rest of the afternoon except as a pesky dot that bounced along the horizon as he and Bubba rode two of his mares to exercise them.

She grew weary in the early afternoon sun and Luke talked her through getting into the back of the wagon without mishap. She unbuttoned her tight dress, unrolled the mattress, and lay down. Lee lay beside her. When she awoke, Luke was bringing the wagon to a halt in the circle with the others.

Quickly she fed Lee and then, putting his crate on the tailgate in the shade, went about building their fire and getting their supper. She took time to tidy up her hair and bathe her arms and face and neck in cool water before Ross returned looking dusty and sweaty.

He looked at the pot of beans simmering over the fire. "I thought we were eating with the Langstons." The greeting sounded cross and critical, but he couldn't help it. The domesticity of the scene before him—the supper cooking, and Lee sleeping contentedly, and her taking the trouble to look nice for him—made him unreasonably angry.

"We are, but I'd been soaking these beans all day and it seemed a shame not to cook them. I sent word to Ma that we'd be bringing them for our part of the supper."

He didn't like the way she said "we" and "our" either, like they were a pair. "You can take the beans for *your* part. For *my* part, I'm helping Zeke reshoe one of his horses after dinner."

"Very well, Mr. Coleman," she snapped. "I was heating this water for you to wash in, but I think I'll use it to start washing out Lee's things instead." She swished past him, moving her skirt out of the way as though not to dirty its hem on his dusty boots.

He had a good mind to yank her around by the hair on her head and tell her that just because she was taking care of his boy, it didn't mean she had anything to do with *him*. But she had already stepped up into the wagon before the right words arranged themselves on his tongue. Besides, if he ever put his hand in her hair, he wasn't sure what he would do.

He turned away angrily, not wanting to think about how good it would feel to wash in warm water. He cursed viciously as he stepped behind the wagon where he was provided some privacy and peeled off his shirt.

Lydia, with the soiled clothes piled beside her, lifted the pot away from the fire before the water got too hot. Then, rubbing a bar of soap over each garment, she dropped it into the water. When all were in, she swished them with a stick.

Her shoulders lifted and fell in a sigh of irritation. He had been hateful again, but then it would be silly for her not to offer to wash his shirt too. Drawing in another deep breath, she rounded the end of the wagon to the far side. Ross was standing in pants and boots. His arms and chest were lathered white. For the few moments before he saw her, Lydia watched his hands sliding over the wet soapy flesh of his wide shoulders and under his arms. His chest was matted with dark, crinkly hair that twined around his fingers as he washed. The muscles of his upper arms bunched and knotted with each economic movement. His ribs were as evenly corrugated as a washboard. His stomach was flat and tapering.

When he saw her standing there watching him, he became stock-still. Soap bubbles dripped from fingers gone suddenly lifeless. For a long moment they stared at each other, each stunned by the sight of the other.

"I'll wash your shirt," Lydia said at last.

Rather than argue and prolong her standing there, Ross picked up his shirt and handed it to her.

Her eyes averted, she whisked it from his hand and disappeared quickly around the end of the wagon. Ross rinsed and dunked his head in the water. Only after he had dried off did he realize that he didn't have a shirt to put on. He went to the tailgate and vaulted up into the wagon, nearly stepping on Lee where he slept in his crate. He cursed as he bumped his head on one of the slats, then grew more agitated when he couldn't locate any of his clothes.

He stuck his head through the open canvas flaps. "Uh . . ." he said, hoping to get her attention as she wrung the clothes out. She turned around, brushing back a strand of willful hair with a damp hand. "I can't find my clothes," he stated simply.

"Oh. I straightened up this morning. I'll get a shirt for you."

Nervously Ross's eyes scanned the campsite, hoping to God no one was watching her climb into the wagon with him shirtless. Damn! There stood Mrs. Watkins, glaring at them across the grassy expanse, her mouth drawn up like a rotten apple, looking for all the world like a witch-hunter. Her daughter Priscilla was standing behind her with a knowing, smug look on her petulant face. Ross had seen her wear that expression before. It made him damned uneasy.

Lydia, oblivious to their audience, brushed past him.

Her brisk movement stirred the hair on his chest and stomach. He ducked out of sight into the wagon. God, the girl was shameless. Didn't she have one ounce of propriety?

"I folded them up over here," she was saying as she rummaged through the supplies which she had neatly stacked out of the way. It occurred to Ross suddenly that the interior of the wagon no longer painfully reminded him of Victoria. All traces of her clutter were gone. Things were more neatly arranged to save space and make room.

Lydia handed him a clean shirt that had been folded carefully. She had almost gasped at the sight of the scar. It was above his left breast and had gouged out part of the muscle. She tried not to let him know she had noticed it.

"Thanks," he said tersely, hoping that she would leave the wagon so everyone could see her outside instead of in there with him.

He should have known that was too much to ask of her. "Mr. Coleman, would you teach me to drive the wagon?" she asked, looking up at him. Even stooped over as he was, she came no higher than his breastbone.

"Drive the wagon?" he repeated vaguely. He was wondering if he should pull his shirt on or wait until she left. Better to put it on now. The way her eyes wandered curiously over his chest was making him perspire even though he had just washed. "I don't think so," he said, cramming his arms into the sleeves. Was she looking at his nipple or at the scar?

"Why?"

"Because the team would probably pull you off the seat, that's why. You're not . . . husky . . . enough." His fingers were behaving as though they had never buttoned a shirt before.

"Did your wife . . . did Victoria drive the team?"

When he reached the last button, he discovered he had matched them all up with the wrong holes. He cursed under his breath and nearly ripped them free before starting all over again. "Yes, she did."

"She was husky?"

"Dammit, no, she wasn't husky!" he shouted. Nervously he glanced over his shoulder. He lowered his voice to a vicious hiss. "No, she wasn't husky."

"And you taught her."

"Yes."

"Then why can't you teach me?"

"Because you've no business driving my team."

"Why?" she repeated.

Unconsciously he unbuttoned his pants to cram his shirttail in. The men Lydia had known wore suspenders to hold up their breeches. Even the dim memories of her father pictured him with suspenders. Her eyes were on Ross's hands as he secured the buttons on his pants and refastened the buckle of his wide leather belt, slapping it lightly when he was done.

"You have to take care of Lee, that's why."

She dragged her eyes up the long length of his torso, not knowing how provocative that sweep of her lashes was to watch. "But he sleeps so much. I enjoyed riding on the seat today. There's no reason why I couldn't be useful while I'm sitting there. That would free you to ride your horses if you wanted to. I'm not saying I'd drive all the time. If Lee was fretful, I couldn't, but I should know how."

More to end the conversation and get out into the open where he could breathe normally again, he said, "I'll think about it. It's not easy, you know." With that he stamped out of the wagon, leaving her with a satisfied smile on her lips.

The noise and general state of confusion at the Langston wagon served to camouflage the tension between Ross and Lydia. The two roosters were honored with hearty appetites that didn't leave one bone unpicked.

Only Bubba didn't enjoy the meal. After eating only half a plateful, he slunk away in the darkness, ostensibly to check on the horses. A few minutes later Luke found him leaning against a tree, absently peeling a twig of its bark.

"What's the matter, Bubba? Got a bellyache?"

"Go away," Bubba sighed. Privacy in a family the size of his was rare and valuable.

"I know what's wrong with you," Luke said cockily. "You couldn't eat on account of lookin' at Lydia's titties."

Bubba sprang to his feet poised for hand-to-hand

combat. "You shut up, you foulmouthed sonofabitch!" he shouted.

Luke only laughed and danced away from his brother, shadowboxing to egg him on. "Can't help but look at 'em, can you? 'Course a body would think you'd have your eyes full after gawkin' at Priscilla Watkins's all the time. Hers are pretty big. I seen the way she pushes 'em out every time you ride by their wagon, which is about as often as you can. You're about the randiest billygoat I ever did see."

Bubba lunged at his brother and managed to connect his flying fist with Luke's jaw. Luke fell back onto the ground, but he wasn't subdued by any means. He grabbed Bubba around the ankle, hauled him down, and a battle royal ensued. Ross came upon them moments later, grappling and rolling and slugging in the dirt.

"What's going on here?" he bellowed. He grabbed the top one, which at the moment happened to be Luke, by the collar of his shirt and hauled him to his feet. Bubba came to his feet of his own volition. They were heaving from exertion and bleeding from noses, mouths, and various scratches. "Is this all you two have to do?" Ross demanded.

He knew what came of fighting. First with fists, then with guns. It became a vicious cycle to see who you could best. If someone had curbed him when he was a youngster, maybe things wouldn't have gone the way they had. But by the time he was Bubba's age, he had already developed an awesome talent with a pistol.

"Bubba, I thought you were going to help me shoe that horse."

Bubba dabbed at his rapidly swelling lip. "Sure, Ross."

"Luke," Ross barked. "Fetch some water to my wagon. Lydia has some clothes to rinse out." He didn't stop to consider how easily her name had come to his lips. "But shake hands with your brother first."

The boys grudgingly did as he instructed. They were both dreading having to explain their bloody, swollen faces to their ma. It would be hell to pay.

Lydia was enjoying herself. She never knew folks could be so cordial. "Neighbors" stopped by to meet her.

Some were openly curious, some were cautious, and she knew she wouldn't have been nearly so well accepted had it not been for the Langstons. Because Ma approved of her, everyone else felt obliged to. It was an unspoken fact that Ma governed much of what went on in the insulated community. Almost as much as Mr. Grayson did. Her maternal instincts carried over to all members of the train. She adored and admonished each one, no matter how old or young, with the freedom she did her own children.

Lydia tried to remember names and put the right children with the correct parents. There were the Sims with their two shy little girls, the Rigsbys with two boys and a baby girl. Lydia met the woman with the twins. They were almost a year old. One was beginning to take tentative steps, invariably in the direction of the campfire. Other names became familiar. Cox, Norwood, Appleton, Greer, Lawson. Everyone ogled Lee Coleman, who slept through most of it.

Mrs. Greer offered her the use of some baby clothes. "My boy has grown out of them. Ain't no sense in them going to waste." Such kindness was unheard of to Lydia, who had seen life as one scraping effort to survive. What one had, one kept and selfishly guarded.

Before Lydia returned to Mr. Coleman's wagon, Ma gave her one of Luke's shirts and an old skirt of Anabeth's. "They ain't as attractive as the dress, and Lord knows it ain't nothin' fancy, but they'll be a sight more comfortable, I 'spect."

Lydia carried Lee back to her own camp and was surprised to find Luke stretching a cord between the slender trunks of two nearby post oaks. He spotted her and averted his head. "Mr. Coleman told me to fix this here so you could hang them clothes up."

"Thank you, Luke," she said quietly. She didn't comment on his bruised, distorted face, sensing his self-consciousness over it.

When all the clothes were hanging on the line, she wearily climbed into the wagon. The camp had grown quiet and dark. She nursed Lee and settled him in his crib. Then she put on the nightgown Ma had told her was hers to keep.

Her head was sore from supporting her hair all day. She shook it out and began brushing it. The brush, too, was a gift from Ma.

She didn't want to go to sleep until Ross returned to the wagon. His presence outside made her feel safe, though why that should be she couldn't imagine. For weeks before she had dropped in the woods to deliver her child, she had slept in the open, sometimes in a barn. But fear had been her guardian then. It had protected her from becoming tired or careless. But she had gotten careless and he had caught up with her. "Never again," she whispered in the darkness. "He's dead."

Just when her eyes were drowsily closing, she heard Ross outside. His movements were easy to follow as he banked the fire and shook out his bedroll.

Walking on her knees to the end of the wagon, she lifted the canvas. He was sitting on his bedroll tugging off his boots. "Good night, Mr. Coleman."

His head came up with a jerk. She was framed in the opening of the wagon, her nightgown reflecting whitely in the moonlight. Surrounding her head, her hair was a riot of curls and waves. Her voice seemed to come toward him out of the darkness to stroke his cheek.

"Good night," he growled and flopped down on his hard bed.

Still grouchy, she thought dejectedly as she settled herself on the mattress spread with soft bed linens. He was anxious to get across the Mississippi. By tomorrow maybe they would see it. He would be in a better frame of mind then.

Chapter Six

They drove the teams hard for the next two days, trying to reach the Mississippi. It was a landmark to all of them. Once they crossed it and left Tennessee behind, they would feel they were truly on their way.

Ross let Bubba Langston lead his string of horses and drove the wagon himself. He never turned the reins over to Lydia, but he showed her how to hold and maneuver them. The instructions were tersely issued and he rarely looked at her directly. Though Luke's shirt and the old skirt left a lot to be desired in the way of fashion, Ross had been vastly relieved to see that she wasn't wearing that dress anymore.

She seemed determined not to foster his bad mood and pushed him into conversation. It became apparent that the girl knew little about anything, and he wondered again if she were mentally deficient. He dismissed that possibility, however. Once told something, she never forgot it, and behind her inquiring eyes he saw an eagerness to learn.

"Did you fight in the war?"

He nodded. "For Dixie."

"You wanted to keep the colored people slaves, then?"

He stared at her incredulously. "No. I don't want anyone to be a slave to anything or anybody."

"Then why did you fight for the South?"

"Because that's where I lived," he said with growing impatience. She seemed to know his sore spots instinctively and went straight to them with probing accuracy.

Patriotism had had little to do with what side Ross had allied himself. The war had provided him, as a reckless young man, with a good excuse to loot and kill without consequence. He had been spoiling for a fight, and he had been granted a dilly of a one. When a group of guerrilla fighters had recruited him to ride with them, nobility had not entered into his joining.

Lydia didn't want him to think her totally ignorant. "One day I watched a column of soldiers ride past our farm. They were all dressed alike. One was carrying a flag."

"Yankee troop. We sure as hell didn't have uniforms and flags toward the end." He had had only one uniform, and that he had taken off a dead soldier at Pea Ridge. He had never ridden in a column of soldiers, either, but struck unsuspecting camps at night. There one minute, gone the next, phantoms leaving death and destruction behind. And Ross hadn't cared if he got killed in the process because to him it was all a game of chance. He was perfect for that kind of soldiering.

"I never saw any more soldiers, but I can remember hearing the guns and cannons sometimes."

"Where was your farm?"

Lydia didn't want to confide too much, but then she didn't actually know where the Russell place was. "Northeast Tennessee."

"Didn't troops from either side ever loot it?"

She laughed bitterly. "No. There wasn't anything there worth stealing."

He had ridden with men who would have passed up food for a chance at the girl. But then the war had ended six years ago. She couldn't have been more than a kid. "How old are you?" he surprised himself by asking.

"I'll be twenty this year. How old are you?"

"A lot older," Ross said grimly. He was thirty-two if one counted chronologically. He liked to think his life had started when John Sachs found him.

Winston Hill rode up to their wagon on a prancing white horse. "Good day to you, Miss Lydia, Mr. Coleman."

"Hello, Mr. Hill."

"Hill."

"I hear that with luck we'll reach Memphis by nightfall."

"That's the rumor," Ross said curtly.

It irked Lydia that Ross was behaving rudely. She didn't want another argument with him concerning Winston Hill, but she didn't want to be a party to his bad manners either. "Do you think we'll have much trouble crossing, Mr. Hill?" She tilted her head back so she could see him from beneath her hat.

"That depends on the flooding they've been having upstream." He paused to cough into his handkerchief. "Once we're across, Moses and I would like to invite the two of you to celebrate with us with a glass of sherry."

Lydia wondered what sherry was. If it tasted as pretty as it sounded, she would like it. She was about to accept his invitation when Ross intervened. "No, thanks. Lydia is busy most evenings taking care of Lee, and I tend to my horses."

Mr. Hill's eyes glanced back and forth between the two of them before he replied with gracious acceptance. "Well, perhaps some evening when all your chores are done." He doffed his hat to Lydia and rode away.

"The next time someone invites me to do something, I'll answer for myself, thank you," Lydia said as soon as the man was out of earshot.

"Not as long as you're sleeping in my wagon and eating the food I provide, you won't," he growled out of the side of his mouth. "I won't have you openly flirting with him or anyone else as long as you're caring for Lee."

"I wasn't flirting!" she said heatedly. "I was being mannerly, an area of your personality that could stand some improvement."

"Manners has nothing to do with it. I don't like the man."

"He has said nothing but nice things about you and Victoria, but every time he comes around you puff up like a bullfrog. What's he ever done to you?"

Ross hunched his shoulders and didn't speak. Winston Hill represented everything Ross wished he could be. Winston was the kind of man Victoria should have married. Ross remembered the night they had met. They had had mutual acquaintances to swap gossip about and had spoken in a cultured language he could barely follow. He had felt like scum.

Though he wouldn't put a name to the emotion Hill aroused in him, he had been jealous of him since the first time he laid eyes on him. Hill carried his aristocratic heritage like a shield in front of him for all to see. Ross felt that his heritage was just as visible no matter how hard he tried to hide it.

"Why does he cough all the time?" Lydia asked. She ignored the working tension in Ross's jaw.

"He's tubercular."

"Tu . . . what?"

"He has tuberculosis. Lung fever. Caught it in a Yankee prison camp. When he finally made his way home, somewhere in North Carolina—Raleigh, I think—the plantation was gone. No one was left but old Moses. Even the house had been destroyed. He moved into town, but the weather there was bad for his lungs. He's on his way to a warmer, drier climate."

Winston had stopped at the wagon in front of them to chat. She studied the slight young man, whose eyes, though kind, were too old to match the rest of him. "I feel sorry for him."

That seemed truly to irritate Mr. Coleman. He didn't talk to her anymore until the noon break.

Her first sight of Memphis was through a veil of mist as she sat in the wagon, staring out over Mr. Coleman's shoulder while he maneuvered the team into the circle for the night. Lydia had never seen so large a city. Even from that distance, it was an awesome sight. She could have gazed idly at it for a long time, but there was work to be done in a hurry.

"We'd better get a fire going as soon as I can locate some dry wood," Ross said, glancing up at the moisture-laden clouds that scurried past on a cool wind.

He finally coaxed a small, sputtering fire out of the damp wood he had gathered. Lydia fried extra meat and made two batches of biscuits, saying, "This may be our last full-fledged fire for days." The rainfall had steadily increased.

Everyone in camp was dejected. They could see the Mississippi below them where they were camped on the bluffs. They had both dreaded and anticipated crossing the river, but now it looked intimidating and ominous. It was swollen from recent heavy rains. One could barely see the Arkansas shore for the gloomy rain that shrouded it. Those who had lived on or near the fierce Tennessee all their lives were impressed into silence by the breadth of the Mississippi.

Despite its awesome proportions, now that they were here and could see it, they were ready to cross. And it appeared they might have to wait, for days, even weeks.

"A group of us are going with Grayson to check on the ferry first thing in the morning," Ross told Lydia as they secured everything they could in the wagon and out of the weather.

"What do you think will happen?"

Ross cursed. "I think we'll have to wait out the rain. Folks who live on this river are superstitious about it. I don't think the ferries will chance crossing it until the next sunny day."

Lydia was sensitive to his mood and didn't provoke his temper. When he came in to get an extra blanket, she spoke to him softly from the other side of the warm, dry wagon. "Do you have to sleep outside, Mr. Coleman?"

He looked at her in open astonishment. She was feeding Lee, but since that morning he had seen her nursing him, she had started draping her shoulder, breast, and the baby's head with a flannel blanket. Ross was glad that she had felt some degree of modesty, but his mind wouldn't forget seeing her cushioning his son's head on that creamy mound of flesh.

"What would people think if the two of us stayed in here together?" he demanded short-temperedly.

"They'd probably think you had the good sense to come in out of the rain," she snapped back. The weather wasn't doing her temperament any good either. Nor was the man's stubbornness. Did he think she was trying to lure him into the wagon? Lying with a man was the last thing she wanted to do.

"Well, I can't sleep in here with . . . with . . . you." He turned toward the opening. "I'll see you in the morning."

He crawled beneath the wagon and rolled up in a

blanket-lined tarpaulin. He was damp and chilled, but it was almost a relief from the hot, fevered feeling that had plagued him for days.

Ross was querulous and bedraggled when he returned to the wagon about noon. Rain was falling in sheets. He, Mr. Norwood, Mr. Sims, and Mr. Grayson had ridden down to the banks of the river and contacted the man who operated the ferry service. As Ross had predicted, he wouldn't consider crossing the flood-stage river in this kind of rain and wind. Hauling twenty wagons with teams, women, and children through the swift current was out of the question.

"He said we would have to wait until the rain subsided," Ross said, grimacing as he tossed down the cold coffee Lydia had saved him.

"Are you hungry?"

He shrugged. His face was dark with stubble. With good reason—he hadn't shaved that morning. "Reckon I could eat something."

She passed him a folded linen napkin in which he found a bacon and biscuit sandwich. "Ma is sending her two boys into town later in hopes of buying some canned food. Can you think of anything Lee needs?" Ross asked.

Lydia shook her head, thinking of a dozen things she needed. Like a chemise, for instance. If she wore one, she could line it with soft cloth so that when her breasts leaked, she wouldn't have to run from Mr. Coleman or anyone else who might see the two damp circles on the front of her dress. "The ladies on the train have loaned him things. He won't need much else until he grows some."

Ross would have loved to go into town himself, but didn't dare take a chance. He had been foolhardy even to go down and talk to the ferryman. He had kept his bearded face averted. It had been three years, but still . . .

The afternoon hours dragged by drearily and interminably. Lee slept, though Lydia sang to him, tickled his tummy, and anything else she could do to keep him awake. She was bored, sitting alone in the wagon without older children or a husband to talk to. Other women were using this day to rest, or mend, or speculate with their families about their new homesteads in Texas or farther west. Ross had left the wagon to see to his horses, leaving Lydia alone.

Luke and Bubba called to her from the back of the wagon just before darkness fell. She scrambled on hands and knees to lift the canvas and peer out, bursting into laughter at the sight of them. Their felt hat brims were drooping low as runnels of water rolled down onto the slickers they wore. But their rain-washed faces were as animated as ever. She imagined that they had enjoyed riding into a city like Memphis and would be full of stories to tell for days to come.

"We spent all the money Ross gave us. Peaches, pears, okra stewed with tomatoes and onions, and a smoked sausage," Bubba said, taking the items from the knapsack tied to his saddle horn and passing them to her.

"The smell of that sausage has been making our mouths water," Luke said.

"Did you buy one too?"

Bubba glanced at Luke with a look that said he would dearly love to murder him. "Naw."

Lydia was appalled at what she had forced the boy to admit. The Langstons couldn't afford a sausage. She and Mama had helped butcher hogs, working all day for a pound of bacon and a sausage. She had no concept of money or any idea how much a sausage or anything else would cost.

"Well, you deserve a reward for bringing it back to me . . . to Mr. Coleman, I mean." Reaching in the cooking-utensil box, she lifted out a butcher knife and, securing the sausage between her body and her arm, cut off a slice for each boy. "Here. Enjoy it."

Luke reached for his slice immediately, unabashedly cramming it into his mouth. Bubba took his portion almost grudgingly. "Thank you kindly, Miss Lydia." He was relieved to see that she wasn't wearing the tight dress anymore, though she filled out the front of Luke's old shirt right nice.

The mysteries of the female body bewitched him and consumed his thoughts. He had been thinking about

Priscilla Watkins all day. He had seen her standing out in the rain yesterday evening. Her dress had been clinging wetly to her body and detailing her figure. When she saw Bubba, she had turned to him, seemingly unaware that the cloth was plastered to her breasts and their impudent nipples. He had lain in misery all night wondering what it felt like to touch a woman's breast.

Now sight of Lydia's warmth and softness caused embarrassing and shameful reactions in his body. "We'd best be gittin' to our own wagon or Ma'll have a posse out after us."

Lydia smiled. "Yes, you'd better." They rode away into the gathering gloom.

She and Ross shared the food when he returned to the wagon. He looked almost as sodden as the young men had. They rationed the food to last for several days. Even eaten cold with leftover biscuits, it tasted delicious to Lydia. Before the Langstons found her, she had never had such good-tasting food, food that everyone else seemed to take for granted.

Lydia dreaded the time when Ross would go back outside. But not as much as Ross did. The ground was good and soaked now and he didn't look forward to another night spent striving to stay dry. The wagon was cozy with the lantern's soft glow, with Lee's new baby smell, with . . . Lydia. Her feminine presence made the wagon alluringly homey.

He stretched out the time he could remain inside by repairing a bridle that could have gone another few days without his attention. It took him an inordinate amount of time to accomplish that simple task, but he made sure that the two shadows cast on the canvas by the interior light were well separated should anyone happen to be watching. When he had run out of excuses to stay, he gathered his damp bedroll and approached the back of the wagon.

"Don't forget to turn out the lantern." He didn't look at her where she sat in a front corner of the wagon with Lee lying on her breast. The baby had finished feeding minutes ago, but she hadn't wanted to put him in his bed yet. She loved his precious weight against her body, loved to feel his rapid heartbeats against her.

"Good night, Mr. Coleman." Guiltily she watched his retreating back. Rightfully he could have booted her out in the rain and taken the wagon for himself. But she had suggested once that for common sense's sake he stay inside. He had nearly bitten her head off. She could be as stubborn as he. She wouldn't offer again.

She hadn't been asleep long when a crack of thunder brought her bolt upright on the pallet. It had been thundering the last time Clancey had crawled into her sleeping loft and clamped her throat with his grimy hand in order to hold her still and quiet. Her forehead and upper lip were beaded with perspiration. She had been dreaming of his grappling hands on her, of the pain, of the sickening culmination of her losing struggle.

Thunder reverberated through the air again, accompanied by a keening wind. Rain pelleted the canvas covering the wagon. It sounded like a thousand tiny beating drums. Lydia shivered, in terror of the elements and with the residual horror of her nightmare. She checked on Lee. He was sleeping soundly. She thought of Mr. Coleman out there in the rain and, before she weighed her reasons, began crawling her way toward the end of the wagon.

About the time Lydia was waking from her dream, Ross decided that he was a damned fool for turning over the warmth and comfort of his wagon to a strumpet who would likely run off any day now. He was soaked to the skin, shivering with each blast of wind and rain that found him where he lay underneath the wagon. The girl could go to hell and take Mrs. Watkins and everyone else on the train with her for all he cared. He was going inside. He inched from beneath the wagon, and was groping for the flapping canvas when Lydia threw it back.

Surprised to see the other, they each stared, frozen for a moment in time, heedless of the rain drenching Ross. It took another fearsome crack of lightning, which cut a jagged bluish scar out of the sky, to jerk them back into the present.

Lydia reached out and caught his hand, pulling him into the wagon. He all but fell inside on his knees, shivering convulsively while a great pool of rainwater formed around him.

Mindless that she was getting the hem of her nightgown wet, Lydia knelt before him and began unbuttoning his shirt buttons. "You're going to catch your death," she said fussily as she peeled the sodden shirt away from his shoulders and down his arms. "Get out of those pants."

Ross was too numb in mind and body to object, and obeyed blindly. Lydia tossed the shirt onto the steps outside. It couldn't get any wetter. She lit the lantern, but only turned the wick high enough to cast a feeble glow. She glanced over her shoulder to see him working with his belt buckle. "Hand me all your clothes. I'll put them outside."

She kept her back turned, but she could hear him taking off the clothes. His pants must have weighed ten pounds with the water they contained, but she managed to take them with her hand stretched out behind her, bring them forward, and heave them outside along with a pair of socks and underwear.

When she glanced around, Ross was wrapped in a blanket. "You're shivering. Are you still wet?" She reached into the hamper where towels were stored and approached him with two of them. "Dry your hair."

He draped the towel over his head and rubbed it vigorously. She placed the other towel on his chest and began to run her hands over it. Ross's actions stilled for a heartbeat, but he resumed as she briskly blotted his shoulders, his chest, and lower to his stomach.

She was struck by how hard his body was. The bronzed skin was stretched tautly over sinew and muscle and bone. There were nicks in it, small scars scattered over him, and the one just below his left shoulder that looked like a handful of flesh had been torn out by a giant fist. She wondered what he had suffered to have put it there, and she ached to touch it, soothe it somehow.

Intriguing to her, too, was the forest of crisp hair that covered his chest. It looked like a dark cloud, damp and curly. But the farther down his torso her hands moved, the silkier and finer the hair became. The growth pattern narrowed toward his navel.

Ross sucked his breath in sharply when she touched his navel and clenched his teeth when he felt her hands climbing back up his ribs. He draped the towel around his neck and caught her wrists in both his fists, yanking her upward and forward. He had been intent only on stopping her hands. He hadn't counted on her being caught totally off guard, on her weighing no more than a hummingbird, and on it taking no more than that swift tug to land her square in his lap with her breasts pressed flat against his chest and her knees . . . Good God! Could she feel him? Naked and hard.

For another startled moment they stared deep into each other's eyes, their breaths rasping together, hearts pulsing as violently as the thunder outside.

Damn those eyes of hers. He searched the jeweled depths of them. The myriad facets made him too dizzy to count them. And did her mouth have to look so goddamned succulent, like a rare and precious fruit that the gods squeezed nectar from? The tip of his tongue ached to dip into it and taste . . . and taste again. Didn't she have bones? Did all of her feel this soft and malleable, with no sharp angles to poke or protude?

He wanted to kiss her, to distort the perfection of her mouth with his lips. He craved to mold that incredible welcoming warmth against his hard desire. He would die if he didn't surrender to the raging, maniacal demand of his body for surcease.

But he would forever regret it if he heeded that cry. He closed his mind to it.

Gradually his grip relaxed and he eased her away. Lydia moved back quickly the moment she gained her release. The sparks shooting from the corners of his green eyes frightened her. When she was sitting on her knees a safe distance from him she whispered, "Are you feeling better?"

That was entirely dependent on one's point of view. "Somewhat."

"Your teeth aren't chattering anymore."

"I'm getting warmer." He was a helluva lot warmer.

Hot, in fact. So damned hot he didn't know why the hair on his body wasn't singed.

"I wish we had something hot for you to drink."

"I do too. Maybe at breakfast I can build a fire."

Neither thought so, but it gave him something to say and something they could nod their heads in agreement over. Now that the immediacy of the crisis was over, they had to come to grips with sharing the wagon.

"I'd better put some clothes on."

"Oh," she said, lifting a hand to still the fluttering pulse in her throat. Why her heart was pounding and why her breath was irregular, she couldn't imagine. But every time she looked at the network of hair disappearing into the shadows of the blanket bunched around his hips, she went to trembling all over. "Of course." She turned her back and pretended to straighten the covers on the pallet.

In a minute he said, "It's all right now." He was sitting on the floor in a pair of breeches, pulling on socks. He hadn't put on another shirt. Even as Lydia watched, gooseflesh formed on his arms and chest.

"Mr. Coleman," she said, moving away from the mattress, "get in here under these covers or you're going to have pneumonia."

"No. I'll bundle up over here."

"No. I've already warmed a spot." That's what he was afraid of. "And it's your bed, after all."

Well, at least the girl remembered that. "No, you go on—"

"Please, don't be stubborn about this."

"I'm not being stubborn."

"You are. If I hadn't been using your bed, you wouldn't have been outside in the first place. Don't make me feel any more guilty than I do." She could see the indomitable thinning of his lips and took another tack. "If you get sick, it might delay you and Lee getting to Texas."

"I won't get sick."

"Or you might die. Then what would happen to Lee?"

"I'm not going to die."

"How do you know?"

"For godsakes, all right!" Ross exploded. He bent at

the waist and made his way to the pallet, falling onto it with more weariness than he wanted to admit to, and pulling the warm covers over his shivering body. "There. Are you satisfied?"

"Yes," Lydia said, smiling.

She mopped the wagon floor with the damp towels, then threw them outside with his clothes. No telling how long it would take them to wring the water out of those things, but she couldn't leave them in the wagon. Turning out the lantern first, she crept to the opposite corner, wrapped herself in a blanket, and leaned against the side of the wagon.

Damn! Ross knew what he should do, but how could he? How could he invite that girl, who had slept with God knew how many men, who represented everything he hated and had tried all his life to escape from, beneath those blankets with him? How could he ask her to lie beside him where Victoria, ladylike and proper even in bed, dressed in her chaste nightgowns trimmed with satin bows and eyelet lace, had lain?

Of course it wouldn't be that way. He didn't want the girl. *Like hell*, his baser side mocked him. All right, he was stiff with wanting her. He ached like hell. It was physical. But he was a man, not an animal. Victoria's love had rid him of all that ugliness inside him. He couldn't control his body, but he could control his response to it.

"Miss . . . uh, Lydia," he spoke into the darkness.

"Yes?" Her voice was shallow with fright. What was he going to do? It was most often in the night when men did things to women. She could remember her mother's weeping as she lay with Otis Russell in their bed. She could remember Clancey's defilement of her own shuck mattress.

"You can't sit there for the rest of the night. If you like, you can lie on the other side of the mattress."

"I'll be fine."

"Don't be ridiculous." He came up on his elbows to address the silhouette huddled in the darkness. "It's hours till dawn. It's cold and damp. You can't sit there all night or you'll be consumptive by morning."

"I have a strong constitution. I'll be fine."

The last thing his shredded nerves needed was the girl's obtuseness and another argument with her. Lately he had been losing every one of them. His temper flared. "Dammit, I said to get over here." He extended his hand, closed it around her upper arm, and hauled her across the wagon.

Tears pooled in Lydia's eyes. She hadn't thought Mr. Coleman would do the bad things Clancey had, but she had been wrong. He was a man. She struggled until she realized that she was fighting empty air. Mr. Coleman had slung the blankets over her and then rolled to face away from her. He wasn't even touching her.

Lydia lay awake for long minutes, letting her body relax by gradual degrees. When Mr. Coleman's breathing had been regular and deep for several minutes, she let herself believe that he wasn't going to hurt her and snuggled down deeper into the blankets.

It was still raining hard, though the thunder echoed now from far away and the lightning flashed no longer. Even though they weren't touching, the heat emanating from Ross's body felt good. She slept.

When Ross awoke, it took him a minute to orient himself. His eyes opened to the side slats of the wagon. Through the crack between the side of the wagon and the canvas covering, he could see that it was light but still raining hard. He was dry and warm and rested and felt pretty damn good about someth—

He rolled over quickly. Lydia lay beside him. She was awake, lying on her side away from him, holding Lee in the crook of her arm. The nightgown was unbuttoned and open. Lee was avidly sucking at her breast.

She turned her head slightly. "I'm sorry we woke you up. You were sleeping so soundly."

"You didn't wake me. I'm used to getting up early."

Ross tried to tear his eyes away from her, from his contentedly nursing son, from her breast, but he couldn't. He didn't think about lying in the same bed with her, neither of them fully clothed. He didn't think about

Victoria. He didn't think about anything except how pretty she was when she smiled drowsily like that.

"No sense in getting an early start today," she said quietly. "The rain is as bad as it was last night."

"Sounds like it," Ross said absently. He wondered how he could have ever thought her hair was unattractive. A compulsion to touch its curly confusion seized him, and only by an act of will did he resist. He propped himself up on one elbow to better peer over her shoulder at his son. "He's getting fatter," he observed.

Lydia laughed, a soft, throaty laugh that brushed every erogenous part of Ross's body. "He should be. All he does is eat and sleep."

They looked on while Lee, unaware that he was something as important as a unifying bond between two strangers, sucked happily. He was greedy and a pearl of milk escaped his lips and rolled down his chin and onto Lydia's breast.

Ross didn't plan it, would have been horrified by the mere thought of doing it. But it was done before he realized he had even moved. He reached across Lydia, lifted the droplet of milk from her breast with his finger, and then brought it to his own mouth and licked it free with his tongue.

Realizing too late what he had done, he lay perfectly still, paralyzed by his own reflexive action. Lydia turned her head on the pillow to gaze up at him with disbelief. Her eyes went to his moustache, to his mouth beneath it, to the finger that still rested against his lips, a guilty culprit caught in a crime.

"I didn't mean to do that." Ross's voice was like a saw against hardwood. Lydia continued to stare at him with wordless inquiry, as though trying to figure out something beyond her reasoning powers. Why he didn't throw the covers off both of them and leave, he didn't know. He only knew that he was powerless to move either his body or his eyes away from hers.

At last she turned back to the baby. "He's already asleep again," she murmured softly as though nothing earthshattering had happened.

Ross fell back onto the pallet, an arm thrown over his eyes. With his ears, he followed each of her motions as she lifted Lee from her breast and tucked it into the security of the nightgown. She rebuttoned it. She positioned the baby safely against her side. She settled into sleep again.

And still he couldn't get over what he had done. And still he couldn't move away. And still he could taste it.

With the essence of her lingering on his tongue, sleep overcame him again. Unconsciously he lowered his arm and sought to warm it under the covers as he rolled to his side. Unknowingly his cheek trapped several strands of russet hair and they in turn ensnared his moustache. His body instinctively curved around the closest source of warmth, a rounder, softer, smaller version of humankind than himself. To his subconscious mind, it felt right.

The three slept on.

That's how Mr. Grayson found them an hour later.

Chapter Seven

Ross Coleman had the quicksilver instincts of a rattlesnake. From years of guerrilla fighting and being a fugitive he had developed a sixth sense about any intrusive presence. It failed him completely that morning. He was still sleeping soundly when the wagonmaster cleared his throat loudly.

Ross opened his eyes to see Hal Grayson standing just inside the wagon's opening. He was staring at the floor, nervously rotating the brim of his hat between his fingers.

Ross's whipcord reactions took over. He leaped from the pallet, slapping his right thigh, reaching for something that wasn't there, and balancing on the balls of his feet in an attitude of attack.

Grayson's eyes opened as wide as his mouth in astonishment. He had never seen a man move so quickly.

He held both hands up in surrender. "I'm . . . sorry
. . . I . . . kn . . . knocked," he stuttered.

Lydia scrambled to the side of the wagon, bringing a
startled and fussing Lee with her. Her eyes were wide with
incomprehension, her hair a swirl of wild disarray around
her head.

"Do your duties extend to entering someone's wagon
uninvited?" Ross demanded of the obviously appalled
Grayson.

"No, they don't—"

"Except when he's about to evict the party."

The smug voice belonged to Leona Watkins, whose
beady accusatory eyes had been level with the floor of the
wagon as she stood on the ground below. Now she stepped
up into the wagon to glare at Lydia and Ross with righteous
outrage.

Ross forced his muscles to relax and his heart to stop
racing. "Evict? What's she talking about?" he asked Grayson, who wouldn't meet Ross's eyes.

"I'm sorry, Ross, but Mrs. Watkins has gotten up a
committee of folks. They voted that you and the girl have to
leave the train since you've . . . uh . . . you plan to
. . . uh . . . cohabitate."

"Cohabitate!" Ross roared. "We shared the wagon last
night because it was pouring down rain."

"I understand—" Grayson began, but Leona interrupted.

"You shared a bed!" she screamed, pointing a bony
finger at them. Then, turning to speak out the end of the
wagon, she addressed the soggy group gathered outside. "I
saw them. They were lying together on the same bed. He
still doesn't have all his clothes on. God will probably smite
me blind for the sinful thing I witnessed."

Lydia had had all she could stand. She saw the dozens
of pairs of eyes curiously gaping at her through the opening
at the end of the wagon. Bounding off the pallet and holding
the squalling Lee to her chest, she said in heaving breaths,
"You witnessed nothing except two people sleeping on the
same bed!" At the sight of Lydia clad only in her nightgown,
her hair unbound and seductively falling about her shoul-

ders, Leona Watkins drew up as tight as a fiddle string.
Lydia didn't notice. "I felt bad about using Mr. Coleman's
bed. I told him to sleep there on the pallet because he was
cold and shivering. That's all. I was only lying beside him
because there wasn't any other place to sleep."

"I know what I saw," the woman hissed, her scrawny
neck stretching out like an angry hen's. Spittle flecked her
narrow, pious lips.

"What in blue blazes do you know about how a woman
sleeps with a man, Leona Watkins?" Ma heaved her bulk
into the wagon, Zeke behind her. He had pulled his pants
on over his longjohns, which he wore year-round. They
were a faded red. With his hair sticking out at odd angles to
his head, he made a comical sight. Leona went even stiffer
when she saw him. "You got only one young'un. That must
mean you got lucky the one time you was with your
husband."

Leona's face drained of color only to be inundated by a
deep blush. Her lips worked wordlessly. "I won't listen to
this filthy talk," she said finally, spinning around to face
Grayson again. "What are you, as elected leader, going to
do about this sinful influence on the children of this train?"

Wearily Grayson sighed, shaking his head. His own
wife, tolerant as she was, had been aghast when this
morning, at the crack of dawn, the Watkins woman had
come to their wagon with the news that Mr. Coleman and
"that disgraceful trollop" were sleeping together in his
wagon. Grayson hadn't believed it at first. He had seen
Ross suffer through Victoria's labor. He had seen the
devastation on the young man's face when they lowered the
undecorated pine box into the ground. Ross had been angry
when Ma brought the girl to him to wet-nurse his son.
Grayson didn't think Ross would be ready to engage in a
carnal act with any woman, especially the girl he obviously
held such contempt for.

Still, Ross was a man. A young man. With more spirit
and, Grayson suspected, a lustier nature than most. And
the girl wasn't bad to look at at all, now that she had been
cleaned up and dressed.

He looked at Lydia, then dropped his eyes in embarrassment. What man in Ross Coleman's situation wouldn't have done the same thing? Or have been sorely tempted at best. The girl, either to her credit or detriment, was of the stuff wicked fantasies were made. He bravely raised his eyes to Coleman, and shrank from the black hatred stamped on every rigid plane of his face. The man's green eyes smoldered.

"I'm sorry, Ross," Grayson said, spreading his hands wide, imploringly. "Left to me, I wouldn't care. But there are the children to consider and . . ." He lifted his arms uselessly as his voice trailed off.

"Forget it," Ross snapped. "I don't want to stay where I'm not wanted. Now if you will all get out—"

"Hold on there just one galdern minute," Ma said. "This here has gone far enough." She turned to Ross. "You're wanted on this train. Who else knows as much about doctorin' the horses?" She addressed Grayson. "And who's a better shot? Who always brings back fresh meat? Huh? You gonna git rid of a man for comin' in outa the rain? Myself, I'd have thought him a fool if he hadn't."

"Really, Mr. Grayson—" Leona interrupted.

"Quiet, woman," Zeke snapped. It was the first time they had heard the easygoing man admonish anyone. Surprise more than anything else rendered Mrs. Watkins speechless.

"Now as to these two young people doin' anythin' shameful, use your God-given common sense. She had a baby not two weeks ago. You think she's in any shape to be bedded?"

Lydia's face went fiery as all eyes speculatively turned on her. She looked at Ross. He was standing as stoic and taut as an Indian, seemingly impervious to what was going on. She turned to Leona and put all the chill she could muster into her eyes. The woman was the first to look away, but she wasn't completely cowed.

"That wouldn't matter to the likes of *her*!" she exclaimed.

"Pain's pain to any woman," Ma said. She crossed her arms over her massive bosom and drew a deep breath.

"There's only one practical answer to this problem. Mr. Coleman and Lydia could get married."

Pandemonium broke out from every direction.

Ross snarled, "Like hell I'll marry her."

Lydia gasped, "I don't want to marry anybody."

Grayson said, "Ma, you've gone too far."

Zeke cackled with delight.

Mrs. Watkins chanted, "Lord, Lord. His sainted wife not even cold in her grave." Actually she had despised Victoria Coleman for her beauty and graciousness, but was now staunchly ready to take up the cause of the wronged late wife.

"Mr. Grayson, if they was to marry up, would that satisfy you?" Ma asked, dismissing everyone's initial dismay over her suggestion.

Hal Grayson rued the day he had ever accepted the appointment of wagonmaster. He didn't know much about anything except farming. His opinion on planting time was valued, but what did he know about who should marry whom? "I suppose so."

"What about you, you spiteful, mean, ol' busybody?" she demanded of Leona Watkins.

The woman sputtered angrily. Her skin seemed about ready to split open for the rage expanding her insides. "I think it would be a disgrace. No telling what we would all see and hear from this wagon."

"If you're so all-fired hepped up on seein' and hearin' what other people are doin' in their beds, why don't you try doin' some of it in yours?"

"Oh!" Leona covered her breast as though Ma had struck her. After glaring at Grayson, silently expressing her severe disappointment in him, she stepped out of the wagon. "The Langston woman has suggested that the two of them get married," she announced to the others. "I wash my hands of the whole affair and think we all should pray that we as God-fearing Christians be protected against the evils that beset us."

"Mr. Grayson, why don't you excuse us?" Ma said, ignoring the confused babble that had erupted outside. "I want to talk to Lydia and Ross. You, too, Zeke. Git along to the wagon and see that those young'uns don't tear it up. They'll git rambunctious if confined too long."

Zeke and Grayson departed. Baby Lee had wailed through the whole fracas. Now Lydia dropped down onto one of the stools, turned her back on Ross and Ma, and began to nurse him.

Ross was seething as he spoke to her back. "I told you I didn't want to sleep on that goddamn bed, but no, you browbeat me into it. Now look what's happened."

Lydia glowered at him over her shoulder. "Me!" They were keeping their voices soft, punctuating their anger with flashing eyes and seesawing inflections. "Yes, I wanted you to sleep in your bed. You were cold and wet and tired. But who dragged me across the wagon to sleep there too? Answer me that. Who nearly rattled the teeth out of my head, jerking me onto that bedroll?" She turned back to the baby and crooned softly.

Ross slammed one fist into the palm of his other hand. "You've been nothing but a pain in my ass ever since I first saw you."

"Oh, and you've been such a joy to be around, with your bad temper and your mean looks and your insulting words. A real pleasure, Mr. Coleman."

"You should have awakened me this morning when you first started nursing Lee. I would have gotten up then and this whole damn thing would have been avoided."

She looked at him again, aghast. "You *did* wake up! It's not my fault if you snuggled and went back to sleep."

"I didn't snuggle," he ground out between his teeth.

"No? Well, you nearly scared the life out of me when you woke up. You jumped up like a scalded panther when you heard Mr. Grayson. You were lying so close, Lee and I nearly came with you. As it was, you practically pulled the hair right off my head."

"Well, if you ask me, it could stand some pulling. Like through a brush and comb. If it weren't a wild, tangled—"

Ma's laughter cut him off. He and Lydia looked at her, bewildered, as she wiped tears of mirth from her eyes. "You two are already arguing like married folks."

Ross began shoving the buttons of his shirt into their

corresponding holes. During one of Mrs. Watkins's harangues, he had pulled on a shirt, but had been distracted from buttoning it. "I like you, Ma, and your whole family. You've been kind to me, and you were nice to Victoria before she died, but this is one time I'm going to ask you to butt out of my business."

"All right," she surprised him by saying. "But first I'm gonna have my say and no one's leaving this wagon until I do."

She planted both booted feet inside the opening and Ross didn't think he could move her with dynamite. He couldn't travel far today anyway with the mud and rain, so there was no advantage to getting an early start. He plopped down on the other stool and dropped his head in his hands.

When Lydia glanced at him over her shoulder, she was struck by his pose. That was exactly as she had first seen him, as though he carried the weight of the world on his shoulders.

"Now, listen to me," Ma said to him, "are you going to let that wicked-hearted old witch Leona Watkins drive you away?"

"No," Ross replied tersely. "She has nothing to do with my decision. I should have left the train after Victoria died. I can make it to Texas on my own and probably move a lot faster."

"With Lee?"

"I'll manage."

"And probably kill the baby in the process. Unless you're plannin' to take Lydia with you. And in that case you might just as well stay with the train and have the protection of the group."

"Staying with the train means marrying her. I can't marry her."

"Why?"

"Why?" He came to his feet and began to pace, though he had to slump to do so. "Because she's trash, that's why."

"I'm sick to death of you saying that, Ross Coleman," Lydia said, whirling away from the crib where she had just put a full and sleepy Lee. She faced Ross with both fists grinding into her hips. "You don't know anything about me."

"That's right. Not even your full name."

"And I don't care to tell you. But I'm not trash," she said with the ferocity of a lioness. "You've told me nothing about yourself either."

"It's not the same."

"Isn't it? How do we know you haven't got some shameful past you're trying to hide? Maybe you don't belong here with these folks any more than you think I do, no matter who your wife was."

If Ross's darkly tanned skin could pale, it did so then. His eyes ricocheted from her to Ma as though the women were enemies about to attack. His whole body tensed. Rather than give himself away, he snatched at his second argument.

"I had a wife," he said to Ma. "Victoria Gentry was my wife, my *only* wife. I loved her. She died not two weeks ago. How can you even suggest that I betray her memory by taking another woman?"

"You'll do no 'taking' with me. I'd kill you first," Lydia spat.

"There, you see?" Ma jumped into the thick of the argument. "There's one problem solved. Ross, you don't want another woman, and Lydia don't want another man. You can live and work together for convenience's sake. She can take care of Lee. You can provide for her. 'Pears to me, it's a simple solution to the problem. The weddin' would only be to settle down them so-called God-fearin' Christians out there anyway," she said, jerking her head backward. "We'll know it don't mean nothin' much. Way I see it, things would go on 'bout the way they been goin'.'"

Ross gnawed the corner of his moustache as he cast deprecating looks first at Ma, then at Lydia. He yanked his hat down from its peg and clamped it on his head. "I've got to see to my horses." He stamped out of the wagon.

"I'm not going to marry him," Lydia said quietly. She knew the misery that could come of marriage. Her mother had lived through years of servitude and degradation until she'd finally died of the shame and humiliation of it all.

Lydia wanted no part of it. "I'm not going to marry anybody."

"Was it as bad as that, girl?"

"What?"

"Gettin' that baby of yours. Was it bad enough to taint your opinion of menfolks in general?"

Lydia stared at Ma for silent seconds before directing her eyes to the outside. Ross should have taken his slicker. It had begun to rain again.

"Yes," she said in a faint whisper. "It was bad." She shivered with repugnance at the memories that crowded her mind, memories that she had sworn never to recall if she could help it.

Ma sighed. "I was afraid it was somethin' like that. But it don't have to be that way, Lydia. Mr. Coleman is—"

"A man. A man who doesn't want me any more than I want him."

"That's debatable," Ma said under her breath. Out loud she said, "But you need each other. Could you stand to let Lee go now?"

Tears blurred Lydia's eyes as she looked toward the makeshift cradle. In a few weeks she would have to find another box to put him in or he would be kicking the sides away. But would she even be with him in a few weeks? Mr. Coleman was a gentle and loving father, but would he see the little things that had to be done to care for the infant? He didn't have the maternal instincts she had.

Ma could see that her persuasion was working, so she pressed on. "What are you going to do if they evict you? I don't even think they would let you stay with us any longer. Not with my two impressionable boys around."

That stung the girl's pride just as Ma had intended it to. Lydia's head came up defiantly. "I can take care of myself."

"Well, you weren't doin' too good a job at it when my boys found you nearly dead from exhaustion and exposure and loss of blood. Your clothes were shreddin' off your back. You had no money any of us could locate. No food. These times, it's hard for a woman to make it on her own." Ma eyed the girl keenly. "'Specially if she's runnin' from someone."

Caution sprang into Lydia's eyes, revealing her fear. Ma saw it and knew she had guessed correctly. "Nobody would be lookin' for a young wife with a baby, now would they?" She turned on her way out, but paused with one last point to make. The girl was sitting on the low stool, staring into space, deep in thought. "You could do a lot worse. I 'spect Mr. Coleman has got a temper mean as Satan's, but he's learned to control it. I don't think he'd ever hurt you like that other man done. Think on it." With that she left.

A lot of what Ma had said made sense to Lydia. By marrying Mr. Coleman she could stay with Lee. She loved the child, and thought he was coming to love her, or at least recognize her. All she had to do was speak to him and his wobbly little head would turn toward her voice.

Mr. Coleman wasn't an evil man, not like the men she had lived with for twelve years. He was a bit high-strung and temperamental and proud, but she agreed with Ma. He might get angry at her, but he would never beat her. He had had ample opportunity and, if he hadn't already, he wasn't going to.

His face was nice to look at. When he smiled, she felt a warm glow spread over her. He had lain close to her all night, but she hadn't been afraid of him. His body didn't repulse her. Indeed, she thought it a very nice body and had felt protected by its size and obvious strength. Physically, she could tolerate having him around her.

If she were Mrs. Coleman, she would have things she had never had before. She would have a title, a position in the world, a place where she belonged. The title carried with it a certain respect that she wasn't likely to get anywhere else, especially as a woman alone without family or background.

She wanted a home. Maybe with curtains in the windows. Several rooms that were light and airy. A home. How could she, a woman without a man, without money, without any means of support, ever have that?

But she wasn't going to beg. If he was dead set against it, so be it. She wasn't going to start out a marriage by asking him for anything.

* * *

Ross held the bucket of oats under the mare's muzzle, wishing she didn't have such fastidious table manners and would hurry up and finish it.

What a helluva of mess. But then it went along with the rest of his life. The only good thing that had ever happened to him was Victoria. The gods must have been napping the day he met her. And when they woke up and discovered him happy, they had killed her.

"Shit," he said aloud.

What was he going to do with the girl? Or, more to the point, what was he going to do without her? Everything Ma had said had been accurate. He wasn't afraid to strike out on his own, leaving the wagon and everything else behind. He had lived out of a saddlebag since he was about fifteen. Fourteen? He didn't remember. But what of Lee? He needed Lydia to take care of the baby.

He rebuked himself for thinking of her by name and took the bucket of oats from the mare. If she were that particular, she couldn't be very hungry. He patted her neck and moved to the other side of the temporary corral to the stallion.

Picking up a brush, he began to comb through Lucky's thick, deep mane. He had won the horse in a poker game, thus the name. Vance Gentry hadn't known that. He had complimented Ross on saving up enough money to buy the animal. What his father-in-law didn't know wouldn't hurt him.

He would be devastated by news of Victoria's death. Ross had sent a letter to him from a rural mailbox. He wondered how Gentry would react to the news that he had a grandson. Gentry hadn't known about Victoria's being pregnant. Ross doubted the man would care about ever seeing the boy since he had made no secret that he thought his daughter had married beneath her. Ross wouldn't be going back to Tennessee. He certainly had no ties there now that Victoria was dead. He would probably never hear from Vance Gentry.

Putting emotional considerations aside and looking strictly on the practical side, it would be to his advantage to marry Lydia. He needed a woman to cook and clean for him. And it would be harder to find someone in Texas who would move out onto his land with him before there was even a cabin to move into. Leaving Lee in town with strangers would be out of the question. He didn't want to be separated from his son even temporarily. No, he needed a woman. Lydia was available.

He could do worse. It wasn't as if she looked like a toad. She was presentable even if her coloring was extravagant and attracted the attention of every man who saw her. Her tongue was as sharp as a razor and her temper testy at times. But most important, she loved Lee. That was a strong point in favor of marrying her. She wasn't someone he had *hired* to care about the baby. She already cared.

From an emotional point of view . . . but there wasn't an emotional point of view, because emotions had no place in this decision. It had to be purely practical.

He hated himself for what had happened that morning. Of course it had meant nothing. It had been a chilly dawn. He had been asleep and couldn't be held accountable for cuddling up with Lydia . . . with *her* . . . like that. He had loved Victoria and would never love that way again.

And what of Lydia's lover, or lovers? Even though he had looked for it when he had clasped her to him last night, he hadn't found any sensuous invitation in her expression. What he had seen in those whiskey-colored eyes was fear. Stark fear, the terror that petrifies an animal caught by a sudden bright light in the darkness. Ross wanted to think the worst of her, but now he wasn't so sure she had had many men. Maybe only one. And he had hurt her.

He cursed. Or was she playing him for a fool? Maybe that frightened expression was only a part of her game to seduce him. Was she a well-trained whore who knew all the tricks of her trade? Did she laugh at him behind his back because she knew he wanted her? Was she ticking off the nights until he succumbed and bedded her? Well, he wasn't going to, by God.

He would never give in to the physical urges that she stirred inside him. Never. He would buy a woman if need be, but he would never sully himself and Victoria's memory by taking that girl.

He could marry her and remain detached. He knew he could. He just wouldn't get too close to her, that's all.

She was alone when he stepped into the wagon. Her arms were raised over her head as she struggled to twist her hair into a prim knot. Pins were sticking out of her mouth when she turned at hearing him enter. He was immediately sorry he had made that snide comment about her hair earlier. But was he sorry because it had been unkind or because she had taken it to heart and was pinning up the riot of curls he had come to like? It was too dangerous a question for him to ask himself.

Hastily she pushed the remaining pins into the collection of hair at her nape and faced him, running her palms down the sides of her skirt.

"I've been thinking it over," he began. His eyes moved from one item in the wagon to another, unable to light, fearful they would stop on her. "Maybe we should consider it."

"Maybe."

Dammit! She was going to start those soft-spoken, short responses that told a man not one goddamn thing about what she was thinking. "Well?"

"I've been thinking too."

Christ! "And?"

She breathed in deeply. "*And* I don't know how you're going to take care of Lee otherwise."

"That's what I was thinking too." Ross felt his muscles melting into a more relaxed stance. "But I want to make it clear that if either one of us ever want to call it off, we can."

Lydia didn't like that. One reason she was doing this was for security and a feeling of permanence. However, if that were one of his conditions, she would have to agree and then see to it that she never did anything that would cause him to send her packing.

"All right. But I have a condition of my own."

The hussy had nerve. Here he was offering her a way to better herself and she was laying down conditions. "Let's hear it." His head tilted to an arrogant angle that annoyed Lydia.

"Don't you ever hit me or hurt me in any way," she warned, her eyes flashing.

"What do you think I am? A savage? I wouldn't hurt a woman," he cried, highly vexed.

"Then there's no problem, is there?" she shot back.

He cursed, pulling on his hat again and painfully scraping his knuckles on the rough canvas ceiling of the wagon. He was still cursing as he turned to leave. "I'll go tell Ma and Grayson."

Things were already off to a bad beginning.

The wedding ceremony was set for three o'clock that day, outside if the weather permitted, inside the Coleman wagon if not. Ma saw to it that everyone was invited. She made it sound like a happy occasion to be celebrated by all, building up the sentimental fact that the Lord had provided a wife to take care of Mr. Coleman and Lee after his poor Victoria had been snatched from him. Who said the day of miracles was over? She actually coaxed tears from the eyes of some of the more romantic souls.

Grayson volunteered to go in to town and arrange a license and to fetch the Baptist minister. An hour before three, Ma appeared at the wagon toting several wrapped packages. She handed them to Lydia.

"For you," Ma said proudly.

Lydia stared down at the packages dumbstruck. She could remember getting presents from her mama and papa, but the memories were dim and she didn't know what was fact and what was fantasy.

"For me?" she asked breathlessly.

"Don't know anybody else around here who's gonna be a bride in an hour. Better get started openin' them up."

Hesitantly at first, and then more hurriedly as treasure after treasure was revealed, she plowed through the contents of each package. There were two dresses, two skirts and two shirtwaists, three pairs of pantaloons, two chemises, one nightgown, and two petticoats, along with a pair of black shoes, and three pair of cotton stockings.

"Mr. Coleman bought it all for you. 'Course he sent Anabeth and me after it. Menfolks get as nervous as a long-tailed cat in a room full of rocking chairs when they go to buyin' stuff for the ladies." Ma chattered on, deliberately not seeing the tears that clouded the girl's eyes. "Now, I thought this yellow dress would be right pretty for the weddin'."

At the appointed time, Lydia stepped out onto the tailgate. She shrank back shyly at the crowd gathered in front of the wagon. All eyes were turned to her. But those who had been her accusers that morning were smiling apologetically at her now.

"Come on, Lydia," Ma said gently, tugging on her arm. "Let's get on with this before the rain starts again."

She took the steps down, loving the rustling sound of her new clothes. The undergarments caressed her skin softly. The skirt of her dress swished around her legs. Thank heaven the bodice fit and her bosom didn't bulge out the way it had in Anabeth's dress, though there wasn't much room to spare. The shoes were serviceable, and laced up past her ankles. The new leather squeaked slightly with each step. For a woman with higher standards, the clothes would have been for a work day. To Lydia they were the clothes of a princess.

She searched out Lee to see that he was all right. Anabeth was holding him, his head covered with a light blanket. The Langston children were clustered around their father, strangely somber. Lydia imagined they had been threatened with a thrashing should they act up. Her eyes glided over the crowd. She was too shy to meet individual eyes. When she had run out of things to look at, she looked at Ross.

He was standing grim and ramrod straight. Her heart did a funny flip-flop on seeing him. He looked so handsome. He was still dressed in his work pants, but had put on a white shirt and string tie. The shirt set off his black hair and moustache and tanned face. His eyes were the only trace of color on him, an intense green that shone from under his thick, dark brows.

A weasely little man with spectacles and a pointed nose, whom Lydia assumed was the preacher, was standing beside him. He smiled at her warmly.

"And here's the bride, so now we can get started. Take your bride's hand, young man," he instructed Ross.

Lydia watched, mesmerized, as Ross's dark hand enfolded hers and placed them both atop a black leather Bible which had magically appeared out of nowhere.

His hand was warm, hot in fact, as it lay on hers. The calluses where his fingers bordered his palm were rough on the back of her hand, but that reality made the whole thing seem less like a dream. She stared at his hand, almost afraid that if she looked away he would suddenly disappear.

She followed only a few of the words, but apparently she made the right responses because in an amazingly short span of time, the preacher was saying, "I now pronounce you man and wife. What God hath joined, let no man put asunder. You may now kiss your bride."

Kiss! The word echoed off the walls of her brain, ringing through the chambers and growing louder until she thought her head would burst. No one had told her about that.

But she didn't have time to ask Ma if she would have to go through with it because Ross had put his hands gently on her shoulders and was turning her toward him.

She saw his face looming above hers. It seemed huge and blocked out everything else. It came closer, closer. She screwed her eyes closed against the recurring nightmare of a man's face bending over her, cutting off her air with his fetid mouth, suffocating her with a crushing weight.

Then she felt the warm brush of Ross's lips across hers. They lingered but for a heartbeat and then withdrew and it was over.

Leona Watkins, peeking from beneath the canvas of her wagon because she wasn't about to be seen at such a flagrant mockery of the institution of marriage, was disappointed. The hypocrites were acting as though they hadn't ever touched flesh to flesh before!

Ma was disappointed. She had hoped for a lengthier kiss, one with more substance.

Bubba Langston lost control of his Adam's apple. It bobbed spasmodically as the front of his breeches filled up. He lapsed into a prayer that no one would notice.

Only Ma's threat of a whipping if he didn't behave himself kept Luke Langston from giggling out loud.

Tears of romanticism came to Anabeth's eyes.

Lydia was wondering how Mr. Coleman's moustache could have tickled not only her lips but the back of her throat and all the way down the center of her body. The place between her thighs had grown strangely warm and swollen and moist with the touch of his mouth on hers. She was vaguely disappointed the kiss hadn't lasted longer.

Ross was swearing that he wasn't going to put himself through any more tests. He had convinced himself that he could kiss her unemotionally for the sake of ceremony and curious eyes. Well, now he knew. He couldn't kiss her unemotionally for the sake of anything.

"It's a shame it started raining so soon afterward."

"Why?"

Lydia sighed. She had hoped that they might have an easier time talking to each other now that they were legally man and wife. But ever since they had returned to their . . . yes, *their* . . . wagon, Mr. Coleman had been acting mad at her. Did he already regret marrying her? Well, she hadn't seen anyone holding a shotgun at his back.

"I got the impression that some of the folks wanted to visit with us, that's all."

He snorted a derisive laugh. "They're just nosy. They came to the wedding for the same reason they go to the circus."

She had wanted to believe that everyone who crowded around her after it was over was glad that she was now Mrs. Coleman, that they accepted her as one of them.

She looked at the bouquet of flowers she had put in a glass jar. She touched the fragile petals. Mr. Hill had given them to her as he kissed her hand after the ceremony. "Congratulations, Mrs. Coleman. I wish you many years of happiness."

"Thank you, Mr. Hill. The flowers are lovely," she had said.

Now Mr. Coleman seemed bent on ruining all the good feelings she had stored up to savor later. "I don't think they only came to gawk."

He shrugged. "Suit yourself."

She checked Lee one last time and lay down on the bedroll. Ross had made himself another one on the far side of the wagon, as far away from her as he could get. *I'm not poison*, she had wanted to say to him, but she had held her temper. She was too elated by the events of the day, by her new name, by her new clothes, to fight with him.

"Thank you for the new clothes."

"You're welcome," he said harshly. "I couldn't have you running around in hand-me-downs." He turned out the lantern and she heard him taking off his clothes, then crawling between his own covers.

The rain seemed noisy now that it was quiet. This morning it had sounded comforting as it lullabied them back to sleep. Now it was a sad sound. Lydia felt more lonely than ever, and she knew that if he had chosen to lie beside her, she wouldn't have said anything to change his mind. In the dark she rolled to her side and sought out the shadowy huddle of his body on the other side of the wagon. "Good night . . . Ross."

Why did she choose this moment to speak my name aloud for the first time? And why does it sound like music coming from her mouth? Ross asked himself. Over the thrumming blood that rushed through his veins to concentrate in his manhood, he could barely hear himself reply, "Good night, Lydia."

Chapter Eight

The man took a chair at an empty table in the smoky saloon and absently spread out the curled, yellow sheets of paper on its nicked surface. His companion took the opposite chair after first scanning the other patrons in the barroom. It was a habit of his profession. "Whiskey?"

"Yes, please," the first man absently replied as he continued to peruse the posters.

He was as unaware of Howard Majors, signaling to the barkeeper for a bottle and two glasses, as he was when they arrived. Only when Majors had poured him a draught and slid it across the table, did he look up. His expression was ravaged, that of a man coming out of a bad dream. He grasped the shot glass and tossed the burning contents down his throat. Usually a gentleman where drinking intoxicants was concerned, he uncharacteristically reached for the bottle himself and poured another glass. When the whiskey had stung a raw path down his throat into his stomach, he raised hate-filled eyes to his host.

"That bastard married my daughter." His fist thumped the table. The fingernails were well manicured, but it was a purely masculine hand, and the way the fingers were tightly clenched reflected his personality. He was a man accustomed to getting his own way, of exercising control on himself and everyone around him, of rarely being duped, of getting revenge if necessary. "God! When I think about him sharing her bed!" He slammed his fist down harder on the tabletop, sending the posters scuttling across it and sloshing the whiskey in the bottle.

"I hated to show you these," Majors said with commiseration. "I immediately thought I recognized him in the wedding portrait you showed me, but I wanted to be absolutely certain by closely comparing that photograph to these posters. There's no doubt it's the same man, even with the moustache. The law has been after him for years. The Pinkerton Agency has been asked on many occasions to try to apprehend him."

"Ross Coleman is really Sonny Clark," Vance Gentry said bitterly. "My daughter is married to a gunfighter, an outlaw, a man wanted for murder, bank robbery . . . God!" He groaned, dragging his hands over his ruddy face, distorting the aristocratic features beneath the snowy white crown of hair. "What has he done with her?"

Wordlessly Majors poured the man another drink and he gulped it down. "If he's hurt her in any way, I'll kill him." His lips barely moved as he made the vow. "I wanted to anyway every time I saw him touch her. I knew he was scum the first time I laid eyes on him. He had a way with horses, otherwise I would never have hired him." His straight, white teeth clamped together. "Why didn't I heed that gut feeling?"

"Well," the Pinkerton detective said with cool professionalism, "we have to locate them before either of us can do anything."

"He could have killed her and run off with that cache of jewelry."

The man was working himself up into a lather and Majors couldn't let that happen. The only way to find Clark was with a clear head and level thinking. The young man was wily and had cagily eluded the finest lawmen for years. Detective Majors was going to bring him in, and he wouldn't let a hothead like Gentry bungle it. "I don't think he has disposed of your daughter. That's not his style. Sonny is wild and reckless and mean, and he did his fair share of killing, but it was always when he was in a pinch, backed into a corner and trying to escape. He didn't kill on whim. Besides, you said he adored your daughter."

"I said he *seemed* to adore her. He fooled us in every other instance, how can you expect me to believe he truly loved her? The servants said they'd been gone for weeks by the time I returned from Virginia. Not a note. Nothing. Is that the behavior of an affectionate son-in-law? No telling where he has dragged her."

"We'll find them."

Majors's platitudes were wearing thin. "Well, you didn't find him before, did you?" Gentry barked. "With these posters scattered all over the Mississippi Valley, you weren't able to find Sonny Clark."

"We stopped looking because we thought he was dead. That's why I had to dig the posters out of an old file. He got shot up in a bank robbery. We felt for certain the rest of the James gang had left him for dead somewhere. Apparently that's exactly what happened, because on all the subsequent jobs Jesse and Frank have pulled, he hasn't been with them. We never heard from Sonny again until you walked into my office the day before yesterday and showed me that picture of your daughter and her husband, Ross Coleman. I figure he holed up somewhere until he was healed, changed his looks, and took on the aspects of a law-abiding citizen."

The glasses on the table rattled again, this time because a man drunkenly stumbled against it. He half fell over Majors before righting himself. "Pardon," he mumbled as he ambled to the next table and collapsed into the chair. "Whiskey," he bellowed.

Gentry eyed him with disgust. He was filthy, his clothes stained with dried blood. Maybe his unsteady gait couldn't be attributed solely to drunkenness. His thin hair and scalp were matted with clotted blood. The man reeked of unwashed flesh. Gentry was about to suggest that he and Majors go somewhere else to continue their discussion, but Majors was already speaking.

"I've been nosing around. The old man who lived up in the hills." Majors checked his note pad. "John Sachs. He was dead and apparently had been for weeks when our men finally found their way to his cabin. No sign of a struggle. He obviously died of old age. No help there as to where Clark might be headed. There was a wagon train organized last month in McMinn County."

Gentry scoffed. "You don't know him as well as you think, Majors. Ross . . . Sonny is restless, active. He's constantly moving. He rides a horse better than any man I've ever seen."

"So I've heard from plenty of posses," Majors said dryly.

"He wouldn't attach himself to something as slow moving as a wagon train."

"But that would protect him too. Traveling with his wife like any other immigrant wouldn't call attention to him."

Gentry was already shaking his head adamantly. "I know the man better than you do. If he's got a pocket full of jewelry, and believe me, its value would amount to a considerable sum, he wouldn't be heading to the frontier with it. New Orleans, New York, St. Louis maybe, places where those jewels could be sold for cash."

"Maybe you're right, but we have no leads."

"That's what I'm paying you for, Mr. Majors," Gentry said in a sour tone. "I'll head for New Orleans. I'm familiar with the city."

"Very well. I'll go to St. Louis. We'll communicate through cables sent to my office here in Knoxville. I'll have posters printed with his 'new' face on them."

"No," Gentry said sharply, causing the man at the next table to peer at them closely with shrewd eyes. "I don't want anyone to know that my daughter is married to a notorious outlaw and that he tricked us both and robbed us of valuable heirlooms."

"That will make our job harder, working alone without the help of local law enforcement folk."

"But it may also save Victoria's life. I've never seen him raise a hand to her or he wouldn't be alive today. But I've never seen him desperate either. I don't want him alerted. We don't want Ross Coleman to panic."

"You may be right at that. Witnesses have tried to describe his hair-trigger reactions. They defy description. Finding Sonny Clark will be my last official duty with the agency before my retirement. I don't want any deaths on my conscience."

"Except his."

The bone-chilling determination in Gentry's tone sent shivers down Majors's veteran spine and he was tempted to remind the man not to take the law into his own hands. He wanted Clark taken alive and hoped that by the time they located Victoria Gentry and her husband, her father's hatred would have subsided. "Let's get started," he said, rising and tossing several coins on the table.

The men pulled on their hats and left the saloon as it was being prepared for the evening crowd. The barkeeper was busy washing glasses behind the bar. A young man was desultorily pushing a broom around the floor as he watched the foot traffic of Knoxville parade by.

The man with the injured head stood, reeling until he gained his equilibrium. Purposefully he let himself stumble into the table the other men had just vacated. As he did, his hand covered the coins and swept them into his palm. It was a far greater amount than what he had left to pay for his own drink. His bleary eyes tried to focus on the outdated wanted posters which still littered the table. He couldn't read, but he knew what the posters signified. And he had heard the mention of stolen heirlooms. Never passing up a chance to get something for nothing, he crammed the crackling sheets beneath his blood-stained shirt and staggered toward the door. No one had seen him pick up the money. No one was paying him any attention. So far so good.

"Hey, mister."

Shit! "Yeah?" Belligerently he turned toward the barkeeper.

"Better have that head seen to."

He relaxed and slid a smile over his uneven, broken yellow teeth. "Sure thing."

"How'd you get your head bashed in that way anyhow?"

He smiled again, the sly, cunning grin of a scavenger. "Got a little too feisty with my woman. She clouted me over the head with a rock."

The barkeeper laughed good-naturedly. "Doubt if I'd let her get away with that."

The grin turned into a malevolent smirk. "I don't intend to." If it was the last thing he did, he would find that bitch and give her what she had coming. He took one more step toward the door, then paused. Something else the two dandies had said came back into his alcohol- and pain-dazed mind. "Say, you hear sumpin' 'bout a wagon train startin' up in McMinn County?"

"No, can't say that I have," the barkeep said, polishing a glass with a muslin towel. "But it wouldn't suprise me any. Had a helluva flood down that way last spring. Folks have been trying to salvage what they could of their farms after the war and the floods and all. Lot of 'em are getting out."

The man at the door rubbed his beard-stubbled jaw musingly. A wagon train of families looking for new homesteads would be a good hiding place. "Think I'll mosey down that way and have a look-see."

He went out the door, chuckling to himself and

wondering when the friendly barkeeper would notice he had been robbed.

She liked the way his hair fell over his forehead. His head was bent over as he cleaned his guns. The rifle, already oiled and gleaming, was propped against the side of the wagon. Now he was working on a pistol. Lydia knew nothing of guns, but this particular one frightened her. Its steel barrel was long and slender, cold and lethal. Ross brought it up near his face and peered down the barrel, blowing on it gently. Then he concentrated on rubbing it again with a soft cloth.

Their first day of marriage had passed uneventfully. The weather was still gloomy, but it wasn't raining as steadily or as hard as it had been. Nevertheless, it was damp and cool and Lydia had spent most of the day in the wagon. Ross had gotten up early, while it was still dark, and had shuffled through trunks and boxes. He seemed intent on the task, and she had pretended to sleep, not daring to ask what he was doing. When she did get up and began to move about the wagon she noticed that everything that had belonged to Victoria was gone. She didn't know what Ross had done with Victoria's things, but there was nothing of hers left in the wagon.

Lydia watched him now as he unconsciously pushed back his hair with raking fingers. His hair was always clean and glossy, even when his hat had mashed it down. It was getting long over his neck and ears. Lydia thought the black strands might feel very good against her fingers if she ever had occasion to touch them, which she couldn't imagine having the nerve to do even if he would allow it. She doubted he would. He treated her politely, but never commenced a conversation, and certainly never touched her.

"Tell me about your place in Texas," she said softly, bringing his green eyes away from the pistol to meet hers in the glow of the single lantern. She was holding Lee, rocking him gently, though he had finished nursing for the night and was already sleeping. They were killing time until it was time to go to bed.

"I don't know much about it yet," he said, turning his attention back to his project. He briefly told her the same story about John Sachs that he had told Bubba. "He sent for the deed and, when it came back in the mail, there was a surveyor's description attached to it."

His enthusiasm for the property overrode his restraint and the words poured out. "It sounds beautiful. Rolling pastureland. Plenty of water. There's a branch of the Sabine River that flows through a part of it. The report said it has two wooded areas with oak, elm, pecan, cottonwoods near the river, pine, dogwood—"

"I love dogwood trees in the springtime when they bloom," Lydia chimed in excitedly.

Ross found himself smiling with her, until he realized he was doing it and ducked his head again. "First thing I'll have to do is build a corral for the horses and a lean-to for us." The word had fallen naturally from his lips. Us. He glanced at her furtively, but she was stroking Lee's head and watching the dark baby hair fall back into its swirls after it was disturbed. Lee's head was pillowed on her breasts. For an instant Ross thought of his own head there, her touching his hair that way with that loving expression on her face.

He shifted uncomfortably on his stool. "Then, before winter, I'll have to build a cabin. It won't be fancy," he said with more force than necessary, like he was warning her not to expect anything special from him.

She looked at him with unspoken reproach. "It'll be fine, whatever it is."

He rubbed the gun barrel more aggressively. "Next spring I hope all the mares foal. That'll be my start. And who knows, maybe I can sell timber off the land to make some extra money, or put Lucky out to stud."

"I'm sure you'll make a success of it."

He wished she wouldn't be so damned optimistic. It was contagious. He could feel his heart accelerating over the unlimited prospects of a place of his own with heavy woods and fertile soil, and a prize string of horses. And he wouldn't have to be looking over his shoulder all the time either. He had never been in Texas. There wouldn't be as much threat of someone recognizing him.

Lost in his memories, he snapped the barrel back into place, spun the loaded six-bullet chamber, and twirled the pistol on his index finger with uncanny talent before taking aim on an imaginary target.

Lydia stared at him with fascination. When it occurred to Ross what he had done out of reflex, he jerked his head around to see if she had noticed. Her dark amber eyes were wide with incredulity. He shoved the pistol into its holster as if to deny that it existed.

She licked her lips nervously. "How . . . how far is your land from Jefferson?"

"About a day's ride by wagon. Half a day on horseback. As near as I can figure it on the map."

"What will we do when we get to Jefferson?"

She had listened to the others in the train enough to know that Jefferson was the second largest city in Texas. It was an inland port in the northeastern corner of the state that was connected to the Red River via Cypress Creek and Caddo Lake. The Red flowed into the Mississippi in Louisiana. Jefferson was a commercial center with paddle-wheelers bringing supplies from the east and New Orleans in exchange for taking cotton down to the markets in that city. For settlers moving into the state, it was a stopping-off place where they purchased wagons and household goods before continuing their trek westward.

"We won't have any trouble selling the wagon. I hear there's a waiting list for them. Folks are camped for miles around town just waiting for more wagons to be built. I'll buy a flatbed before we continue on."

Lydia had been listening, but her mind was elsewhere. "Would you like for me to trim your hair?"

"What?" His head came up like a spring mechanism was operating it.

Lydia swallowed her caution. "Your hair. It keeps falling over your eyes. Would you like me to cut it for you?"

He didn't think that was a good idea. Damn. He *knew* that wasn't a good idea. Still, he couldn't leave the idea alone. "You've got your hands full," he mumbled, nodding toward Lee.

She laughed. "I'm spoiling him rotten. I should have

put him in his bed long ago." She turned to do just that, tucking the baby in with a light blanket to keep the damp air off him.

She had on one of the shirtwaists and skirts he had financed the day before. He wasn't going to let it be said that Ross Coleman wouldn't take care of his wife, any more than he was going to let it be said that he was sleeping outside his own wagon when he had a new wife sleeping inside. It was hell on him and he didn't know how he was going to survive many more nights like the sleepless one he had spent last night. But his pride had to be served. After a suitable time when suspicions would no longer be aroused, he would start sleeping outside. Many of the men did, giving up the wagons to their wives and children.

She liked those new clothes. She had folded and refolded them about ten times throughout the day. Ross couldn't decide if she was a woman accustomed to having fine clothes who had fallen on bad times, or a woman who had never possessed any clothes so fine. When it came right down to it, he didn't know anything about her. But then, she didn't know about him either, nor did anyone else.

All he knew of her was that a man had touched her, kissed her, known her intimately. And the more Ross thought about that, the more it drove him crazy. Who was the man and where was he now? Every time Ross looked at her, he could imagine that man lying on her, kissing her mouth, her breasts, burying his hands in her hair, fitting his body deep into hers. What disturbed him most was that the image had begun to wear his face.

"Do you have any scissors?"

Ross nodded, knowing he was jumping from the frying pan into the fire and condemning himself to another night of sleepless misery. He wanted badly to hate her. He also wanted badly to bed her.

He resumed his seat on the stool after he had given her the scissors. She draped a towel around his neck and told him to hold it together with one hand. Then she stood away from him, tilting her head first to one side then the other as she studied him.

When she lifted the first lock of his hair, he caught her

wrist with his free hand. "You aren't going to butcher me, are you? Do you know what you're doing?"

"Sure," she said, teasing laughter shining like a sunbeam in her eyes. "Who do you think cuts *my* hair?" His face drained of color and took on a sickly expression. She burst out laughing. "Scared you, didn't I?" She shook off his hand and made the first snip with the scissors. "I don't think you'll be too mutilated." She stepped behind him to work on the back side first.

His hair felt as good coiling over her fingers as she had thought it would. It was coarse and thick, yet silky. She played with it more than she actually cut, hoping to prolong the pleasure. They chatted inconsequentially about Lee, about the various members of the train, and laughed over Luke Langston's latest mischievous antic.

The dark strands fell to his shoulders and then drifted to the floor of the wagon as she deftly maneuvered the scissors around his head. It was an effort to keep his voice steady when her breasts pressed into his back as she leaned forward or glanced his arm as she moved from one spot to another. Once a clump of hair fell onto his ear. Lydia bent at the waist and blew on it gently. Ross's arm shot up and all but knocked her to the floor.

"What are you doing?" Her warm breath on his skin had sent shafts of desire firing through him like cannon-balls. His hand all but made a garrote out of the towel around his neck. The other hand balled into a tight fist where it rested on the top of his thigh.

She was stunned. "I . . . I was . . . what? What did I do?"

"Nothing," he growled. "Just hurry the hell up and get done with this."

Her spirits sank. They had been having such an easy time. She had actually begun to hope that he might come to like her. She moved around to his front, hoping to rectify whatever she had done to startle him so, but he became even more still and tense.

Ross had decided that if she were to trim his hair, it was necessary for her fingers to be sliding through it. He had even decided that it was necessary for her to lay her hand along his cheek to turn his head. He had decided that this was going to feel good no matter how much he didn't want it to and that he might just as well sit back and enjoy her attention.

But when he had felt her breath, heavy and warm and fragrant, whispering around his ear, it had had the impact of a strike of lightning. The bolt went straight from his head to his loins and ignited them.

If that weren't bad enough, now she was standing in front of him between his knees—it had only been natural to open them so she could move closer and not have to reach so far. Her breasts were directly in his line of vision and looked as tempting as ripe peaches waiting to be picked. God, but didn't she know what she was doing? Couldn't she tell by the fine sheen of sweat on his face that she was driving him slowly crazy? Each time she moved, he was tantalized by her scent, by the supple grace of her limbs, by the rustling of the clothes against her body which hinted at mysteries worth discovering.

"I'm almost done," she said when he shifted restlessly on the stool. Her knees had come dangerously close to his vulnerable crotch.

Oh, God, no! She leaned down closer to trim the hair on the crown of his head. Raising her arms higher, her breasts were lifted as well. If he inclined forward a fraction of an inch, he could nuzzle her with his nose and chin and mouth, bury his face in her lushness and breathe her, imbibe her. His lips, with searching lovebites, would find her nipple.

He hated himself. He plowed through his memory, trying to recall a time when Victoria had been such a temptation to him, or a time when he had felt free to put his hands over her breasts for the sheer pleasure of holding them. He couldn't. Had there ever been such a time?

No. Victoria hadn't been the kind of woman who deliberately lured a man, reducing him to an animal. Every time Ross had made love to Victoria it had been with reverence and an attitude of worship. He had entered her body as one walks into a church, a little ashamed for what he was, apologetic because he wasn't worthy, a supplicant for mercy, contrite that such a temple was defiled by his presence.

There was nothing spiritual in what he was feeling now. He was consumed by undiluted carnality. Lydia was a woman who inspired that in a man, who had probably inspired it as a profession, despite her denials. She was trying to work the tricks of her trade on him by looking and acting as innocent as a virgin bride.

Well, by God, it wasn't going to work!

"Your moustache needs trimming too."

"What?" he asked stupidly, by now totally disoriented. He saw nothing but the feminine form before him, heard nothing but the pounding of his own pulse.

"Your moustache. Be very still." Bending to the task, she carefully clipped away a few longish hairs in his moustache, working her mouth in the way she wanted his to go.

Had he been looking at her comical, mobile mouth, it might have made him laugh. Instead he had lowered his eyes to trace the arch of her throat. The skin of it looked creamy at the base before it melded into the more velvety texture of her chest that disappeared into the top of her shirtwaist. Did she smell more like honeysuckle or magnolia blossoms?

Every sensory receptor in his body went off like a fire bell when she lightly touched his moustache, brushing his lips free of the clipped hairs with her fingertips. First to one side, then the other, her finger glided over his mouth. The choice was his. He could either stop her, or he could explode.

He pushed her hands away and said gruffly, "That's enough."

"But there's one—"

"Dammit, I said that's enough," he shouted, whipping the towel from around his neck and flinging it to the floor as he came off the stool. "Clean this mess up."

Lydia was at first taken off guard by his rudeness and his curt order, but anger soon overcame astonishment. She grabbed his hand and slapped the scissors into his palm with a resounding whack. "You clean it up. It's your hair. And haven't you ever heard the words 'thank you' before?"

With that she spun away from him and, after having

taken off her skirt and shirtwaist and carefully folding them, crawled into her pallet, giving him her back as she pulled the covers over her shoulders.

He stood watching her in speechless fury before turning away to find the broom.

The sun shone from dawn till dusk the next day. And on the following day they crossed the Mississippi.

Everyone was at a pitch of excitement as the wagons rolled in file down the bluffs to the banks of the muddy river. Mr. Grayson collected each wagon's toll, which, like everything else postwar, was inflated. Two steam ferries would be working, carrying two wagons, their teams, and their families at a time.

Lydia was as excited as everyone else. Until she saw the river. It could have been an ocean and not appeared more vast, limitless, life-threatening. Holding Lee protectively against her pounding heart, she watched as the first wagons were guided onto the ferries and their wheels secured between braces. She saw the murky water slapping at the hull of the ferry.

The hateful memory from her childhood came rolling over her. The brackish taste of river water flooding her mouth and throat was real. She couldn't breathe. Just as she hadn't been able to that day.

They had been taking one of their rare trips to town. For once old man Russell had agreed to let her and Mama go along. She had looked forward to the day for a week. They had to cross a branch of the Tennessee on a poled ferry. She had been leaning over the railing, watching the sunlight dancing on the water. Clancey came up behind her and nudged her lightly enough to appear accidental and yet hard enough to make her lose her balance and send her plunging into the water.

She clawed her way to the surface, sputtering and screaming. The water sucked at her skirt and the one petticoat she owned. Through water-filled eyes she could see Otis and Clancey laughing hilariously, slapping their thighs, hooting over her distress. Mama had both hands clasped to her head, screaming for them to pull Lydia out.

She reached for the splintery edge of the bargelike ferry, but Clancey kicked at her hand with his boot. For a full minute, she had struggled to stay on the surface, and they wouldn't help her. When Mama tried to, Clancey held her back. Finally, he grabbed a handful of her hair and pulled her out. "Enjoy your swim?" he had taunted.

She had been about eleven when that happened, but she could still remember the terror she had known when the water had closed over her eyes, her nostrils, her mouth, cutting off her air supply. Now she stared entranced into the opaque waters of the Mississippi and wondered how she would ever force herself to step onto the ferry.

She was still trembling when Ross, who had been busy helping secure the wagons, came up to her. "Our turn next. You stand with Lee there against the engine house. The Langstons are crossing with us."

"Ross," she called out when he turned and strode away.

"Yes?" He looked back, a trace impatiently.

"Wh . . . where are you going to be?"

"With my horses."

She nodded, pale and nervous. "Oh, yes, of course."

He stared at her for one intense moment, then went back to the chore of getting the two wagons secured onto the ferry with as little delay as possible. Lydia stepped onto the gently rocking ferry, hastened toward the engine house and plastered herself to the vibrating walls, clutching Lee tightly. Ma joined her there, though the children stood as close to the railing as they could. This was an adventure they would remember for the rest of their lives, and after one cautioning lecture, Ma let them enjoy themselves.

The ferry was about a third of the way across when Marynell called, "Come here, Lydia. Look." She was pointing down into the water at something that was riding the current of the river and entertaining the children with its bobbing course.

"No, I've got to stay with Lee."

"Go on," Ma said, taking the baby from her before she could object. "You ain't much more than a kid yourself. Have some fun."

Not wanting to appear a coward, she inched closer to the edge of the craft. Frantically she tried to catch sight of Ross, but he had seemingly disappeared. Though she executed a shaky smile for the children's sake, the apple crate riding in the ferry's wake did little to rid her of her fear. All she truly saw were the unfathomable depths, the swirling patterns of currents, the foamy water licking the sides of the boat. She began to shiver. She could feel that dark water closing over her head again, could feel her lungs burning.

Panic engulfing her as surely as she imagined the water to be, she whirled away and searched out a haven. She ran, heedless of knocking the astounded Langston children out of her way, toward the wagon. Nostrils flared, eyes wide, her lungs pumping like a bellows, she scrambled up the wheel of the wagon and worked her way around to the back, climbed over the raised tailgate, and fell inside, panting laboriously.

Ma had seen the whole thing and began shouting to her children, who were chasing after Lydia like scattering baby chicks, to stand where they were. "Go get Mr. Coleman, Atlanta. Tell him to turn his horses over to Luke." Bubba was holding the lead horse of Ross's team as his father was doing to their own.

Within seconds Ross was running over the rough planks of the ferry. Out of habit his hand was on the holster strapped to his thigh. "What is it?"

"Lydia. In your wagon."

"Lee?"

"Is fine. See to your wife, Mr. Coleman."

Ma caught his eyes and held them for one telling moment before he bounded toward the wagon. When he flung his long leg over the tailgate and stepped inside he saw her huddled in a corner, her head covered with her arms. She was weeping hysterically.

"Lydia!" he barked. "What the hell—" Taking off his hat and tossing it aside, he pulled the rest of his body through the opening and crossed the floor to crouch down in front of her. He extended his hands, intending to place them on her comfortingly. But they hovered for a moment before he withdrew them.

"Lydia," he said more gently. The weeping was bitter, from the soul, from hell. "You've scared the stuffing out of everyone. What's the matter with you?"

As with most men, tears without a logical explanation were beyond his ken. And as with most men, he became angry when no explanation was forthcoming. "Lydia, for godsake, tell me what's wrong. Are you hurt? In pain?" Had she bumped her head? Why was she covering it that way? He tried to prize her hands away, but her arms were as rigid as death.

Desperate, he gripped her shoulders and began to shake her hard until she brought her arms down. Dazed, she looked at him with unfocused eyes and clutched handfuls of his shirtfront between numb fingers. "Don't push me . . . in the . . . water . . . the river. Please, don't . . . push . . ."

Ross stared at her in mute dismay. He had seen men about to die, staring down the barrel of a pistol, seconds away from having their brains blown to smithereens, and he had never seen such stark terror on any face. The pupils of her eyes were so drastically dilated that only a ring of amber encircled them. Her lips were chalky. There seemed to be not one drop of blood left in her face.

"Lydia, Lydia." His voice was a soothing purr and he never remembered lifting his hands to cup her face between his palms. "What are you talking about?"

"The river, the river," she said deliriously, clutching the fabric of his shirt tighter.

"No one is going to push you in the river. You're safe."

She swallowed. He could see her forcing the knot of fear down her throat. Her tongue came out to wet her lips. Her chest rose and fell dramatically with each rasping breath. "Ross?" His name was a question. She peered deeply into his eyes as though trying to identify him.

"Yes."

Her body sagged with relief and her head fell forward to thump against his breastbone. Because his hands were still pressed to her cheeks, he drew her closer until she rested against his chest. They remained motionless until her breathing returned to normal. "Why would anyone want to push you in the river?" he asked at last in a rough whisper.

She lifted her eyes to his, but she didn't speak, only stared back at him in that habit he found both irritating and captivating. "We were all right there . . ." His thumbs stroked her cheekbones, ridding them of remnant tears. "Ma . . ." He watched her eyes fill again, but this time the tears weren't terror induced. Her whiskey eyes were cleansing themselves of the nightmare she had just relived. "Ma wouldn't let . . ." His thumbs alternated as they skimmed her lips. They were damp from the recent licking she had given them. The moisture collected on the pads of his thumbs. ". . . anything happen to you."

He knew then he was going to kiss her and there wasn't a damn thing he could do about it. The choice had been taken away from him long ago. The moment had been ordained, predestined, and he would be jousting with fate to resist it. So he submitted his will and let the gods dictate that his head move slowly downward toward her waiting mouth.

At first he merely touched his lips to hers. Her fingers curled tighter into his chest. He waited until he could deny himself no longer. Then, tilting her head farther back to accommodate him, he rubbed his lips against hers, dusting them with his moustache, applying more pressure until they parted.

His heart was pounding erratically, but he didn't rush. He hesitated, taking time to breathe in the flavor of her breath and anticipate what he would find beyond this first soft portal.

He touched her upper lip with the tip of his tongue, lightly, so very lightly he wasn't even sure he had made contact until he heard the soft, choppy rush of air that escaped her lips and feathered his.

The wake of another boat on the river caused the ferry to wobble. They lost their balance. Ross was on his knees, and when she fell back against a pile of bedding, his body followed hers down. Hot emerald eyes roved her face, her hair, down her throat, over her chest, then back up to her mouth that he hadn't gotten near enough of. She lay motionless, soundless, sacrificial.

The fingers of one hand tunneled through her hair to settle on her scalp. His other hand cradled her jaw. He eased himself down until his chest touched the gentle slopes of her breasts in repose.

When his mouth aligned with hers again, instinct took over. He had been taught to kiss at thirteen by one of his mother's friends in the brothel. The whore had taken the boy into her room on a boring afternoon and had teased him mercilessly even as she demonstrated the finer points of kissing. She instructed him on how to apply just the right amount of suction to seal two mouths together, on how to swirl his tongue as though gathering honey with it, and how to thrust and parry with it in ever-changing tempos. Her pupil was brilliant. He had a natural talent for it and before the afternoon was out, he had perfected the art. The whore had learned a few things too.

Ross applied that knowledge and years of practice to this kiss, for never had he dreaded or anticipated one more.

Only, his anticipation hadn't prepared him for the soul-jolting thrill of it. The reality far exceeded his imagination. She had a marvelous mouth. It was a sweet, wet chasm he explored thoroughly. He tasted it all because he had been so consummately hungry for it. He dragged his tongue along the straight ridge of her teeth. He touched the roof of her mouth, investigated the slick lining of her lips, playfully prodded the tip of her tongue with his. And he applied that sweet, sweet suction that intimated he would draw all of her into himself if he could.

He wasn't aware of the low rumbles of arousal that issued out of his throat, not until the ferry bumped into the dock on the Arkansas side of the river. That animal growl reached his ears and for a moment he wondered where it had come from.

When he realized its source, he pushed himself off her. Her eyes were just as large, just as inquiring as before he had kissed her. But they were less afraid. Her mouth was red and wet, shiny with his kiss. The skin around her lips was abraded by his moustache.

He had been totally lost in the kiss, in her. She had made him forget everything—who he was, who she was . . . who Victoria was.

He shoved himself to his feet and retrieved his hat. Crushing it onto his head and not daring to look back at Lydia, he stepped through the wagon's opening and dropped to the deck of the ferry just as Ma came bustling up.

"Well?" she demanded.

"She's fine," he said crossly before he stamped off.

Ma smiled broadly.

There was a celebration in camp that night. They had reached a landmark and everyone was glad it was behind them. Fiddles were taken out of cases and played. Songs were sung. A jug of whiskey was passed around for the men who imbibed. Few refused that night. Children were allowed to stay up later than usual. The long trek would began again tomorrow, but tonight there was call to celebrate this momentous day.

It had been a momentous day for Lydia too. Ross's kiss had taught her that not all kisses were loathsome, that some intimacies between a man and a woman could be wonderful.

She would also remember the day for another reason. It was the day her milk stopped coming.

Chapter Nine

$\mathcal{A}$t first Lydia thought Lee was fussy because of the unusual commotion in the camp. It wasn't until later, when she was nursing him before putting him to bed, that she realized he was hungry. He wasn't getting enough milk.

She squeezed what milk she could out of her breasts and he finally fell asleep against her chest. Too tired and emotionally frazzled after what had happened on the ferry, she fell asleep holding him on her pallet, not even garnering enough wherewithal to put him in his crib or to undress herself.

She stirred when Ross came in much later. In that netherland between sleep and wakefulness, she noticed only that he smelled of whiskey. The next morning he complained of a splitting headache when Lee set up a hungry howl.

"Get him fed, for godsakes," he said as he tugged on his boots.

Lydia didn't think she had any milk, but she unbuttoned her shirtwaist and offered Lee her breast anyway. Fearful of what Ross would do if her milk had dried up, she self-defensively lashed out at him.

"Your head wouldn't be hurting if you hadn't gotten drunk last night."

He stood, blinking his squinted eyes against the pain as he wavered toward the wagon's opening. "I didn't get drunk. But I sure as hell tried," he grumbled as he went out.

Within minutes Lee was wailing lustily out of a beet-red face, thrashing his arms and legs in frustration and hunger. Lydia didn't know what to do. She knew nothing of babies except her short experience with Lee. What did a mother do when her milk stopped coming? Cow's milk? Yes, but how would she get that without Ross's finding out?

Sitting on the floor holding Lee to her chest, she rocked him soothingly, singing him what few songs she knew. For a while he would doze fitfully, then instinct would send him rutting for her nipple, reminding him that he was hungry, and his crying would start again.

"What's the matter with him this morning?" Ross asked, stepping into the wagon after he had shaved.

"I don't know," Lydia lied. "Maybe a tummy ache. Or maybe all the excitement yesterday got him out of sorts."

Their eyes met briefly, each remembering the kiss. Then both looked away guiltily.

"Don't bother with breakfast," Ross said. "I'm not hungry. I'll just make coffee. You take care of Lee."

Lee's problem couldn't be solved with time. Indeed,

the longer the morning stretched out, the worse his crying became. While Bubba drove, Lydia sat in the stuffy wagon with the baby, trying to soothe him the best she could and knowing that nothing she was doing would eliminate his problem.

At the noon break, Ma came lumbering over to the wagon. "That young'un's been cryin' all mornin'. What's the matter with him?"

Ross was adjusting the harnesses on the team. Lydia spoke in a frantic whisper, tears rushing to her eyes. "Ma, you've got to help me. My milk is gone. He's hungry."

Ma stared at the girl, for once at a loss for anything to say. "Ya sure? When did ya notice?"

"Last night. He didn't get enough before he finally went to sleep. This morning he's had nothing. What am I going to do?"

Ma saw Lydia's worried glance toward the front of the wagon where Ross was chatting with Mr. Cox. The girl was right to be concerned, but Ma didn't want her to fret any more than she already was. "I'll get some milk from the Norwood's cow and we'll get it into young Lee if we have to ladle it down his throat. Don't you worry now, or you'll be in as bad a shape as he is. You just keep calm, keep talkin' quiet-like to him. He can sense that you're upset and that don't help none."

"You won't tell—"

"No. Not right now," Ma said, leaving.

She came back just as everyone was rolling out.

"I'm staying back here with Lydia and Lee this afternoon to see if we can get him to feelin' better."

"Thanks, Ma," Ross said over his shoulder. He had relieved Bubba. "Is he sick?"

Worry furrowed a deep groove between his dark brows and Ma smiled gently at the vulnerability of the man who tried so hard to be cold and indifferent. "No, just fussy. I 'spect he's gonna feel better real soon."

It took some doing, but Lydia finally managed, by holding Lee against her as though he were nursing, to get him to suck on the nipple Ma had tried to get him to take the day after he was born. It was fashioned out of an oilskin glove and stretched over the mouth of a small Mason jar.

After much sputtering and choking and coughing, Lee and the contraption seemed to come to a meeting of the minds and he sucked hungrily until his stomach was at last full and he fell peacefully asleep.

Ma and Lydia worked out a schedule. Ma would bring fresh milk every morning when Ross went to tend his horses. If Lee awoke and began fussing before that, he would just have to fuss. Another bottle would be brought at noon and two in the evening. Somehow Ma would smuggle them to Lydia.

The first morning while Ross was shaving and Lydia was getting his breakfast and ignoring Lee's bellows, he commented on it.

"What's wrong with you, letting Lee cry like that?"

She brushed back a mass of curling hair as she straightened from bending over the fire. The long fork she was holding dripped bacon grease as she waggled it at him. "Nothing's wrong with me and I'll thank you not to start a conversation with me in that tone of voice. It sounds like you're accusing me of something." Her own guilty conscience and the heat from the fire had painted a healthy color on her cheeks.

Ross wished to God she didn't look so healthy. His body was responding to her vitality with a burgeoning strength of its own.

"It's good for a baby to cry now and then without someone rushing to pick him up," she went on. "That way he won't get spoiled." At least that's what Ma had told her to say if Ross should notice Lee's unusual fussiness.

Ross wiped his face of shaving soap. She was right, of course, but he knew what it was like to be neglected, to have a scraped elbow and no mother to take care of it because she was busy with someone else. "Just see to it that you don't let him cry too long without checking on him."

"Do you think I would let him cry if I didn't know he was all right?"

Ross tossed down the towel and pulled on his hat. "You're to take care of Lee, first and foremost. Or have you forgotten that's the reason I was forced into marrying you?" He stalked off in the direction of the temporary corral.

"Bastard," Lydia hissed through her teeth.

"He just might be," Ma said from behind her. Lydia spun around, unaware that anyone had heard her epithet. "And touchy as a boil about it too. But whatever he is, that man's actin' stranger and stranger every day. Like the other day when we crossed the river, I never seen a man so scared as when he thought somethin' had happened to you. And when he come out of that wagon, he looked like he'd been poleaxed right between the eyes." She stared after Ross's anger-straight figure as he went into the cover of the trees. "Makes a body wonder what's ailin' him, don't it?" she said musingly. "Well, let's get that young'un his breakfast."

Their schedule worked out fine during the day, as Ross was always busy. It was the nighttime bottle that was tricky. Lydia would turn her back and open her dress just as if she were nursing, then sneak the bottle of cow's milk out from where she had secreted it earlier. So far, thank God, Ross was none the wiser. But Lydia expressed another concern to Ma.

"What are you telling the Norwoods?"

"Told 'em one of my own was lookin' puny and I thought he could use some fresh milk."

"You're having to pay them for it, aren't you?"

"I got some coins tucked away. Don't you worry about it none. You can pay me back once Mr. Coleman finds out."

Lydia shivered. "Not yet, please."

"The man'll find out sooner or later, Lydia. You can't go on pretendin' forever."

"Yes, but later, Ma, please."

They successfully carried out the charade for a week.

After a particularly arduous day of travel, the train had gratefully camped near a running stream that was crystal clear and cold. Ross was talking to Scout over cups of coffee when Ma came up to the wagon, hiding a bottle of milk in her apron pocket.

"Let's walk a piece and find some cool shade near the water."

Lydia heartily approved the suggestion. Eastern Arkansas was beautiful. Wildflowers abounded in the meadows, and the forests were thick with undergrowth. Finding game was no problem. Rarely did Ross or the Langston boys, or any of the men who hunted for the train, come back empty-handed. The evening menus were far from monotonous. When they passed a town, they would send emissaries to buy staples, potatoes, and occasional treats like fresh eggs.

Lydia and Ma found an immense oak and sank onto the shady green turf beneath it. Lydia placed Lee against her and offered him the bottle. He had adjusted to the cow's milk amazingly well and was getting plumper every day.

Ma launched into a tale about one of her pet peeves, her disappointment in Bubba for trailing after the Watkins girl. Lydia was listening, but her mind was wandering. That's why she looked up with lazy indifference when she noticed movement behind Ma's shoulder. Her whole body jerked to rigid attention when she saw Ross. He was staring down at his son, fury turning the green eyes as sharp as nails that pinned Lydia to the ground.

Ma, seeing Lydia's sudden reaction, turned around and assessed the situation immediately. She heaved herself to her feet.

"What the hell is *that?*" Ross spat, pointing at the bottle.

"What does it look like? It's a bottle of cow's milk," Ma said. "Lydia, give me the boy. I'll take him down to the river and let him finish his dinner in peace. I fear if he stays here, he'll likely get indigestion."

Lydia's arms and hands were trembling so spastically, she could barely lift Lee into Ma's outstretched arms. And all the while her eyes remained fearfully on Ross's glowering face. His scowling brows all but obscured his eyes. His lips had sternly disappeared beneath his moustache, and every muscle in his body was straining against his skin.

"Why is Lee sucking on a bottle?"

Beneath his burning gaze, Lydia's eyes lowered to her lap where she was twisting the fabric of her skirt between white, bloodless fingers. "My milk stopped coming," she muttered.

His vile curse made her flinch. "When?" he barked.

"The day we crossed the river. Ma said—"

"Over a week ago?" His roar disturbed the family of blue birds in the tree overhead. They jay-squawked back at him angrily.

"Yes."

"The day after we got married." He laughed then, an ugly, self-deprecating laugh.

Lydia looked up at him and licked her lips nervously. "A few days after."

He slumped against the tree trunk and looked up through the branches as though imploring heaven to tell him what terrible sin he had committed to deserve such punishment. "So now I'm saddled with you, an unwanted wife, and you're not even good for the reason I married you?"

"That brought Lydia surging to her feet. "Well, did you ever stop to consider that I'm *saddled* with you too?"

"It isn't the same."

"You're damn right it isn't. It's a helluva lot worse."

"See? What kind of man wants a wife who talks like a tramp?"

"I learned it from *you!*"

He taught her a new, extremely explicit word before he asked, "Why did your . . . you know . . . your milk . . ." When he glanced at her breasts, he began to flounder. He drew himself up straight and said harshly, "A woman's supposed to be able to nurse her baby indefinitely. What's wrong with you?"

"Nothing."

"Something sure as hell is or you'd still have milk."

"Ma said the river crossing caused it to dry up. I got too excited and upset. I . . . ." Her voice trailed off as once again they were reminded of those tumultuous minutes in the wagon.

Annoyed because she had reminded him of what he had tried for a week to forget, he turned away so he wouldn't have to look at her. He didn't want to see her eyes wide and eloquent because he remembered so well how they had looked up at him before and after that kiss. He didn't want to see her hair surrounding her head like a flaming halo because he knew what it felt like to sink his fingers into it. He didn't want to see her mouth because even now he could taste it. He didn't want to see how her front filled out the bodice of her dress because he could remember how soft and feminine she had felt lying beneath him.

Damn! He didn't want to remember any of it and he remembered all of it. The memory had stalked him for a week, sleeping and waking, every luscious detail haunting him.

Lydia took advantage of his silence. "Ma said it's not unusual. Sometimes if a woman gets scared, like I did on the ferry, this can happen. But Lee's doing fine," she rushed to add. "He learned to suck from the nipple. The cow's milk hasn't given him a stomachache or anything. He's growing every day. He—"

Ross whipped around. "But the fact remains that I'm still married to you and I don't want to be. I had a wife. A wife who was even-tempered and soft-spoken, who was a lady and wore her hair as ladies should, who wouldn't—" He broke off. He had started to say that Victoria wouldn't have let him kiss her with the unbridled lust with which he had kissed Lydia, but he didn't want to tell her that. He didn't want to admit he even remembered it.

If he had intended to cut her to the quick, to hurt her as best he could, he had succeeded. Lydia wished he had belted her as Clancey used to, because then the pain would only be physical and would eventually go away. But Ross had inflicted the worst kind of pain. He had reminded her of what she was, and of what she would always be, no matter how many fine clothes she wore or whose name she carried. She would still be trash on the inside.

Like a wounded animal, pain made her vicious. Her eyes gleamed with the fiery gold of a sunset. She tossed back her mane of hair with a haughty flick of her head. "Well, I haven't made too good a bargain either. I hate you and your bad moods and the way you hurt people for no good reason. I've got a notion you aren't any better than I am, and that's what you can't stand, Mr. Coleman."

With a low growl, Ross advanced toward her. Lydia's

impulse was to flee him and his murderous eyes, but she was too angry in her own right to heed common sense. "I can't think of anything worse than spending the rest of my life as your wife," she shouted, "you . . . you . . . you fornicating hillbilly."

Ross stopped dead in his tracks, his mouth falling open as though the tendons holding up his lower jaw had been clipped.

"Evenin', Mrs. Coleman, Mr. Coleman."

Winston Hill's drawl wafted over the sulphurous air shimmering between Lydia and her husband. His greeting had been spoken pleasantly enough, but he eyed them narrowly as they turned to face him. They had looked like two fighting cocks about to fly into one another, spurs sharpened.

The woman was trying to compose herself and cover her embarrassment by smoothing her hands over her skirt. Ross Coleman was gnawing at the corner of his moustache with his lower teeth.

"Hill," he said tersely, then nodded toward Moses. Lydia let a quick nod of greeting include them both.

"Beautiful countryside, isn't it?"

"Yes, it is, Mr. Hill," Lydia said breathlessly. She had been ready to slap Ross's smug face. What if Mr. Hill hadn't happened upon them? Had he heard the insulting way her own husband had been shouting at her? She could easily die of mortification and hoped that the stinging heat in her cheeks was invisible. "The wildflowers are so pretty," she said with a futile attempt to set things right.

"I just picked these down by the river. Would you accept them, Miss Lydia?" Moses offered her the bouquet. "They'll perk up your wagon."

She hazarded a glance at Ross. His face was as hard and implacable as granite. "Thank you, Moses," she said softly, taking the cluster of flowers and automatically sniffing them. They tickled, and she embarrassed herself further by sneezing.

Mr. Hill and Moses laughed. Ross shifted from one foot to another in apparent vexation.

"Moses admires the way you handle your horses, Mr.

Coleman," Winston said. He wasn't as tall as Ross, but his posture was dignified and gave the illusion of height. "Moses has always worked in the house. I rode, of course, but never handled a team of six. Would you mind showing Moses a few pointers on handling the team? They've been engaged in a battle of wills since we left."

Ross cleared his throat uneasily. "I suppose I could."

"I surely would appreciate it, Mr. Coleman. I couldn't ask for a better teacher," Moses said deferentially.

"I'll see if I can spot your trouble."

"Good, good." Winston beamed at Ross, then addressed Lydia. "Have you seen the river yet? It's cool and pleasant down there. I'd love to escort you. With Mr. Coleman's permission, of course."

"I . . . uh . . . I was about to take Lydia down there myself."

Lydia jerked her head around to look up at her husband, who had spoken the sentence with the casualness of a man who often takes his wife out for an evening stroll. When his arm slid protectively around her waist to draw her closer beside him, she could have been knocked over with a feather.

"We'll bid you a good evenin' then," Winston said graciously, tipping his hat to Lydia.

"Evenin'," Moses said before accompanying his employer back toward the train.

Ross's arm was immediately dropped from her waist and Lydia was vastly disappointed. For just a moment, walking to the river with him had sounded like a good idea. He had walked in the twilight with Victoria, hadn't he? she thought dismally.

There would be no enjoyable stroll. She supposed now that Mr. Hill and Moses were gone, they would start fighting again. She didn't think she had the energy, but she looked up into his face with a challenging expression just in case he lit back into her.

"*Fornicating hillbilly?*" he asked in a soft whisper.

"What?" Was he deliberately confusing her? He wasn't angry. A grin was tugging at one side of his moustache.

"Where in the world did you ever hear such a thing and how could you bring yourself to repeat it?"

It had been an insult often flung at Otis and Clancey by their "neighbors." Lydia had thought that if it fit them, it must surely be the worst of insults. "Is it bad?" she asked timidly, her eyes rounding.

Ross threw back his head and laughed. It was the first time she had ever seen him laugh that way and, after looking at him in slack-mouthed wonder for several moments, she joined him.

"Bad?" Ross said at last, wiping his teary eyes with the back of his knuckles. "Yes it's bad. If I were you and wanted to be treated like a lady, I wouldn't say it in front of anyone again." He started chuckling again and when the laughter finally subsided, he slouched against the tree and slid down its trunk until he was sitting on his heels. He looked up at her with an expression she had never seen before. It was almost tenderly affectionate.

"Goddammit, Lydia, what am I going to do with you?" He ran his fingers through his hair and then hung his head dejectedly, shaking it in bewilderment. "One minute I'm mad as hell at you, ready to strangle you with my bare hands. And then the next minute you're giving me the best laugh I've had in a long time."

He stared at the ground for an interminable length of time while she looked down at his head, wishing she dared touch his hair, iron the creases of worry from his brow. When he looked at her again, his face was void of expression. "I guess we don't have much choice but to stay together until we reach Jefferson."

"I guess so." Then what? She was afraid to ask. Marriage to a stranger with volatile moods wasn't ideal, but he didn't beat her. She preferred having him around to being alone as she had been a month ago. In fact, she was coming to miss him when he wasn't in sight, whatever his mood. "I'm really sorry about my . . . my milk. I had no way of knowing when we married."

Unerringly his eyes went to her breasts. They were as lush, as full, as seductive as ever. "No, you couldn't have known," he said. "I wasn't angry with you, only at fate."

He had been angry because his wife had died prematurely and unjustly. He had lost his temper because he had married this girl, telling himself she was trash and vowing that he didn't want her. And he was furious because, in spite of all those claims, he wanted her very much.

"Why did you tell Mr. Hill you were taking me to the river? Why did you put your arm around me?" The last two words were spoken to her shoes because by that time she had shyly bowed her head.

Because I wasn't about to let him court you. Because I was jealous as hell that he even mentioned taking you for a walk. Because it provided me with an opportunity to touch you. "He and Moses probably heard us fighting. I didn't want it to get back to anybody that I was treating you badly."

"Oh," she said around a mouthful of bitter disappointment.

"Let's get back to the wagon. Ma'll be along with Lee in a while." Surprising both of them, he closed his hand around her upper arm to guide her along.

"If that isn't the most pitiful sight I ever did see."

Bubba Langston's light head cleaved the surface of the water and he came up sputtering. Only a few feet from him Priscilla Watkins was lounging on the grassy bank of the stream. She sat with her arms braced behind her, her knees drawn up, heedless that a good bit of shin and petticoat were visible to the boy in the shallow rushing water.

"What are you doin' spyin' on me? And what's pitiful?" Bubba asked, treading slowly toward the bank. He had been tempted to shuck all his clothes before going into the water. He thanked his stars now he had left his breeches on.

"I wasn't spying on anybody," she retorted petulantly. "I just came down here to the river to cool off. It gets so hot and stuffy riding on that ol' wagon all day." Priscilla drew her mouth into a pout she knew no man could resist looking at and sat up straight. She brought her arms up high over her head and stretched languorously, pulling the cloth of her dress tight over her well-developed breasts. Her lashes lowered over sultry gray eyes as she looked at Bubba commiseratingly.

"And what's pitiful is your chest, Bubba Langston. It doesn't have any hair on it. Nary a one. I saw Mr. Coleman once when he was bathing in the river. He's got hair all over him. Under his arms, on his chest. Some places a young woman shouldn't even see." She yawned broadly, feigning boredom while she slyly watched Bubba's Adam's apple bounce uncontrollably.

"You know what would feel real good?" she asked, becoming animated. "I think I'll take off my shoes and stockings and dangle my feet in that cool water. Girls aren't as lucky as you boys. We can't just strip off to the buff and go swimming whenever we want."

Bubba watched in silent fascination as she unlaced her shoes and pulled them off. Hiking her skirts up, she began to roll her stockings down slowly. Bubba's whole body thickened as her hands slithered down over her knee and calf, taking her stocking with them. She eased the stocking over her slender foot and when Bubba saw the white, naked length of her leg and foot he thought he would die.

Closing her eyes and taking on a rapturous expression, she eased that foot into the swirling water. Lasciviously, she licked her lips with an indolent tongue. Bubba moaned miserably and took another three steps toward her, his legs leadenly pulling through the water. "Priscilla."

She ignored him and went about peeling down the other stocking until her skirts were bunched around her waist and she had both feet swishing in the water. "That feels almost as good as some other things I know about, doesn't it, Bubba?"

He wasn't thinking clearly and what she said didn't register. "It does, too, have hair on it."

She smiled coyly. "Does not."

"Does too." Bubba stood within inches of her now. With the current of the water, her feet bumped against his thighs and the fly of his pants. God, he was going to die! "See?"

She leaned forward to peer closely at his chest. "Well, I do declare. I do see a few hairs sprinkled here and there." She looked up into his feverish face from under her lashes.

Lowering her voice to a seductive purr she asked, "Can you feel them growing there? What do they feel like?"

Bubba's tongue felt too big for his mouth and it had forgotten how to move. He couldn't have worked up a spit if his life had depended on it. Still he managed to garble out, "Touch it and see."

Priscilla's eyes glowed triumphantly and she glanced over her shoulder cautiously. "If I do, you won't tell anybody, will you? Not even that snoopy little brother of yours?"

"I swear," he said, with all the wholeheartedness of a saint vowing obedience.

"All right, then." She extended her hand and, just when she was about to make contact, snatched it back. "I can't."

God, she was killing him! "'Course you can," he panted. "Just touch it."

"You're a beast for making me do this, Bubba Langston," she said chastisingly. Bubba was too far gone to notice the role of seducer had just reverted to him. All he knew was the firebrand touch of her fingertips on his chest. It sent white heat coursing through his body. His manhood throbbed painfully inside his wet pants. If the water hadn't been waist high, she would have seen the tremendous power she was working over him. As it was, the toes of one foot had somehow become lodged in his crotch.

"Oh, Bubba," she cooed, closing her eyes and letting her fingers wander farther afield. "You feel so good. Manly."

"Do I?"

"Um-huh." Sighing with regret, she took her hands away. "But I shouldn't have let you talk me into such a thing. I'm getting hot all over."

"You are?"

She nodded, letting her wheat-blond hair cascade over her shoulders. "I think I'll dip some of this water over me to cool me off." Studiously ignoring his avid eyes, she nonchalantly opened the first two buttons of her dress and leaned toward the stream, making sure he could see her bosom swelling over her bodice. Then cupping water in her hands, she poured it over her chest and let it trickle down.

"Ooooh," she squealed softly. "I didn't think it would be so cold." She continued to ladle water over herself until the front of her dress was wet and clinging.

When she straightened, she gasped in mock surprise at Bubba's dilated gaze. She followed it to her breasts. The cotton molded over them tantalizingly. The cold water had brought her nipples to hard distention, just as she had planned.

"Oh, mercy me," she cried and covered them with her hands. "Don't stare at me like that, Bubba. That gleam in your eyes makes me want to swoon."

"You stared at me," he said thickly.

Gradually she lowered her hands, making sure they dragged with deliberate leisure over the globes of her breasts and that her fingertips grazed the rigid nipples. "So I did, didn't I? You're a cad to take advantage of a girl this way, but fair's fair, I suppose."

He stood there gaping at her breasts and didn't see the frustration that thinned her lips. The boy was dense, of that she was certain. If Scout hadn't hightailed it out for the nearest town as soon as they had made camp, she wouldn't be here with this lout who apparently didn't know what that tool in his pants was for. But she knew what it was for and she could barely sit still for wanting it.

He needed prodding. "I touched you too," she said softly, letting her voice sound tremulously on the verge of tears. "But I know you'd never hold me to that, would you, Bubba?" Her toes pointed downward, bringing the high, arching vamp of her foot to lie along the buttons of his pants.

He brought his blue eyes piercingly up to hers. "You said fair was fair."

She wet her lips with her tongue, making sure he saw the gesture. She batted her eyelashes, coaxing a few tears to form. "You truly are beastly. But if you promise not to tell."

"I swear," he repeated, his eyes fastened again on the puckering nipples showing so plainly through her dress. Awkwardly his hands came up out of the water. "I'll get your dress wetter."

"It won't matter!" she fairly screamed. If this had been Scout they would have already been at it for an hour or more. And here she was having to instruct this fool every step of the way.

Bubba's hands closed over her lightly, then, testing her reaction, more firmly. He rubbed, squeezed, kneaded, not quite believing something could feel so good. He gathered enough courage to let his thumbs drift back and forth over her nipples.

"Ummm, Bubba. I do believe you've done this before," Priscilla said. She had opened her legs and he had naturally stepped between them. Her heels found the backs of his knees and pressed him closer.

"No, never."

"Come on, Bubba, you can tell me."

"Never. I swear it, Priscilla. You're the first girl I've ever loved."

"Harder," she rasped. "Rub them harder, Bubba, and step closer so—"

"Bubba Langston!" The name echoed off the heavens and came right back down on Bubba's head, sending him backward into the water. Had Priscilla not caught a handful of grass, she would have fallen in after him.

"Yes, Ma?" Bubba said, slipping on the rocks of the stream bed as he clambered toward the bank.

"I think your pa needs some help back at the wagon."

"Yes, ma'am," he said, pulling his shirt off the bush where he had hung it after rinsing it out. His wet breeches squished and sloshed as he scampered through the trees.

Ma, looking as indomitable as a fortress even with baby Lee Coleman in the crook of her arm, bore down on the girl, who was hastily pulling on her stockings.

When Bubba was out of earshot, Ma grabbed a handful of Priscilla's hair and hauled her to her feet. "I'm raisin' a decent boy and I aim to see that he stays decent, you hear me, girl?"

"Let go of me," Priscilla said, twisting her head to no avail except to prickle her scalp. Ma's grip didn't lessen.

"You're a hot little hussy and I seen that the first time I

laid eyes on you, but I'm tellin' you now to stay away from Bubba."

"He—"

"He's maturin' and feelin' his manhood and you're just the bait he needs to get hisself in a heap of trouble. I ain't a'gonna let it happen."

"I'll tell my ma about you talking to me like this."

"No you won't, 'cause then your fun with Scout would come to a screechin' halt."

Priscilla ceased her struggles abruptly and Ma, knowing she had the girl's undivided attention, released her. "The next time you feel that twitchin' in your tail, wag it in someone else's face and leave the Langston men alone."

When Ma had returned Lee to Lydia and gone to her own wagon, Bubba was there. She didn't vocalize her rebuke, but her eyes told her son just what she thought of his dalliance with Priscilla Watkins. Bubba, swallowing convulsively, his face flushing hotly and turning the roots of his hair white, said, "Need any help with supper, Ma?"

Chapter Ten

"Yep. I surely do recollect that," the ferryman said, passing a plug of tobacco to the man who was inquiring after the wagon train. "'Bout two, three weeks back, it was."

The man bit off a generous chew and crammed it into his mouth. Pinching off another, he put it in his shirt pocket for later. The ferryman yanked his tobacco back. Prices being what they were, generosity only went so far. "Two or three weeks, you say?" the man repeated.

"'Bout that, yeah. I remember 'cause they had to camp up there on the bluffs before the rain stopped and the river was safe to cross."

"You remember seein' anybody lookin' like the girl I told you 'bout?"

The ferryman shot a wad of tobacco spittle into the current of the river. "'Spect I do. Had a heap of hair, she did. And a young'un. A sucklin' babe."

"A babe?"

"Tiny little mite. Not more'n a month old, I'd say."

The other man grinned with evil satisfaction as he gazed toward the Arkansas shore. "Reckon she's the one, all right."

The ferryman chuckled. "She's not a sight a man could forget like yesterday's piss, but how come you're after a little ol' gal like that, who's already got a babe and all?"

The other man sent flying a nasty string of chewed tobacco into the muddy water. "She's the she-bitch what give me this here scar on my head."

The ferryman had already assessed the man as one of the orneriest, dirtiest, ugliest bastards he had ever seen, but the scar that sliced across his hairline and down into his brow was only part of it. He figured the man was ugly clean through to the marrow.

"I aim to make her pay for it," he was saying about the girl.

The ferryman took off his wide-brimmed hat and brushed his sleeve across a sweating brow. "Well, if I was you, I'd be careful of that man she's with. He—"

"Man!"

The ferryman backed away cautiously from the sudden menace in his companion. He didn't invite trouble with anyone, especially with this kind of renegade who looked like he would just as soon kill a man as look at him and for no better reason than the fun of it. "Yeah, her husband, I 'spect."

"She ain't married," the man growled.

"Well, she was carrin' a sucker and travelin' in a man's wagon, so I reckoned they was a family. I remember 'cause 'bout halfway across, she got scared-like and went scramblin' back into the wagon. Everybody panicked for a minute, the horses too. The man went runnin' after her and they stayed in the wagon together for the rest of the crossin'."

Eyes, black and beady and threatening, were scanning

the opposite shore. The ferryman spat again, glad this man wasn't after him. But he wouldn't have an easy time of getting that woman away from the big man with the moustache and flashing eyes.

"He 'peared to be a mean sonofabitch. His eyes were shifty-like, know what I mean, like nothin' escapes his attention. Pulled a Colt out of a holster quick as lightnin' when he thought somethin' had happened to his lady. Kind of a dark and broody type, he was. Didn't say much, that one, but didn't miss anythin' either. I wouldn't want to tangle with him."

The other man was listening intently, still staring at the opposite shore.

"Had a fine string of horseflesh. Knew what he was doing with 'em too. One sound, one hand motion, and they responded. Spooky-like, it was, to watch the way those horses listened to him. 'Course he left them in the charge of a kid when his woman went flyin' into that wagon like all the devils of hell was after her. Never seen anybody so scared of the river."

The grin the other man turned on him was demonic. "Scared of the river, was she?" His scratchy laugh made shivers run up and down the ferryman's spine. "But she ain't his woman, she's mine."

"Might have a hard time convincin' him of that." He spat again. "It was me, I think I'd let him have her, fine piece of womanflesh though she be, 'fore I'd fight him."

"Well, I ain't you, am I?"

The ferryman shrank from the maniacal calculation in the other's eyes. "You gonna cross now?" he asked nervously.

"Tomorrow. I got some supplies to buy first." He began to walk away before he turned back. "Any hints where they was headin'?"

"All I heard was Texas."

The man nodded, glanced toward the western shore, grinned, and started back toward Memphis on foot, a happy whistle sifting between his tobacco-stained teeth.

"Mornin', Mrs. Coleman." Winston Hill tipped his hat to the young woman driving the team of horses as he rode up beside her wagon. He could appreciate her good posture, dainty figure, and lovely profile. Most of all he could appreciate that she didn't realize how lovely a picture she made.

"Good morning, Mr. Hill."

"When will you start calling me Winston?"

"When you start calling me Lydia."

"Do you think your husband would like that?"

Lydia sighed, keeping her eyes forward as her shoulders lifted and then lowered gradually with the soft expulsion of breath. Her husband approved of little she did. One more transgression, real or imaginary, wouldn't matter. Besides, she was tired of trying to please him.

"If I give you my permission, there's nothing Ross can say about it," she said defiantly and flashed the young man a smile. She was unwittingly flirtatious and Winston's heart leaped inside his chest at the brilliance of her face.

Reaching inside his saddlebag as he maneuvered his mount with one hand, he said, "I brought you something."

"Something for me?" Lydia asked, pleased.

"You called attention to the book I was reading the other night when you were strolling with Lee around the camp. Remember? You stopped to eat some of Moses's apple pie—"

"Only because he acted like he'd be hurt if I didn't," she interrupted.

Winston laughed. "He would have been."

Ross had been furious when he came upon the happy scene a few minutes later. He had all but dragged Lydia back to their wagon, his whole body tense with anger. Sometimes she wished he would shout at her, anything except fume and stew silently like a kettle about to blow its lid off.

Winston was saying, "I saw you looking at the book I'd been reading." He took it out of his saddlebag and stood in his stirrups, reaching to set it beside her on the wagon seat. "So I'm loaning it to you. Keep it as long as you like."

She flushed hotly, embarrassed and grateful at the same time. "Mr. . . . Hill . . . Winston," she stuttered. "I did admire your book. I only wish I could . . . read it."

He was silent for a moment as he stared at her averted face. What a ghastly error he had made. The other night, she had eyed the book with such longing that he was certain she could read and didn't indulge for lack of time or reading material. It had never entered his head that she couldn't read at all.

"Forgive me, Lydia. I didn't mean to give offense. I assumed you knew how to read."

"I did once," she said slowly, shyly. "Mama was teaching me to read when Papa died and . . ." Her voice dwindled away to nothingness with sad, heart-wrenching memories. "Anyway, she didn't teach me anymore after that and I never went back to school. I still recognize the letters and I might be able to read some. I don't know. I haven't seen a book in . . . a long while."

Winston's eyes lit up brightly. He was about to speak when a coughing fit seized him. He coughed wrackingly into his spotless linen handkerchief before he could resume the conversation. "I'll bet you remember more than you think you do. Please take the book, read what you can, and if you have any trouble, ask me for assistance."

"I couldn't. It would be such a bother and—"

"No bother. I would enjoy it." He would enjoy talking to her for any reason. He didn't like being in love with another man's wife. His feelings offended his code of honor. And if the situation weren't hopeless on that account, it certainly was on another. Until he knew he could survive in a warmer, drier climate, he couldn't think of subjecting any woman to the aggravation of his illness. He was sick, but he wasn't dead yet. He was still a man. He loved looking at Lydia, listening to her quiet way of talking, enjoying her innocent charm.

"Lee might not give me much time to read. And I have my duties to my husband."

Now it was Winston's turn to blush hotly as he mistakenly assumed what duties she was referring to. "Of course, I didn't mean to imply that you weren't busy with . . . with being a wife and . . . and mother. I only thought that if you had some spare time, resting time, you might enjoy the book."

Lydia gazed down at it longingly. She could remember

the room where Papa used to sit and read. It had been stocked with books. She had liked the way that room smelled, of Papa's pipe tobacco, of ink, of aged paper and dusty bookcovers. She hadn't thought of that room in years and now the memory was piercing and poignant. "I can't tell you how much I appreciate your thoughtfulness, Winston. Maybe I will have a chance to read it, if I can. I hope so. I don't want to be ignorant the rest of my life."

"I'd hardly call you ignorant, Lydia," he said softly.

Just then Ross came thundering up on Lucky. Like the man, the horse always seemed impatient for motion and he pranced arrogantly when Ross reined him beside Hill's horse, who respectfully gave the stallion room.

"Mornin', Ross. Got some rabbits, I see," Winston remarked with a friendly smile.

"Winston just stopped by to say hello," Lydia said nervously as she pulled on the team's reins. "He brought us a book to read." Maybe if Ross thought the loaned book had been for both of them, he would let her keep it.

"Yes," Winston picked up smoothly. "I brought a whole box of books with me. No sense in them going to waste."

"Thank you kindly, Hill," Ross said.

"I wonder if I might go hunting with you one morning? I'm a fairly good shot," he said with a certain wistfulness. "My daddy and I used to go hunting all the time together. Before the war."

"Sure," Ross said. God, he wanted to hate the man, but Hill never did anything one could hate him for. He even made a big fuss over Lee. Ross couldn't hate anyone who admired his son. "I usually leave as soon as the train pulls out."

"Let me know the next time you go. I'd like to accompany you. And thank you for helping Moses with the team. I knew they were good horses, but until you showed him how to line them up so they weren't pulling against each other, they were giving him trouble."

"I didn't mind," Ross said, shrugging. He glanced at Lydia and wished he hadn't stressed sitting straight on the wagon seat when he was teaching her to drive. Her posture detailed her proud breasts to the havoc of his senses, and he imagined to those of any man who happened to ride by. Hill included. "Lydia, I'll hang these rabbits on the back of the wagon and dress them when we stop at noon."

She couldn't believe what she was hearing. Dressing game was one duty he usually delegated to her, though he knew the process made her stomach queasy and that she hated doing it. "Thank you, Ross," she said softly, staring at him solemnly for a long moment before he snatched his eyes away and wheeled Lucky toward the end of the wagon.

"Have a pleasant day, Lydia," Winston said, tipping his hat and riding off.

"You, too, Winston. And thanks for the book," she replied absently, her mind still on Ross and his strange behavior. Just when she thought she had him figured out, he did something unexpected that made her think she didn't know him at all.

During the past two weeks, ever since they had decided to stay together until they reached their destination, he had successfully been teaching her to drive the team. At first she had been terrified and awkward. But, by following his brusque instructions, she began to get the hang of it.

After the first day, when he had cursed her ineptitude and the futility of teaching her, he had ridden into the nearest town and bought a small pair of leather gloves.

The camp had settled for the night and most fires had already been burned down by the time he stepped into the wagon. Lydia was lying on her bedroll, but wasn't asleep. She had left the lantern on, turned down low. He tossed the wrapped package at her. "You'll tear your hands to ribbons if you don't wear these," he said before turning away to pull off his shirt and boots. Her hands were red and hurting with water blisters and abrasions but she didn't know he had noticed.

She peeled the wrapping away, and when the buttery soft leather gloves fell into her lap, tears came to her eyes. "Thank you, Ross."

"You're welcome." Without looking at her, he turned out the lantern and slid onto his own pallet.

"Does this mean that no matter how bad I was today, you'll still try to teach me to drive?"

"I reckon today was the worst. You're bound to get better."

It wasn't much, but it was a step up from his frowning and cursing at her awkwardness. The next morning she was wearing the gloves when he climbed up beside her on the wagon. She loved them, not only because they felt good against her hands but because Ross had given them to her. And he had picked them out himself.

They were getting along better each day, sometimes in the evenings laughing and talking together like normal married couples. Then something had happened that brought that dreaded frown to his mouth and that deep, stern cleft between his thick dark brows.

One evening Scout had warned the drivers about a ravine they would have to cross the next day. "It's deep, but dry," the young man had told the group collected around him. "No one will have trouble as long as you take it slow and easy. The ground is soft and you won't have much traction. It's shallow on the other side, so getting out will be no problem."

Despite Scout's cautioning words, one of the drivers hadn't ridden his brake enough and his team had been given too much rein. They had run upon the wagon in front of them on the steep decline, causing a potentially dangerous situation and a commotion that frightened both teams. Ross had been sent for to help get the horses calmed.

He was still trying to quiet them and get them lined up on the other side of the ravine when Lydia's turn came. She drove the Coleman wagon to the lip of the steep ravine. The height was dizzying as she looked over the brink. She didn't want Ross or anyone else to criticize her for holding up the rest of the train. Taking a deep breath, she clacked her tongue and slapped the reins against horseflesh and urged the leads to take that first plunging step.

She was about halfway down when she felt the wheels beginning to slip on the soft earth. She gradually applied the brake but nothing happened. Pulling on the reins only seemed to confuse the team and they began to balk at her command to slow down. Anxiously she glanced over her shoulder to see that Lee was sleeping in his crate just inside the wagon's opening behind her. Even that short break in her concentration was enough to make the horses become more skittish. She pulled up on the reins sharply.

"No, Lydia," Ross shouted. He had led Lucky down beside the wagon and sensed the trouble immediately. Out of the corner of her eye, she saw him swing one leg over his saddle horn and leap onto the wagon. With a piercing whistle he gave his mount a command to get out of the way.

"Don't saw the reins, pull in gradually."

The muscles of her arms and back and shoulders ached as she tried to regain control of the team, but they only became more fidgety and the wagon gained momentum on its rolling descent to the rocky floor of the ravine.

"Here, let me," Ross said. He put one arm around her back to take her hand under his and covered her other hand as well. "Easy, easy." He was speaking as much to her as to the nervous team. His cheek was so close it almost lay against hers. She heard his words, felt his breath in her ear.

Her hands followed his whispered instructions. "See? Give them just a little. You're still in charge, easy, easy, don't jerk the reins, just a steady, strong pull. That's it, Lydia, that's it. Good girl. Just a little farther."

When they reached the bottom without mishap, she turned her head to him with a triumphant laugh. "I did it! I did it! Didn't I, Ross?"

The brim of her hat tipped his and slipped off the back of her head. The mass of hair she had piled beneath it came tumbling down over her shoulders. The heart that beat in the breast pressed by his forearm was rapid and irregular with excitement.

The face that was tilted up to his was animated and eager and possibly the loveliest he had ever seen. It was surely the most alluring face, with its rare combination of innocence that a new sprinkling of freckles enhanced, and a blatant sensuality that could never be acquired but was innate. Her smiling mouth looked soft and moist and kissable. And God, how he remembered its sweetness melting beneath his lips.

In the sunlight her eyes were of a color that was indefinable, hovering somewhere between brown and gold. He saw reflected in them a man hypnotized. A man starved for the taste and touch of her. He saw a lonely man wanting a woman, not just any woman, this woman. A man craving the solace that her soft voice and lush body promised.

He saw himself. And what he saw scared the hell out of him.

He released her quickly and said in a gravelly voice unfamiliar to them both, "Yeah, you did just fine." He picked up the reins, scooting along the seat to put inches of space between them. "I'll take it the rest of the way."

Lydia couldn't read his thoughts. For one breathless moment she had thought he was going to kiss her again. She felt an emotion like a gigantic flower opening inside her chest. She wanted him to kiss her. She wanted to feel his moustache against her lips again, his mouth opening over hers, his tongue inside her mouth. Her insides curled with delicious pleasure at the thought.

But it hadn't happened and he had been cross and cranky ever since, until this morning when, in front of Mr. Hill, he offered to dress the rabbits so she wouldn't have to.

He drove the team after the noon break, but didn't seem inclined to engage in conversation. Lydia made several brave attempts, but his responses were clipped and obligatory. So, to help pass the hours of the bumpy ride, she opened Winston's book and began to peruse the gilt-edged pages. She managed to decipher the title.

"I-van-hoe," she whispered.

"Ivanhoe." Ross corrected her misplacement of the accented syllable.

She brought her head around. "You can read, Ross?"

He shrugged in the way she knew meant he didn't want to elaborate. And she was right. He didn't want her to know that it had only been since he had met Victoria Gentry that he had known how to read. Victoria had been aghast when she learned of this deficiency in him, and had set about teaching him in the evenings when his work for the day was done.

Once Victoria had taught him to read, he had read

everything the Gentry library had to offer, and his education had extended to other subjects. She taught him a smattering of geography and history, how to add a column of figures and how to subtract. If he hadn't loved Victoria for any other reason, he would have loved her for teaching him without mocking his dismal ignorance.

"What does that mean?" Lydia asked him now.

"What?"

"Ivanhoe."

"It's a man's name."

"Oh," she said, running her fingers reverently over the smooth leather. "Is there a lady in the story?"

"Two. Rowena and Rebecca."

"What happens to them?"

Ross looked down at the inquiring face and answered the way Victoria used to answer him. "Read it and find out."

A challenge issued by Ross was one she wouldn't refuse. Winston Hill couldn't have induced her nearly so easily with his gentle coaxing. Lydia's chin lifted proudly. "All right," she said. "If I miss a word or don't understand something, will you help me?" He nodded.

So for the rest of the day, he listened as she stumbled through the first two pages. When they pulled into the circle of wagons for the night, they were both tired, but Lydia was aglow with her accomplishment.

Ma visited with her, feeding Lee his bottle, as Lydia sliced potatoes and set the rabbits to roasting. Bubba came running up, breathlessly interrupting them. "Ross needs some shoeing nails. He said there was a sack of them in the wagon."

"I'll get them," Lydia said.

When she had fetched them, Ma said to her son, "You go help your pa and let Lydia take them nails to her husband."

Bubba was disappointed that he had been reassigned chores. He liked spending as much time with Ross as possible. But he wasn't one to argue with his ma these days, not after she had seen him with Priscilla. "All right," he said dispiritedly, ambling toward the Langston wagon.

"I need to finish feeding Lee so you can get your own

family's dinner," Lydia said, objecting softly, when indeed her heart had started beating faster at Ma's suggestion. She and Ross had so few moments alone. He was always the last in the train to retire, sometimes long after she had fallen asleep. More mornings than not he was already up and tending his horses before she awoke to feed Lee and get their breakfast. She was beginning to think he hated being around her, especially in the privacy of the wagon.

"Anabeth's gettin' supper tonight. I'd rather take care of Lee anytime than break my back over that hot campfire. Go on," she urged.

Lydia smoothed her hair and took off her apron. Those vanity-inspired gestures made Ma smile secretly as she watched the young woman crossing the camp in the direction of the overnight corral. The people of the train accepted Lydia now as Mrs. Coleman, and she was politely addressed as such.

Ross was alone at the corral, everyone else having returned to their wagons. When she sighted him he was standing beside one of his mares, brushing her mane and speaking to her softly. Lydia was taken with how handsome he was. His hat was off and the late afternoon sunlight cast iridescent streaks on his black hair. His rugged masculinity harmonized with the forest setting.

Lydia was so absorbed in watching the way his hands smoothed over the mare's flank that she didn't see the stone in her path. She stumbled, falling to her knees, spilling the nails and scattering them over the rocky ground. Embarrassed and cursing her own clumsiness, she rushed to gather them up. Just as she extended her hands to scoop them toward her, she heard the telltale rattle. She froze. The rattlesnake was coiled against the very rock she had stumbled over.

Lydia's scream tore through the evening air and she flung herself backward. Waiting for the pain of the rattler's strike, she turned her head to take one last look at Ross.

At her scream he dropped to the ground, whipping the pistol out of his holster at the same time he rolled over twice. Then, seemingly without even taking aim, he fired the pistol. Lydia screamed again as the snake's head was cleanly severed from its body by the accuracy of Ross's bullet. The body writhed and slithered only a few inches from her shoe before it finally lay still.

Frozen in time, her eyes wide, she stared at Ross. He had fired the pistol with the same second-nature reflexes that compel a rattler to strike at anything that moves. Lydia didn't know which had frightened her more.

Speechless, motionless, awed, she watched as he sleekly lifted himself off the ground and came toward her. She shrank from him as he knelt beside her. Lethal as the snake had been, this man could be just as deadly.

"Lydia, did he get you?" The question could have been ripped from his throat for all the pain it caused him. His features were contorted with the agony of having to know.

Another reversal. He had gone from killer to consoler even as she watched. The trauma was too much for Lydia's frayed nerves. "No, no," she stuttered, beginning to shake all over, uncontrollably and violently.

She reached out for him and crawled her way up his chest until her arms were folded over his shoulders and she was crying into his shirtfront. His arms had long since gone around her, bringing her to her knees, locking her small body against the bulwark of his. He buried his face in the wealth of her hair, murmuring reassurances that everything was all right. He felt the shuddering upheaval in her breasts and pressed her tighter against him, cushioning her residual terror and taking it into himself.

Lydia raised her head, her eyes laden with tears. "Only a few weeks ago I wanted to die. But when I saw that rattlesnake, I didn't want to die and leave Lee. I didn't want to leave . . . you, Ross."

"Lydia," he moaned softly before his mouth came down hard on hers, twisting, grinding, releasing all the pent-up tension he had stored inside him for weeks. Their mouths met with the urgency of the moment, with a fierce need to be reassured that they had survived a near disaster. Their breathing was labored and harsh as his tongue thrust undeterred and deep into her mouth. Her hands, the heels of them braced against his shoulders, opened wide with fingers extended, tensed, held, then gradually began to relax as they closed tightly around his neck.

Low animal sounds emanated from him as his hands scored her slender back. He was insane with the primeval male instinct to claim, to possess, to protect, to mate. His hand curved under her hips, lifting her to his heat which found a harbor in her softness. He rubbed himself against that vulnerable pocket that housed her femininity.

Ross thought the low rumbling sound in his ears was the thundering of his own heartbeat. But Lydia realized it was the thudding of running footsteps and tore her mouth free of his. Members of the train were coming to see what the pistol's firing had been about. Ma, having shoved Lee into Anabeth's unsuspecting arms with an order to take care of him, was leading the pack that congregated around the couple kneeling together, wrapped around each other.

Everyone stared at the grisly body of the snake, which spoke for itself.

"Goddamn lucky if you ask me."

"Could've been any of us. We were all trampin' 'round here not five minutes ago."

"Lucky it wasn't one of the children."

"Lucky Ross got off that shot."

"How'd you do it, Ross?"

"How'd you get off a clean shot like that?"

Lydia looked into the green eyes. They were shimmering with a silent, urgent plea. She read it. He was begging her not to tell them about his precision with the pistol. At that moment she had new insight into the character of her husband, something she had sensed before, but had had no real evidence of. He had something to hide too. Handling horses wasn't his only talent, but he didn't want anyone to know it.

"I . . . uh . . . I hadn't taken off my gunbelt since my hunting trip this morning. The pistol was still loaded. When Lydia saw the snake and called me over, I was able to get right on top of him." He didn't look at his rapt audience, but kept searching Lydia's eyes, beseeching her not to tell them he was lying, that he had taken the snake's head off from a good forty feet away.

"Well, it's all over now, and speakin' for myself, I've had enough adventure for today," Ma said, coming to their rescue. She didn't know what, but she sensed something important happening between the two of them. She recognized lying, too, when she saw it, and Mr. Coleman had lied. "Mr. Sims, you got any of that brandy left? I'll bet a good swig of it would calm Mrs. Coleman while her husband's gentlin' those spooked horses. Some of you stay with him and comb the area for other snakes."

Reluctantly Ross pulled his arms away from Lydia.

Reluctantly she let herself be turned over to Ma and led back to camp.

Chapter Eleven

L ydia awoke the next morning with a nervous stomach and fluttery heart. She longed to see Ross and yet she dreaded it too. For some absurd reason she had pretended to be asleep when he returned late to the wagon the evening before. She couldn't quite gather up enough courage to face him then. She didn't know if she could now.

What had happened yesterday after the incident with the rattlesnake? She had never felt such heart-stopping, roiling emotions before. Like tiny hatching eggs, secret sensations had opened up inside her. Timed perfectly to respond to Ross's touch, his kiss, they had cracked, opened, released a new and wonderful emollient that had flowed through her body slowly like warm, golden honey. She had wanted that kiss to go on forever until . . .

What? What did that kind of embrace culminate in? Certainly not what she had experienced with Clancey. They were two different things entirely. The distinction wasn't clear to her yet. She only knew that being with Ross would be nothing like what she had endured before.

Recollections of those detestable times with Clancey were more painful now than ever. Even though her nemesis was dead, the emotional wounds he had inflicted

lived after him in her heart. Ross had kissed her yesterday.
Only then had she realized the full extent of Clancey's
abuse. Should she and Ross ever do . . . that . . . she
wished to be new for him. She wanted him to be the first to
have knowledge of her body. She yearned to offer him
purity. It was a gift no longer hers to give.

Regret over that ate at her until she actually felt pain.
If it plagued her that much, what must Ross feel about her
having had a man before?

Those thoughts were with her as she smoothed down
her hair, inspecting her reflection in the scrap of mirror and
sadly wanting to be more conventionally pretty. Just then
the canvas was flung back and Ross stepped inside the
wagon. Startled, she jumped back from him. He loomed
large and close, consuming all the available air.

"Good morning," she said breathlessly. She found it
easier to speak to his shirt buttons than to his eyes. "Did I
oversleep?"

"No. I was up early." When she hazarded a glance up
at him, she noted that he wasn't meeting her eyes either.
"Did you sleep all right? No aftereffects? From the . . .
uh . . . the snake?"

"No," she said, wetting her lips. "I'm fine."

"Ah, good." He turned to leave. "Well—"

"Ross?" She took a step toward him.

"What?" He spun around on the heels of his boots,
nearly colliding with her.

"Thank you." This time she dared to raise her face to
his.

"For what?" From some internal fire, his eyes shone
brightly and warmed her whole body.

"For saving me from the snake." The words were only
a tripping rush of air past lips suddenly gone wooden.

"Oh."

How long they stood there staring at each other, they
never remembered. And what would have happened had
Luke Langston not stuck his head inside calling, "Anybody
home? I got the young'un's milk," they could only guess.

It was like that all day. They spoke in clipped sentences
as if afraid to say too much. But they spoke often in fear of

not saying enough. They watched each other covertly, but found it difficult to meet each other's eyes. They were overly polite. They were both strangely happy. They were both abysmally miserable. They walked a tightrope. That kind of tenuous balance couldn't last long. At one point one must fall to one side or the other.

As usual, after they camped that evening, Ross went to the far side of the wagon to wash up while Lydia prepared their evening meal. She had come to appreciate the sight of him stripped to the waist as he soaped and rinsed, and had begun inventing excuses for stepping around the wagon to speak to him while he was about it.

Still experiencing aftershocks from his kiss the day before, seeing him that way took on a new dimension. Lydia's insides quivered when she remembered the way his hands had intimately conformed her body to his. Perhaps the thought of mating with him wasn't hateful because he was more physically attractive than Clancey. For whatever reason, she admitted to a frank interest in the way he was made.

She decided she would ask his opinion of the stew. *Taste this and tell me if it needs more salt, please*. That was a wifely request, wasn't it? A plausible excuse for her to talk to him while he was washing? Taking a spoonful of stew with her, she rounded the end of the wagon.

Ross was bending over the basin. The supple groove of his spine separated his back into two toasty loaves of flesh. The muscles rippled with each movement of his arms as they brought handfuls of water up to his head. Suddenly he straightened, wet head thrown back, his hands covering his eyes. Droplets of water splashed on his chest and rolled down the furred expanse to that fine line of dark hair that disappeared into his pants where his sex was a full bulge.

Lydia forced a swallow past her beating heart. At that moment she wanted nothing more than to touch him. All of him. Because he was beautiful.

But then she saw Priscilla Watkins lounging against one of the trees nearest the wagon. Her eyes were glassy and drowsy behind half-lowered lids, her expression rapt, as she watched Ross.

Lydia went hot all over and she had an overpowering temptation to fling the scalding stew into the girl's lascivious face. How dare Priscilla stand there gaping at, lusting for, her husband!

When the girl saw Lydia, her lips curled into a knowing smirk before she slipped back into the cover of the trees.

Irrationally Lydia took her anger out on Ross. "Aren't you done yet?" she demanded haughtily.

He lowered his hands and looked in her direction, realizing for the first time that she was there. Endearingly, his wet hair dripped onto his ears and neck. "No," he snapped back. "Are we on a schedule?"

"Hurry up. Supper's almost done." With a flourish of her skirts, she turned on her heel and stalked back to the fire, wondering what she was so mad at. "And for heaven's sake put some clothes on," she called back over her shoulder.

That's all the provocation Ross needed. His nerves were stretched to the breaking point. If he couldn't find sexual release, losing his temper would suffice. He stormed around the end of the wagon, pulling on a shirt.

"You may not have noticed, but I rarely wash with my shirt on."

After slinging the spoon back into the stew, she spun around to face him. "No, you'd much rather parade around half naked so the likes of that Watkins girl can get an eyeful of you."

He shook his head, trying to muddle through what she had said, and trying to rid himself of the need to crush her body to his and silence her with another soul-rending kiss. "What the hell are you harping about. I wasn't parading anywhere. I can't help it if that hot-blooded little twit comes snooping around when I'm washing."

Lydia's face went furiously pink. Her dainty hands balled into ridiculously fragile fists. "You mean she's done it before?"

He shrugged and the gesture was full of pure conceit. "Sure. Lots of times."

"Well, she won't see any more of you. You're a married man. You'll wash inside the wagon."

He took a step toward her, which necessitated her bending her head back to look up at him. "The hell I will," he ground out. "Marriage doesn't give you ownership of me. I'll continue to do what I've always done, which is whatever I damn well please, and you'll have absolutely no say in the matter."

"I *do* have some say in the matter," she hissed back. "I'm your *wife*."

"My wife is dead."

The instant the words left his lips, he regretted them. Lydia reeled backward as though he had actually struck her, and he had to curb an impulse to reach out and catch her back to him.

He had said those hateful words because he had been reciting them to himself all day. Since he had kissed Lydia yesterday, he had carried on mental conversations with Victoria, apologizing to her for wanting another woman with a need that left him weak. To the ghost that haunted him, he had justified his desire for the woman who now bore his name. He was only a man. Not a very stalwart man at that. Could Victoria blame him for wanting, needing, another woman?

He felt guilty as sin. But that didn't keep him from wanting to take what rightfully and lawfully was his to take. He was in a moral dilemma. And though he had lifted himself out of a life of crime, moral dilemmas were still new to Ross and he hated them like hell. He had to blame somebody for the war being waged within his conscience. Lydia was a convenient whipping post on which to vent his frustration.

Tears of hurt and fury sprang into Lydia's eyes. "Oh, yes. You'll never let me forget that I follow in Victoria's hallowed footsteps, will you?"

Bubba Langston saw the air between them fairly crackling with animosity. They looked like hunger-crazed wild animals, straining against invisible leashes, ready to tear into each other. He knew he was stepping into a lion's den, but he had been sent to fetch Ross. Swallowing his caution, he said a trifle too loudly, "Uh, Ross?"

The man's dark head swiveled around and Bubba was lashed by razor-sharp green eyes. "Yes?"

Bubba quailed under Ross's hard stare. "They sent me for you," he said in a rush. "There's a wagon of . . . ladies, sort of . . ."

Luke, who had tagged along, snorted a laugh behind him. Bubba turned around and glared at him warningly. Luke's laughter was reduced to a shaking of his shoulders and muffled sounds.

"They're broke down by the river. Mr. Grayson asked you to come help."

Ross looked at Lydia long and hard before taking up his hat and saying to the boys, "Show me where they are."

Lydia watched him stalk away. Disconsolately she picked up Lee, who had been perfectly happy lying in his crib, and held his small warm body to her chest in hopes of finding comfort from him. She sank onto the small stool and stared dejectedly into the fire.

An hour passed. Most everyone else had eaten supper and was getting settled for the night. Lydia noticed that folks were avoiding her, casting furtive glances in her direction. She wasn't hungry, but she ate anyway, determined not to let Ross and his hateful words destroy her healthy appetite. She could have been eating sawdust. Lee was sleepy, and after keeping him up as long as she could for company, she put him down for the night.

She was stepping back into the evening air when Ma, looking as tight-lipped and foreboding as any Indian chief on the warpath, came marching up to her. "You best see to your husband," she said stonily, giving Lydia a sound push.

"But—"

"Git. That wagon full of floozies is over yonder by the creek."

"Floozies?"

"Yes, floozies," Ma came close to shouting impatiently. "Git. I'll stay with Lee."

Lydia was puzzled as she crossed the camp. Everybody was looking at her like they all knew something tragic, but didn't want to be the one to tell her.

The wagon by the river didn't look like any other Lydia

had ever seen. It was gaily decorated with a garland of wild roses, hearts, and doves painted on its sides. The wheels were red with white hearts painted over the hubs. Even the canvas top seemed frivolous with underthings hanging from it on pegs. Lydia had never seen such lacy, transparent, frilly garments and wondered what purpose many of them served.

Ross was sitting on Lucky, one leg raised and hooked around the saddle horn. He was indolently leaning over the saddle, he was smoking a cigar, his hat was pushed back, his teeth were flashing whitely against his moustache as he tossed back his head and laughed—all of which made Lydia furious. His attitude of cocky self-assurance reminded her of Scout. And Scout's conceit had always irritated her.

He was chatting with the five women who were languorously draped on the wagon seat or sitting barelegged astride the team horses. The one who had his eye now was fanning herself with a broad purple plume fan. Her dress was scandalously low-cut, revealing twin white mounds of bosom.

Lydia strode up to the wagon like a tiny soldier, her back straight, her head high and tilted at a disdainful angle.

The madam was the first to see her. Her fan stopped its lazy waving and she admired the girl marching toward them with such determination in her bearing and expression. She was a good assessor of womanflesh and she recognized a potential money-maker when she saw one. Made up, corseted, and dressed in something besides calico, this girl could earn her a fortune. What fabulous coloring.

Ross realized his audience's attention had lapsed. The young women were looking at something beyond his shoulder. He turned his head to see Lydia coming toward them. She stopped a few feet from his stirrups and looked up at him.

"Are you taking supper at the wagon, Mr. Coleman?"

He drew on the cigar and blew a cloud of smoke into the air over his head. He studied the cigar as he answered slowly. "Ladies, this is Mrs. Coleman. Lydia, Madam LaRue and her . . . wards."

Lydia's cheeks flamed scarlet as the girls twittered behind their hands. She heard one of them say, "Have ya eveah in ya life seen hayeh like that?"

Her eyes were glacial as she let them gloss over the covey of girls and then the buxom madam, who was still surveying her through narrowed, speculative eyes.

With a dismissive sniff, she looked back up at Ross. "Well? I asked you a question."

Ross stared down at her and wished to God she didn't look so beautiful with the last of the sunrays filtering through her hair. Why did her body look more voluptuous with its slender curves wrapped in plain cloth than did the variety of flesh being so generously displayed for him in scanty satins and laces? She looked like a sulky lioness who needed taming very badly. He felt like vaulting off his horse, hauling her to him, and starting the taming process right then and there. The first thing he would do was kiss that contemptuous curl off her lips.

"No, I'm not having supper in camp. These ladies," he tipped his hat at them and the girls giggled again, "had bogged down in the mud. I helped to pull them out. I've offered to escort them into town where they are looked for by the proprietor of the Shady Rest Saloon."

"Looked for by all those railroad men with loose change filling their pockets," one of the girls drawled seductively.

"That ain't all they got filling their pockets," another added. They burst into ribald laughter, Ross included.

Lydia's teeth ground together and her fingernails made half-moons in her palms. "Suit yourself," she said before she swung away and went tromping through the tall grass and wildflowers back to camp.

Ross clamped down on the cigar and watched her go. If she had acted like she cared, if she had begged him, he wouldn't have gone. But she didn't care, didn't give a goddamn, and he was due a good time. He didn't realize until that moment how much he had missed drinking and gambling and whoring. Yes, whoring! First Victoria wouldn't let him touch her for months. Now he was living with a woman he couldn't stand, who deliberately flaunted herself at him when she knew damn good and well he wouldn't take her.

He had had it with family life. With marriage. Damned if he would put up with it any longer. He had his choice of women tonight and by God, if he couldn't walk tomorrow as a result, he was going to bed them all.

He turned back and let his green eyes slide over each of the girls, resting finally on Madam LaRue. "Whenever you're ready, ladies."

"I see you're findin' the book interestin'."

Lydia looked up from the pages she was holding close to the lantern. "Hello, Winston. Yes, it's fascinating."

He smiled in the dark stillness. "May I sit down?" he asked politely, indicating the other stool. She swallowed a lump of gratitude that Mr. Hill was speaking to her as though nothing had happened. By now everyone in the train knew that Ross had gone into Owentown with the whores. They were giving Lydia wide berth, as though she were in mourning. If only they knew how little she cared, she thought defiantly.

She was lying to herself. Her heart had felt like a lead ball in her chest ever since Ross had scorned her in front of the whores.

"Please sit down, Winston," she said with a forced smile. "Would you care for coffee?"

"Thank you, yes."

After she had poured him a cup and he had sipped at it, he commented, "You must not be having any trouble reading, or you're too proud to ask for my assistance."

She smiled at his gentle rebuke. "I remember more than I thought I would. When I do have trouble with a word, Ross—" She broke off suddenly, having spoken his name. She gazed into the fire, wondering if he was kissing one of those women the way he had kissed her only yesterday. "Ross helps me. He knows how to read," she said proudly.

"How fortunate for you both," Winston remarked quietly. He wished he had the strength to fight the man who had brought that look of despair to her face. But even if he did, it was none of his business. Still, what was the man thinking of, insulting her this way in front of all the train? He should be horsewhipped. "Lee's sleeping already?" he asked, changing the subject.

It worked to lift her eyes from the depths of the fire and to replace a great sadness with one of animation. "He's an angel, going right to sleep after his last bottle every night. And he sleeps straight through, but he wakes up early."

"He's a fine boy."

"Yes, he is. Sometimes I forget that he's not mine."

She hadn't intended to admit that. Winston saw her distress immediately and stood up. "Thank you for the coffee," he said, setting the half-full cup on the tailgate of the wagon. "I must turn in. Like Lee, we all must get up early in the morning."

Where will Ross be in the morning? Lydia wondered. "Yes."

"Do you need help with banking your fire?"

"No," she said quickly. She still held out hope that Ross would come back tonight. "I'll do it in a bit. I want to read a while longer."

Winston raised her hand to his lips and kissed it softly. "Good night, fair Lydia."

Then he disappeared in the darkness and Lydia was left alone to wait for Ross.

It was the kind of place he used to frequent, and he knew before he went in that he was courting disaster. Yet he went anyway with an almost compulsive need for self-punishment. The "ladies" were getting on his nerves by the time they reached Owentown. They giggled and simpered and managed to maul him with soft, well-placed, accidental touches that, rather than inflaming his desires, quenched them. He kept thinking about Lydia and the valiant way she had stood her ground both with him and with the women who had all but promised to seduce her husband. She had made them all look pathetic.

Combating guilt and dissatisfaction, Ross swung open the doors of the Shady Rest and entered the clamorous racket. The air was thick with smoke and the stink of stale beer and unwashed bodies. The red wallpaper had long since been peeled away from the clapboard walls and the naked girl reclining in the badly painted portrait over the bar had had both eyes shot out. The floor was sticky with tobacco spittle. The pianist was an abomination to anyone with half an ear for music, and the drinks were watered down.

The clientele didn't seem to notice these deficiencies. They were there to have a rambunctious good time and the arrival of five new whores had everyone's blood pumping and tempers flaring.

It was just the kind of squalid atmosphere Ross needed to convince himself he was unhappy in his new life.

He picked up a bottle of whiskey at the bar and waded his way through a maze of foul-smelling bodies to a table where a poker game was in progress. Thankfully the stakes weren't high, and he got in on the next deal and won it. He had taken the next few hands and had drunk numerous glasses of the whiskey when he noted a man across the room watching him closely. The man was too innocuous not to alarm Ross immediately.

Every instinct he had groomed over the years went into play. Even after three years of living straight, his whole body was trained to react to potential danger. When he looked up again the man had turned his back, but Ross knew he could have been recognized. He gathered up his winnings, left the bottle to the others as a token of fair play, and wended his way to the side door of the saloon.

He entered the dark alley cautiously, his eyes darting around the myriad places a sniper could lurk. He knew them all. Damn! The man he had noticed watching him in the saloon was standing at the corner of the building, lighting a cigar. It might mean nothing or it might mean everything, but Ross didn't take chances. He had left Lucky at the front of the saloon. He would have to whistle for him later. For now he had better lie low.

He flattened himself against the wall and, keeping his eyes on the silhouette at the corner, soundlessly crept along it to the rear of the building. He saw Madam's wagon parked at the back door. The soft lantern glow from within revealed her standing on the tailgate.

He walked toward her on silent feet. "Why aren't you inside with the others?" he asked in a whisper.

"Why aren't you?" she returned.

She was smoking a cigar, the smoke wreathing the mass of coal-black hair piled high on her head. Her cheeks and lips were rouged. Her face was pasty with makeup that, if one didn't look closely, camouflaged the hard-earned lines surrounding her eyes. Her arm was lying across her stomach holding together the front of a black satin robe with a garish dragon embroidered over the shoulder, his fire-breathing nostrils and red, mad eyes crawling down her generous bosom.

Ross glanced over his shoulder at the saloon. Squeals of pleasure, the thumpingly brash piano, and the roar of anger and laughter mingled offensively. "Too big a crowd."

Madam dropped her cigar into the dust. "That's what I thought. I was too tired for it tonight."

Ross was lonely. He thought of the man in the front of the saloon. Pursuers, always, for the rest of his life, pursuers. He thought of Victoria dying and leaving him mercilessly to fall back into the life he had tried to escape. He tried not to think of Lee. And Lydia. *God, don't think of Lydia.* "You got a bottle?"

"Yes." She let her arm drop and when it did the wrapper fell open to reveal a body that must once have been desirable, but that now sagged and lumped in unfortunate places. Only her breasts were fine. She had magnificent breasts with nipples rouged to match her mouth. The nest of hair between her thighs was coarse and thick and dark. Her thighs were heavy, but her ankles trim. "I've got plenty of whiskey and everything else you need right now, Mr. Coleman."

She was an old whore. But what was he? A whore's son. And one took comfort where one could find it. He climbed into the wagon and let the canvas flaps close behind him.

It was stygian when Ross drunkenly stumbled out of the wagon. He blinked against the moonless darkness and took a few halting steps before he gave up the endeavor to walk as useless. Lifting his fingers to his mouth, he placed them just right and whistled through numb, flaccid lips. It pierced the night, slicing through the stillness like the blast of a bugle. He tensed, but relaxed when his horse rounded the building. That was the only movement. The saloon had long since closed its doors for the night.

After several aborted attempts, he managed to climb onto his horse and guide him in the general direction of the train. God, he felt miserable. Each clop of Lucky's hooves slammed against his skull. He was never so glad to see the faint, shadowy outline of the circle of wagons.

He slid down Lucky's side, taking the reins and guiding him into the roped-off corral. "You're a friend," he muttered as he clumsily took the saddle off. "A real friend."

When the horse had been seen to, Ross ambled around the circle of wagons trying to decide which was his. The venture made him dizzy; the whiskey he had drunk churned in his stomach, and before he knew what had hit him, he was racing for the bushes where he vomited it up violently. God, at one time what he had drunk tonight would have seemed only a thimbleful.

He reeled toward the wagon, feeling badly about the way he had treated Madam . . . uh . . . Madam whatever the hell her name had been. He had thought he could go through with it, thought that it didn't matter which female body he spent his frustration on. But he had been wrong.

She had been accommodating, telling him how smart and witty and handsome and strong he was. She had praised his body even as he drained the bottle of whiskey while trying to conjure up desire for hers. He had even kissed her. Compared to Lydia's mouth, hers tasted sickeningly sour. He had buried his face in the folds of flesh at her neck and nearly gagged at the cloying fragrance. Drunkenly he had fondled her breasts, but instead of finding them firm and ripe, he had only been handling globs of loose, pudgy flesh that he found repugnant.

She neither looked, nor felt, nor tasted, nor smelled like Lydia. No, goddammit. Not Lydia, Victoria. Victoria.

Say it. Victoria. Remember? Your wife. The woman you loved. The woman you still desire.

But it had been Lydia's face he had seen, not Victoria's. Even as Madam had patiently stroked and manipulated him, he had tried to envision Victoria, but could see only Lydia, staring up at him with censure on her golden face and in those amber eyes. When Madam's perseverance paid off and he became hard and throbbing in her hand, it had been Lydia's name he had moaned, and Lydia's name he had repeated, even as he pulled on his clothes and left Madam cursing him to perdition.

Swaying precariously, he gained the back of the wagon and pulled himself inside, bracing his hands on the floor in a futile attempt to keep it from tilting. Then, on all fours, carefully placing one palm and one knee in front of him, making no jarring, hasty motions, he crawled to the place in the wagon that offered him the solace he craved, and he lay down.

He sighed once with immense pleasure, then let the blackness that obliterated conscious thought engulf him.

Lydia awoke to a pleasant heaviness on her breast. At first she thought she was holding Lee against her as she slept, as she had done when he awakened at night and wanted to suckle. But even Lee, after he had begun gaining weight, wasn't this heavy. Cocooned in that hazy cloud between sleep and wakefulness, she lifted her hand to the delicious weight and touched silky hair. As her fingers imbedded themselves in the thick mass, the strands curled around her fingers in their own caress.

She sighed with a sense of well-being and shifted slightly, realizing that the heaviness extended down her torso and onto her legs. Curiosity was beginning to overcome sleepiness, but still she didn't come fully awake. She didn't want this rare pleasure to be disturbed.

Something stirred over her breast and her flesh responded. Her nipple beaded into wakefulness and a mysterious tingling was generated there and radiated throughout her body. It was the most profound pleasure she had ever felt. She made to bend her knee and a soft moan, not unlike the one she felt rising in her own throat, vibrated from the heaviness atop her.

Yawning, she opened her eyes. Then, blinking them rapidly, she lay perfectly still, looking down at the long body sprawled over hers. His head was pillowed on one of her breasts, his large hand covered the other. He was snoring softly through his mouth. The moisture of his breath had dampened her gown and the skin beneath it. One long leg, still booted, was stretched along the floor of the wagon, the other was bent and lying across her thighs. Her knee was tucked firmly against his crotch.

Lydia stared at her own hand moving through the dark waves of his hair of its own volition. And she looked at his hand, curved protectively, almost lovingly, around her breast. She had an impulse to cover that large hand with her own, to trap it there, even as she pressed his head deeper against her breast.

Maybe then he would wake up, and look at her, and kiss her the way he had the other day. Maybe he would slide his tongue between her lips again and she would feel its hard, velvety length inside her mouth. She would taste him again and feel his hard body close to hers, feel his moustache brushing her lips.

But then she remembered the way he had looked down at her from his horse the evening before, all but laughing at her in front of the prostitutes. He had probably spent the night in their company and had just minutes ago returned. Didn't she smell whiskey? And something else that was overpoweringly sweet? Cheap cologne?

His hand moved and he murmured something in his sleep. Lydia watched, not daring to breathe, as his fingers sought out the taut peak of her breast. He brushed against it with his fingertips. They stilled, then moved again, gently rolling over the tightening flesh. He lifted his head to move his mouth nearer. His lips made seeking motions.

A tight constriction claimed Lydia's throat. Blood pounded in her veins. If she didn't stop him now, she wouldn't be able to.

She put all last night's anger and loneliness and embarrassment into the blow her fist gave the middle of his back and the shove she gave his shoulder. "Get off me, you drunken . . . bull!"

Startled awake out of an alcohol-induced sleep, Ross rolled to his back, caught himself on his elbow with a loud crack, banged his head against a trunk, and sat up cursing.

"Sonofabitch!" he said in a scorching hiss. He clutched his head while the whole Union army seemed to tramp through it. The pain from his elbow shot like malicious arrows through his whole body. "Goddammit," he muttered, squeezing his eyes against the pain that wouldn't stop.

"Shut your foul mouth," Lydia said in a harsh whisper. Dawn was just breaking and she didn't want their neighbors to hear his vile curses.

He blinked bleary, bloodshot eyes in her direction, trying to get her four images to congeal into one. His look was as black as the stubble sprouting from his chin. "Are you the one responsible for waking me up like that?" he growled.

"You wouldn't get off me," she said haughtily, standing up and checking to see that Lee was still asleep. "I woke up and thought there was a fallen tree lying on me."

Ross rubbed his throbbing temples. He had been sleeping on her? Vaguely he remembered getting into the wagon and finding the softest pillow he ever remembered putting his head on. He had slept better than he had in months. He looked at her now and let his eyes focus on her breasts. He felt his blood heat and glanced away before she could see his fixation.

That damn cheap whiskey had made him sleep like a dead man. He felt like a fool. Worse, he knew he looked like one. "Don't you ever wallop me like that again, Lydia," he said, pointing a threatening finger at her and trying to look stern, though arranging his face into any expression brought on such intense pain he wondered if it was worth it.

"Don't ever weigh me down like that either. Especially after you've been in the company of whores all night. If you wanted to sprawl on top of somebody, why didn't you stay with them?"

They were still whispering, but it was going to be a helluva fight just the same and both of them were spoiling for it. Bad as he felt, Ross managed to get to his feet, hating the way he had to bow his back in order to stand in the wagon, while she faced him standing straight as a flagpole, her fists digging into her hips, her chin pointing defiantly toward his chest. "Why didn't you ask me not to go?"

"Because I didn't care if you went or not."

"No? Then what are you mad about?"

"*I* didn't care, but other people on this train will. I was only worried about the appearances you were so all-fired anxious that *I* maintain. Apparently the same rules don't apply to me as apply to you."

"That's right. I'm the man."

Lydia made a sound of total disgust as she whirled away. Lost in anger she whipped the nightgown over her head and stood with her back to him wearing only her pantalets.

And he, with some demented demon pounding the eyeballs out of his head from the inside, couldn't help but notice how neat and enticing and rounded her butt was, and how slender and shapely her calves were. Still befuddled, he was about to reach out and touch her skin to see if it was as soft as it looked when she spoke.

"Take off that shirt. It stinks of your whores' perfume."

"They weren't *my* whores. They were just women in trouble and I only helped them."

She struggled into her camisole, then turned around. As she grappled with the buttons, she glared up at him. "How kind of you. You were ready to boot me out of this very wagon when you thought I was a whore and I needed help. Why were you so generous with them?"

His eyes were riveted to her breasts as she pulled the cloth together and secured the buttons. Even so, her breasts spilled over the lacy border. Plainly he could see the dusky circles of the areolas and nipples. He was still entranced as she plopped down on the bedroll and began to pull on her stockings, her breasts jiggling softly with each hurried movement.

Only the sudden hardening of his manhood jerked him

out of his daze. "I'm a fast learner. I helped them because I didn't want to get stuck with them the way I've been stuck with you."

Lydia's head came up and she stared at him fiercely from where she sat on the bedroll. He was the first to look away, tearing at the buttons of his shirt and balling it up angrily when it was off. He searched for a clean one, wreaking havoc on the neatness with which Lydia had folded all his things in his trunk.

She rose to her feet when she had shoes and stockings on and reached for her petticoat. "I was the one stuck here last night to face the decent people on this train, not you."

He wheeled around and was brought up short by the sight of her squeezing her breasts together and peering over them to button the waistband of her petticoat. He cleared his throat and wished he could clear the congestion in his manhood as easily. "If you want to run off anytime you get a notion, I won't be the one to stop you."

She faced him belligerently, the petticoat finally buttoned around her narrow waist. "I don't want to make a fool out of myself like you did by getting stinking drunk and sleeping with whores."

His jaw went rigid and he strained his words through clenched teeth. "I told you I didn't sleep with any whore. If I had wanted to do that, I could have stayed here."

The residual silence was heavy and thick, palpable. It filled Lydia's air passages, smothering her. Ross nodded his head tersely as though he had made his final, triumphant point.

It was that smug satisfaction lifting his moustache that brought her hand up. Her fist swung wide and connected with a resounding smack against his cheekbone.

He stood stock-still as the waves of pain rolled over the ones already undulating in his head. He blinked against encroaching blackness. He also balled his fists at his sides to keep from wrapping them around her throat and killing her.

"I'm not a whore," she said softly, each word deliberately enunciated. "I never was. I've told you that."

He fought off another attack of nausea and said, "You weren't married when you conceived that baby of yours, were you?"

"No," she said, shaking her head, willing away the tears that seemed intent on filling her eyes.

That brought Ross to the crux of his dilemma and he had to face it. Whose baby had she had? What man had had her, touched her? It haunted him, drove him crazy. He had to know. Despite his good intentions not to put his hands on her, they came up to shackle her upper arms. He brought her up against his naked chest and lowered his face to within inches of her.

"Who was the man? Who was he, Lydia? Dammit, answer me."

"Who are *you*, Ross Coleman?"

Everything in him went still as death, though his hands didn't loosen their grip on her arms. "What do you mean?" he asked huskily.

She almost backed down from that cold, feral glint in his green eyes, but she had gone this far. "You live like an ordinary man with a wife and child, you go about the day-to-day things like an ordinary man, but you're not. You've got the eyes and reflexes of a predator, Ross Coleman. You're not ordinary at all, though you pretend to be. Who are you?"

He released her gradually, pushing her back slowly, and all the time staring into the depths of her eyes. Then he turned away without speaking. They finished dressing in antagonistic silence.

Lydia stepped into the pink morning light and began to stir the coals of the fire to life. She was scooping coffee into the pot when she heard Ross come out of the wagon and start to shave.

When he stepped beside her a few minutes later and reached for the coffeepot, she glanced at him and gasped softly. His skin had a greenish cast. His cheeks were sunken and his eyes were ringed with blue shadows. Forgetting her anger, Lydia touched his sleeve. "I'm sorry I hit you. I know you don't feel well. Actually I had no right to be angry. You're free to do what . . I mean, this isn't a real marriage." She lowered her eyes. "And . . . and I want you to know that, in spite of the fuss I made, I really didn't mind the way you . . . you slept on me last night."

"Lydia—"

"Miss Lydia?" Her name was repeated by Moses. "Oh, good mornin', Ross," he said, stepping around the wagon and seeing them standing by the campfire. "Winston asked me to bring this book to you, Miss Lydia. He said he meant to bring it last night when he came to visit, but forgot it."

Lydia's eyes swung from the black man to Ross. She watched as his mouth went hard and his eyes turned cold again. He was angrily pulling on his gloves when he stamped away without another word to her and only a brusque "Moses" to the messenger who had unwittingly timed things so badly.

"Ross," she called after him, but either he didn't hear her or he ignored her.

The cigar butts in the ashtray were as stale as the coffee. The air in the cramped office was stifling. Howard Majors ran a hand over his oiled hair and drew in a deep breath, loosening yet another button on his vest. He was tired. So was the man at the window, but Vance Gentry showed his tiredness by pacing.

"Dead ends, all of them." He banged the grimy window glass with a frustrated fist. "Where the hell are they?"

Majors shuffled through the reports on his desk. "God knows," he said wearily. "There hasn't been a trace of the jewelry, though we've got every informant on the payroll searching through pawnshops." One report attracted his attention. At first it had seemed insignificant. "Here's one from Arkansas . . . Owentown, wherever the hell that is. A railroad town. One of our agents is working undercover there. He saw a man who looked familiar playing poker in a saloon. The agent thought the guy noticed him, so he turned his back for a minute. When he looked again the man was gone. He waited around, but the poker player had disappeared."

Gentry was already shaking his head vehemently. "If he's trying to unload that jewelry, he wouldn't be in an out-of-the-way railroad town. Who could afford to buy it in a place like that? I still think he would head for the major cities. Maybe even out of the country."

Gentry was becoming more of a handicap than a help. If the missing couple could be found, the Pinkerton Agency could find them, but it didn't need a hysterical father interfering. Majors stood and walked around the corner of his desk. "Why don't you go home for a week or two, Mr. Gentry. If anything turns up—"

"No. I can't go home without Victoria."

"But they might have come back. You might have word of her waiting for you there."

"I telegraphed my attorney in Knoxville to check on that. He rode out to the farm, and the only ones there were the servants. They hadn't heard a word since the day Clark left with Victoria, not telling where they were going."

Majors lit a fresh cigar and studied the burning ruby tip as he asked tentatively, "Could your daughter have taken the jewelry? If she were leaving a life she'd always known, maybe she wanted that security with her."

Gentry whirled on the detective angrily. "You miss the point, Mr. Majors. She wouldn't leave her home, *me*, unless this outlaw coerced her to do so. I know my own daughter. She wouldn't do it." He tore his coat and hat off a clothes tree as he stamped toward the door. "I think I've wasted enough time—"

Just as he was reaching for the door, it was opened from the other side. Majors's assistant rushed in. "Excuse the interruption, Mr. Majors, but this wire just came in. It might be pertinent and I knew you'd want to see it."

"Thank you," Majors said, taking the extended telegram. As the assistant went out, Majors's eyes scanned the paper. He put it on his desk, his eyes staring sightlessly for a moment before he raised his head.

"It's from Baltimore. A young woman's body was discovered."

"Body?" Gentry wheezed.

Majors nodded. "She was found dead in a hotel room she had shared with a man for several weeks. She had been stabbed." Majors, who thought he could stand anything, could barely watch the anguish that distorted Gentry's face. Yes, he was getting soft. It was time for him to retire. "The man has disappeared. Their descriptions fit. Of course, positive identification—"

"Yes." Gentry cleared his throat gruffly. "When can we leave for Baltimore?"

Chapter Twelve

L ydia was hanging laundered clothes on the line Ross had stretched between the corner of their wagon and a young cottonwood tree when Anabeth came running up to her, panting from exertion, excitement dancing in her eyes. "Guess what just rolled in down by the river?"

Without waiting for an answer, she continued, "A peddler's wagon. He's toting more goods than a body can shake a stick at. 'Course Leona Watkins is raisin' Cain on account of it bein' Sunday and sayin' folks ain't supposed to buy nothin' on the Lord's day, but Mr. Grayson said this wasn't like normal times and folks couldn't just run into town on a Saturday. I seen that Priscilla buy a candy stick with my own two eyes, and she hid it in her pocket. And Ma said for you to come on down there 'cause she already spotted a bolt of cloth that would make you a right pretty dress for the Fourth of July."

Lydia had paused in her chore to listen as the girl rattled off the exciting news seemingly without taking a breath. Ross, who was mending a bridle, had stopped to listen to the tale too. Simultaneously, they burst into laughter.

Things had been so strained between them since the morning after Owentown that their laughter surprised them both. When they looked at each other, it dwindled until they turned their heads away, embarrassed.

"Well, ain't you gonna come down and see what he's got?" Anabeth demanded disbelievingly when Lydia calmly returned to hanging up the wash.

"I don't need anything," she said quietly.

"But Ma said this material would look better on you than anybody 'cause it's kinda gold and with your hair and all . . . I mean . . . you just gotta come see the wonderful things he has."

"I've got chores to do, Anabeth," Lydia said patiently and glanced toward Ross. He set the bridle aside and went into the wagon. She didn't need or want anything, but it would have been nice if he had offered to walk her down to the peddlerman's wagon just to look.

She should have known not to expect any kindness from him. He had barely spoken to her since he had learned that Winston Hill had called on her while he was gone. Every night he made sure she and Lee were settled, then he unrolled his bed beneath the wagon. No one on the train noticed. Many of the men slept outside where it was cooler.

Lydia noticed. She missed the sound of his breathing across the wagon floor. She missed his presence. She missed watching him take off his shirt and boots.

"Is your ma going to let you buy something?" Lydia asked, trying to ignore the ache in her throat.

"Pa give us each a dime."

"You'd better get on then and do your own shopping before Priscilla Watkins buys everything up."

Anabeth laughed, then her spirits collapsed again. "Reckon I'd better. Sure you won't come along?" She had been so delighted to be the one appointed to inform Ross and Lydia about the peddler. Now it had been ruined because they weren't excited about him at all.

Lydia shook her head. "Come show me what you bought when you get back."

Anabeth's feet shuffled in the dust as she walked away. But then her initial jubilance caught up with her and she began running toward the river.

"Lydia." She looked over the improvised clothesline at Ross.

"Yes?"

Taking her hand, he pulled her through the damp clothes. He opened her fingers and dropped several coins into her palm. "Go buy yourself something."

She looked at the money shiny against her hand, then up into the wagon. She knew Ross kept his money hidden in there somewhere, but had no idea where and didn't care. Money wasn't important to her because she had never had any before, and the value of it meant nothing. The only reason it meant something now was because Ross was giving it to her.

"I don't need anything."

"Don't buy something you need. Buy something you want."

Hopefully she stared up into his green eyes as she asked, "Why?"

The question infuriated Ross. Whenever Hill came around with one of his little presents, a honeycomb he had found dripping honey as sweet as his speech, a book of poetry he thought she might enjoy, a fresh peach tart Moses had just baked, she never asked the reason behind the gift. Of course that gentleman with the sterling manners had always asked Ross's permission before he presented his wife—yes, goddammit, *his* wife—with one of his gifts. Lydia always thanked him shyly, humbly, with a demure lowering of her eyes. But him, her own husband? Oh, no. She couldn't simply accept his generosity with one of the sweet thank-yous and radiant smiles she showered on Winston Hill.

Ross would never have confessed to jealousy. But that was what crawled through him like a serpent poisoning his whole system. Jealousy was what impelled him to say, "Because everyone will think I'm a lousy husband if I don't let my *wife*"—he slurred the word—"buy herself a trinket from the peddler."

She bristled at his scorn. Brushing past him, she picked up Lee. She would be damned before she would spend any of his money on herself, but she might find something for the baby.

"Leave Lee here. I can watch him."

"No!" She whirled around and shook the fist that held the money. "I'll take care of him. That's what I'm paid for, isn't it?" She didn't give him time to reply before she marched away.

* * *

Independence Day dawned clear and hot. There was an air of expectancy about the entire camp. Today was a holiday, a time for rest from the grueling hours of travel, a day for baking goodies, a day for laughing, music, and gaiety. If anyone grumbled that it was a Unionist holiday, his mutterings were soon squelched. The Southern states had won their independence from British rule same as the Northern. After long weeks of travel, the immigrants would use any occasion to take a holiday.

Ma had convinced Lydia to buy from the peddler enough of the gold cloth to make herself a dress. Lydia wasn't much of a seamstress, but with Ma's help and a dress pattern borrowed from Mrs. Rigsby, the dress had been cut out. Ma stitched on it nearly every evening. Lydia felt badly about it. Ma insisted that she would rather spend a quiet evening in the Colemans' wagon sewing, than in the chaos that reigned in her own. So, despite Lydia's objections, the dress was ready for her to step into when the time came.

They were camped on the Ouachita River. As a result of a wet spring, the surrounding countryside was green despite the summer heat. The ladies were allowed use of the river first and, as soon as morning chores were done, they trooped down to its grassy banks with towels and bars of soap for one of the few real baths they had taken since leaving home.

The festivities began at sunset. The men came back from the river, having been granted their privacy in the late afternoon while the ladies napped in their wagons. Some of the men were unrecognizable with their hair plastered down, wearing a string tie, a shiny belt buckle, or a Sunday-only pair of suspenders. The womenfolk, too, had added touches of finery to their calico and had taken extra pains with their hairdos.

Ross had bathed in the river and dressed in a pair of black pants, white shirt, and black leather vest. Instead of a tie, he wound a bandanna around his throat. He brushed his hair, leaving off the oil most of the other men had used.

He noted that his hair was growing long again. He would
have to get Lydia to trim—

He pulled himself up straight and stared at the
hairbrush in his hand as though he didn't recognize either it
or the man who held it. How easily her name came to his
mind now, when Victoria's rarely did. How natural it
seemed that he would ask her to trim his hair again, an
intimacy expected from a woman who lived with a man.
Damn!

"Lydia, are you ready?" he called into the wagon.

She surveyed herself in the mirror, wetting her lips
and pinching her cheeks as Ma had told her to do. She had
dressed with Ma's and Anabeth's help, Lee having been
turned over to Marynell and Atlanta to watch.

Lydia ran her hands over her skirt to convince herself
it was real. The gold broadcloth had been sewn into the
most beautiful dress she had ever owned, even nicer than
the ones Ross had bought for her in Memphis. The neckline
was scooped to reveal her throat and the upper part of her
chest. The short sleeves were puffed and barely covered
the top of her arm. The bodice buttoned to her waist,
where a wide sash, tied in a bow in the back, separated it
from the full, gathered skirt. She didn't have enough
petticoats to make it stand out far, but it swayed against her
ankles nicely.

Ma was determined that she wear her hair "the way
nature intended it," which was wild and free and curly.
They had decorated it with wild yellow roses found on the
riverbank that morning. She had been liberally splashed
with cologne.

"Lydia?" Ross let all his frustration go into that
summons.

"Coming," she said shyly and stepped out onto the
tailgate.

Had Ross not been grinding his teeth in agitation, his
mouth would have dropped open when his wife presented
herself. Her petite figure had never been so clearly defined
as it was in the soft cotton. Her skin was glowing the color
of ripe apricots from the suntan she had acquired despite
the straw hat she always wore while riding on the wagon

seat. Her hair . . . well, it occurred to him that at one time he had been appalled that she would let it go unbound. Now it neither shocked nor offended him. Indeed, he preferred it that way.

He wiped his palms on his pants legs and extended his hand up to hers, guiding her down the steps of the wagon, something she did on her own a hundred times a day. "I think they've already started eating," he said inanely.

"I'm sorry I made you late. You should have gone on. I could have caught up."

"It's all right."

Her brave smile sagged with disappointment. He wasn't going to say anything about how nice she looked, as Ma had promised her he would. Feeling dangerously close to tears, she wanted to return to the wagon, but they were soon caught up in the party. Each woman had contributed to the buffet supper, bringing her specialty dish, and Lydia and Ross were handed plates heaped with food.

Even before they were finished eating, those who could fiddle, including Moses, were rosining their bows and applying them to the strings.

By the time the leftover food was stored away and the dishes cleared, several of the less self-conscious couples were whirling to the lively tunes being played on fiddles and harmonicas. Ma, clapping her hands in time to the music and watching fondly as Zeke dipped his cup again into the barrel of beer somebody had brought from the nearest town, said, "You two go on and dance. I can keep an eye on Lee."

Lydia looked up at her husband, who had a long, slender cigar clamped between his teeth. She had never danced, but it looked like fun.

"I never learned how to dance," Ross said dismissively.

Ma, wishing she could give him a good swift kick in the seat of the pants, was undaunted. "It don't matter none. Them's not experts out there. Just take your lady on your arm and start movin' to the music."

"I don't know how to dance, either, Ross," Lydia said, hoping that her own lack of experience would encourage him to try it.

He gazed down at her face, at her body, and knew that he couldn't put his arms around her, looking as beautiful as she did, and keep the vow he had made to himself not to make love to her. "Then there's no call for us both to make fools of ourselves, is there?" He strolled off in the direction of the beer barrel.

"Well," Ma said huffily. "I seen stupid, pigheaded men in my day, but that one takes the cake."

Lydia, humiliated, her cheeks flaming with embarrassment, was staring at the ground when the toes of two polished boots came into her range of vision. "May I have the honor of dancin' with you, Lydia?"

Her eyes came up to meet the warm, open, appreciative gaze of Winston Hill. He scanned her face, not with the open hostility or the frightening intensity Ross often did, but with an unqualified liking for what he saw.

Ma, smiling once again, urged her. "Go on, Lydia. The gentleman asked you to dance."

"I don't know how," she muttered. On the one hand she wanted to, but she knew it would incur Ross's wrath.

Winston laughed and swept his hand wide to indicate the enthusiastically bobbing couples who were keeping time to the music without worrying about form. "I don't think anyone does." He extended his hand to her. "Dance with me, Lydia."

He spoke so urgently, so compellingly, that without thinking of the consequences, she thrust her hands into his and let him lead her into the melee. He curved one arm around her waist and, lifting her hand with the other, began to move in the circular pattern of the other dancers.

At first Lydia felt like she had six feet, all lame and unable to go in the same direction. But Winston was patient and instructive. Soon she relaxed and began to get the hang of it. By the time they had made the circle four times, she felt like she was flying and never wanted to stop.

When Ross spotted his wife in the arms of another man, especially Winston Hill, who was dressed fit to kill in a white linen suit and soft brown leather boots, his fingers automatically tensed around the tin cup he was bringing to his lips.

Without even realizing that his eyes had narrowed dangerously, becoming green slits, he watched their movements like a hawk. He made cursory responses to the conversation going on around him. But Lydia, with her skirts flying, her mouth smiling, her hair swirling, had his undivided attention. Each time she whirled past him, oblivious to him, laughing up into Hill's face, Ross's fingers squeezed his cup. He tossed down another draught of beer, and the coil inside his gut wound a little bit tighter.

"Come on, you silly boy," Priscilla giggled, tripping through the darkness on the far side of the wagons. "I tell you no one saw you steal that beer."

"We'd be in a passel of trouble if anyone had," Bubba said, cautiously glancing over his shoulder.

"Shoot! No one was paying us any mind." They're all having too good a time at their stupid party." She leaned against a tree, making sure her breasts thrust forward beguilingly. "I had in mind a private little party just for us, Bubba," she drawled, drawing him close. "Give me a sip of beer."

She had been anticipating the dancing all week. Then Scout had informed her that he wasn't going to spend his Fourth of July with a bunch of sod busters and had gone in to town, leaving her alone. She would show him, the sonofabitch. Did he think he was the only man in the world? Not by a long shot.

"Stand close in front of me now, Bubba, so no one can see." She positioned him where she wanted him, then raised his hand that held the cup of beer to her mouth. She tilted it, sipping some, but letting most dribble down her chin and chest. "Oh, Bubba, give me a handkerchief, quick. If my ma smells beer on me, no telling what she's liable to do."

Entranced as his eyes tracked the rivulets of beer disappearing into Priscilla's bodice, Bubba whipped a handkerchief out of his back pocket and handed it to her. He watched, stupified, as she unbuttoned her top.

"Mercy me," she said. "It's run clear down to my waist. I'm going to unbutton my camisole, but you're not to do anything you'll be ashamed of later. You hear, Bubba?"

He nodded dumbly. Every word of caution his mother had drilled into him slipped from his mind as easily as the buttons of Priscilla's camisole slipped through their holes.

Eyeing him slyly, Priscilla dragged the handkerchief over her bared breasts, lifting them, moving them, rubbing the nipples until they hardened, wiping away the imaginary spilled beer.

When the handkerchief slid over her one last time and then left her completely bare as she lifted it away, Bubba groaned. It was a sound that originated in his loins and worked its way up into his throat and out his body.

"Priscilla, you're beautiful," he rasped.

"I'll bet you're just saying that," she crooned, arching her back and lifting her breasts for his closer inspection.

"No, no, Priscilla. I love you. I told you that."

"If you loved me, you'd kiss me and . . . stuff."

Bubba looked at her in wordless wonder before he moved in closer. He pressed his body against hers and touched her mouth with his. Priscilla adjusted herself, curling upward to rub her mound against the swelling in his pants. Bubba cried out softly and ground against her. He put his hands on her naked breasts and caressed them gently.

"Oh, Bubba, that feels so nice." She flicked her tongue along his lips. The boy pulled back quickly. He was shocked, but he saw her sultry eyes and felt her hand pulling him back to her breasts. With a hopeless moan, he sealed their mouths together again.

This time his mouth was open, too, and following her lead, he pushed his tongue into her mouth. He plucked at her nipples with fingers acting strictly on instinct. Not much finesse was employed. Priscilla didn't want gentleness. She writhed between him and the tree, moaning her pleasure.

"I've got something to show you," she said breathlessly, pushing him away.

His blood boiling, Bubba wasn't ready to stop. He tried to recapture her mouth, but she dodged him, laughing softly and batting his hands away when they reached for her breasts again. "Bubba Langston, you behave," she said with mock severity. "Promise not to tell a soul. I been hiding these from my ma." She lifted her skirt and petticoats and raised her knee to prop against his thigh. "I bought these red satin garters from that peddlerman. Can you see them? Aren't they beautiful?"

He didn't look at the gaudy garters. He gaped at the smooth expanse of white thigh above them. "Yeah, I see 'em," he said thickly. He touched the garter with his finger, then trailed it up to touch her thigh.

"Shame on you, Bubba," she said on a gust of rushing breath, but she didn't try to stop him.

Encouraged, Bubba explored higher, his breath soughing loudly through his lips when his fingertips encountered fleecy hair. "Priscilla, you don't have on any—"

"It was so hot today. I wanted to feel cool. Oh, Bubba, you shouldn't, oh, God, are you touching me *there*?"

"Let me, Priscilla," he begged. "I won't hurt you. Am I hurting you? I'll stop."

"No!" He made to withdraw, but the arching of her body urged him back. "I mean, a man can get violent if a lady lets him go so far and then . . . Oh, right there, Bubba." She shuddered. "Yes."

"Priscilla," he sighed, burying his mouth in her neck.

"Feel how wet you're making me, Bubba."

"I'm so hard I hurt," he mumbled into her breasts.

"Let me help you." She groped at the front of his pants and encircled him with knowing fingers. She stroked.

"Jesus, Jesus," he groaned. He was going to die and his ma and everybody else would know how he had died and he didn't even care. He sent his fingers delving into her warmth.

"Oh, Bubba, that's good," she sighed. "But not here. Down by the river. Come on. Hurry."

Dazed, he withdrew his hand and stepped back. She lowered her leg and pulled her bodice together. Then, looking at him with dreamy promise, she took his hand and turned toward the river. They both came to a reeling halt when they saw Luke Langston lounging on a nearby tree stump. Seemingly indifferent to them, he was whittling down a stick with his pocketknife.

"Hidy," he chirped. "Nice evenin', ain't it?"

"You snooping little bastard," Priscilla screamed. "How long have you been here?"

"'Bout as long as that thing in Bubba's pants has grown. When did you start sproutin' gourds in your breeches, Bubba? That one is 'bout the biggest one I ever did see."

"I'm gonna kill you," Bubba said and flew toward his brother, who leaped off the stump and went tearing through the trees, whooping like an Indian. Bubba tore out after him.

"Goddamn stupid hillbillies," Priscilla muttered as she fumbled to rearrange her clothing. She kept up the scathing litany until she reached her wagon and flopped down on her bedroll to lament her frustration and the sad plight of her life.

Ross turned his back to the dancers and dipped his cup into the bottom of the beer barrel. He was stonily furious. He was green with jealousy. He was more than a little drunk. The latter was the only one of those conditions he could control, but he didn't want to. He tossed down another cup of beer, wishing it were whiskey so he would get drunk quicker.

What the hell did he care if she flaunted herself in front of a Milquetoast like Hill? Let him have her. As soon as they got to Texas and established residency, he would start divorce proceedings. Everything was still haywire in this part of the country since the war. Surely a divorce wouldn't be that hard to obtain.

Reflexively, he rocked back and forth on the balls of his feet, his fury building as he tried to attune himself to the ribald tale Mr. Appleton was telling. Everyone else seemed to be hanging on to every lewd word. All Ross concentrated on was keeping his gaze off Lydia who smiled up into Hill's face. She had never looked at him like that. He found her sensuously curving mouth and the voluptuous way her body swayed to the music repulsive. At least, that what's he told himself.

She was deliberately making a fool of him, that's what she was doing. Dancing with her highfalutin' friend was her way of pointing up her husband's shortcomings. Well, by God, he wasn't going to stand here and be made a fool of by that chit he had been roped into marrying. If he had to carry her off by that wild head of hair—

Where was she?

Ross had turned around to scan the frenzied dancers. His intoxicated eyes tried to focus on the couples, but after several minutes passed and he couldn't locate either Lydia or Winston, he dropped his tin cup in the dust and began to shove his way through the noisy crowd.

"Hey, Coleman, watch out—"

"Where you goin', Ross?"

"Ross, get enough to drink?"

"Where's your lady—"

He was impervious to everything around him. He felt the familiar tension building. The violence in him rose and filled his pores, seeking an outlet. He hadn't felt it so powerfully since that last job he had pulled with Jesse and Frank. His fists balled mechanically; automatically he felt for the holster and its lethal cargo. It wasn't there, but still he stalked through the crowd, intent on finding his betraying wife and her paramour.

"Ross, I told the girls to take Lee back to our wagon and put him to bed so you and Lydia can stay at the party as long as you like," Ma said, when he passed by her. He gazed down at her with unseeing eyes. "Leave him in our wagon till morning. No need to—"

"Where is she?" he hissed.

Ma had been watching him for an hour and knew that he was reeking with jealousy. She had the wisdom not to smile. Instead she let her eyes wander over the dancers. "Who? Lydia?"

"Yes, Lydia." Ross spat out the name as though holding it on his tongue too long was hateful to him.

"Don't rightly know. She was dancin' with Mr. Hill last I saw."

Ross pushed his way past a celebrating group and stumbled in the direction of the wagons, which for the most part were dark and deserted. If she had gone to his wagon . . . If he found them together . . . He didn't want to know . . . He had to know . . . Where was she . . .

* * *

Lydia had never had such a good time in her life. Winston was treating her like she hadn't grown up with trash, living in a hovel, forced to submit to the sexual abuse of her stepbrother. Winston treated her like a lady, complimenting her on the way she looked and on her dancing, fetching her cups of punch, laughing with her, sharing her exuberance.

When he started coughing, she asked if he were all right. He insisted he was and she took his word for it until they had to stop dancing and draw outside the circle of couples. He had a coughing seizure, the likes of which Lydia had never seen.

"Winston?" she asked, placing a hand on his shoulder as he bent at the waist, his whole body convulsing as he strangled. "What can I do?"

"I'm sorry," he gasped. "I'm fine."

But he wasn't. There were flecks of blood in the corners of his lips and his face had gone to the color of old wax. "Do you want me to fetch Moses?"

He shook his head, clapping a handkerchief to his mouth again. "He's having fun," he choked out when his coughing subsided. But the next attack was worse than the last and Lydia became truly alarmed.

"Winston, tell me what to do."

"My medicine," he said in a garbled voice.

Her eyes searched out Ross, but he was standing with the throng of men crowded around the beer barrel and she would have to wend her way through the dancers to reach him. She didn't want to leave Winston alone that long. She clutched his sleeve. "Where is it? Your medicine. Where is it, Winston?"

"Wagon," he gasped out.

"Come on," she said, making up her mind to take care of him herself rather than run for someone else. He might choke to death before she could get anyone's attention and she knew he would be embarrassed if she caused a commotion because of him. Putting her arm around his waist and splaying her other hand over his chest, she led him into the deep shadows where the wagons were stopped for the night. "Where is yours?" she asked.

Weakly he pointed it out and they made stumbling progress across the camp. "I'm sorry, Lydia," he kept repeating.

"Hush, now. Don't talk or you'll start coughing again."

"I hate myself for this."

"It isn't your fault." At the tailgate of his wagon, she asked, "Can you get inside?"

He nodded and by a sheer act of will pulled himself up, taking wheezing breaths and pausing to cough. At last they gained the inside and Lydia blinked against the darkness while Winston crawled toward his bedroll. He fell upon it heavily and rolled onto his back, seized by another fit of coughing.

Lydia, her eyes growing accustomed to the darkness, searched out a lantern and match and had soon lit the wick, keeping the flame turned down low. "Where's the medicine?" she asked him softly, while he struggled for air with collapsing lungs.

He pointed to a small wooden chest. Lydia lifted it toward him, raising the lid to reveal several dark bottles of tinctures in the velvet-lined teak box. With a shaky hand he pointed out the one he needed.

She set the chest aside and uncorked the bottle. Raising his head with one hand, she pressed the dark brown vial to his lips. He drank a generous amount, then lay back weakly.

"Thank you, Lydia."

"Are you better?" she asked. Her brows wrinkled with concern and her mouth puckered with anxiety.

Wisps of hair surrounded her face like filaments of light. Her skin was dewy from her overexertion. The scent of her cologne permeated the interior of the starkly masculine wagon. She had no idea how beautiful she looked to the ill man who would have given anything at that moment to be strong and whole.

"I'm better," he replied sadly, wishing the look she bestowed on him could be one of passion rather than pity.

"Let me help you out of this." She untied the silk tie

from around his neck and unabashedly unbuttoned his vest and shirtfront.

Catching her hands, Winston stilled her. "Moses can do that when he comes in. Go back to the party. I'll be fine."

"Should I go and get him now?"

He shook his head on the fine linen pillowcase. "When he notices I'm not dancing, he'll be along." He tightened his grip on her hand. "Thank you, Lydia."

"It was nothing." Instinctively, maternally, her fingers brushed back the damp curls that lay on his forehead. At the same time, Winston raised her other hand to his lips and kissed it softly.

Ross plunged through the opening of the wagon like a pillaging vandal, flinging open the canvas flaps and holding them wide. Startled by the sound, Lydia whipped her head around, but not before Ross had seen what looked to his jealousy-crazed mind to be a tender, loving scene.

Lydia shrank from him. He was no longer wearing his vest or bandanna. Several of his shirt buttons had been opened to reveal each rippling muscle and a carpet of dark hair. His face was fearsome. Green eyes impaled her from beneath hooding black brows. Lying in damp disarray over his forehead, his hair was as untamed as his fierce expression. Beneath the frowning moustache, his mouth was a hard, straight line. His legs were planted wide apart, the muscles in his thighs contracting and bulging in the tight-fitting black pants.

Even the bravest of souls would cower under that magnificent physical presence. His fierce countenance portended disaster for anyone he considered his enemy.

"Ross?" Lydia squeaked.

"A touching scene," he snarled.

Winston struggled to sit up. "Let me—"

"He's sick. I looked for you. He was choking. There was—"

"You're my wife," Ross growled, taking two lunging strides to reach her. He wrapped his fingers around her upper arm and jerked her to her feet. "I didn't want you to be. I still don't. But as long as you are, goddamn you, you'll act like it."

"Ross, please listen to me," Winston pleaded faintly. The last thing he wanted was to bring trouble to Lydia for treating him kindly. "The circumstances are deceiving. Nothing unseemly happened here—"

"Yet," Ross snapped. "But I think I was just in time."

"No!" Lydia cried, trying to wrench her arm free of Ross's hold.

"Come on." He lifted her toward the wagon's opening and thrust her through it.

"He's sick," she said, digging her heels in the dirt and pulling on her arm. "I should get—"

"You'll get what's coming to you, what you've been begging for. But you'll get it from me, your *husband*," he sneered.

She stumbled against him and caught at his belt for support. The glittering anger in his eyes terrified her. Her teeth began to chatter and her bones threatened not to hold her up. "W . . . what do you mean?"

By now they were at his wagon. He scooped her in his arms and lithely took the steps up to the tailgate. He bent almost double over her to get inside the canvas opening.

"Lee—"

"Ma's got him." He laughed and the sound sent a cold chill of fear down her spine. "Till morning."

Unceremoniously he dropped her onto her bedroll and she scrambled to cover her legs with her skirt. His lips curled in a nasty smile. "Don't bother with that modesty act, Lydia. If I had any doubts before, you proved tonight what you are."

"No," she whispered and sat up, scooting away from him into the corner of the wagon. She had seen this expression before. On Clancey's face. It was indomitable. It meant that no amount of begging or pleading would stop the man from taking what he wanted. Ross's eyes were alight with too much drink, fury, and lust. "No, Ross, please," she whimpered, covering her chest with her arms.

He peeled off his shirt, leaving his chest and stomach bare. Lydia watched the play of muscle and sinew. The vicious scar looked like an angry red eye winking at her. He unbuckled his belt and whipped the wide strap of leather out of the loops. She hunched forward protectively, thinking he meant to beat her first. But he only dropped the belt at his feet and began slowly to unbutton his pants.

She lifted her soulful eyes to his. Silently they pleaded with him not to do this, not to hurt her, not to use her with no more feeling than Clancey had done. "Please, Ross."

"You wanted a man?" he asked silkily, lowering himself to the bedroll. "Well, that's what you're going to get."

He moved so swiftly that one moment she was balled into the corner of the wagon, and the next she was being pulled beneath him by hands that moved with uncanny speed and skill.

Panicked, wild with the need to escape, she fought him, bucking violently, thrashing with arms and legs, curling her fingers into claws. "No, no," she chanted as she struggled against his unyielding strength that pressed her down.

"Oh, yes. How many have you given it to, huh? What makes me so different?"

The rose petals in her hair were crushed beneath her head as she rolled it from side to side. Her hair tumbled around her face, neck, shoulders. "No, Ross, Ross. God, don't let him do this to me," she cried helplessly.

"God won't help you, Lydia. God doesn't listen. He's never around when you need Him."

He caught her hands in one iron fist and stretched them above her head. Greedily his fingers worked at the buttons on her bodice until they came undone. Once the dress was pushed aside, he ripped at the ribbon on her camisole, then unfastened the tiny buttons. His breathing was loud and harsh as he pulled the garment aside and bared her breasts to his ravaging eyes.

Lydia moaned, squeezed her eyes shut, and turned her head away. If only he had asked her, she might have consented. She might have bartered this for his future kindness. Had he treated her gently, she might have offered it without his asking.

But he was going to hurt her, violate her, bruise her, just like Clancey had. It would be worse this time. Ross had the power to hurt her in a way Clancey never could. She cared for Ross, and that he could treat her with so little regard hurt her to her very soul. He wouldn't think of physically abusing one of his horses.

He didn't let himself touch her breasts. A remnant of sanity in his alcohol-ridden mind warned him that if he caressed her, he might begin to feel tenderness for her. That mustn't happen. She needed punishing and he was going to punish her.

He shoved her skirt and petticoats to her waist and laid hold of the waistband of her pantalets. Yanking hard, he broke the fastening and pushed them down her thighs. She groaned wretchedly and tried to lock her thighs together. Brutally he tore her underdrawers down the length of her legs and prized her thighs apart with his knee. Freeing his erect manhood from his pants, he positioned himself above her.

Had it been Clancey, Lydia would have stared up at him defiantly, showing him all the hatred she felt. But she didn't hate Ross and rather than give him that haughty, damning stare of her dark golden eyes, she kept her head averted as he thrust inside her. She didn't anticipate the tearing pain that shot through her. Her body arched off the pallet and she uttered a sharp cry.

Ross buried all of himself deep inside and burrowed farther. When she had taken all of him and absorbed all his weight, he held. Sucking in great amounts of air, his head began to clear. And when that happened, he was aware, for the first time since seeing her in Hill's wagon, of what he was doing. The jealous rage that had bathed his whole world red lifted like a mist and he was left face-to-face with bitter regret. So much regret.

And pleasure. The immensity of which he had never felt before.

He didn't want to feel the pleasure. Yet it saturated him, his mind, his heart, his belly, his manhood snugly gloved by her. He had to test it to see if he were still conscious. Maybe this was a fantasy, the erotic product of a drunken stupor.

He moved slightly, not wanting to awaken from the

dream, should it be one. But it was real. He rocked over her, and the miracle sensations washed over him in time to his rhythmic movements. "No," he whispered, "she can't feel this good."

His voice belied his words. It was the voice of a man experiencing the highest physical gratification he had ever known.

It was wrong. He couldn't let it feel so good. He wouldn't. He withdrew, planning to move away, but his body wouldn't let him and he sank into her sweet depth again. "Damn it all to hell, it's not supposed to be like this with you," he mournfully sighed into her neck.

Breaking his own best intentions, his hand worked its way between their bodies. He found her breasts ripe and malleable and fondled her with the inquiring sensitivity of a blind man. He measured her plump fullness in his palm. He stroked the smooth flesh. He examined the nipples with his fingertips, loving the nubby texture of them when they hardened against the pad of his thumb.

Without his realizing he had moved, his head replaced his hand and he began kissing her breasts. His moustachioed mouth moved over her in an aimless caress until his lips found a nipple, pebbly and flushed. They closed around it loosely while his tongue appreciated it with fleeting licks. Then he suckled it gently, taking all of it into his mouth and tasting, tasting, tasting the woman—

His head came up and he looked down into whiskey-colored eyes that were wide and uncomprehending. He saw his own fingers, white with pressure, wrapped around her wrists. He released them immediately. His hands came up to her hair and he plowed his fingers through it until he had closed all ten around her scalp.

Tilting her head back, he fused their mouths as intimately as their sexes were adhered. The heat of the kiss intensified until his lips were grinding over hers, until his tongue was mating with hers, until he couldn't control his kiss any more than he could control the burst of fire from his loins that melted through the gate of her womb.

His lips fashioned her name out of the low, soft staccato sounds of his supreme satisfaction.

For a long time after the crisis had shuddered through him, he lay atop her, suspended in a state of the sublime. He never remembered rolling off her, gathering her to him closely, and slipping into peaceful unconsciousness.

Chapter Thirteen

"**H**i," the whore said tiredly. "My name's Pearl."

God! This was her last customer of the night and that bitch Madam LaRue was paying her back for smart-mouthing this morning by sending her this scum. It had been a hellish day, the Fourth of July. The streets of Owentown were swarming with railroad men in for the holiday. They were a rowdy bunch, randy as a herd of buffalo bulls, and she felt like every one of them had had a go at her. She was tired and sore. And now she had to service this, the worst of the lot. "You railroad?" she asked with a weary attempt at conversation.

Clancey Russell snorted derisively as she shut the door behind him. "Got better sense than to bust my balls for somebody else. Got better use for 'em too." He caressed himself suggestively.

Putting all her professionalism into practice, Pearl smiled despite her repulsion. He was filthy and smelled to high heaven. "Let's see your money," she purred. She would make sure this scum had cash before she would let him touch her.

Clancey dug into his pocket for the money he had heisted from a poker table when the players had gotten into an argument over a dealt hand. It had been enough to buy him a good meal and a bottle of whiskey. Both were making his stomach feel fuller and warmer than it had in weeks. He tossed the fee down on the aged dressing table covered with a yellowed crocheted scarf.

"You seen my stuff," he said arrogantly. "Now let's see yours."

Though she let her mouth take on an aroused pout, on the inside Pearl was shuddering with revulsion. He pulled down his suspenders and began to unbutton his shirt. When he shucked out of it, she saw the rings of dried sweat circling his armpits on the faded red underwear. Stalling for time, she pointed to the scrap of folded paper that had fluttered out of his shirt to the foot of the bed. "What's that?"

"Somethin' I picked up. Bounty poster. Never know when somethin' like that can come in handy. Come on now, girlie, take that thing off."

Pearl came up on her knees on the rickety bed and shrugged out of the old ratty robe a veteran whore had given her. Even the sad row of feathers she had sewed along the neckline hadn't improved it much.

She was naked. Clancey's eyes glazed with lust and his mouth twisted cruelly. Pearl was known to be a good sport, giving a man whatever he paid for as long as he didn't hurt her. But her heart began to race when she saw the feral malice in Clancey's colorless eyes as they toured her. He unbuttoned his pants to reveal a swollen, angry sex that even to Pearl's jaded eyes was hideous.

"If that paper is so important, let me see it," she said, lunging for the poster. Anything to stall this animal climbing on her.

"Hellfire," Clancey said, falling atop her. " What you wanna—"

"Why, that looks like . . . oh, shoot, what did he say his name was? The man from the wagon train."

Clancey clapped his hands over her breasts and pinched the nipples hard. "Ouch! That hurts, stop it. Don't you understand what I'm trying to tell you? I saw this man just a few days ago."

Clancey raised himself up and peered first at her, then at the poster. "That's just a piece of trash." He couldn't read the writing on it. He hadn't even known why he had picked it up that night off the table in the Knoxville saloon, except that those two fancy men had been talking about how they had thought this man was dead, but it seemed now he was passing himself off as somebody else. Stolen some jewelry too. Is that what they had said?

"It's worth five thousand dollars," Pearl said, her tiredness fading into excitement. This might be her ticket out of Owentown and away from Madam LaRue.

"Five thousand dollars?" Clancey sat up and jerked the poster out of her hand. "You say you saw this guy? Recent-like?"

Pearl wasn't all that astute, but she was cunning. Two years with Madam LaRue hadn't been completely wasted. She would keep what she knew about the man on the poster to herself. If there was five thousand dollars in it, she would be damned before she would let this dirty sonofabitch get it in her stead.

She blinked her eyes seductively and allowed her hand to trail down past his waist. "Shoot, I was just funning with you. I thought you wanted to talk about me, not some old poster."

Clancey swung a mighty fist at her jaw. It cracked sickeningly and she fell back on the dingy pillow, dazed and wracked with pain. "You'll wish you'd never funned with me, whore, if you don't tell me where you seen this here man? You understandin' me?" He slapped her hard on each cheek and with the meaty fingers of his other hand pinched the inside of her thigh. "Understand?"

Pearl, her vision clouded and ears roaring, nodded. "All right, I'm waitin' to hear." His hand moved up her leg threateningly. She whimpered. "Talk." He bruised the white flesh between his fingers.

"We . . . we broke down and he . . . I think it was him . . . helped us and followed us in to town. He's older now, doesn't have long hair and has grown a moustache. It might not even be the same man." But Pearl had little doubt that it was. Who could forget those eyes? And the way he had of looking at somebody, like he was going to remember them for the rest of his life and how they had treated him, good or bad.

"Did he call himself Clark?"

"No, no . . . it was . . . I don't remember."

Clancey knotted his fingers in her pubic hair and pulled hard. "That jostle your memory?"

Tears spurted from her eyes and she yelped, but he only slapped her again. No one would hear her cries for help. The barroom downstairs was in celebratory pandemonium. She could hear the laughter, the thumping of the piano, the raucous sounds of revelry. No one could help her. "Co . . . Coleman. He said his name was Coleman."

Bejesus! That was it. That was the name of the fella the two gentlemen in Knoxville had been after. He was on that wagon train Lydia was hiding in. Kill two birds with one stone. Isn't that what Pa had always said?

He chuckled evilly to himself while Pearl made pathetic efforts to shove him off her. She had told him she had seen the man only a few days ago. He was getting close. First thing tomorrow, he would start after that train again. Hell, he would start tonight. He could travel miles a day faster than that wagon train. But before that, he had something else to do.

"Pearl? Is that your name?" he cooed, taking her breast in his hand and massaging it. "Right pretty name, Pearl. And you're a right pretty girl too. And you done right by ol' Clancey. You surely have."

She sniffed back her tears. Maybe if she let him do his deed, she could contact the sheriff before he did with news of the wherabouts of that Mr. Coleman. "Thank you," she whispered.

"I mean to pay you back, Pearl. Yes, sirree. Clancey Russell always gives back what he thinks someone has comin' to 'em." His dirty hands were scouring her belly, slipping down between her thighs, fondling her roughly.

Pearl gritted her teeth and forced her swelling lips back into a travesty of a smile. She wasn't smiling seconds later when Clancey rammed into her like a driven spike, painfully, tearing her insides as his fingernails brutally dug into the soft flesh of her breasts.

"You're hurting me," she screamed.

"And you like it, bitch," he panted as sweat beaded on his oily forehead. "You love it." One of his hands wrapped around her throat and pressed against her larynx. With each thrust of his hips, he pressed harder, until her eyes bugged out and her mouth opened wide. Clancey, lost in satisfying his lust, didn't even notice until he had spewed his seed into her that she wasn't struggling anymore.

Pearl wasn't missed until early the next afternoon. Madam LaRue couldn't remember what Pearl's last customer had called himself or even what he had looked like. It had seemed that the entire male population of Arkansas had paraded through the saloon last night.

How was she supposed to remember them all? she asked the harried sheriff. She couldn't provide him with a description. One sweaty, stinking man wanting a woman looked the same as another.

But Madam knew that wasn't true. She had had a hankering for that one a week or so back. The tall one with the black hair and green eyes. She had thought by the way he moved and the way he handled himself that he was different. But unfortunately for her, he had been just another sod buster too much in love with his wife to bed a whore. She had been mad as hell when he left her wagon that night. But then Madam had remembered that girl with the unique hair and unusual eyes and proud carriage. Maybe the man couldn't be blamed for loving her.

Every muscle in Lydia's body ached. She tried to move to a more comfortable position, but there didn't seem to be one. The wagon was dim, awash with the first blush of dawn. Everything was still. After the celebration the night before, everyone was sleeping later than usual.

The man lying with Lydia was still. The arm stretched across her waist was like a lead weight. His breathing was soft and steady, barely stirring her hair as he held it trapped beneath his cheek. The gentle cadence of his breath was reassuring, testimony that she hadn't spent the dark hours of the night alone, but that someone stronger had lain beside her protectively.

A lone tear rolled from the corner of her eye and into her hair. It wasn't at all unpleasant to wake up beside him. And now he would despise her. More tears followed the course of the first.

Maybe he was right about her. Maybe she was a born whore. Clancey had seen her wantonness, like a sickness growing inside her even as her body matured. He had responded to it. Ross had known it all along. Last night had proved him right. Because when she should have fought him the hardest, she hadn't been able to. She had liked what he was doing to her too much.

She tried to turn her head away from his, but her hair caught and she had to lie looking straight up at the canvas overhead or risk waking him.

Something had happened to her last night when Ross began to move over her. Something strange and terrible and shameful and wonderful. When his tongue exercised the same artistry in her mouth that . . .

She closed her eyes and sank her teeth into her bottom lip. When he released her hands, instead of fighting him off, she had rested them on his shoulders and had enjoyed the feel of his naked skin under her palms. Her fingers had tightened around the corded muscles to pull him nearer and deeper. Her thighs had closed tight against his hips.

She had actually been disappointed when he eased away from her and fell into a dead sleep. What she had thought she would despise, her body now grew warm and restless with the memory of. He would taunt her and hate her for what she was.

She was unsuccessful in stifling a sob and he stirred beside her. He came awake by degrees, shifting his legs and stretching. The arm across her waist contracted, then relaxed. He drew in a deep breath, then let it go on a long shuddering sigh.

Lydia knew the instant his eyes opened. She could feel their gaze on her profile. He lay still for an interminably long time while her heart thudded achingly in her chest. At last he lifted his arm from around her and sat up. He stared down at her.

A compulsion to touch him seized her, a compulsion so strong she had to struggle not to reach up and smooth the furrow from between his brows, to push back the unruly hair that fell over his forehead, to lift the frown from his mouth. But she couldn't. After last night he wouldn't want her touch. So she lay immobile and let her eyes gaze back at him without one trace of expression that would betray the tumult inside her.

She watched as his eyes scanned her breasts, left exposed because she hadn't had the initiative to move and rebutton her clothing. Nor could she have. His arms had kept her imprisoned all night. Shamed, she crossed her arms over her chest.

In his throat, he made a sound that might have been a blasphemous curse. He looked away, but his eyes fell on the skirts still rumpled around her waist and the underdrawers lying in a heap just beyond her feet.

Awkwardly, with uncoordinated motions, he rearranged her skirts more modestly. Her hands were lying limply on her stomach, and when he allowed his eyes to look at them, at the purpled wrists, a grimace twisted his mouth. Though it was the hardest thing he had ever had to do, he forced his eyes back to her face. There were no visible signs of suffering there, except for that haunted vagueness in her eyes.

"Did I hurt . . ." *Stupid question, Coleman*, he said to himself. *Look at her, man. She's bruised all over.* He amended his original question. "Are you in pain?"

She shook her head no, still not blinking or relieving him of that accusatory stare. He stood unsteadily. Without another word, he fastened his breeches, picked up his discarded shirt, and left the wagon.

Lydia rolled to her side, buried her face in her hands, and wept. It was a long while before she could force herself to get up and go about routine things. She washed herself thoroughly, not a little alarmed to find traces of blood on her thighs. She scrubbed herself hard as though to wash away the impurities inside her and make herself acceptable. Ruthlessly she raked her hair back and pinned it tight to her head like it was a symbol of her wickedness that should be hidden.

When she garnered enough courage to step outside the wagon, Ross was hunched down in front of the fire sipping the coffee he had brewed. He had already shaved, but he looked haggard.

She laced her fingers together tightly. "I'll go get Lee

and then see to breakfast." When he didn't say anything, but only stared into the fire, she took a few steps in the direction of the Langston wagon.

"Lydia."

Her name, spoken sharply, brought her up short and she turned back. He was standing facing her, but she found it impossible to look directly into the green heat of his eyes.

"About last night," he began.

She shook her head in denial even before he made the indictment. "Nothing happened between Mr. Hill and me. I swear it. He was sick. He couldn't stop coughing. He coughed up blood. I helped him back to his wagon and gave him his medicine. That's all."

Ross tossed the remainder of his coffee on the ground, cursed, and crammed his hands into his pockets. "That's not what I'm talking about." Another tense silence ensued in which they couldn't look at each other. "I don't think this is going to work out," he said with a deadly calm that chilled her. "As soon as we get to Texas, I'll figure out a way for us to get divorced." Her head was bowed so he couldn't see her shattered features. "It shouldn't be too difficult."

"No," she said raspily. "It shouldn't be."

"Things are in a turmoil all over. Federal troops occupying—"

"Yes."

"I'll make the arrangements."

"All right."

"Goddammit, Lydia, would you look at me?" he ordered on a note louder than their whispered conversation had been. Exasperation was stamped all over him as she raised her forcibly restored face. She wouldn't cry. She wouldn't. She stared back at him levelly, letting none of her heartache and despair show. "Say something," he commanded angrily.

How did she expect her to respond when he had just informed her she was going to be dumped in the middle of nowhere just when she had become accustomed to living with him? What did he want her to say? That she would be happy to give up Lee? That she would be happy to be alone again, without family, without anyone to look after her in a strange place, without means of supporting herself? Of course he thought she could support herself. By whoring. Tears welled in her eyes, but she wouldn't give this arrogant man the pleasure of gloating over them. She could take care of herself. She had done it once before.

Her chin went up a notch. "I'll go get Lee now" was all she said before hurrying away.

When she returned to their camp, he was standing beside a saddled Lucky, strapping down a full saddlebag. He glanced at her over his shoulder. "I'll be gone for a day or two. Scout and I are going to ride up ahead and look things over. If you need help with anything, ask Bubba."

Her heart rolled to her feet. "All right, Ross." He finished tying down the leather straps and came to her, the spurs buckled onto his boots jingling musically with each step. The merry sound was jarringly out of place.

He patted Lee on the back and ducked down to kiss his temple. "Good-bye, son." Lydia could feel his warm breath against her shoulder and on her neck. He was so wonderfully close and smelled so good, of horses and leather and shaving soap and man.

When he raised his head, his eyes locked with hers and for a long moment they held. She willed one kind word from him, one tiny gesture that would let her know that he didn't despise her. He did nothing. Turning away, he pulled on his hat and vaulted easily into the saddle.

He clicked his tongue and the mighty stallion wheeled. "Ross," she called quickly, taking two running steps toward him. He reined in and looked down at her. "Be careful," she whispered. From under the brim of his hat she saw his eyes widen appreciably before he nodded and led his horse away.

The day was hot and everyone was glad that the train didn't try to travel far. Especially Lydia, who had driven her own team. They made camp early. Ma instructed Bubba and Luke to gather firewood. "Hurry up so I can get supper started. Lydia's eating with us. She looks a mite peaked to me and I'm gonna make her go to bed early."

The boys were a good way from the camp when Bubba

pulled Luke to a stop and whispered. "I got a proposition for you."

Luke took off his hat, wiped the sweat from his forehead, and asked suspiciously, "What?"

"How'd you like to take care of Ross's horses tonight? Feed and brush them, everything."

The idea was attractive. He was still jealous of his brother's friendship with the older man they both idolized. But such generosity wasn't without its price. "What do I have to do?"

"Finish this here chore of gettin' the firewood and forget where you last saw me when Ma asks."

Luke's eyes narrowed as he considered his brother suspiciously. Bubba's hair was brushed and he had on a fresh shirt. "Just like I forgot all about last night? You gonna meet Priscilla again? 'S that it?"

"Ain't none of your business. You wanna make a deal or don'tcha?"

Luke laughed at his brother's anxiety. "Well, hell, don't rush me. Lemme think on it for a second here," he said, stroking his chin. Bubba's fists balled at his sides, but he held his temper. It wouldn't do him any good to get angry. That would only make Luke more stubborn. "How about I do the chores and keep my mouth shut, and you gimme that pocketknife you bought off the peddler."

"Aw, shit," Bubba said fiercely. "That ain't fair. That's a brand-new knife."

Luke shrugged. "You must not want to diddle that gal very bad then." He gave Bubba his back and began to walk away nonchalantly.

"Wait!" Bubba cried, rushing after him. "I didn't say no, I just think you're a goddamn crook."

Luke's eyes danced mischievously. "Businessman," he said, tapping his temple with his index finger. "And I'll take my new knife now, thank you."

Bubba gave him the knife, all the while his face working angrily. Priscilla had told him not to be late or he would have shown this snot-nosed brother of his who was smarter. Bubba thrust his index finger into Luke's face. "You remember now. You ain't seen me"

"Have a good time," Luke said in a singsong voice. "Oh, Bubba, one more thing. You're gonna tell me all about it, ain'tcha?"

"That ain't proper."

"Then I just might remember that I seen you sneakin' around in the woods with Pris—"

"All right, I'll tell you. I gotta go now." He thrashed his way toward the appointed place, leaving Luke laughing behind him.

Priscilla was vexed. She had wanted to get there late and make Bubba wonder if she was really going to meet him. Instead it was the other way around. When he came rushing up to her full of apologies, she tossed her head angrily. "Well, I'm sure my ma will be bearing down on us at any time. You sounded as noisy as a moose coming through the trees," she said with not a little asperity.

Bubba was disconsolate. "I'm sorry to be late, Priscilla, but I had to make a deal with Luke."

"That little—"

"He won't bother us this time. I swear it."

She had been simmering in anger all day. Scout had left again without so much as a good-bye. Her body had been afire since last night and, even if it had to be a lout like Bubba Langston who quenched it, she wanted no further delays. She put her hand against his chest and said, "I'm sorry I was cross with you. It's just that I'm so anxious for you to kiss me again." She pressed her hand to him. "I swear to goodness, Bubba, but your heart is pounding."

"Yeah, it is. Is yours?"

She was wearing her prettiest dress, but one she had almost outgrown. Her ma had threatened to give it away numerous times, but Priscilla had insisted she keep it. She liked it because it had a scooping bodice that fit snugly over her breasts.

With her eyelids half closed, she lifted his hand and carried it to her breast, placing it palm down over her and pressing hard. "Feel for yourself," she whispered.

Bubba had wised up. He had caught on to the fact that Priscilla could lead a man a merry chase. All day his body had been rioting with thoughts of her and the way she had been primed and ready for him the night before. That morning, when she sidled up to him while Ma wasn't looking and suggested that they meet, he had decided he wasn't going to let her get the upper hand anymore. Ross Coleman wouldn't let a woman get to him this way. If he wanted a woman, he would take her. Bubba wanted to do everything the way Ross would.

Now, to Priscilla's surprise, he pushed her back on the soft grass and swiftly unbuttoned her dress, pulled down her chemise and ran his hands over her breasts, grinning his pleasure when her red nipples peaked and hardened. He lay down beside her, sacrificing one exploring hand to unfasten his breeches.

Then he was kissing her, pushing his tongue into her mouth, even as he rubbed his manhood against her skirts and played with her breasts. Priscilla was thinking that she might not have made such a bad choice after all. Bubba's newfound aggression thrilled her. It added an element of danger to it, like he might go a little insane at any moment.

She had managed to wrestle free of her bloomers and now had his hard and pulsing shaft in her hand, guiding him. His mouth was on her breasts, kissing, sucking, making low animal noises.

"No!" he said when she would have done the task for him. "I want to do it." He braced himself over her and thrust inside, driving himself deep and hard into her flesh. She arched reflexively and cried out, but was soon matching her thrusts to his. It never occurred to Bubba to prolong the pleasure. Within a moment, he was exploding inside her, emptying all the desire that had plagued him for months.

"Damn you, Bubba," Priscilla seethed. "You didn't make it last long enough."

He didn't hear her, he didn't hear anything. He only lay sprawled atop her heavily, thinking that it had been about the best thing that could ever happen to a body and that as soon as he got his second wind, he was going to do it again. And again. He couldn't wait to brag about it to Luke.

* * *

Ross gave little heed to his surroundings as he rode alongside Scout. The man was taciturn and insolent and reminded Ross of himself a few years back. He didn't like the young man but had agreed to accompany him so he could think, and so he wouldn't have to look at Lydia and remember last night and how good it had been and how much he wanted her again. Only willingly. He would never take her violently again.

Rape. My God! He had done many things in his lifetime he could be ashamed of, but he had never forced himself on a woman. He had killed men—too many. He had been a thief with no compunction about stealing. He had vandalized property. Lied. Cheated. But he couldn't remember a time when he felt more disgusted with himself.

"All right with you if we camp here?" Scout asked him.

"Fine," Ross said, reining in his mount.

"I'll haul water if you'll get the fire goin'. Ain't much of a cook. If you'll do that, I'll clean up."

Ross nodded as he heaved the heavy saddle off Lucky and dropped it to the ground. Methodically he went about setting up the temporary camp, something he had done a thousand times when on the run. The division of labor, the roughhousing, the cursing of bad luck, the plans for the next big job, the fighting among comrades in crime, were familiar memories. And during all those years of carousing with the meanest of outlaws, he had never assaulted a woman.

He had been putrid with jealousy when he saw her with Hill, though common sense told him that even if Lydia were of a mind, Hill's code of honor would never let him take another man's wife. Before leaving that morning, Ross had made amends, asking Moses after his employer's health and offering to take over some of his chores so he could take care of Winston. Winston had sent his heartfelt thanks through Moses.

But to Lydia he couldn't make amends. He was too ashamed. He couldn't bring himself to face her with an apology. No matter what she had been, she was now his wife, virtually mother to his son. She had said no, and it hadn't made one goddamned bit of difference. He had had to have her and he had taken her like a savage.

Waking next to her this morning had felt so good. But then he had remembered the night before. When he saw the bruises on her upper arms and wrists as she crossed them over her defenseless breasts, saw the residue of his rape dried together with her blood on her thighs, he had never felt so wretched.

He hadn't even considered that she would be almost as tender as a virgin after having her baby. It was a wonder he hadn't permanently injured her. He cursed himself as he stirred the pan of beans. Maybe he had injured her beyond healing. Maybe even now she was slowly bleeding to death.

"Smells good," Scout said, hunkering down beside the fire and pouring himself a cup of coffee.

"It's ready when you want it." Ross leaned against a tree and stared into the sunset. When he left she had looked dispirited, but she didn't look sick. Hopefully he hadn't hurt her too badly.

It was no wonder she hadn't even looked at him when he spoke to her. He had searched for one glimmer of forgiveness in her eyes. He would have grasped at her faintest protest that it was too soon to talk about divorcing when they had only been married for a few weeks. But she had only stared back at him with those eyes of hers that could burn as bright as firelight or turn as hard as stone depending on her mood. The contempt she had for him was all too apparent.

"You ain't eatin'?" Scout asked around a mouthful of beans.

Ross shook his head. "I'm not hungry just now. Maybe later."

What the hell did he care if she forgave him or not? She was a tart. Surely she had had it rough before. Why should he feel sorry about it?

Because she was afraid of you, you bastard. You knew that but went right on with it anyway.

She could have fought harder.

She fought as hard as she could. Have you looked at her? A strong wind could blow her down. What chance did she have against a brute like you?

Well, she had asked for it.

For rape?

Maybe not rape. But she let you know she wanted it by brushing up against you and doing nice little favors for you and wearing her hair to look like she had just had a most satisfactory tumble. And what about all those glimpses of flesh she gives you?

Accidents.

Are they?

Yes. I think.

Did you ever think of Victoria like this? To the point of thinking if you didn't see her, touch her, make love to her, you would explode?

I don't remember.

You remember. You didn't. You loved her, but she didn't consume your every waking thought and that's what's really troubling you, isn't it? It was ten times better with the girl than it ever was with your wife. With any woman. And you can't forget it.

Yes, I will.

I doubt it. You're hard as a pike now with thinking about it.

Yes, yes, yes! It was goddamn great and I want it again. Dammit, what am I going to do?

"It's good to get away from them sod busters for a spell," Scout said.

"Yes," Ross answered laconically. It would be suppertime. She would be bending over the fire and her cheeks would be flushed from the heat. He would step around the wagon after washing and they would look at each other and then she would wet her lips the way she did when she was nervous.

"That little Watkins gal is drivin' me crazy. Hot bitch," Scout said, tearing off a plug of tobacco. He offered a chew to Ross, who shook his head no. "Know what she did?"

"What?" Ross asked when he couldn't have even said what they were talking about.

God, sinking into Lydia's body had been like finding home for the first time in his life. He had intended to take her hard and fast and dispassionately, but once encased in her, he found that he couldn't. It had been too good. Had she put her arms around his shoulders, or is that just what he wanted to remember?

Scout was embroidering a luscious tale. "Well, I played the stud for her a few times and now she's talkin' weddin' and babies and all." He chuckled in gross amusement. "I'll tell you one thing, she's as tight as ol' Dick's hatband. You ever dipped into that honeypot? Naw, 'course you ain't. Not with that juicy little piece you're married up with now waitin' for you every night."

Ross moved with the speed of lightning. He kicked Scout in the chest with both bootheels and sent him reeling backward. Before the younger man had recovered, Ross rolled him over, planted his knee at the base of his spine and arched him backward with a forearm beneath his chin. Scout heard the deadly click of a pistol hammer at the back of his skull. How the hell the man had gotten it out of his holster, Scout would never know.

"Have you got anything else to say about my wife?" Ross asked, and his dulcet tones did more to terrify Scout than the lethal quickness with which Ross had moved.

"N . . . no," he stuttered. "I didn't mean nothin'. Swear to God I didn't . . . Awwww," he yelled as Ross pressed his knee harder and brought his arm back farther. "Swear to God I meant no disrespect."

Gradually the deadly hold relaxed. Ross stood slowly, released the hammer of his pistol and put it back in his holster. "I think I'm hungry now," he said with a voice as cold and steely as the long barrel of his gun, which Scout could still feel tickling the back of his neck.

He fearfully eased himself over and saw Ross indifferently spooning beans into his tin plate. Scout had never thought Coleman belonged with the rest of them. Now he was certain. There was more to the man than anybody thought and damned if he wanted to find out what it was.

Ma's face was as hard as stone as Bubba came gliding dreamy-eyed into the circle of firelight. His feet barely touched the ground. He was floating in a state of euphoria.

"Where, might I ask, have you been?" Ma's booming

voice cracked through his state of well-being and brought him hurtling back to earth.

"Uh . . ."

"I'm gonna thrash the both of you," Ma said, shaking an intimidating willow switch in Bubba's face. "Sent you out for firewood hours ago and ain't seen hide nor hair of you since. Where's that no 'count brother of yours? Might as well whip both of you at the same time."

"Luke's not back?" Bubba was having a hard time getting his head on straight. Priscilla had not only wrung his body dry, but seemed to have pickled his brain as well. When he realized that Luke hadn't lived up to his end of the bargain, he went almost as livid as Ma.

"No, he ain't back. What have you two been up to?"

"I . . . we . . . we went after the firewood and Luke said he was gonna bring it back."

"Which he didn't, 'cause I had to send your hard-workin' pa after some. Well?"

"And he said he was gonna . . . I know . . . I'll bet he's at the corral with Mr. Coleman's horses . . . he said—"

"No, he ain't. I done sent Marynell lookin' down there and Lydia's taking care of them horses. Atlanta said Luke ain't nowhere in camp. If you're covering up for some of his mischief . . ." She shook the switch at him again.

Bubba hoped to God Priscilla wasn't listening to this. She would laugh at him. Diddlin' all afternoon like a man and gettin' a whippin' in the evenin' like a kid.

"No, Ma, I swear . . . he . . ."

Bubba's voice dwindled off when he realized his ma wasn't listening anymore. She had suddenly dropped the switch she had been brandishing. Her red, work-rough hand flew to her mouth, and for the first time in his life, Bubba saw his ma's cheeks go pale as she knocked him aside and took stumbling steps forward.

"Mrs. Langston," Moses said quietly. "I found him over yonder in the woods."

He was carrying Luke, who looked amazingly young and small cradled in Moses's arms. There was a handkerchief tied around Luke's throat, but still the gaping slash was visible. His shirtfront was stiff, sticky, red—drenched in blood that had dried quickly in the summer heat.

Bubba collapsed against the wheel of his family's wagon and began to vomit.

Chapter Fourteen

*L*ydia stared into the gaping square hole in the ground and refused to believe that the quilt-wrapped bundle at the bottom of it was the vivacious, mischievous Luke Langston. The mourners stood grim and silent as Mr. Grayson officiated at the brief burial service. This was the second mortality among them since the outset of their journey. There was no coffin. There hadn't been time to make or buy one.

Lydia let the tears roll down her cheeks without attempting to wipe them away. Thankfully Lee was being quiet and still as she held him. Could he sense the tragedy of the situation, the tension in the adults around him?

How Ma Langston was holding up so well, Lydia didn't know. The woman looked as she did every day, sparse hair sleeked back, dressed in calico and the perennial apron. She stood erect, with her face set into an expressionless mask. Her hands were clasped together at her shapeless waist. The white rigidity of her knuckles was the only giveaway to her grief. Her family was clustered around her. Zeke was bent, looking far older than he had this time yesterday. Anabeth was trying to imitate the dignity of her mother, but the other girls were clinging to each other, weeping copiously. Samuel looked bewildered and on the verge of tears. Little Micah, uncomprehending, stood beside his mother, her skirt clutched tightly in his hand as he solemnly watched the proceedings.

But Bubba, Bubba was the most pitiable to behold. His eyes were hollow as he stared down into the grave. He was several degrees more pale than the body that had been carefully washed and wrapped for burial. While Luke's face had looked peaceful in death, that of his older brother was ravaged by grief and despair.

"They were so close, those two young fellas," folks murmured.

"It'll take a long time for him to stop missing Luke."

Mr. Grayson finished reading the Twenty-third Psalm and closed the worn leather binder of his Bible. He cleared his throat softly. "Ma, if you're ready . . ."

Ma bent down and picked up a handful of the dirt that had been emptied out of the ground for her son's grave and sprinkled it over the body. "Children," she said. One by one the brothers and sisters of Luke Langston came to the rim of the grave to toss down a clump of earth. When it came Bubba's turn he looked down into the grave with eyes too dismayed and an expression too stark to weep. He uttered one anguished cry, turned, and ran through the people gathered around the grave. Ma looked after him as he fled toward the wagons, her expression as bleak as his. "Zeke," she said, nudging her husband's arm. Zeke stirred, mechanically taking up a handful of dirt and letting it sift into the grave as though it had no relevance to him.

The family stood solemnly as everyone else took a turn and started a slow, sad procession back to the camp. Soon only Lydia and Mr. Grayson were left standing with them.

"Take as long as you like. I don't reckon anybody feels up to traveling today. I'll have some of the men come back to finish here"—he gestured toward the open grave—"when you're done." Ma nodded.

Lydia hugged each of them in turn and then let Mr. Grayson accompany her back to the wagons. She longed for Ross. If he were here with her, maybe she could stand the thought of Luke's brutal death. Ross could help Bubba get through the horror of seeing his brother viciously and senselessly slain.

She grieved for young Luke. She had liked him for his sense of humor and his mischievous nature, his zest for life, and his quick mind. She wanted to weep for the wasteful taking of his life. She wanted Ross to hold her as she did.

But he was gone and she needed to be strong and helpful to Ma and Zeke. Never would she be able to repay them for taking her in when no one else would have, but she could try and help them through this tragedy.

Arriving back at the camp, Lydia realized at once that Luke's murder was going to have serious repercussions that extended beyond grief. Last night after Moses first brought the body in, it was too late in the evening to send a rider after a peace officer. The nearest town with a sheriff was twenty miles away through unfamiliar territory. And no one wanted to get mixed up with the Federal troops that still occupied Arkansas.

Mr. Grayson had dispatched an emissary before sunrise that morning. Now he was back, reporting to the avid, restless listeners that the sheriff hadn't been available. He was on the far side of the county and wasn't expected back for days. The deputy refused to leave the office.

"They haven't heard of any such crimes in these parts," Mr. Sims said gravely. "He said . . . uh . . . for us to think about someone in the train—"

"You can't mean he suggested that one of our own killed the boy?" Grayson asked.

Miserably, Sims twisted his horse's bridle in his fingers. "That's what he hinted at. I told him I didn't agree, but—"

"Well, I been giving it some thought," Leona Watkins said shrilly. When all eyes turned on her, she pulled her shawl around her, lifted her shoulders back haughtily, and let the suspense build. "I saw somebody sneaking through the woods yesterday. I didn't think anything about it till the Langston boy turned up dead, but now I feel that it's my Christian duty to report it."

Her husband Jesse was glancing around nervously. Lydia had always thought the man was as afraid of his shadow as he was of his wife. He looked now like he desperately wished she hadn't opened her mouth. Priscilla stood nearby in sulky boredom.

"Leona, you don't know—"

"Quiet, Jesse," she snapped and her husband cowered. "These folks ought to know if they're harboring a killer."

Everyone gasped, including Lydia. "Mrs. Watkins, surely you don't think someone on this train killed Luke," Mr. Grayson said.

Leona let her ferret eyes dart around the circle of people. She had everyone right where she wanted them—held in breathless suspense. "Who brought him in? Hmm? Covered in blood himself."

"Moses?" Lydia exclaimed on a high note. "You're accusing Moses of killing Luke? Of killing *anybody*?"

"We don't need interference from outsiders," Leona said, not even deigning to look at Lydia. Instead she turned hard, colorless eyes on the black man. Those who had been standing nearest him moved back on shuffling feet, giving him wide berth and looking at him suspiciously. It was as if they had never seen him before, though they had been traveling in the man's company for weeks.

"I saw him slinking through the woods yesterday on my way to the river," Leona Watkins whispered loudly. Her eyes were glittering malevolently, seething with hate and prejudice. "I say he's the killer."

There were murmurs of consideration and Lydia's heart began to pound. Surely this was all a terrible dream and she would soon wake up, wake up with Ross's arm heavy and secure over her waist.

"Why would Moses want to kill anybody?" someone in the crowd asked.

"He's a former slave," Leona reasoned loudly, spreading her arms wide. "Now that he's been freed, he's got the lust to kill white folks. There have been times when I've felt his eyes crawling over me and my daughter. One look from those evil, dark eyes is enough to make my blood run cold."

"That's ridiculous," Lydia shouted, but she couldn't be heard over the rumblings of speculation.

Moses was beginning to glance around nervously. He had been protected by the Hill family all his life but knew enough about the night riders who terrorized freed Negroes to be afraid. He had witnessed mobs incited to lynching blacks on trumped-up suspicions, suspicions much less incriminating than the bloody murder of a white boy.

"I say we tie him up and try him ourselves," Leona

screamed. "There's no telling when that sheriff might decide to come help us. In the meantime, others could be killed. Do you want him running loose with your children around?" she demanded of Mrs. Norwood, who was standing beside her.

"Wait!" Mr. Grayson commanded, holding up both hands. Everyone respected him enough to stop their hostile advance toward Moses and look toward their wagonmaster. "We haven't heard anything from Moses. Were you in the woods yesterday?" he asked the black man.

"Yes, sir. I was picking healing herbs to make a tea for Mr. Hill. It's good for his consumption."

Lydia had visited Winston only that morning. He was looking better. She only hoped that from his bed in his wagon, he couldn't hear what people were accusing his friend of.

"Did you see Luke Langston?"

"No, sir. Not until I found him the way I brought him in."

"Lies," Mrs. Watkins shrieked. "You're going to believe him? He was probably picking poisonous weeds to kill Mr. Hill with. I saw him, I tell you, creeping around like he was just waiting to pounce on a poor unsuspecting soul. Jesse, get the rope." The man rushed to obey and several others surged toward the black man.

Everything happened at once then. Lydia, frantically looking around her, pushed Lee into Mrs. Greer's arms. She cried out to Grayson, "You can't let them do this."

He was overwhelmed to see people usually so civilized behaving in so barbaric a fashion and only stood and watched helplessly. Moses, seeing the enraged men striding toward him, panicked and, turning, began to run.

"He's gettin' away," someone screamed.

"Stop him!"

"No, Moses, no!" Lydia shouted and charged after him, knowing that his running away would be as good as an admission of guilt to these people gone temporarily mad.

"Stop him, Jesse. Get the shotgun," Leona yelled to her husband.

It was at that instant that Ross's horse leaped over the

tongue of a wagon and came streaking into the circle like a ruthless black dart. No sooner had Lucky's hooves landed than he was turned about, deftly separating Lydia and Moses from the others. Ross had the barrel of his rifle trained into the crowd and his pistol pointing at Jesse Watkins, who had frozen in the act of catching up the shotgun at his wife's shouted order. Everyone froze, as much out of surprise as fright. But anyone having the misfortune of meeting Ross's eyes at that moment tasted fear, acrid and vile.

"I wouldn't if I were you." Those were the only words he uttered, and he spoke them in a sibilant whisper, but Watkins's hand came away from the shotgun as though a puppeteer's string had jerked it back. "Everyone stay real still now until I find out what the hell is going on."

"I'd like to know that myself." That came from Ma. At hearing the commotion, the Langstons had come back to the camp. Ma was relieved that whatever the trouble was, Bubba didn't seem to be involved. The boy wasn't himself and the drastic change in him went deeper than grief.

The members of the train stood stunned. They had all respected Ross Coleman as an upstanding man, a man who minded his own business, who had been devoted to his first wife and now seemed to be making the adjustment to being a parent with a new wife to cope with. He was helpful when asked for help, but didn't give unsolicited advice. He had never been known to invite confidences, but he would laugh at anyone's joke and take a swig of whiskey when the womenfolk weren't watching, same as any other man. He was all right, not as friendly as some, more handsome than most, a tad standoffish, but hardworking.

Now, however, they were seeing a side of the man they had never seen. His voice could have stopped an avalanche with its quiet persuasion. And those eyes, as all-seeing as an eagle's, were fearsome and hypnotizing. No one moved for fear that he might misinterpret the motion and fire the pistol. Everyone had seen him whip it out of his holster even as that horse of his sailed between the wagons. They could almost believe they had seen that. What they couldn't believe was that at the same time, with his left hand, he had pulled the rifle out of its saddle scabbard.

Not a muscle in his face flickered as Ross slung his right leg over his saddle horn and slid to the ground, still keeping his two guns poised and ready to fire.

"Lydia?"

"Yes?"

"Come here."

Lydia had never been so glad to see anyone in her life. She felt compelled to run toward him and wrap her arms around his waist and let his strength ebb into her. Instead she gave Moses a reassuring glance and walked forward slowly until she was even with Ross. His eyes didn't waver off the others as he asked, "What's going on?"

She swallowed, not sure she could keep herself from stuttering, and then commenced to tell him about Luke's murder and what had transpired that morning. At hearing of the boy's death, Ross's whole body spasmed and he glanced toward the Langstons, who were still grouped together. Otherwise he didn't flinch. When Lydia finished giving him the relevant details, Ross, sensing that violence was no longer about to erupt, let go the hammer of his pistol and sheathed it in its holster. He lowered the rifle to his side.

Walking through the subdued members of the train, his spurs the only sound in the camp, he came face-to-face with Mr. Grayson. "Do you think old Moses is capable of killing anyone?"

"No," the man said abashedly, shaking his head. "The local sheriff's deputy more or less left it to us to settle. I didn't know what to do."

"I know what I'm going to do." Ma had listened to Lydia's explanation as closely as Ross had. Now she strode toward Leona Watkins and, without the least hint of warning, slapped the woman hard across the cheek. "I've buried three children, and I might have to bury other loved ones before my own time. I only pray to God you ain't around to contribute to my family's grievin' then. Besides bein' a mean old witch, you're a fool, Leona Watkins. Why would Moses have brung me my boy if he'd been the one what killed him?" She drew herself up taller. "You're heartless and ain't ever been acquainted with joy. I feel sorry for you."

Leona glanced around the group, seeing only hostility where moments before she had seen allegiance. Sweeping her skirts aside, she turned toward her wagon. When Jesse and Priscilla only stared at the ground, not following her, she turned to them and said, "Well?" Meekly they followed her into the wagon.

Ma was the first to stir. She turned to speak to everyone at once. "I'm not surprised by her behavior, but it 'pears to me some of you others got some apologizin' to do." Guilty eyes were lowered as everyone began shamefacedly to shuffle back to their wagons. Some cast embarrassed eyes toward Moses, who stood with quiet dignity, but no hauteur.

Lydia retrieved Lee, then crossed the dusty ground to speak to the black man. "I'm sorry, Moses. That was a terrible thing they did to you. Are you all right?"

"I'm fine, Miss Lydia. Thank you for standin' up for me."

She smiled at him and touched his arm. "It was no more than you and Winston did for me when I was the outcast." Then in an encouraging tone she said, "If you could watch Lee for a while this afternoon, I'll cook supper for you and Winston."

The gesture was intended to invest confidence and it did. Tears glossed the old man's eyes. "Thank you. That would truly be appreciated, I'm sure."

Feeling his presence behind her, she turned to Ross and said softly, "I'll have coffee waiting for you at the wagon."

He looked down at her and she felt the look straight through to her soul. "I'll be along as soon as I pay my respects to the Langstons."

She didn't want to leave him even for a moment. She wanted to look at him, to assure herself that he had really returned and was gazing at her like he had missed her. But if she stayed with him one more moment, he might see the tempest in her heart through her eyes. She turned away quickly.

His fatigue was evident when he came to the wagon a while later. He nodded his thanks for the cup of coffee she handed him as he sank down on a stool. "Helluva mess to come back to."

"I thought you'd be gone for several days." The casualness in her voice was acquired. Actually she was consumed with curiosity as to why he had returned to the train early.

"So did I, but . . ." He shrugged evasively. "I decided before dawn to come back. Scout will go on ahead."

Why didn't he just say it? Why didn't he just come right out and tell her that he couldn't stay away, that he had tossed on his bedroll last night until he had decided he was wasting his time trying to sleep? He had packed and saddled his horse, had awakened a surprised, sleepy Scout to tell him the change in plans, and then had ridden hell-bent on getting back to her as soon as possible?

"It's a good thing you came back when you did." She didn't have anything to do with her hands. Lee was taking his morning nap. Her chores were done. The best thing she could think to do with them was massage away the tiredness she could see weighing down Ross's shoulders, to erase with soothing fingers the lines wrinkling his brow. She wanted badly to touch him, but she didn't. Her hands held each other.

He was staring into the cup as he swirled its contents in a tiny whirlpool. "I can't believe someone killed that boy in cold blood. Why?" he asked rhetorically. "Dammit, *why?*"

"I don't know, Ross. What is Mr. Grayson going to do?"

"He thinks we should look around today, see if we can find any evidence as to who could have done it."

"We?" she asked tremulously.

"I volunteered."

"Oh." She sat down on the stool facing his and laced her hands together tightly. She had seen Luke's body, the gash that had almost severed his head. She shivered. "What do you think you'll find?"

"Nothing," he said succinctly. She watched fascinated and terrified as he methodically began to check his pistol and rifle. "It could have been Indians, but I doubt there are any warrior tribes left this far east. Besides, this wasn't a noble killing, not for food or to serve any purpose. It was wanton, a murder for the hell of it. In that case, it could have been any renegade Luke happened upon. There are thousands of them roaming the South since the war, fighting their private battles, getting their own brand of revenge, taking out their hate on someone as innocent as Luke. This kind of killer is crafty, used to striking and disappearing. He's probably miles from here by now."

"Why do you have to go after him?"

His busy hands stilled and his head came up. The anxiety in her voice was genuine. "Why did you have to defend Moses, nearly getting yourself shot?"

She lowered her eyes from his inquiring gaze. "Of course you have to go," she mumbled. Only, please don't let anything happen to you, she wanted to beg. "You're tired. I can tell."

"Yeah. I rode hard this morning." To see you. To smell your hair that even on a gray day like today smells like sunshine. To see if your body is real or only a figment that keeps haunting me. To hear your voice.

As he stood, he slid the pistol into its holster. She couldn't help but notice the practiced ease with which he did it, or how automatically he tied it to his thigh with leather thongs. He pulled his hat down low on his brow and picked up his rifle. "Don't look for me until well after dark," he said as he worked his hands into leather gloves.

Forgetting to keep her emotions a secret, she rushed to him and put both hands on the forearm that was crossed over his stomach as he held the rifle. "Ross, you'll be careful?"

When had anyone cared like this about him? In his whole godforsaken life, when had anyone worried about his safety? Even Victoria had taken it for granted that he could look after himself. If anyone needed protection it was she, not he. When had anyone looked at him with such apparent concern, not for what it meant to them if he survived or not, but concern exclusively for his safety?

He thought of the night he had spent dreaming of her,

of the hours of riding when he had spared neither himself nor Lucky to get back to her. He thought of how his body raged to be held tightly in hers once more . . . and the hell he had gone through trying to forget the splendor of that.

Now she was looking up at him with those eyes that reminded him of the finest whiskey. Her hair was begging to be caressed away from her cheeks. Her mouth was moist and inviting and looked as if it wanted to be kissed.

By the Almighty, he was owed one.

In plain view of God, and Leona Watkins, and anyone else who wanted to watch, his hand cupped the back of her head and lifted her up and against him. His mouth met hers with tender temperance. Sipping lightly until he felt her lips go pliant, his tongue then slid between them and sank into the sweet hollow that closed about it.

Lydia went weak. His kiss robbed her of conscious thought save how marvelous it was to share this intimacy with him. She left her hands where they were on his forearm trapped between their bodies, but leaned closer so that the backs of her knuckles were digging into the muscles of his stomach.

Repeatedly, on delicious forays, his tongue dipped into her mouth. She heard her own murmur of desire and need. The impulse was strong to open her knees and hug his between them. She settled for pressing her thighs against his.

Ross was made dizzy by the weight of her breasts on his arm. He wanted to drop the rifle, to carry her into the wagon, to see her naked, to touch her softness, to forget about everything except losing himself in her again. But he couldn't, so he spared himself further pain.

He withdrew slowly. First his tongue left her mouth, but paused to flirt with her upper lip. Then he brushed her mouth with his lips and moustache. Finally he pulled away and opened his eyes to meet a gaze as slumberous and confused as his own must be. "I'll be careful," he said hoarsely. Then he eased his arm free of her hands, let go of the curls that were tangled in his fist at her nape, and left.

* * *

He was gone for the rest of the day and well into the night. Lydia passed most of the time with the Langstons. Ma held her children close and they wept. It was both wonderful and horrible to see. Lydia had had no one to cry with over her mother's death. At least the Langstons could help each other bear the sorrow. Zeke found solace in working and busied himself around the wagon, periodically moving to Ma and resting a gnarled hand on her shoulder in silent communication. The family shared their grief.

Everyone except Bubba, who sat alone within sight of the wagon but detached from everyone else. Lydia's heart twisted every time she looked at him. The boys had fought between themselves, but they had loved each other. Bubba's grief frightened Lydia. It absorbed him. To the point that he forgot to care for Ross's horses.

Lydia did the chore. It was tiring, but she felt a great sense of satisfaction that she could do it for Ross. She tried not to dwell on recollections of his kiss that morning. For when she did, her knees liquefied and she felt flushed and shaky all over. She wanted to touch her breasts, to rub them until the nipples, which seemed inclined to pout embarrassingly, relaxed. The place between her thighs ached each time she thought of the way Ross's mouth had moved over hers and the surging power she had felt in his thighs. She thought about him without his shirt, about the way his body hair grew in swirling patterns over hard muscles. She speculated on how the rest of him was made and her face would go hot with color and shame. But it was a thought she couldn't leave alone, and at intervals throughout the day, she would indulge her fantasy and think on it.

Try as she might, she couldn't put out of her mind the way he felt when inside her, thick and hard and warm and pulsing. She couldn't forget the sensations that had rushed over her with each thrust of his body into hers. Ma had been right. With the right man, it could be very good.

Moses came to her wagon at sunset, shyly asking if she had meant what she said about his watching Lee while she prepared dinner for him and Winston. She assured him she had been serious and sent him to walk Lee around the camp while she fried cornmeal batter in bacon grease to go with the rabbit stew she had had simmering since early afternoon.

When she, Moses, and Lee went to the Hill wagon, they were surprised to see Winston sitting outside sipping sherry. Lydia declined his offer for a glass, but commented on his apparent good health.

"I'm feeling much better." He sampled the stew and complimented her profusely. When he was finished eating and had set his plate aside, he said, "Lydia, Moses has told me about what happened this morning. I don't blame anyone. I know how these things can get started and how ordinarily peaceful people get caught up in them. However, I do want to say thank you from the bottom of my heart for defending Moses in my absence."

She glanced down shyly. "No thanks are necessary. The two of you are my friends."

"An ex-slave and a consumptive. Moses, you'd think a lovely young woman could find finer friends than us."

She laughed with them, but little did either know that they were among the few friends she had had in her life.

Ross returned to the wagon late, but Lydia was still awake. She had heard the men ride in and waited until she heard him outside the wagon. Crawling to the rear of it, she called out softly, "Ross?"

"I'm sorry I woke you."

"Did you find who killed Luke?"

There was a long silence while he sighed loudly. "No. It was just as I thought. No camp. No tracks. Nothing."

He was spreading his bedroll. "Why don't you sleep inside?" she asked hesitantly. "With the sides rolled up it's as cool as outside." When he didn't reply she added, "I know you're tired."

"Very."

"Then you'll rest better in here."

He seriously doubted that, but he climbed inside the wagon anyway. The moment Lydia saw he had made that decision, she scooted back to her own bedroll, not wanting him to think she expected anything. But hoping, praying . . . She watched through the shadows as he took off his shirt and boots and lay down on the other side of the wagon.

"How was Lee today? I didn't get to see much of him."

Squelching her disappointment that he hadn't lain beside her, she said, "He got his fingers tangled up in my hair and I thought I'd never get them out without scalping myself."

He laughed, and in the darkness it was a nice, comforting sound. "I can see where that might happen." Dammit, he hadn't meant that the way it had sounded. The words hung in the still night air while he held his breath and hoped she hadn't taken offense.

Lydia, sensitive to her unconventional appearance, took his remark the wrong way. "I know my hair is . . . different . . . wild. It's not like . . . corn silk." Not like Victoria's, she thought.

"It's very pretty," he said softly, flexing his fingers, remembering what it felt like to have the russet strands coiling around them.

"Thank you," she whispered, tears gathering in her eyes. He had said few complimentary things to her. She would cherish this one.

"You're welcome." You goddamn hypocrite, he thought to himself. You're lying here reciting polite phrases when you're thinking about what it was like being with her and how you wish you had another excuse like drunkenness to do it again. Irritated with himself, he said a terse "Good night," and turned away from her.

For a long while they lay in the darkness, knowing that the other wasn't asleep, but not saying anything. Tired as Ross was, his eyes seemed full of grit every time he tried to close them to sleep. At last he heard her gentle breathing that let him know she had fallen asleep.

This is no good, he thought as he rolled to his back once again, hoping to relieve the part of his body that was adamant about keeping him awake. His sex was hard and angry with him for this stupid, self-imposed denial. In the long, dark hours of the night, Ross began to think it was stupid too.

So she had a past. So had he. She wasn't all that

Victoria had been. She was many things Victoria hadn't been. They were married legally. Unstable as local governments were these days, it might not be that easy to obtain a divorce. They might be married for a long time. What was he going to do? Live like a monk or buy women by the hour?

He thought of the lonely night in Owentown and knew he didn't want that.

He wanted Lydia.

And maybe once he had her, he would be over whatever ailed him. The night he had taken her, he'd been drunk. Maybe his imagination was making him remember it better than it actually had been.

Who are you kidding? No one has ever been that drunk.

But it was a good arguing point when he was trying very hard to convince himself to move over to her now, kiss her awake and . . .

No. Then she would think that was all he wanted from her. And, much as his body craved surcease, that wasn't exclusively what he needed. He had come to depend on her quiet efficiency, the meals she prepared for him, the way she always knew where things were, her loving care of Lee. He wanted those things too. And he liked the way she listened to him when he talked. It made the things he said seem important. He wanted her to worry a little about him when he rode off as he had done today. It wasn't just her body he wanted surrounding him, but her spirit as well.

One thing was certain, he couldn't go on like this, with a constantly stiff rod in his pants and a mind torn in two. Sooner or later he was bound to do something obscene like he had done the night of the Fourth and he didn't want to see that fear on her face ever again if he could help it.

Tomorrow. He would start treating her more like a wife tomorrow, and then maybe she would start feeling more wifely and one thing would eventually lead to another. First thing in the morning he would launch his campaign. Maybe he would kiss her good morning. Yes. In the morning.

He fell asleep tasting that kiss.

But in the morning she was gone.

Chapter Fifteen

He awakened at once, feeling fully rested after only a few hours of sleep. It wasn't yet dawn. The sky was dove gray, with no streaks of light yet showing in the east.

Ross sat up, his eyes flying immediately to the bed on the other side of the wagon. He blinked against the dim light, thinking that his eyes were playing tricks on him, because it looked like the place where Lydia always slept was empty. He moved closer and his heart stopped before beginning again to pound rapidly. He touched the linens to confirm what his brain refused to accept.

She wasn't there.

He checked the crate and Lee was still sleeping peacefully.

Lydia would never leave him alone. Not voluntarily. And there was a killer about.

Ross lunged for the back of the wagon and ripped open the canvas flaps. Nothing. No one in the camp was stirring. Last evening's fires were only gray mounds of cold ashes. He reached for his pistol, mechanically checked to see that it was loaded, and crammed it into the waistband of his pants. Forgetting his boots, his shirt, his hat, he swung himself over the tailgate and landed on silent feet on the dew-damp ground. He glanced around the camp once more, but he didn't see any movement anywhere, not even in the Langston wagon where he thought Lydia might have gone.

He took off at a swift trot, knocking tree limbs and grapevines out of his path as he thrashed his way through the dense woods in the direction of the river. That was the only place she might have gone alone. He heard nothing except the rushing of his own breath in and out of his chest and the thunder of his heart as he imagined Lydia at the hands of a man who could maliciously slay an adolescent boy.

Or had she simply run away, as he had thought she was likely to do one day? Had she tired of him and Lee and gone back to whatever she had been doing before the Langstons found her? And what was that? Why would she just sneak away in the dead of the night?

She wouldn't, Ross told himself. The thought gave him no comfort because the alternative was worse. He began to run faster. He came to the creek, his chest heaving with exertion. He propped his arm against a tree trunk and gulped in deep breaths. His eyes scanned the banks on either side. At first he didn't see her, only her dress hanging on a forsythia bush. Then he spotted her diminutive figure on the far bank. She was lying on her side facing away from him. Her knees were curled up to her chest.

Was she hurt? Unconscious? Dead? *God!*

Taking the pistol from his waistband and holding it high, Ross ran into the river and splashed his way across the shallows. He came out on the other side, dripping oceans from his heavy cloth pants. "Lydia!" he cried.

She sat up, startled, and whirled her head around to see him emerging from the river. The clear water rolled down his chest and arms, molding his pants to his form. She had crossed the river after she had washed, and her chemise was clinging damply to her torso and thighs. The morning humidity had brought her hair to an uncontrollable curling wreath about her face and down her back. Upon seeing him, her tear-laden eyes overflowed and the crystal drops trickled down her moist cheeks. Surprise parted her lips and she mouthed his name.

Ross stopped dead still. He tried to regain his breath, but it seemed to accelerate, as did his heartbeat, at seeing her near nudity, the dewiness of her exposed skin, the wildness of her hair unrestrained, the air of expectancy about her. He dropped his pistol on the ground and advanced toward her. His knees hit the soft, grassy turf as he rested his hand along her cheek and picked up a tear with his thumb.

"What are you doing here? Jesus, Lydia, you scared

hell out of me when I woke up and you weren't anywhere to be found."

"I'm sorry. I didn't think you'd wake up before I got back." She didn't realize that she was speaking as rapidly and breathlessly as he, or that her hand had gone to his hair, or that she was threading her fingers through the dark strands. "I didn't get to bathe yesterday because everything was . . . I didn't sleep well last night . . ."

"Why were you crying?" His other hand was at her nape, lifting the heavy mane away from it and caressing the soft skin beneath with his fingertips.

Her tears began to cascade again. She couldn't explain them to him any more than she could to herself. "Luke, I suppose. It was so awful yesterday, Ross, before you got back. I was sad and then afraid when they . . . Moses . . . and I wanted you here and was so glad to see you."

"Don't cry, don't cry," he chanted even as he lowered his head and began picking up the tears with his moustache, his lips, his tongue. When his mouth took hers it was with the desperation, the urgency, that boiled inside both of them. He slanted his lips over hers and they parted. Then his tongue was swirling inside her mouth, plundering gently, taking, giving. She made a purring sound in her throat.

His hands scaled down her shoulders to cup her under the arms and lift her up. He held her against his chest and his wet nakedness redampened her chemise. Her nipples beaded against his, already erect from the cold water. She trembled slightly, and he hoped that the shudder wasn't from fear, but from a desire as rampant as his. He buried his face in the curve of her neck. She let her head fall back, allowing him access. Her generosity made him bold; he skimmed the satiny length of her throat with his mouth, planting kisses along it.

Lydia couldn't imagine what was happening to her or where this feeling of weightlessness was coming from. On the one hand she felt that she could fly. On the other, her whole body seemed anchored to his by a delicious lassitude she hoped never to recover from. She felt more alive than ever in her life, but wasn't sure how she was to respond to

this new awareness of her being. Naturally her arms curled
around his neck and she pressed closer to him.

"Ah, Lydia," he groaned and resealed their lips with a
blistering kiss that bespoke his leashed passion.

He maintained enough reason to realize that anyone
venturing out early to get water would see them. He lifted
her with him as he half stood, half crouched, and stumbled
toward a clump of honeysuckle. The vine had climbed to
the lower branches of a post oak and draped down to the
ground. When they were on the other side of that natural,
fragrant screen, he lowered her to the ground.

The damp chemise detailed her form for his avid eyes.
It clung to the full mounds of her breasts. Through the
sheer fabric he could see the darker areolas and the sweetly
puckering nipples. His eyes followed the row of dainty
buttons down her body, over the narrow column of ribs to
the concavity of her abdomen. The cloth dipped alluringly
into the dimple of her navel, then molded to the gentle
mound of her sex and outlined its V shape and curly down.
Her slender thighs didn't escape his rapacious eyes.

Her eyes were wide and dilated as she watched him
unbutton his pants. He could see the agitation in her
breasts as they vibrated with each heartbeat that matched
his own in tempo.

"I won't hurt you again."

"I know."

He felt compelled to justify the act, to justify himself.
"I married you. You're my wife."

"Yes, yes."

Her hair was fanned out on the grass beneath her head
and on either side of it lay her hands, palms upturned,
fingers slightly curled, defenseless. Ross knelt above her,
straddling her legs. He leaned forward and placed his
palms against hers. His large hands covered hers completely. With that discovery, he smiled, and she answered it.

Moving slowly, he rubbed her palms with his, caressing. The contrast electrified them both. His were rough
and callused, hers fragile and soft. He matched the length
of his fingers to hers and moved them up and down,
marveling over how small hers felt against his. His middle

fingers trailed into the hollows of her palms and massaged them gently.

He felt her sudden intake of breath, saw her violet eyelids flutter and her lips part. Lacing their fingers together tightly, he levered himself down to cover her. Belly cushioned belly and her breasts absorbed the weight of his chest. He nestled hard and throbbing in the cradle her thighs formed for him. He bent his neck, letting his head fall against her shoulder. His mouth found her ear.

"You feel good against me, Lydia. Goddammit, but you do."

"Didn't you want me to?" she asked. Was her voice wavering because she was afraid of what was going to happen, or because she was afraid it wouldn't happen?

"No," he rasped. "No, I didn't."

She wanted to know why, but he had begun moving his mouth against her ear and she forgot to ask. His moustache tickled along the rim. His breath rushed in. Her earlobe was flicked by his tongue, wet and frisky.

"Ross . . . ?" she gasped, gripping his hands tighter.

He squeezed her hands, then released them. Cupping her jaw in one hand, he pressed his lips against hers. "I couldn't forget how it was. God knows I tried. I couldn't." He kissed her then, deeply and thoroughly, making love to her mouth with his brazen tongue, darting and delving, promising and granting.

"I couldn't forget it either." She sighed when his mouth began to meander over her cheekbones and his fingers stroked her neck.

"Please forget it. I was drunk and had no right to come at you violently like that. Forgive me."

"Forgive?" she asked, not understanding.

He touched the corner of her lips with his tongue, then let his moustache caress the spot. "I raped you, Lydia."

She wasn't familiar with the term and was about to ask its meaning when his mouth claimed hers once again. This time her arms came around his back and he moaned when he felt her first tentative caresses with shy fingertips on his bare skin.

He propped himself up on one elbow and dipped his head to scour her throat with voracious kisses. Hungrily his mouth moved over her, as though she might disappear and he would be left wanting. He examined the fragility of her collarbone with his fingertips. His hand closed around the upper part of her arm gently, remembering the bruises he had left there before. His thumb rubbed the sensitive underside of her arm and she quivered reflexively. Encouraged, he let his hand coast down, over her chest to her breast.

He placed his hand over it, loving the way it fit. Even through the covering of her chemise, he could feel her skin's warmth, feel the irregular beats of her heart which his palm absorbed. Easing his hand lower, he molded it around the undercurve and pressed upward, causing her breast to swell above the top of her chemise.

His lips were waiting to graze the sweet plumpness. Lydia shivered at the scratchiness of his moustache and beard stubble on her skin. The sensations that were foreign to her only weeks earlier, but were now achingly, blissfully familiar, feathered up from the depths of her body into her breasts, to the back of her throat. Her femininity flowered open, scandalously moist and throbbing. But she felt no shame as she instinctively arched against his male counterpart that offered to assuage this vague longing that plagued her.

He whispered a garbled curse and rubbed her nipple with his thumb, at the same time parting his lips to touch her cool skin with his tongue's wet heat. Her back bowed off the soft grass and she called his name plaintively. She closed her arms tighter around him as she pressed against his hardness. Her thighs opened and Ross settled himself firmly between them. He kissed her as if he wanted to draw all of her into himself.

His hand worked its way down between their bodies to raise the hem of her chemise. As he withdrew his hand, the backs of his fingers brushed her mound. The hair was fleecy soft, tightly curled, lavish. Lydia's breath stopped at the same time Ross's was slammed back into his throat.

His head began to ring clamorously. He wanted to go

on touching her. He wanted to sift his fingers through that sweet nest, to explore what lay beyond. But he had sworn to treat her like a wife. And wives didn't like to be fondled there. No decent woman would let a man touch her there unless he was an old and trusted physician. Victoria would have pretended the accidental touching hadn't happened. Regretfully Ross withdrew his hand.

The head of his shaft probed her hesitantly and he felt the tensing of her thighs around him. "I won't hurt you," he whispered. He thought that if he waited much longer, he would likely die.

Slowly her thighs relaxed, parted wider. He penetrated her slowly with one long, steady stroke. Her name broke over his lips as he sank into the wet, silken casing of her womanhood. It surrounded him, entrapped him, housed him, and he knew such peace and exhilaration that he wanted both to weep and shout.

It hadn't been a product of his drunken imagination. It was as euphoric as he remembered. Better. Because this time she was moving with him and her hands were delicately scaling his back. In random whispers that caressed his ears, she repeated his name.

She opened her eyes when he braced himself above her on stiff arms. Her small, white hand came up to touch lovingly the scar on his chest, and he groaned and clenched his teeth with the intense pleasure that engulfed him. He rocked his hips against her, plowing ever deeper into her receptive warmth. Striving for control, for endurance, he moved slowly. It wasn't enough.

He knew his climax was upon him and he submitted to it. Gathering her close, he held her tight as his body went rigid and he bathed her womb with molten fire.

When it was over, he lay heavily atop her. The scent of the new day, the dewy grass, the honeysuckle, and the issue of his own body filled his nostrils. He breathed deeply of her, burrowing his nose in her hair and letting his body relax. Silence prevailed. Nothing stirred in the wilderness setting they had converted into a temple of love, nothing but the rushing shallows of the river. Its gurgling was a song, a lullaby that lulled them into deeper languor.

He had almost fallen asleep when he felt her fingers touch his hair. "Ross, Lee will be waking up soon."

He sighed and eased out of her. Sitting up, he turned his back. The waistband of his pants fell low on his hips. Lydia noted the indentation of his waist, the slight flaring of his buttocks, the dusting of hair on the small of his back.

"We've stayed too long already," he said shortly.

She sat up, adjusted her chemise over her thighs, and touched the smooth skin of his back, unmarred save for the scar beneath his left shoulder blade. "Not for me."

He jerked his head around to pierce her with eyes the same brilliant shade of green as the grass on which they had lain. Her skin was rosy with the aftermath of loving. The dark amber eyes were limpid, and her lips were swollen and moist from his kisses. Her expression was guileless, innocent, unselfish.

Ross knew in that moment that he didn't give a damn about her past or how many men she had had. He only knew that no woman had ever satisfied him more. Not just with her body had she touched him, but with a kindred spirit that would draw him back to her time and again.

He extended his finger and grazed a spot on the top curve of her breast that his stubbled chin had abraded. He raised his eyes to hers and smiled sheepishly. She smiled back, then out of sheer joy laughed. He began laughing, too, and they collapsed, holding each other as they fell back onto the grass. He kissed her mouth, richer, better-tasting now than before. She responded, closing her hands around his neck and sliding her fingers through the hair on his nape. She smelled of him and he wanted to taste himself on her skin.

"Oh, dammit, Lydia." He stood up and hauled her after him. "If I don't stop now, I won't be able to."

Shyly she looked away as he clumsily buttoned his pants over a growing bulge. "Come on," he said, taking her hand when he was done. "Let's get back before Lee sets up a howl and alerts the whole camp."

He retrieved his gun and dragged her into the river. They waded in the waist-high water to the other side. When they came out, the chemise was plastered to her, revealing everything that Ross had recently touched. In the morning light, her breasts were creamy swells over the lacy border of the garment. Her nipples thrust blatantly against the wet batiste. The dusky shadow of her sex was clearly revealed through the cloth that sealed her like a second skin. "You'd better dress," he said thickly.

After gathering the fresh clothes she had brought with her, Lydia modestly slipped behind a screening bush and peeled off the wet chemise. She glanced down at herself and was amazed to see that she looked exactly the same except for the red marks his beard had made on her breasts. She felt totally different. Her body was tingling with life from the top of her head to the soles of her feet. But deep inside her there was a gnawing dissatisfaction that she couldn't pinpoint. An unnamed yearning was still with her. It wasn't unpleasant, but rather something to savor.

She stepped into her underwear and clean chemise, then her dress. Her shoes and stockings had been left at the wagon. When she came out from behind the bush, Ross was shoving his pistol back into his waistband. When he saw her anxious look, he teased her, saying, "Don't worry. I'm not going to let it shoot off anything valuable."

To the roots of her reddish brown hair, she blushed furiously.

"Ready?" he asked.

"Yes." She was suddenly shy of him, and despite his joke, she thought he was nervous, too, now that it had happened again. They didn't converse as they made their way back to the camp. When they broke through the trees, Ma was coming toward their wagon toting a pail of milk. She stopped in her tracks and surveyed them with open curiosity.

Ross was uncomfortably aware of the gun in his waist, his bare feet, and his bare chest with its incriminating scar. Lydia was holding the wet chemise she had wrung out. It felt like a hundred-pound weight in her hand when Ma looked at it.

"Excuse me," Ross mumbled and hoisted himself onto the tailgate to disappear into the wagon.

Ma watched him and then turned her inquiring eyes

back to Lydia. "We . . . we went swimming," she stammered, dropping her wet chemise onto the tailgate like it was something hot.

"So I see," Ma said.

"Ross is . . . uh . . . teaching me to swim."

"Is he now?"

She felt like a fool as she bobbed her head to confirm her lie. "You shouldn't have bothered with Lee's milk this morning. I was planning to fetch it myself."

"We been doin' this for you for weeks. I see no call to change."

"I was thinking about Luke."

Ma sighed deeply as she set the pail on the tailgate. "I'll always miss him. Till the day I die, I'll miss him. But he's dead, Lydia, and nothin' I do can bring him back. For some reason the good Lord seen fit to take him and I ain't one to argue with Him."

Lydia thought she would do battle with any power in heaven or on earth that tried to wrest Lee or Ross away from her, but she didn't say anything.

"Life goes on. All of us talked about it and decided to leave our grief at Luke's grave. All but Bubba. The boy's in a bad way."

"I'll ask Ross to talk to him."

"Ain't sure it'll do any good, but I'll appreciate it. He's down there carin' for the horses." As Ma looked wistfully in the direction of the corral, Lydia wondered if she knew Bubba had forgotten his chores last night. Ma shook off her worry and smiled at Lydia. "Git on in there to your husband. He might need some help gettin' out of those wet pants." She was laughing softly as she walked off in the direction of her own wagon.

Lydia found Ross dressed and bending over Lee's crib. "Is he still sleeping?"

"Just waking up. He's growing so big. I guess I'll soon have to invest in a regular cradle for him."

"There's probably not much sense in that until we get settled." She gasped softly when she realized she had voiced her most urgent prayer. Two days ago he had said they would stay together only until they could obtain a divorce in Texas.

"You want to stay married then?" he asked brusquely.

"It would be all right with me. If you want to."

Ross had hoped that she would profess some kind of feeling for him, that she would indicate that the thought of their separating was as bleak to her as it was to him. After what had happened this morning, couldn't she force herself to show some enthusiasm for their staying together? Again she had lit the short fuse of his temper. "Well, from now on we're going to live like a married couple," he stated firmly. He placed his finger beneath her chin and tilted her face up to him. "A husband has rights, you know. Do you understand what I'm telling you?"

"I think so."

Just so there would be no doubt, he slid one arm around her waist and yanked her forward to collide with his chest. At the same time he ground his lips against hers in a searing kiss.

When he released her, she stepped back and covered her breasts with a fluttering hand. "What's the matter?" he asked, instantly contrite over his roughness.

"My heart's beating so fast."

His glazed eyes fastened on her breasts. "Is it?" he asked huskily.

The kiss had been intended to teach her that he was still boss, that out of the benevolence of his heart he was going to keep her around under the condition that she serve as his bed partner. But his composure had been as shattered by the kiss as hers. All he could taste now was her mouth. Her scent assailed him. He could feel her as she felt this morning beneath him, pliant and feminine, accepting all of him.

"Lydia," he murmured gently. He was reaching for her again when he was summoned by a call from outside the wagon. Cursing and frustratedly passing a hand over the fly of his pants, he grabbed his hat and stepped outside.

He told Lydia at breakfast that he had been asked to ride point so he could direct them to the campsite he and Scout had selected. Lydia thought he had more than likely

been asked because of his precision with a gun. The entire
train was still edgy about Luke's murder. She was both
proud that Ross had been chosen to help look after the rest
of them and worried that something would happen to him.

"Will you be all right driving today?" he asked her
from the back of one of his mares, who was prancing and
eager to be off.

"Yes," Lydia said, smiling in answer from her seat on
the wagon. "I asked Anabeth to ride with me. I thought if
she had me to visit with, it might help get her mind off
Luke."

He nodded solemnly. "I tried talking to Bubba when I
went to the corral this morning. The subject of Luke is
closed." He glanced toward the front of the train where the
first wagons were pulling out. "I've got to go."

"I'll see you at sunset."

Her message, spoken with such quiet emphasis, was
clear. Ross's heart expanded in his chest. His eyes wandered leisurely over her face before he doffed the brim of
his hat and rode off in a cloud of dust.

She saw him many times before sunset because he
invented excuses to ride back along the train just to catch
sight of her. People began to comment on how conscien-
tious Mr. Coleman was in his job as vigilante. It gave them
a sense of security to know that a man with his soldiering
experience—because where else could he have acquired
that talent with guns?—was guarding them.

Their confidence was to tax Ross more than he could
have imagined.

That evening he rushed through his chores, returning
to the wagon in record time, washing quickly but thoroughly, humming to himself. When he went in the wagon
to fetch clean clothes, he noticed Lydia had swept it out and
tidied things. It was roomier somehow . . .

Only one bedroll was in evidence. She had combined
the two they had been using to make one, and it was thickly
padded and neatly turned down. There was a bouquet of
wildflowers in a glass of water sitting on the oak chest of
drawers.

She was as nervous as he during supper and seemed in

a hurry to clean up afterward. Lee was fed and sponged down, so he would sleep easier, and then put in his bed. They were sharing one last cup of coffee and giving the sun plenty of time to set so they could go into the wagon when Mr. Grayson approached them.

"Good evening, Mrs. Coleman."

"Good evening, Mr. Grayson."

He marveled over the young woman who now bore little or no resemblance to the dirty creature Ma had brought to Coleman's wagon weeks ago. She was a pretty little thing, if her hair was a bit too free and her eyes a bit too eloquent. Her coloring was remarkable, the likes of which a man couldn't ignore. As was her shape. He had a hard time dragging his eyes off her to speak to her husband.

"Ross, I hate to ask you this, but would you mind patrolling the camp tonight?"

"Patrolling?" he echoed dismally. He wanted to go to bed with Lydia, as soon as it was good and dark.

Grayson cleared his throat and shifted his weight from one foot to the other. "Some of the folks got together and figured they sure would feel safer if someone with your . . . skills . . . was looking out for all of us. They offered to swap off, but I'm afraid if we do that, one of them will accidentally shoot the other. Everybody's edgy about Luke Langston's murderer still being on the loose. Would you mind too terribly much?"

He minded like hell. But how could he say no? "All right. Just for tonight."

Grayson coughed lightly. "Well, they were thinking maybe for a week or so. They've offered to pay you," he rushed to add.

A curse sizzled through Ross's thinned lips and Grayson cast another embarrassed glance in Lydia's direction. "How am I supposed to stay up all night and then ride point every day?"

"Not all night. The others will take turns relieving you after midnight. That'll give you a few hours to sleep."

But no time with my wife, Ross thought.

"Please, Ross. Just until we're out of this area and everyone's nerves calm down a little."

Ross really had no choice but to agree. What excuse could he provide for not wanting to? Certainly not the true one.

The days passed. The train made progress through southern Arkansas. All of them began to relax as they put more distance between the train and the site of Luke's murder. Everyone but Ross, who seemed to grow meaner by the day. Folks began to dread meeting him face-to-face. Invariably they were glowered at by green eyes that now had lines of fatigue and tension radiating from them.

By the end of the sixth day, Ross was at his wit's end. As soon as he put his horses up, he stamped to his wagon and slung open the canvas. He caught an unsuspecting Lydia washing from a basin. Her hair was pinned precariously to the top of her head. Disobedient strands had escaped to lie on her neck and shoulders that were still damp where she had just washed. In her surprise she dropped her washcloth and it splashed in the china bowl. It went unheeded. Her arms fell to her sides. Her unbuttoned chemise barely covered her nipples. Twin half-moons of flesh filled the space between the opening.

Without his uttering a word, Ross's eyes traveled from the base of her throat, where he could see a rapid pulse beating, down to the valley between her breasts, down her stomach to her navel. He stared at the spot for a long, silent moment before he whirled out of the wagon and went striding across the camp toward Grayson's wagon.

"I want to talk to you," he virtually growled to the man.

"Of course, Ross," Grayson said, taking Ross aside to keep Mrs. Grayson from hearing any unfortunate words the man might choose to use.

Ross wasn't good at speeches. He wanted to say, "Look, Grayson, I'm horny as hell and want to tumble my wife, if it's all right with you and everyone else on this goddamn wagon train." But he was no longer a hellion and couldn't talk like one. He forced a modicum of control over himself and said tightly, "I've had it, understand? No more nights away from my . . . family. I haven't had time to piss this week." A man was entitled to one slipup. "I'm tired. The extra money is nice, but . . ." He pulled in an exasperated breath when the vision of Lydia's clean-smelling flesh came back into his mind. "I resign."

"That's fine, Ross. I think everyone's assured that it was an isolated incident and that the rest of us are in no danger."

Ross willed his body to relax. He had counted on an argument. Now that he didn't get one, he was ashamed of the way he had stormed at Grayson.

"All right, then. See you tomorrow."

He walked downstream from where everybody was getting water, shucked off all his clothes, and plunged in.

"Do you think that's what it was? An isolated incident?"

They were in the wagon, having eaten supper, cleaned things away, gotten Lee to sleep, and waited a decent interval to go inside. Now they were passing time until the rest of the camp settled into sleep.

Ross gazed at Lydia as she dragged the brush through her hair. "Yes, I think it was a renegade, long gone by now. I told you that from the first."

Putting her hairbrush aside, she began unlacing her shoes. "Ma and the others seem to have accepted Luke's death. I don't know how anyone gets over losing a child." She was thinking how she would feel should anything happen to Lee. That's why she looked up in speechless shock when Ross said incisively, "You got over losing yours."

She ducked her head and took off her shoes. That hadn't been a child. It had been a lifeless product of shame and abuse. "That was different," she muttered.

"Was it? How?"

"It just was."

"Lydia." He waited until she was looking at him before he spoke again. And when he did it was with a gravity that told her he demanded an answer. "Who was the man?"

Chapter Sixteen

Barefoot now, she walked to where he sat on a stool. As she knelt in front of him, she placed her hands on his thighs, just above his knees, and peered up into his face. Tears made her eyes shine like mellow wine in the dim lantern light.

"He was no one, Ross. No one. Unworthy of even thinking about." She tilted her head to one side as she pleaded with him. Her hair swept across her back to fall in a heavy cascade over one shoulder.

"I hated him. He was cruel. He took pleasure from hurting other people, from hurting me. By leaving him I didn't desert him, I escaped him. To save my life, to save my soul. Believe me, Ross."

She was weeping now, but only from her eyes. Tears rolled down her cheeks in a silver stream, but her voice didn't waver. It was full of supplication.

"He was the only one, Ross, I swear it. The only man to have me. I fought him every time. I was never with him willingly. I didn't want his baby. It was good that it died." Her fingers curled tighter around the outer edges of his thighs. "I wish I had never known him. I wish I could have been pure and new for you."

"Lydia—"

She shook her head, not letting him finish. Now that she had gone this far, she wanted to tell him how she felt. She might never have the courage again.

"You thought I was trash when the Langstons took me in. It's true that's how I had been living, but on the inside I knew I wasn't like that. I wanted to live among decent folks. When you married me, I made up my mind not to dwell on my past. I had been given a new life and was determined to put the old one behind me.

"The times we've been together have nothing to do with what happened to me before. I learned from you that what passes between a man and a woman doesn't have to be shameful and painful and horrible."

His hands came up to frame her face. With his stroking thumbs, he smoothed away the tears. He ran his hand from the crown of her head to her shoulders, loving the feel of her hair against his palm.

"Nothing in my life has been as fine, as good, as the time I've spent with you and Lee. I can't change the past, though I wish I could forget it. But don't hold it against me. Please. I want to be a good mother to Lee. I want to be a good wife to you. I'm ignorant and awkward and have so much to learn. Teach me, Ross. I'm trying hard to forget where I came from. Please, can't you forget it too?"

Who was he, Sonny Clark, to pass judgment on anyone? Hadn't he thought of himself as a victim of his heritage, and forgiven himself of past transgressions on those grounds? If he could absolve himself from guilt using his sordid upbringing as the reason, how could he condemn Lydia? Obviously she had been a victim too. And did he really care anymore what she had been, who had fathered her baby?

With her head now resting on his knee, her hair spilling over his thigh like a skein of knotted silk, he couldn't deny himself loving her because of some muddied principle. What she might have done before he ever met her seemed of little consequence.

Gently he raised her head. Opening his knees wider, he drew her close to him. He laid his thumbs vertically along her windpipe and curved his fingers around her neck to intertwine at her nape. Softly he said, "You're beautiful, Lydia."

She shook her head as much as his strong fingers around her throat would allow. "I'm not."

"You are."

She gloried in the hooded eyes that bathed her face with emerald heat. "Not until I met you."

He urged her toward him as he bent slightly and placed his lips against hers. He kissed her softly with his moustache. His hands fell away from her throat and glanced over her breasts to her sides. His lips roamed her face, dropping light kisses on the tear-damp cheeks, on her eyelids, her nose, her temples, and then back to her mouth. His hands slipped around to the middle of her back.

He applied a constant, gradually increasing pressure, until she was molded against him. "I've dreamed of this all week," he confessed against her lips. "I've wanted you so damn much." He sighed. "From the very beginning I wanted you and hated myself for it. I took all my anger and frustration out on you." That admission cost him dearly. Lydia couldn't even appreciate how far Ross had come to be able to admit such a weakness in himself. None who had witnessed the hot-tempered young gunman drawing on a man for the merest slight, real or imaginary, would recognize this man who now reverently stroked his lover's cheek.

"I thought you hated me," she whispered.

She moved her head from side to side, loving the feel of his mouth against hers. *Ross's mouth*. It was a heady thought that made her stomach quiver and her breath quicken.

"I tried to. I couldn't. I'm tired of punishing both of us."

Then the aggressive side of his nature reasserted itself. His mouth slanted over hers possessively as his hands splayed wide and held her immobile against his chest. Her lips were acquiescent as his tongue pressed between them and caressed the soft, wet lining. She moaned and raised her arms to encircle his neck.

They indulged the desires that had bedeviled them for the past few days. They celebrated each other's mouths, letting their tongues engage in playful combat.

When at last Lydia pulled away and laid her cheek against his chest to regain her breath, she whispered softly, "I never knew people did that with their mouths."

He tilted her chin up and smiled mischievously. "Few people do."

Her heart thumped erratically against his ribs. "Why?"

He shrugged. "Don't know any better, I guess."

"I'm glad you do. Know better, I mean."

He laughed then, a rich, rumbling sound that rolled out of his vibrating chest. "Are you?" She nodded vigorously. "Let's get back to it then," he murmured before pulling her close for another deep, passion-inducing kiss.

Keeping their mouths sealed, he put space between their bodies and let his hands find the buttons on her high-necked bodice. Her response had made him confident. As a youth, he had been too eager to employ finesse. When he had been an outlaw, time hadn't permitted leisure, and it hadn't been necessary, because whores had found his lustiness exciting. Victoria's primness had made him nervous and clumsy. He had been afraid of offending her with every move. But Lydia . . .

When all the buttons were undone, he lowered his mouth to her neck and nibbled it gently as he peeled the dress off her shoulders and down her arms. "You always smell so good." His breath fanned her skin, eliciting that tumbling weightlessness in her stomach.

With her arms free of the sleeves of her dress, she lifted her hands to his head, sank her fingers into the black richness of his hair, and held him close as he continued to nuzzle her.

Raising his head, he looked at her. The lantern had been turned down low to eliminate telltale shadows on the canvas, but it burned brightly enough to cast a golden glow over her skin. The lacy edge of her chemise rode low over the top curves of her breasts. The shadowy cleft between them intrigued him with its texture, which he imagined velvety against a man's fingers, a man's tongue.

His index finger ran along the top of her chemise from one side to the other and back again, slowly, while his eyes tracked its progress. When he lifted his eyes to her melting gaze, he smiled his pleasure in her. He unbuttoned his shirt and pulled it off. His belt came next and then he unbuttoned his pants. She remained entranced and looked at nothing save his eyes. Her own were wide and darkly amber.

"Do I frighten you, Lydia?"

She shook her head. "No. At one time, yes. No longer."

"Well, you frightened me too." He laughed softly.

"I?" It was incomprehensible that he could be frightened of anything.

"Didn't you realize how hard it was for me to spend the night in here with you, especially when you were nursing Lee, and not touch you?"

"Do you still want to touch me?"

He squeezed his eyes shut as though in pain. "Very much."

Taking his hand in hers, she guided it to her breast and pressed. "Like this?"

"God, yes." He groaned. He brought his other hand up to join the first. He massaged the soft globes lovingly, lifting, pushing them together, then letting their plumpness settle in his palms. She sighed his name when his fingers circled her nipples. With gentle fingertips he explored and implored until they budded to hard contraction.

"You opened my chemise that first night," she whispered dazedly.

Incredulous green eyes sprang up to meet hers. "I was drunk," he said hoarsely.

"Oh," she replied, ducking her head in shame. By his expression she knew she had said something terribly wrong. "I'm sorry. I don't know about these things. I thought you would like—"

"I would, but . . ." Hell, if his wife was one of the few on the whole damn continent who didn't demurely shrink from her husband's caress, he would be a sap to tell her.

He cursed the tiny buttons as his fingers grappled with them. After a frustrating moment, she gently closed her hands over his and moved them aside. Her movements were slow and unconsciously seductive as she released the buttons one by one.

Only a ribbon of skin showed at first, then the inside curves of her breasts, finally the shallow groove that divided her stomach. She leaned forward, the top of her head almost touching his chin, as she pulled the chemise off. Her hair fell forward, so that when she straightened, it covered her bewitchingly.

There was a roaring in Ross's ears that hadn't been there since he had taken his first woman so many years ago. He had been no more than a boy, yet he could remember the dryness in his mouth, the sweat lubricating his palms and beading his upper lip, the drumming of his heart. He felt that way now.

He brushed aside her hair and gazed at her breasts. They were full, coral tipped, beautifully shaped, high, rounded, maternal, sexy. The breasts of a madonna—and of a mistress. He remembered the first night he saw her, saw those milk-laden breasts and his son's avid mouth sucking on the nipples. A new surge of blood filled his manhood and he grew hard to the point of pain.

He put his hand on her and it burned with a thousand sensations that shot up his arm and straight into his heart. Beguiled, he caressed the soft flesh, loving the way it conformed to the shape of his hand and the movement of his fingers. His skin looked dark against its creamy whiteness.

He fanned the nipple lightly and it pearled temptingly; the dusky areola surrounding it wrinkled sweetly. Whispering a curse, he folded his hand around her breast and lowered his head.

First Lydia felt the silky-scratchy touch of his moustache, then the moist kiss. She placed her hands on his cheeks and held him fast. Her head fell back. His tongue rolled over the bead of rosy flesh, again and again, bathing it with the dew of his mouth. Then he trapped her in the scalding, wet vise of his mouth and sucked lightly.

Gasping with surprised delight, she inched closer, instinctively aligning her body to his. A serrated cry escaped his lips. His arms formed a brace across the small of her back and she arched backward over it. He devoured her sweetly, savoring every morsel of flesh he had dreamed of tasting for weeks. He sponged her nipples with his tongue, dried them with his moustache. His mouth was hot and fervent when he drew her between his lips, tugging rhythmically.

It was a carnal rhythm and they were both responding to the beat. Ross knew that if he didn't curb his desire now, he would take her savagely again. He lifted her up and cradled her head beneath his chin, hugging her damp breasts against his naked chest.

"Lydia, Lydia," he repeated over and over as he rocked her against him until they had both quieted. He didn't want it to be quick and rough this time, but slow, lingering.

She pushed away from him and ran her hands over his hairy chest. "This tickles," she said, wrinkling her nose comically.

"I'm sorry. I'll shave it."

"No!" she said. Her earnestness made him laugh, but he sobered when she quietly observed, "You've got so many scars." She touched the puckered scar above his left breast. Then her fingertips wandered over him to find every other nick and scar on his chest and shoulders.

"I'm afraid so."

"The war?"

He lifted her hand away and kissed the back of her fingers. "Some of them, yes." He said it in the voice she knew meant he wasn't going to say any more. He had been idly studying how her breasts swayed when she made the slightest movement and how strands of hair that fell over her shoulders flirted with her nipples. Lydia seemed not the least shy at his absorption, but was almost childlike in her curiosity about him.

"Let's go to bed," he said huskily.

Ross had already made up his mind that he wasn't going to sleep in his breeches. And he sure as hell wasn't going to drag out one of those ridiculous nightshirts Victoria had insisted he wear in their bed. He was going to sleep the way God created him and if Lydia didn't like it . . . Well, she would just have to like it. He pulled off his boots and socks and stepped out of his pants, tossing them to the other side of the wagon.

Lydia scooted to the bedroll and remained motionless when he blew out the flame of the lantern, plunging the wagon into darkness. Her ears were now trained to follow his movements and she knew that when he lay down beside her he would be naked.

She was both thrilled and terrified at the thought. Clancey had obscenely exposed himself to her through the fly of his pants, but she had never seen a grown man totally naked before. Of course Ross was beautiful from the waist up. She couldn't imagine the rest of him being ugly. Still, she was stiff and afraid when he lay down beside her.

Ross countenanced no resistance when he pulled her to him. His arms went around her tightly as he found her mouth in the darkness and captured it with his. Under the expertise of his kiss, Lydia felt her fear dissipating.

Her bare feet touched his legs, and that wasn't so awful. Her breasts were cushioned against the furred wall of his chest and the contact was thrilling. Ross naked was still Ross. She knew she had nothing to fear from him.

Her arms went around him and smoothed over the rippling muscles of his back. She let her hands slide past his waist and then touched what she had admired that morning at the river. Her palms coasted past the indentation at the small of his back and over the taut curves of his buttocks.

"Godamighty," he groaned as he eased her to her back. He was grateful for the moonlight that aided him in untying the waistband of her petticoat and pantalets. Bunching the material in one fist, he pushed down dress and underthings all at one time to form a bundle of calico and linen at the foot of their bed.

Then his eyes wandered up, admiring the small feet and trim ankles, the shape of her calves, the slender columns of her thighs. His breath rushed in on a sharp inhalation when he saw the nest of tawny curls. The shadowy delta defined womanhood, as did the gentle roundness of her hips, the slope of her belly, and the perfection of her breasts. Her beauty captivated him and he stared at her for long, ponderous moments, drinking it in.

Since puberty Lydia had never been completely naked in front of anyone, not even her modest mother. Ross was so engrossed, it alarmed her. Didn't she look like other women? Was she horribly ugly and didn't even know it? Was something wrong with her? "Ross?" she questioned shakily and covered her femininity with a shielding hand.

He shook himself out of his trance and lay beside her, pressing his rough body to the silkiness of hers to feel the sheer eroticism of the contrast. "My God," he sighed, resting his head on her breasts. Several minutes ticked by while he held her, just held her, disbelieving that such a gift had been granted him. That he had ever thought her coarse and common was inconceivable to him now. She was rare and beautiful . . . and his.

He propped himself up and leaned down to kiss her mouth. He barely let his tongue enter the sweet recess, but twirled it lazily against the lining of her lips. Lydia put her hand on his head, matching his touch for lightness.

Cupping her breast with his hand, he bent down and brought it to his mouth. He kissed the warm fullness in ever-closing circles that drew his mouth closer to the peak. He caressed her nipple wih a circular motion of his lips until it was a perfect bud of arousal. Then he drew back slightly and laved it with his tongue.

Lydia shuddered and lifted herself off the pallet before falling back restlessly. Deep inside her, between her thighs, she felt that familiar stirring, that craving for something undefined and unknown. With such a heralding as this breathless anticipation, the culmination couldn't be less than splendored.

His hand was at her waist, and he squeezed her lightly before sliding his palm down the curve of her hip to her thigh. Her skin was like warm satin. Caressing it was the same as being caressed. His fingers stroked up her thigh, and he paused but a heartbeat before he let them feather over the luxuriant tangle of tawny hair.

He heard no objection, only a soft moan from Lydia's lips. Tentatively he pressured her thighs to part and wedged his hand between them. Pliant flesh, warm and wet, enclosed his fingers.

"Lydia." He grated her name between his teeth as he acquainted himself with the mystery of her.

"Ross!" she cried sharply.

Immediately he withdrew his hand and laid it on her knee. "I'm sorry. I'll stop. I only wanted to touch you."

"Do you have to?" she asked timorously.

"No," he whispered soothingly. "I don't have to. I'll never touch you that way again if you—"

"No," she said a bit hysterically. "I meant, do you have to stop?"

His rasping curse singed her lips a moment before he kissed her. His hand was bolder now, but no less gentle as it fondled. Two of his fingers found the snug cleft and slipped into its liquid embrace. His thumb massaged the tiny, magical hood.

He watched her face take on that expression of sublimity he had seen once before when she was nursing Lee. He had coveted that expression and wanted it to be of his making. Now he watched her nipples tighten, her stomach convulse, her breathing quicken, and he nearly burst with his own desire that was now demanding release.

He covered her, replacing his fingers with his sex, pressing forward until he was swallowed by her body. For moments he lay perfectly still, panting into her neck, wrapped tightly inside her. Then he raised his head and looked into her eyes.

"I've never felt this way before, Ross. Is this the way it's supposed to be?" she whispered, running her fingertip over his moustache.

He closed his eyes and shook his head, willing himself not to move yet, not to rush it. "No. It's not supposed to be this good."

Then his control scattered and his hips began to pump against hers. He practiced every technique he had ever heard of, whether in brothel parlors or around a campfire. He withdrew until he was barely inside her, then delved deeply to meld them together. He stroked the walls of her body, rapidly, slowly, in tempos that sent her spirit spiraling above her.

He teased the tips of her breasts with his chest, stroked her belly with undulations of his, caressed her thighs with strong hands. He was lost in her womanhood, in her sweetness, and he never wanted to be found.

Her face was rapt with supreme pleasure and that served to intensify his. When the tumult came, he felt her own shuddering response beneath him. They clung together tightly as a nameless, benevolent god of love hurled them into the skies and then let them coast gently back to earth.

Lydia passively trailed her fingers up and down his sweat-sheened back as they lay exhausted in each other's arms. Ross finally recovered himself, lifted himself away from her, and turned onto his back, taking in great gulps of air.

When he didn't move for a long time, Lydia put her hand on his stomach beneath his rib cage and asked hesitantly, "Are you all right, Ross?"

He garnered enough strength to chuckle. "Lydia, how can you be both so expert and so innocent?" He rolled to his side and looked at her tenderly. Curly strands of hair clung damply to her cheeks. Her skin was glowing with the rosiness of sexual satisfaction. Her eyes were limpid and drowsy as she smiled at him self-consciously. *God, she's beautiful,* he thought. He gathered her close, despite the warm night. "Let's sleep now."

She snuggled against him, loving the protective feel of his large body. He covered her breast with his hand and she placed hers in the hollow of his waist. As they drifted off to sleep, they were both smiling.

Ross awoke with uncharacteristic lethargy. He never remembered having a better night's sleep. Before he even opened his eyes, he covered his face with Lydia's hair and breathed deeply of its scent. She was still asleep. He eased up, hoping not to awaken her. He wanted to study what darkness had screened from him the night before.

He let his eyes wander at will over her form. Her skin was as luscious to look at as it was to taste. The taste of it lingered on his tongue. There was a light dusting of freckles across her cheekbones. He smiled, thinking they made her look incredibly young. But the uptilted eyes, with their sweeping, thick lashes that now lay like ruffled fans on her cheeks, were a woman's eyes. Multifaceted, bright with tears one moment, smoky with passion the next. They bespoke so much, promised much, and arousal sparked his dormant manhood again as he remembered the sensuous way they had looked at him.

Her lips were slightly parted. At that moment he wanted nothing more than to drag his tongue over them, to penetrate them. She had the sweetest mouth. And she knew how to kiss.

What else did she know?

A frown wrinkled his eyebrows and his moustache twitched with irritation. Why the hell did he keep thinking about it? She seemed so innocent, but then . . .

Last night had been a man's sexual dream come true. She hadn't been faking. He had heard that some women could experience that little death the way men did. Prostitutes had pretended it because they thought he expected them to. He doubted Victoria had ever heard of such a thing. If she had, she would have been aghast.

Victoria. Memories of her bothered him most of all. He missed her. He loved her still. But how could he still love her and enjoy Lydia's body with such abandon? Was it possible to love one woman and be obsessed with another? He hated the comparisons his mind forced on him.

While Victoria's body had been cool alabaster, Lydia's was ivory infused with molten gold. Victoria had been modest sometimes to the point of aggravating him. She had never let him see her completely naked. Lydia was lying naked with him now. Beautifully naked. She had gone beyond immodesty. She had been giving, generous with herself, allowing him unlimited access, anything he wanted to do. Victoria would have fainted had he moved inside her the way he had Lydia. She would have lain still and accepted him, but afterward she would have left the bed to wash herself, as though what he had left behind was nasty.

Lydia had clung to him, milking him with her body, moving with him, making those baritone musical sounds deep in her throat that seemed to purr through his body and stroke his manhood. When it was over, she had covered her belly with both hands and hugged herself, as though treasuring that essence of him that had become a part of her.

Thinking about it now brought him erect. He cursed himself and her. Because while he adored her sensual nature, it haunted him. How had she come about having those tendencies, that talent for loving which had taken him into a realm of sexuality that even he, with all his escapades, hadn't known existed?

He studied her breasts. Even in repose her nipples were slightly flared. Her stomach rose and fell gently with each breath and he wanted to plant his mouth on it, to dip his tongue into her navel. He wanted to again trail his fingers through that silky delta of hair.

Who are you, Lydia—

He didn't even know her last name.

But she didn't know his either.

He gazed at her loveliness in the early morning light and knew he could forgive her her past as she had asked him to. If only she wasn't lying to him about forgetting it. If he ever found out that she had lied to him about putting it behind her as he had his, he would never forgive her.

He didn't allow himself to touch her, or he couldn't have made himself leave. He pulled on his pants and crept outside.

Minutes later Lydia awoke and reached for Ross. The bed beside her was empty and she heard him moving around outside. Rising, she checked on Lee, who was still sleeping, and began to wash from the bowl on the chest. She dabbed the cool, damp cloth over her femininity. Her cheeks flamed as she remembered the way Ross had touched her, the way she had reacted to his touch.

Would he think badly of her?

What had happened to her? For one frightening moment, she had thought she was dying, but at the same time, she had never felt more alive. Joy had gushed over her like a waterfall. The pleasure had been so intense, she hadn't thought her body could contain it. Jealously she had clutched at it to remain. She had closed her limbs around Ross, writhing to take as much of him inside her as possible.

Covering her face with both hands, she breathed deeply, praying she hadn't done something married ladies shouldn't.

She pinned her hair away from face, but left it to riot down her back. Hadn't Ross told her it was pretty, that she was beautiful? When she was dressed, she stepped outside the wagon. Ross wasn't in sight and she was glad. She wasn't ready to meet him face-to-face yet, with last night now an embarrassment.

He came up behind her as she was pouring a cup of coffee. "Good morning," he said softly.

She turned slowly and warily raised her eyes to look at him. Her breath stumbled through her throat when she saw him in the new sunlight. He was the most handsome man she had ever seen, his hair glistening with the dunking he had just given it after his shave. The light twinkling in his eyes and the tender curve of his smile told her that everything was all right. He didn't hold last night's wanton behavior against her. She was certain now that she had only done what wives were supposed to do with their husbands. She had performed as Ross had expected her to. Her relief was vast.

"Good morning." She felt like laughing.

"For me?" He nodded toward the coffee.

Wordlessly, she extended the cup to him and smiled, her face rivaling the sun for radiance. He took the coffee from her, but at the same time curled his free hand around the back of her neck and pulled her up to meet his descending mouth.

He was still kissing her when Ma Langston came to the wagon a few minutes later carrying the pail of milk for Lee. She watched them for a moment, beaming like a proud parent, then cleared her throat loudly.

"Another false lead," Howard Majors said as he took off his hat and hung it on the rack in his Baltimore hotel room.

"You almost sound disappointed that the girl in the morgue wasn't my daughter, Majors. I'm sorry to have wasted your time."

"Christ," Majors muttered disgustedly to himself and did something he rarely did in the middle of the morning. He poured himself a generous drink.

Vance Gentry was beginning to wear on his nerves. He could almost empathize with the young couple who had sneaked away from him. Maybe Sonny Clark hadn't kidnapped his own wife or coerced her into stealing the jewelry. Maybe she had been all too willing to leave her home in order to get away from this disagreeable tyrant.

For the week it had taken them to reach Baltimore, Gentry had been truculent, but Majors had tolerated his mood and understood it. After all, the man had believed that the girl found murdered in that hotel room near the waterfront would turn out to be his daughter. Majors had doubted it all along, even though both physical descriptions had fit Clark and Victoria Gentry.

The murder didn't sound like something Clark would do. He was whiplash-fast with a gun, and violent when backed into a corner, afraid of nothing, but he never had been a ruthless killer, especially to the point of stabbing a woman long after she was dead. That didn't fit Clark's clean, quick eruptions of violence at all.

Majors had put up with Gentry's belligerence out of deference. Now he was good and sick of it. "It wasn't a waste of my time, Mr. Gentry," he said with more diplomacy than he felt the man deserved.

"No, just a waste of my money."

"At least now we know your daughter could still be alive."

"Then where the hell is she?"

"I don't know."

"You don't know." Gentry was so furious that his white hair seemed about to pop out of his scalp as he whirled on the detective. "Goddammit, man, what do you think I'm paying you for? I'm paying you to track down my daughter and that outlaw husband of hers."

Majors counted slowly to ten, reminding himself that after this case was laid to rest, he was facing retirement. "You can fire me at any time, Mr. Gentry. I'll still go on looking for Sonny Clark now that I know he's alive. He's wanted for five counts of murder that we know of, bank robberies in several states. The list of his crimes is as long as my arm. And even though he hasn't ridden with them in several years, he might bargain for his life and help us find the James brothers. So, do you want me to work with you, or do you want to go it alone?"

Gentry rocked on the balls of his feet, angry but subdued. His anger wasn't directed so much toward the Pinkerton detective as it was at the situation. He despised not being in absolute control, but he knew that the detective had a network of informants and communication that he couldn't begin to duplicate even if he could afford to pay for it. "I see no need to separate now."

"Very well, then, I'll politely ask you as a gentleman not to insult me with any more snide remarks. Of course I was glad to know that that cadaver wasn't your daughter's body." He tossed down another drink and passed the bottle to Gentry, silently stating that if the man wanted one, he could damn well pour it himself.

Gentry accepted the rebuke and after pouring his drink asked, "What now?"

"Back to the office in Knoxville, I suppose. We start at square one again, putting out feelers and seeing what turns up."

Gentry swallowed his whiskey in one gulp. It burned no more than the rage in the pit of his stomach. When he did get his hands on Ross Coleman, or whatever the hell his name was, to hell with the Pinkerton Agency, the governments of several states, and anybody else who wanted him taken alive.

He was going to kill the bastard.

The days passed slowly for Lydia and Ross because they couldn't wait for the evenings. Ross was constantly busy with his horses or with someone else's, or hunting, or some other occupation that prevented him from driving his own team. And it was just as well. On the days he sat near her during the long hours, he was in misery. Each brush of his arm against her, each touch of her hand on his sleeve, each glance, each stolen kiss, only made him long for sundown.

The evenings belonged to them. They visited with other members of the train, but as soon as decently possible they went into the wagon and let its privacy embrace them as they embraced each other. Each night their intimacy was enhanced a further degree. They became less shy of their emotions, freer with their shows of affection.

Lydia didn't think she could be happier. She didn't put

a label on what she felt for Ross. She only knew that she would never be whole again without him. They didn't communicate their feelings verbally, but she didn't know enough to miss that particular intimacy. The way he looked at her, the way he touched her, told her all she wanted to know.

As usual, she was in a haze of contentment one afternoon as she washed, preparing for Ross's return to the wagon in time for supper. She had beans boiling over the fire and cornbread batter ready to fry. Moses had picked blackberries that day and shared them with her for Ross's dessert.

When the knock came from outside the wagon, she finished buttoning up her dress, made one last passing sweep of her hand over her hair, and pushed aside the canvas flaps.

She recoiled in horror as she looked into the mean, ugly visage of her stepbrother, Clancey Russell.

Chapter Seventeen

*L*ydia opened her mouth to scream, but terror had frozen her voice. That gave Clancey the time he needed to step into the wagon and clamp his hand over her mouth and against her teeth.

"Now, now, you ain't gonna go and start a ruckus, are ya, Miz Coleman?" He was waving a bowie knife just beneath her nose. "'Cause if you do, whoever comes through that openin' first is gonna get this right through the gizzard. And it just might be that husband of yours."

Lydia's eyes went wide over the ridge of his hand and he cackled. "I see that got your attention."

Gradually he lowered his hand, though he didn't replace the knife in its scabbard. Lydia was too stunned to move. He was the fiend of her nightmares embodied, a ghoul resurrected from the dead. The wound on his head had left a hideous scar that made him even more repulsive to look at. He stank. She wondered how she had lived with him for ten years, much less . . .

She swallowed the scalding bile that filled her mouth. How could he still be alive? How? She had seen him fall against that rock, heard the crack of his skull, seen the blood.

"Thought I was dead, didn't ya?" He leered, reading her thoughts. "You fought me real good when I caught up with you just this side of Knoxville. Like a she-wildcat you kicked and clawed till I lost my balance and fell down. I like spirit in a woman. As you no doubt recollect." His reptilian eyes slithered down her lecherously and she shivered with loathing and fear.

"But I'm mad as hell at you, little sister, for making me fall against that rock and bust my head open. Hurt like hell for weeks, made my eyes all blurry. But I can see clear now. Yes, sirree. I can see clear." His eyes scaled her once again. "And ain't you somethin' to look at all gussied up like this."

"If my husband finds you here, he'll kill you," she said with far more bravado than she felt. Inside she was quaking with fear. Fear that Clancey would even now get his revenge for her fleeing and almost killing him, and an even greater fear that Ross would discover what she had been to this man. The thought sickened her.

"*Your* husband, huh? Did you know he has another wife?" he asked slyly. "A rich one?"

"Victoria? She died."

"Died?" he repeated stupidly. Clancey was nonplussed for a moment, then he shifted his shoulders back arrogantly. "Don't see that that makes much difference to my plans."

"Well, if your plan was to tell me my husband was a bigamist, you've wasted your time. You can leave now."

"Not so fast," Clancey said silkily. "We got a lot of visitin' to catch up on." His eyes wandered around the wagon, nodding his approval. When he spotted the crate where Lee was sleeping, he stepped over to it and looked down. Lydia, free to bolt out of the wagon, didn't dare. She couldn't leave Lee alone with Clancey and she didn't want to alert anyone that he was here for fear he would tell them who he was.

"This my kid?" he asked, pointing the knife down at Lee.

"No!" she cried softly and shoved the man out of the way, putting herself between him and the child. "Your baby was born dead. This is Ross's baby. Victoria died birthing him."

Clancey scratched his thick, whiskered neck with the blade of the knife as he studied Lee. He laughed chillingly. "Likely story."

"It's true!" Lydia cried, sensing his suspicion. "The baby you got on me was dead when I delivered it in the woods. It was buried."

Clancey shrugged. "It don't much matter. This is a right smart cute kid. I'd just as soon have this 'un. 'Course if he ain't mine, I don't rightly care if he's took good care of or not."

Lydia's heart stopped only to start banging against the cage of her ribs. Her throat went dry. "What do you want?"

Clancey laughed. "Now you're gettin' neighborly. I always said you wasn't no dumb bunny. Always did say that."

Lydia was frantic, terrified of what the man might do, and terrified that Ross would return and find him there. It was time for him to come back to camp. The others were at their fires cooking supper. Would she be missed? Would someone come looking for her? Would Ross come back and find her here with Clancey?

No! God, please, no.

"What do you want?" she repeated.

"You stepped up in the world, little sister. Sure enough you did. Now I was thinkin' you could give your poor ol' stepbrother a boost up, so to speak." His beady eyes bored into her as he said quietly, "By turnin' over to me them jewels your husband stole from his first wife's pa."

Lydia stared at him blankly. "What are you talking about?" she asked in a thready voice. "What jewels? There are no jewels, and Ross is not a thief."

Clancey propped himself against a crate and fished in

the front of his shirt for the wanted poster he had been carrying for almost two months, the one that had cost the Owentown whore her life. "Clap your eyes on that," he said, shaking out the creases that had almost worn the paper through. "This fine, upstandin' husband you're puttin' so much stock in ain't the saint you believe."

Lydia stared at the sketch and compared it to her husband's face. Younger, longer hair, no moustache, but undeniably Ross Coleman's eyes and brows and jaw. Sonny Clark. She read the list of crimes he had allegedly committed and the blood drained from her head. She felt dizzy and gripped the edge of the chest to keep from fainting.

She wasn't sure, but the numeral five followed by the three zeros must represent a sizable amount of money offered as a reward to the person knowing Sonny Clark's whereabouts.

She lifted defeated eyes to Clancey. "You're going to turn him in for the money."

He scratched his greasy hair. "I ain't a greedy man. I figure them jewels must be worth more than that five thousand, and there would be no involvin' the law, if ya take my meanin'. So what I figured is that you could turn over that jewelry to me and I'd be on my way. We'd part friends and I'd leave your husband and the young'un in peace."

Lydia spread her arms wide. "But there aren't any jewels. I told you I don't know what you're talking about."

He grabbed her then and hauled her up to him, thrusting his face into hers. "I tell you there is, girlie. I seen his dadddy-in-law talkin' to some fancy gentleman what looked like the law to me. They're after your husband for kidnappin' his own wife and takin' the jewelry to boot."

"Ross wouldn't—"

Clancey shook her hard. "Stop sayin' that. He's a killer, ain't he?"

Lydia tried to think. She couldn't. Ross a killer? The way he handled guns. But a killer? Murder. Bank robbery. Train robbery. It wasn't possible, and yet the poster said it was. "There are no jewels that I know about. Ross loved his wife. They were going to Texas to start their own stud farm. He didn't kidnap her."

"Well, that's what her daddy thinks. And he's just hankerin' to hear what happened to 'em. And I'll see that he knows, unless you find that jewelry and turn it over to me." He pinched the fleshy part of her arm. "You ain't lyin' to ol' Clancey, are ya, gal? 'Bout them jewels."

"No," she said, and he knew she was telling the truth. His hands around her arms relaxed but slightly. "If there is any jewelry here, I don't know where it is."

"It'd be in your best interest to find it."

"Ross got rid of Victoria's things when he married me. I think he buried them or gave them away. I don't know. There would be no way to track it down now. Besides, I can't steal from my own husband!" she exclaimed.

"You rather him end up like that towheaded young'un I had to kill? Huh? He was a friend of yours, weren't he?"

Lydia went completely still and white. "Luke?" she gasped. "You killed Luke?"

"Was that his name? We didn't get acquainted 'fore he went chargin' toward the camp, gonna tell somebody 'bout my trailin' y'all. I had to stop him, didn't I? And stop him I did." He chuckled maniacally.

Lydia covered her mouth as it filled with bile once again. Luke Langston had died because of her. After he had found her in the woods and seen to it that she was nursed back to health, the boy had died senselessly.

"I'd hate to have to do somethin' so messy again. I truly would, but if that kid there ain't mine, as you say . . ." He trailed off threateningly, fingering the blade of the knife as he looked at Lee, who had awakened and was happily gurgling and thrashing his limbs. "And if I turned your husband over to the law, well, then that'd only leave you and me again. Not that that'd be too bad." He ran the evil tip of the knife down her breast and circled the nipple tauntingly.

With misplaced bravery, she swatted his hand away. "I . . . I'll look for the jewelry, but I don't think I'll find anything. If I don't, you'll leave us alone, won't you?"

"You look real hard, little sister. 'Cause if you can't find nothin', then I guess I'll have to get me some cash somewheres else, like from the law when I tell 'em I know where Sonny Clark is." He bent toward her and breathed his fetid breath hotly over her face. "He as good at humpin' you as I am? Huh, little sister?"

"Stop calling me that! I'm not your sister."

"No, I reckon you're not," he said, scratching his stubbled chin. "Maybe a common-law wife, though." She paled considerably, and he let go with that repugnant laughter again. "I ain't thinkin' 'bout that now, though. I got to look after my future." He sheathed his knife and stepped toward the opening of the wagon. "I'll be comin' to see you fairly often. You got your work to do." He looked once again toward Lee. "Sure is a cute young'un. Shame if somethin' bad was to happen to him."

Then he was gone.

Lydia collapsed to the floor of the wagon, her muscles finally giving way to the debilitating shock she had sustained at seeing Clancey alive and back to make her life a hell on earth.

She crawled to the bedroll and lay down, bringing her knees up to her chest protectively, the way she had done after the times Clancey had brutally assaulted her. And now, as then, she wept, for he was violating her just as thoroughly this time. He was violating the new life she had made with Ross. He had soiled her on the inside before she even knew what loving could be about. He had tainted her. Because of his vileness, she had felt herself unworthy until Ross had made her feel clean and valuable as a human being.

Now Clancey Russell was going to destroy her life again.

"Lydia?"

She heard Ross calling her from outside and hurriedly wiped away her tears. He mustn't know. If at all possible she must keep him from finding out. He would despise her. It would make him sick to learn that he had turned the care of his son over to a woman who had been intimate with someone like Clancey. Not to mention the revulsion he would feel at having been with her himself. She would do everything possible to keep him from finding out.

He parted the flaps of canvas and peered inside. "Lydia, what—" He saw her lying on the pallet and was immediately concerned. "What's wrong?" He leaped inside and knelt down beside her, taking her hand and pressing it tightly.

He was beautiful to her, even with his clothes dusty from the trail, with his hair mashed down from wearing his hat all day, even with the red stripe the hatband had made across his forehead, he was beautiful and she loved him.

She loved him. The emotion washed over her, filled her, flowed into the outer extremities of her body. Even if he had been a killer, an armed robber, no matter what he had done or what his real name was, she loved him. He must never know about Clancey. Never.

He saw the tears standing in her eyes and swallowed with difficulty. A fear he couldn't have imagined before gripped him. "Lydia, are you sick?"

She shook her head vehemently, and pressed his hand against her cheek. "I'm not feeling too well, but I'm not sick. Just tired, I think."

He was visibly relieved. His shoulders relaxed as he released a pent-up breath. "Everyone deserves a nap now and then." He touched her throat and felt the pulse pounding there. "You're sure you're all right."

"Yes, yes," she said, sitting up. "I'm fine now. I'll just feed Lee and then I'll get supper—"

"Hold on," he said, laughing and placing restraining hands on her shoulders. "Before I think about supper, I'd like to sample something I've been thinking about all day." With her chin lightly pinched between his thumb and forefinger, he lifted her mouth to his. He applied gentle pressure at first, then opened his lips and claimed hers with that sweet suction that was uniquely his.

Lydia, feeling sullied by Clancey's presence, freed her mouth and pulled away. She considered her stepbrother a disease that had infected her for ten years and she didn't want Ross to catch it. "I think the beans are burning." Before he could stop her, she left the wagon.

Her mood was such for the rest of the evening. Ross couldn't figure it out. She was nervous, jumping at the least little sound. Usually she was talkative. Tonight he couldn't coax a complete sentence out of her. She was even cross with Marynell and Atlanta, who came by after supper offering to babysit Lee so she and Ross could take a walk together.

He rose from his stool expectantly. The last time they had taken a walk after sundown, they had gone far enough away from camp to make love in a field of clover.

As they had rolled in the sweet-smelling pasture, kissing madly, he had fumbled with her bloomers beneath her skirt. She hadn't objected to his fondling hands, but had been dismayed when, still clothed, he had rolled her atop him.

Exclaiming his name, she asked, "What are you doing?"

"Can't you tell?" he asked devilishly as he molded his hands over her bottom and pulled her over him.

She gasped with delight as he speared into her, touching her in a new way and making her senses sing. She looked so maidenly with her skirt spread out in a circle around her as she straddled him. But there was nothing demure about the sexy quality in her eyes when her body's instincts dictated that she rock above him.

Ross had stroked her thighs, up, up, to the place where their bodies were joined. Watching as her head went back and her hair tumbled down her back, he drew his thumbs through the tuft of hair to the very apex of her body and ever so gently massaged the key that unlocked all her womanliness. The pads of his thumbs seductively worried that enchanted kernel and he felt her body closing around him like a squeezing silken fist.

She cried his name to the heavens and fell forward, bracing herself above him with her arms. He pulled the shirtwaist from the waistband of her skirt, shoved it up and opened her camisole. He kissed her breasts, tracing the shape of her nipples with his tongue. Such tenderness was contrary to the violent explosion in their loins.

Long afterward, she had lain like a beautiful ragdoll draped over his chest. He had smiled up at the sky, breathing in the scent of clover, of her, of him, of a summer evening, and realized that he had never known such peace and fulfillment and happiness in his life. His arms had folded over her back and he held her close. He had this woman to thank for that happiness.

So when the Langston girls mentioned their taking a walk, Ross's pulse quickened and his body reacted in the most profound way.

Lydia squelched both the suggestion and his rising desire with a terse "I don't want anyone watching Lee but me." They looked at her with peculiar expressions. "He's been cross all day. I think he might have a stomachache."

That night, she went to bed before Ross came in. He knew she wasn't asleep, though she pretended to be. He cursed women in general as he lay down beside her. What the hell was the matter with her?

Then he knew a moment of guilt. Her monthlies. By God, he had almost forgotten that Victoria would go to bed for several days at that time and here Lydia had been driving the wagon all day, taking care of Lee, cooking over a hot fire.

He turned to her. "Lydia?"

She lay facing away from him, mentally reliving her encounter with Clancey and trying to suppress the fear that was twisting her insides. "Yes?" She wasn't fit to be his wife. She had been Clancey's whore. Not willingly, but his whore just the same. A sob escaped her lips.

Ross heard it and turned her to him, not heeding her momentary resistance. He pressed her face into his chest and smoothed her hair. "Go to sleep," he whispered, touching a soft kiss to her temple. He no longer resented the tenderness she inspired in him. Its source was a part of himself he didn't know. He couldn't control it, so he gave in to it. He still loved Victoria and always would, but she was dead and he was alive and a civilized man needed a companion. "You'll feel better in the morning."

Ross was the first to fall asleep. Lydia lay there, loving him, listening to the steady beating of his heart, and wondering how she was going to escape Clancey this time.

*   *   *

She began to relax somewhat after the third day when he didn't appear again. Maybe he had only been toying with her to frighten her. Maybe something had happened to him. Maybe—

She searched the wagon just the same.

"I'm still not feeling too well," she lied to Ross that next morning after Clancey's appearance. "Do you think Bubba would mind driving for me today? I think I'll stay in the back with Lee."

Ross peered at her closely, but she wouldn't meet his eyes. Was she truly ill and wouldn't tell him? He hadn't made love to her, guessing correctly it wouldn't be welcomed. Was she about to run away from him? A million possibilities paraded through his mind and he couldn't tolerate any of them. "Fine," he said tightly and stalked away.

Lydia knew she was testing his temper, but she couldn't help it. She was fighting for her life, and for his and Lee's.

That day she looked through every packing crate, every drawer in the chest, any place where Ross or Victoria could have hidden jewelry. She didn't think Ross knew anything about it, though he had hidden money in the wagon. She uncovered it in a china sugar bowl that had been packed away in a nest of newspaper. But no jewelry.

Clancey must be wrong. But if she couldn't produce what he was determined to have, then what? What would he do? Turn Ross in? Harm Lee? Tell Ross that she was his common-law wife?

She found out soon enough.

On the fourth day, while she was bending over their cookfire, she looked up to see him standing inches from her. She didn't know where he had come from. He had simply materialized out of nowhere.

"Find it?" he asked.

"No. There's nothing. I looked."

"Don't go feedin' me that cock-and-bull story. It's there, I tell ya."

"It isn't, Clancey," she stressed, glancing around nervously. What if anyone saw her talking to him? Everyone was going about their business as though this were any other evening and not the one when her world was going to come to an end—again. "I tell you I looked."

"Everywhere?"

"Yes," she said earnestly.

He scratched his crotch. "Well, then, I reckon I'll have to mosey into the next town and alert the sheriff that this here wagon train's shelterin' a wanted man. It'll create quite a stir, I 'magine." He took two ambling steps away before she stopped him with a sharp "No, wait!" He turned around and nailed her to the ground with the twin beads of his eyes.

She wrung her hands and licked her lips. "I . . . Maybe there are places I haven't looked. It's not easy."

"I didn't say it was gonna be easy. I just told you to do it or else."

"Give me a few more days, Clancey, please."

He came around the fire and started toward her with predatory footsteps. "And for me being kindhearted, what're you aimin' to give me? Hmm?"

She backed away from him. He stalked her. "Ain't had time to get into a town. Understand? I've had a powerful itch for a woman for days and—"

"You'd better have a goddamn good reason for backing my wife into that wagon, mister."

The deadly voice came from within two feet of them as Ross stepped around the end of the wagon. Clancey, reacting with an animal instinct, reached for the scabbard at his belt where the bowie knife was sheathed.

"I wouldn't," was all Ross said. It was enough. Before Clancey's hand was halfway to the scabbard, Ross's pistol had been drawn from its holster and the barrel of it was resting on the bridge of Clancey's wide, flat nose, directly between his eyes. Clancey raised his arms wide to extend out from his sides.

"Now, unless you want me to blast your brains to kingdom come, I suggest you move away from my wife."

It was the first time in her life Lydia had seen Clancey obey anyone. He had never paid any attention to Otis Russell's drunken orders. He was pale now and sweating profusely as he shuffled backward away from her.

"Easy with that Colt, mister," Clancey stuttered, striving for a chuckle. "Your woman here is as jumpy as a pony. All I done was ask her where you was at and she went all a-tremble."

Ross didn't believe him for a moment. Lydia looked like she had seen a ghost. "Well, you got me. What do you want?"

"A job. You're Coleman, ain'tcha?"

Lydia fixed her disbelieving eyes on Clancey. What was he up to?

Ross was immediately wary. Lydia saw his eyes flicker and his lips thin beneath the moustache. "Who wants to know?"

"Name's Russell." He paused, watching for some reaction from Coleman. There was none. So the gal hadn't told him about her past. He wished he had the courage to gloat that it was him who had swelled her belly up with a baby. "I heard you had a fine string of horses."

"Where did you hear that?"

"Can't rightly recollect," he said, screwing up his face as though trying to remember. "I'm good with horses, ya see, and figured ya might hire me on to help ya take care of 'em."

Ross eased down the hammer of his pistol and reholstered it. "I don't need any help," he said tersely.

"Sure must be a handful, all them fine horses. Can't ya give a poor man down on his luck a break?"

"I said I don't need any help," Ross repeated in a voice that would have sliced through a brave man's veins and made them bleed. "I've already hired on a young man to help me."

Clancey made a regretful, smacking sound with his mouth. "Well, now, that's a real shame, ain't it? Story of my life. Day late and dollar short."

"You can get on your way now, Russell," Ross said.

Lydia saw the momentary flash of hatred on Clancey's face. He didn't like being told what to do and Ross had already bested him once. "All righty. Sorry to have bothered you." He tipped his hat toward Lydia. "Sorry to have frightened you, ma'am. I avoid trouble whenever I can." He put his hand on his shirtfront and she heard the crackle of paper. He was reminding her of the wanted poster. "I always give folks the benefit of the doubt." He would be back to see if she had found the jewelry.

"Get going, Russell." Ross's lips didn't even move as he pushed the words past them.

Clancey glared at him hatefully before he grinned foxily and sauntered away toward a mangy horse tied up not far from the wagon. They watched until he had ridden out of sight.

Ross turned to her and took her gently by the shoulders, bending his knees to better see into her face. "Did he hurt you? What did he say? Are you all right?"

Her teeth were chattering and she stuttered as she answered. "Yes, I'm fine."

"You were scared out of your wits. I saw the expression on your face."

"I was silly to be so afraid. He was uncouth, but harmless, I think."

"Well, I don't think. I'm going to follow him—"

"No!" she cried, catching his sleeves in her fists. "No, Ross. He . . . he might be dangerous."

She didn't seem to notice that she had contradicted herself. Ross regretted not shooting the man when he had had a chance, for no other reason than for terrorizing Lydia. He had never seen her so discomposed. Placing his palm along her cheek he said gently, "Just until he's well on his way. I'll send Bubba to stay with you here."

Ross was anxious to make sure this Russell fellow was only a drifter. It bothered him that the man had known so much about him. Did he know more than that Ross Coleman owned a string of breed horses? Did he know about Sonny Clark? It bore checking out.

Ross was still worried hours later when he returned to camp, having lost Russell's tracks after nightfall. He went around the camp, asking if anyone had seen or talked to him. He was relieved a bit when Mr. Lawson told him Russell had been at the corral that afternoon as they were making camp.

"He asked me whose horses they were. I told him your name. I even pointed out your wagon to him. Sorry, Ross."

"It's all right. I think he was just a drifter looking for work. But I don't think he's anyone we'd want joining us."

"I agree," Lawson said. "Ugly varmint."

Ross went back to his own wagon, resolved that he had let his imagination run away with him. It had been more than three years since he had gotten shot up and left for dead. Sonny Clark had died as far as Ross Coleman was concerned. But there would be bounty hunters and lawmen who would love to know that he lived under a new identity. He couldn't be too careful.

Bubba was sitting on the steps of the wagon, staring into the dying embers of the fire. He jumped to his feet and reached for the rifle propped against the tailgate when he heard Ross approach.

"Careful. It's me," Ross said. "Where's Lydia?"

"Already asleep," Bubba said with the same moodiness that he had shown since Luke's death.

"Lee all right?"

"Yep."

"Anything happen while I was gone?"

"Nope." He couldn't tell Ross that Priscilla Watkins had sneaked up on him, begging to talk. She had come up behind him on the far side of the wagon as soon as Lydia had gone inside and turned out the lantern.

"Bubba," she had whispered from the cloak of darkness.

He had spun around and, seeing who had startled him out of his depression, glowered at her. "Go away," he had muttered, resuming his seat on the steps of the wagon.

"I want to talk to you, Bubba," she whined. "You've been avoiding me since . . . since . . . since the day Luke was killed."

"That's right. Get the message?"

She mashed her fingertips against quivering lips. "Why are you treating me so mean, Bubba? I let you do it to me, didn't I? I was nice to you and now you're acting so hateful. Just like a man, begging and pleading to satisfy his own lust, and then turning on the poor girl who let him use her."

Bubba felt miserable enough without her harping at him. He knew he was treating her badly, but every time he looked in her direction, he was reminded of Luke's body, draped lifelessly over Moses's arms.

If he hadn't been diddlin' Priscilla that afternoon. If he hadn't had his hands all over her. If her breasts . . . and her mouth . . .

In spite of himself he had felt his passions taking over again. They commanded his body, not his heart or his brain. How could he want to do *that* again, even while he grieved for his brother? He must be wicked. He hated, too, that Priscilla knew his misery. She had sidled up to him, put her hand on the front of his pants and rubbed kittenishly.

"Don't you like me anymore, Bubba?"

Even in the darkness he could see that she wasn't wearing anything underneath her calico dress. He had hardened beneath the manipulation of her fingers, and a groan of self-loathing issued out of his throat.

He shoved her away. "Leave me alone."

Furiously, she had tossed back her hair and stamped her foot, fists clenching at her sides. "All right. But I'm warning you, if you put a baby in me, you'll regret it. My pa'll kill you."

With that dismal, though ludicrous, threat, she had stamped away in the darkness, leaving Bubba more miserable than ever. He had thought that would be impossible.

Now he roused himself out of his disturbing reverie to ask Ross to repeat his question. "I asked if there was any coffee left. Never mind. I think there is." Ross poured himself the last of the brew and took the pot off the fire.

"Lydia said to tell you there are beans left if you want 'em."

Ross shook his head. "This is fine. Thanks for keeping an eye on things. You can go on to your wagon now. I'll bank the fire."

Bubba hesitated and Ross, sensing that the boy's distraction came from his distress over Luke, waited as he casually sipped his coffee. He wouldn't press the boy to tell him what was bothering him. But if Bubba wanted to get it off his chest, Ross was willing to listen.

"I remember this bull our neighbors in Tennessee had. We borrowed him for our cow," Bubba began without preamble. He cleared his throat and ran his hands down his pants leg before idly picking at a loose thread on the cuff of his shirt. "And anyway, each time they . . . uh . . . you know, every time he mounted her, she calved."

"Yeah," Ross said, taking another sip of coffee and staring into the shimmering coals.

"I was wonderin'"—he coughed—"if that's the way it is with us. Humans, I mean."

Ross tossed the dregs of his coffee onto the ground and stood up. He took off his hat and hung it on a nail at the back of the wagon, peeled off his shirt, and poured water into the tin basin he used to wash in. After sluicing several handfuls over his face and neck he said, "If you mean, does a woman conceive every time she's with a man, the answer is no." He blotted his face dry with a towel.

"How many times do you figure? I mean . . . if you was to . . . you know, go off inside her several times, three or four maybe, could it be—"

"Bubba," Ross said, placing a hand on the boy's shoulder. "Why don't you tell me what's bothering you."

Pitiably Bubba looked up into Ross's face, then bowed his head dejectedly. Ross felt the thin shoulders begin to shake beneath his hand as Bubba dissolved into wracking sobs.

The whole story poured out then, about his wanting Priscilla, going crazy with want of her, about his bribing Luke to do his chores while he met her that day by the river. He confessed how they had spent that afternoon. He also confessed that it had been his first time and how good it had been.

He was openly weeping when he wiped his nose and eyes on his shirtsleeves. "But if I hadn't been diddlin' her, Luke would still be alive. It's all my fault. I was a horny bastard ruttin' my guts out while my brother was gettin' his throat cut."

Ross cursed at the sky. Why did this boy have to suffer this guilt? Wasn't it enough that his brother had been so ruthlessly butchered?

He looked down at Bubba's ravaged face and almost envied him his ability to care that much about someone. When he was Bubba's age he had killed his first man. He had felt nothing except a sense of elation. He had felt not one twinge of remorse, much less the tormenting despair that this young man was feeling. Bubba didn't know how lucky he was to be able to cry.

"It wasn't your fault, Bubba," Ross said levelly. "Luke was always wandering off by himself. It could have happened anytime. It was purely a coincidence that you were with Priscilla at the time." Ross remembered the days he had wanted Lydia so bad he had thought he would die if he couldn't have her. "Any man understands what it's like to want a woman."

"Hell, I wish I'd never touched her. Now she's saying that she might get a baby. My ma'll kill me. If hers don't kill me first."

Ross laughed then, and Bubba looked up at him, surprised. "How much do you like Priscilla?" Ross didn't want to malign the girl if the boy was in love with her, or thought himself to be.

Bubba shifted uneasily. "At first I thought I wanted to marry her. I truly thought I loved her." He cursed again. "She's right. She said all I wanted to do was mate her and that now I have, I don't care nothin' 'bout her no more. I guess I'm gonna have to marry her," he said unenthusiastically.

"You'll have to get in line."

"Huh?"

"Scout told me she was pressuring him to marry her. Bubba," he said gently, "she's had plenty of other men." He didn't tell the boy that the invitation had been extended to him many times. Subtly, but one a man couldn't fail to recognize. "And if she does get pregnant, she'd have a helluva time proving who the father was. She's a clever little tart to string you along like this." When he saw the dismay on the boy's face, he patted him on the back. "There's a Priscilla in every man's life, the girl who initiates him, who lures him under her skirt, then acts offended afterward."

"Did you have a girl like that, Ross?"

Ross scoffed and wondered what Bubba would say if he knew Ross had been tutored by a whole harem, who would gladly oblige him on lazy afternoons or evenings when business was slow. He grinned in the darkness and his teeth flashed brightly. "That's the second lesson you need to learn. A gentleman never tells."

He was relieved to see Bubba smile. He looked like himself for the first time since Luke had been killed. "Don't blame yourself for what happened to Luke. It was not your fault."

"I'll always feel bad about it."

"Sure you will. It'll hurt for a long time," Ross conceded. "But a man puts his mistakes behind him and tries to do better the next time." He pointed a finger at the boy and said sternly, "And stay away from tramps like Priscilla Watkins. If she let you do it to her, she'll let any other man. Someone special will come along for you in a few years."

"Like Lydia."

"*Lydia?*" Ross's head snapped up. He would have thought Victoria would be a young man's ideal woman.

Bubba swallowed, afraid he had raised Ross's ire. "Meanin' no offense, but Lydia's 'bout the prettiest woman I ever did see. Luke and me both thought so that first day we found her in the woods, though she didn't look too pert then."

When his hero did nothing but stare at him expressionless, he rushed on. "She's all soft and neat, but don't look like she'd mind bein' touched, messed up, you know?"

Lydia, languishing in the clover, her clothes rumpled, laughing over the green stains on her stockings and swatting him playfully when he teased her about a muddy spot on her knee. Lydia, never fussing at him for tangling his fingers in her hair. Lydia, her face wrinkled in concentration as she pored over the pages of a book, struggling to read it correctly.

"She's dainty and all, but brave too."

"Brave?" Ross echoed. It was as if they were talking about someone he didn't know but wanted an opinion of.

"Yeah, like the way she took over carin' for the horses when you was away and I was feelin' poorly. She was scared of 'em at first, but she didn't let that stop her. Maybe I shouldn't tell you this, but she sneaks sugar down to 'em and they heed the little words she whispers to 'em almost as much as they heed you. She's been after me to teach her how to ride too. I said I would if you didn't mind, but she said she wanted to keep it a secret until she could surprise you. I been settin' her up on one of the mares now and again whenever you ain't around to see. You don't mind, do you, Ross?"

Dumbly he shook his head. Lydia riding horseback? "No, I guess she should get used to the horses since she'll be around them once we get settled on our place." She had wanted to surprise him?

"That's what I thought," Bubba said, relieved that Ross wasn't mad at him for taking the liberty of teaching his wife to ride. "You should see her, holdin' on to that saddle horn for dear life." He chuckled softly. " 'Course she's learning to ride astride on account of you ain't got no sidesaddle."

"Of course."

"Don't let on like you know when she springs that surprise on you."

"No, I won't."

Bubba looked toward the wagon wistfully. "Hope I meet up with a woman just like Lydia someday." Then, afraid he had overstepped the bounds of friendship, said quickly, " 'Night, Ross, and thanks for the . . . uh . . . thanks for everythin'." He disappeared into the darkness.

" 'Night," Ross said absently.

The wagon was dark and he felt his way across the floor to the pallet. He tugged off his boots and pants and lay down beside the sleeping form of his wife.

"Ross?" she questioned sleepily.

"I'm back."

"Did you follow him?"

"Lost him after dark. I don't think he stuck around, though. Nothing to worry about."

She only wished that were true. "Did you eat something?"

"I'm not hungry." To belie what he said, his stomach rumbled and gurgled noisily.

"You are!" she exclaimed softly, reaching in the dark and rubbing her hand on his stomach. Except she missed her mark and her fingers brushed the satiny arrow of hair that she knew pointed from his navel downward.

He moaned as his body reacted instantly. His abstinence during the days when her mood had been so volatile was catching up with him. Reflexively, when she started to pull her hand back, he caught it and dragged it back to press against his abdomen. He kicked himself free of his underwear and, turning to face her, rid her of her nightgown with his free hand.

"I *am* hungry, Lydia. Nourish me."

He kissed her rapaciously, her mouth the prey of his starving tongue. He nibbled his way down her throat. His mouth settled on the plump curve of her breast, wandering at will and taking lovebites until it found her nipple.

She whimpered her gratification. "You tasted my milk once. Do you remember?"

"Yes. God, yes," he murmured. He took as much of her in his mouth as possible.

"I wish I still had milk. I would gladly feed you, Ross."

His moan was heartfelt, soulfelt, and he urged her hand down. She resisted only a moment before she let him guide her past the wiry thatch of hair to his masculinity. Then he released her hand, letting her choose what she would do.

He whispered her name in entreaty, chanting it as he kissed her breasts, caressed them with his tongue and moustache and softly plucked at them with his lips. Thinking only about how much she loved him, she trailed the backs of her fingers along the hard, velvety length of him, then closed her hand around it.

His curse was blasphemous, or was it a prayer he spoke, as her fingers began to learn the shape, the feel, the textures, the strength of him. She discovered the first beads of moisture at the tip and used them to lubricate the spearhead.

"Oh, God, Lydia. Yes, yes." His words were disjointed, his breathing ragged. "Faster, my love. That's it. Oh, sweet . . . I . . ."

He rolled her to her back, frantically apologizing for his haste. He needn't have, for her body was dewy with desire and her heart was leaping for joy for this gift she could give him. He sheathed himself in her snug warmth, and after it was over, when he was resting in a golden haze of exhaustion and supreme satisfaction, he thought about what Bubba had said. The boy was right.

Lydia was a very special woman.

Chapter Eighteen

Madam LaRue stared indifferently at the pen and ink sketch lying on her desk in the cluttered, gaudy parlor that her girls referred to as "the front room." Idly, she twined a strand of raven hair round and round on her finger. If she was surprised by the face looking up at her from the parchment, it didn't show. There was no telltale flicker of her penciled eyebrows, no revealing movement in her powdered face, no spot of rising color on her cheeks save the rouge she had applied earlier.

"No, gentlemen. That's not the man I sent to Pearl's room the night she was killed. Are you sure you won't have some sherry?"

Gentry flew out of the pink brocade chair and went to the window, rudely pushing back tasseled curtains. Majors, diplomatic and patient and thorough as always, spoke kindly to the madam, who had made quite a name for herself and her stable of girls in the short time she had been in Owentown. Pearl's murder, seemingly without motive, had served to surround them with an aura of intrigue that Madam had capitalized on.

"Madam LaRue," Majors said, "please remember that this is only an artistic rendering from a photograph. Look again and tell us if you've ever seen this man in your . . . uh . . . place of business."

"That's not what you asked me, Mr. Majors. You asked if he was the man I sent to Pearl and I told you no."

"This is a goddamn waste of time," Gentry exploded, whirling away from the window and thumping his meaty fist on Madam's desktop. "Why are you fencing words with this whore?"

With utter contempt curling her painted lips, Madam's shrewd eyes slid up and down the tall, distinguished gentleman. She had known so many of his type. These self-appointed moral monitors of the community led campaigns against establishments like hers, yet they frequented them more regularly than most men and usually preferred the most sordid whores.

She dismissed Gentry with a delicate sniff of her nose. The Pinkerton man was a true gentleman even though he was associated with the law. She didn't discriminate because of that. Some of her best friends and steady clients had been lawmen.

"Mr. Gentry, please." Majors sighed wearily. He regretted even mentioning the trip to Owentown to Gentry. When they had returned to Knoxville to find that nothing new had been reported, he had begun to sift through what meager information they had.

They had previously dismissed the undercover agent's mention of a man resembling Sonny Clark in the Owentown saloon as not substantial enough to follow up on. But the report of the prostitute's murder was too much of a coincidence to overlook. Lacking any better leads, he and Gentry had come to the railroad town and were now interviewing the infamous Madam LaRue, though this, too, began to look like a dead end.

"Who is this man?" Madam queried silkily, measuring Majors's attractiveness. Maybe she would give him a free treat for his kindness after they had finished their business. As for the other man, he could go to hell. "Someone I should be wary of?"

"Don't tell her—"

"Gentry!" Majors barked. "Shut up."

When Gentry had sunk back into his chair, fuming but silent, Majors continued. Gentry was embarrassed by anyone finding out that Clark was married to his daughter, but Majors decided to give Madam LaRue the whole story.

"His name is Sonny Clark. He rode with the James gang up until a few years ago. Then he disappeared. He's pulled no more jobs that we know of, though he's still a wanted man. Mr. Gentry here didn't know his true identity when he hired him to work on his stud farm."

Her eyebrows shot up eloquently and she swept a smirking gaze in Gentry's direction. Her derision made his ruddy complexion grow even redder. "He is now married to Gentry's daughter. They ran away with a cache of jewelry, leaving no word or trace of their whereabouts. Mr. Gentry, naturally, is concerned about his daughter."

"Why?" Madam asked calmly.

"*Why?*" In spite of Majors's warnings, Gentry bolted out of his chair again. "The man's a criminal, a murderer, a thief. No telling what he's putting her through."

Madam thought back to the stunning young woman walking proudly and haughtily through the tall grass, and well imagined that she could take care of herself.

"He's not the man who went to Pearl's room that night," she repeated.

"Then we've taken up enough of your time." Majors began to rise. "Thank you—"

"However, he *was* here."

Not telling the law about a tall, good-looking man who had spurned her because he was obviously too much in love with his beautiful young wife was one thing. But keeping quiet about a tall, good-looking man who was indeed a notorious criminal, who had ridden with the James gang, was stretching Madam's limited generosity too far. After all, she had her business to consider. And gossip, strategically circulated, that she had unwittingly entertained the outlaw Sonny Clark in her own wagon, well . . .

Looking at the sketch still lying on her desk, she thought about the man's gifted touch. The green fire in his eyes could melt the heart of even the coldest woman, and Madam had been dubbed that by more than one man. His caresses combined just the right amount of roughness to lend excitement and sufficient tenderness to make a woman feel cherished rather than used. She had wanted him. When he had fondled her breasts, she had purred her contentment.

But she also remembered him fighting off her clinging arms, jumping free of her, wiping her kiss from his mouth, and looking down at her exposed body with disgust aimed both at her and at himself. How could any woman be expected to defend a man who had rejected what others paid a premium price for?

She had the two men's attention as she reached for the sherry decanter on her desk. Slowly, respectfully, they lowered themselves back to their chairs. Madam poured the wine into a crystal goblet and extended it to Mr. Gentry. Her lips were curved into a congenial smile, but her eyes remained frosty.

"Sherry now, Mr. Gentry?"

Gentry, mercilessly gnawing the inside of his jaw, reached for the glass. "Yes." When she didn't release the glass right away he humbly added, "Please."

Lydia paused to take a deep breath. Time was of the essence and it was running out. Ross would arrive any minute for supper. Atlanta Langston had taken Lee for a walk around the camp and would soon be bringing him back.

She mopped her perspiring forehead with her sleeve and braced her arms against the chest once again. It moved, but only a few inches. She tried again, putting her entire weight behind it. This time she managed to move it away from the side of the wagon.

If the jewelry did exist and if it were in the wagon, Lydia knew it had to be hidden under this chest. She had looked everywhere else. For days, in every spare moment, she'd searched, finally resorting to prying up the floorboards and looking for possible hiding places. Nothing had turned up and she was getting desperate.

If she could help it, Ross wasn't going to be caught with stolen jewelry in his possession should he be apprehended. She would explain to him how she knew about the jewelry when the time came—if it ever did. She still didn't believe he knew anything about it. In the meantime, she would do all she could to protect him from both Clancey and the men pursuing him.

She dropped down onto her knees, picked up the file that had facilitated her dislodging other boards, and wedged it between the cracks. She began working it up and down, sweat rolling into her eyes, until the section of board could be levered up. Mechanically and without optimism, she slipped her hand underneath it.

Her breath stopped at the same time her hand became motionless. For instead of feeling only the rough underside of the wagon, her hand contacted something soft.

Bending down, she peered under the board, at the same time clasping the soft object and extracting it. In her hand was a black velvet bag about ten inches long and six inches wide, tied with a braided black silk cord at its top. It was heavy.

Perspiration poured down Lydia's sides and rolled between her breasts as she pulled open the cord and tilted the bag into her palm. She shook the contents out. Her gasp was loud in the hot, still wagon. She wasn't even aware of the outside noises over the thundering of the pulse inside her head.

Beautiful things filled her hand. She had never seen jewelry, except for the cheap merchandise on the peddler's wagon and an occasional cameo or locket the ladies wore on Sundays. She was awed by the glistening stones in myriad colors. They threw rainbows on the walls of canvas as they caught the bright afternoon sunlight filtering in. Rings, earrings, bracelets, necklaces, brooches, some with gold and silver settings so intricate they were as fragile looking as spiderwebs. Lydia didn't appreciate the monetary value of them. She only delighted in their beauty.

She shook off her entrancement and shoved the pieces into the pouch. What to do with it? If she hid it somewhere else until she could turn it over to Clancey, there was the possibility that Ross would discover it gone. But then Ross didn't know about it, did he? *Did he?* In any event it was better to leave it where it was even if it meant having to move the chest again.

She had just returned the cache to its hiding place and moved the chest back when Ross slung wide the canvas flaps, surprising her. "What are you doing?"

She had been leaning over the top of the chest, regaining her breath, when she guiltily spun around at the sound of his voice. "Nothing," she said quickly. She swallowed and willed her heart to stop pounding. Was her husband a thief?

"Your cheeks are red."

"Are they?" she asked, clapping her hands to her fiery face. "I'm hot. There's not a breath of air anywhere. I haven't had time to wash."

He smiled, swinging a long leg inside and drawing the other one in behind him. "Let's go swimming." He came to her and folded his hands around her neck, linking the fingers at her nape. His mouth was hot as it covered hers, drinking in her taste, bathing her damp upper lip with his tongue. "You taste salty."

Her muscles were liquefying, just as they always did when he kissed her. Despite the heat, she leaned into him and splayed her hands over his chest. His shirtfront was damp too. "I told you I haven't washed."

"Neither have I. I'm dusty. So, let's go to the river," he murmured into her neck. His hands had found her breasts and were massaging them with appreciable talent. "We'll take off all our clothes and—"

"No," she said, pushing him away and shaking off his hands. "I can't do that. Someone will see us."

He laughed at her indignation, which made her curls bounce around her head and her eyes flash like comets. "All right. I'll take off all my clothes and you can swim in your chemise."

"I can't swim," she said prissily.

Only recently had she learned to flirt. She didn't know what it was called, or even that she was doing it. She only knew that when she acted saucy and made him reach for her, he seemed to like the embrace all the better. She turned her back on him and headed for the end of the wagon.

His arms came from behind to enclose her. He drew her back against his chest, thrusting his hips against her bottom. One hand closed over her breast and fanned the nipple with his thumb. The other fit over the bowl of her belly and his fingers curled into her. "Then we'll do something you can do. Something like this. You can do this, can't you?"

"Hmmm," she purred, nodding. "You taught me how." She turned in his arms and for long minutes they were lost in their kiss. Not only their mouths participated, but their bodies as well. Her breasts flattened against his chest and she massaged the hardness in his trousers with her middle.

"Goddamn," he muttered and pushed her away. "You're right. It's hotter than hell in here." His face was drenched with sweat. "Let's get Lee and go to the creek."

He led her out of the wagon, their hands clasped, and as they went looking for Lee, Ross wondered when even the thought of having sex had started being so much fun.

The next morning he was still sleeping when Lydia awoke. They had had quite an evening. First, they had spent an hour splashing in the shallows with Lee. Then Ross had showed off by diving in and scaring her half to death when he didn't come up for what seemed a full five minutes. She was calling his name frantically, clutching Lee to her and scanning the sunset-dappled surface of the water, when she was soundly pinched on the bottom and Ross came roaring out of the water like a sea monster.

"Oh, I could kill you," she shrieked and started after him, fighting both the current and the slippery stones, and trying to maintain her hold on Lee, who was thrashing his arms and legs in glee at being cool for the first time that day.

"Kiss me instead," Ross said, laughing at her aquatic efforts. He grabbed her slippery arms and pulled her to him. Fastening his mouth on hers, they swayed in the current, delighting in each other's warm taste. Lee fussed between them. He was ignored.

"You know," Ross said softly when he released her

mouth, "swimming in that chemise has its benefits." She glanced down to see the thin cloth plastered to her, enhancing far more than covering. Her nipples were impudent and rosy enticements. Just then, with a particularly vigorous kick, Lee's foot caught on the lacy border of her chemise and pulled it down over her breast. Her skin was white, wet, shiny in the late afternoon sunlight, smooth as marble and crowned with that delicate peak.

It was too much for Ross to resist. He made a low, growling sound in his throat as he slipped his hand beneath her breast, lifted it free, and lowered his mouth to it. He kissed the smooth curve, then took the nipple in his mouth and tugged gently even as his tongue painted circles around it.

"Ross, Ross," Lydia murmured, tears of love and happiness welling in her eyes. She wanted the moment to last forever, but she could feel Ross's arousal against her thigh. She put her hand on his cheek and lovingly lifted his head away from her. "We're not that far downstream. Someone might see us. And there's Lee here."

His eyes reflected the green canopy of tree branches overhead as he smiled down into her face. She would never ask him outright to stop, but he read her pleading message. He reverently recovered her breast and said, "I think Lee's ready for supper anyway. I know I am." He took the boy from her and held him tight against his chest as they walked back to camp. And again Lydia had wanted to weep with the love she had for both of them.

Now Lydia gazed at the sleeping form of her husband and couldn't believe God had been so good as to give him to her. As if in rebuke, her eyes went to the chest and she knew an instant sobering. When would Clancey come again?

He appeared that very morning as soon as Ross had left to fetch fresh water.

"Mornin', Miz Coleman," he drawled.

Lydia, not wanting him to know she was afraid of him, turned slowly and looked at him with a haughty disdain that had always made him furious. She didn't say anything.

"Did you find it?"

"Yes."

His eyes lit up greedily, but she didn't move. "Well, ya stupid bitch, git it 'fore someone sees me."

"I can't. It's hidden too well and will take some time to get out."

He cursed irritably and was tempted to slap the aloofness from her face. But all around him the camp was beginning to stir and he knew it wouldn't behoove him to attract attention.

"This evenin' then."

"Not at the wagon."

"Near the corral after everone's put their horses up for the night." She nodded and he turned to slink away through the trees. Before he went, he turned back to her. "You better be there, gal, if ya know what's good for you." She nodded again.

That was one sunset she would dread.

But it arrived, lavender and crimson and gold. She had supper waiting for Ross when he came back to the wagon. It hadn't been easy but she had managed to retrieve the pouch of jewelry during the noon break.

There was an air of expectancy throughout the wagon train. In only a few days they would arrive at their destination. Scout was anticipating their crossing the Red River in two days. Then possibly three more to Jefferson. Of course most had much farther to go, but they would be disbanding there. All of them were already exchanging addresses of relatives where they could be reached until they had permanent addresses of their own.

Ross went to talk to Grayson after supper. Ma had taken Lee for a stroll and stopped to chat with Mrs. Sims while her two twins toddled around. Lydia had no problem in sneaking off toward the corral.

She walked straight and dignified, even though she was quaking with fear. Would she finally be rid of Clancey after this? She had thought he was dead, and he had resurrected himself to torment her again. The thought of turning over Ross's late wife's jewelry was odious. But even more so was the thought of Ross's being caught with it.

Surely if Clancey had such wealth in his possession, he would leave and never bother them again.

Lydia didn't see him before he came up behind her. He brought her to a painful standstill by grabbing a handful of her hair. "Boo!" he said softly.

She tore her hair out of his fist and whirled on him. "Get your hands off me." They were speaking in whispers and had slipped into the cover of a copse of trees. Even the horses corralled nearby didn't so much as twitch an ear in their direction. "If you touch me again, Ross will kill you."

Clancey revealed a disgusting display of rotting, tobacco-stained teeth with a sly grin. "But he ain't gonna know, now is he? You gonna tell him? I ain't. Not if you brought that jewelry."

"I brought it," she said tersely and took the velvet sack out of her pocket. She thrust it at him. "Don't ever bother me again." She made to brush past him.

He barred her way by placing his hand on the trunk of a tree, almost catching her under the chin. She reared back and was put off guard. When she recovered she was being held imprisoned against the tree, Clancey's thick body pressing against hers.

"You're gettin' mighty feisty, girlie. Mighty feisty. Don't know if I like it or not."

"Let me go," she ground out, struggling and trying to get her knee up. She had accidentally caught him in the groin with it once and learned quickly that that was a sure way to prevent his assaulting her.

Adroitly he dodged her knee. "You're makin' me mad, gal, that's what. Makin' me good and mad and horny."

His breath was foul as it struck her face in huffing pants. He groped for and squeezed her breast cruelly. "No," she sobbed, fighting. She wouldn't let this happen to her again. Not after Ross. Clancey would have to kill her first.

"I figure you been wishin' you had me 'tween your legs instead of that outlaw you're hitched up with. Reckon he's better at ridin' his horses than he is at ridin' you."

"Oh, God, no." He had ripped her bodice and was reaching inside her chemise to pinch her nipples painfully.

"Been missin' this, huh?"

Lydia wouldn't scream, for one scream would alert the camp and everyone would come running. They would see Clancey. They would know what he had done to her. He would tell them . . . Oh, God. What could she do? Ross must never know about Clancey. But could she stay with him if Clancey defiled her again? No. She struggled harder, clawing at his face with her nails.

He grappled with the buttons of his pants and pushed her skirts up. "No, no, no." He clamped a hand over her mouth, banging her head against the tree.

"Lydia!"

Her name came from nowhere and sounded much louder than it had been spoken. Clancey spun around. He and the man stared at each other for a ponderous second, both rendered motionless by mutual surprise. Then the man threw back his head and emitted an outraged yell as he charged toward Clancey, aiming for his throat.

"Winston, no!" Lydia screamed.

The warning came too late. Clancey, with almost lascivious delight and not a little scorn for the soft-featured man in the white suit, pulled the long-barreled pistol from the waist of his pants and fired point-blank into Winston Hill's chest.

The sound of the firearm's discharge reverberated on the windless evening air. "Goddamn it to hell," Clancey cursed viciously. He glared with undiluted hate at the fallen man, then at Lydia, who screamed, "Winston," and fell to the ground beside the prone, bleeding figure.

"Shit!" Clancey spat before running pell-mell into the cover of the trees.

Lydia didn't even notice his flight. She was watching in horror as the scarlet bloom flowered with alarming haste over Winston's white suit. "Winston, Winston," she sobbed, bending over him.

She thought he was dead, but his eyes opened laboriously. "Lydia . . . you're safe?"

"Yes, yes." Tears streamed down her face, dropping off her chin to strike the pooling blood on his chest like raindrops. "Don't talk," she said fretfully, anxiously fluttering her hands over his chest as though to hold it together.

"Haven't felt . . . much a . . . a man . . . recently." She clasped his searching hand and brought it to her cheek. "Died like . . . like one . . . anyway."

"Please don't talk. Don't *die!*"

He smiled at her then. "Better . . . far better this way, my friend."

His eyes drifted closed then and, after one wheezing breath, that hideous gurgling sound in his chest ceased. Lydia whispered his name, knowing he wouldn't hear her. Aimlessly her eyes wandered over his body, as though searching for a way to revive him.

That's when she saw the velvet pouch clutched in his fingers. That was the only handhold he had got on Clancey. Her stepbrother had been so surprised by Winston's attack that he hadn't even noticed that Winston had jerked the pouch from his belt.

Someone shouted her name. Ross. Ma. Running footsteps through the trees. Leafy branches being knocked aside. Closer.

Acting mechanically, she wrested the velvet bag from Winston's hand and crammed it back into the pocket of her dress just as Ross came plowing through the trees.

"Lydia!" he cried raggedly. He pulled up short when he saw her bending over Winston.

Ma, right behind him, cried out, "Good Lord have mercy." She turned around, barring the path. "Get the children back to camp. It ain't pretty."

Lydia looked at Ross over the body of her friend. Her eyes were liquid with tears. "Ross," she croaked, reaching for him.

Several others stepped around him as he stood stock-still, staring at his wife with her hair hanging untidily down her back, her bodice ripped apart, her chest and neck scratched and bruised. He felt the feral snarl working its way up his chest before it came out of his mouth. Shoving the others aside, he lunged for her and pulled her to her feet.

Unable to stand alone, she clutched his shoulders for support. "Cover yourself," he said gratingly in her ear.

Miscomprehending his anger, she looked at him

blankly. Roughly he grasped the edges of her bodice and pulled them together over her breasts.

"Mrs. Coleman, what happened?"

Grayson had to repeat his question several times before it penetrated her shock-benumbed brain. Why was Ross scowling at her? Didn't he realize she had been trying to protect him? *My friend has just died because of me*, she wanted to scream at his cold, mask-hard face.

Dazed, she turned toward Grayson and the others standing by quietly, waiting to hear. "What? Oh, a man," she stammered. "I was walking. A man . . ."

"What man? Had you ever seen him?"

She looked through Mr. Grayson as though she had never met him. Why were they worried about Clancey? Winston Hill was dead. He had lent her books. Ross had helped her to read the books. "Uh . . . no, no," she said, shaking her head. "He attacked me. Mr. Hill . . ." Her voice began to wobble uncontrollably. "Mr. Hill tried to help me."

"That's enough, gentlemen," Ma said, going to Lydia and enfolding her in her stout arms. "I'll take care of Lydia. Seems to me somebody's got in mind to take out vengeance on this wagon train. You'd best go after him. He can't be far."

No one had noticed Moses as he came through the trees. He had stood beyond the rest, looking at the body of his former owner, his friend. He could remember the day Winston was born. There had been a celebration in the big house. He had been only a houseboy then, but he had taken a shine to the young master. He had loved him always because Winston had treated him like a man. Not like a black man.

Grayson, feeling that the weight of the world had just resettled on his back, said, "I guess we need to get Mr. Hill back—"

"I'll see to him." With enviable dignity, Moses weaved through the others and knelt beside Winston's body. With the care of a mother for her child, he lifted the body in his arms, stood straight, and carried it back in the direction of the wagon. The only evidence of his heartache was the unshed tears making dark mirrors of his eyes.

Once ensconced in the Langstons' wagon under Ma's watchful care, Lydia surrendered to her grief and despair. First Luke, now Winston. They had died because of her. Her. White trash. Not worthy of any of them.

"Where's Ross?" she asked. Where is he? Why had he looked at her with such hate? Could he know about Clancey?

"He's out beating the bush for your attacker, and I 'spect Luke's murderer too. Here, drink this tea."

"Lee?"

"Anabeth already has him put to bed. Now you try to get some sleep and forget all about what happened."

"I can't. It's my fault they're dead."

"You ain't makin' sense, Lydia. 'Course it's not your fault."

She wasn't to be consoled and finally Ma left her alone to cry until she fell into an exhausted slumber.

They buried Mr. Hill the following morning. Lydia was dry-eyed and stoic beside her grim husband. She had cried herself out. They didn't speak.

No one blamed her. Rather, they commiserated, saying that she had been lucky not to have been murdered too. "Or worse," the ladies whispered behind their hands. Their condolences over the horror she had experienced only made Lydia more miserable. She was to be blamed, not comforted. There were no words of comfort from Ross.

They traveled that day. They were too close to their destination to take a day off and everyone's fears had been stoked by the second killing.

Moses drove the team of the Hill wagon just as he always did. The others went out of their way to be kind to him. He came to Lydia's wagon that evening.

"I'm sorry, Moses," she said.

"He would have preferred it, Miss Lydia. He was dying of the sickness, and he saw that as a death without valor. It was better this way."

"That's what he said," she whispered hopefully, grasping at anything that would relieve her guilt. "He told me that before he died."

"He meant it. He thought a great deal of you. If he died protecting you, he died as he would have wished to."

"Thank you, Moses." She took the man's hand and squeezed it gratefully between hers.

She invited him to eat supper with her and Ross, but he declined, returning to the wagon he had shared with Winston. When Ross appeared for the evening meal, he was as silently brooding as he had been since he'd seen her leaning over Winston's body. They ate in silence. She could barely see his eyes under the shelf of dark brows he kept lowered over them, but she knew he wasn't looking at her. It was as it had been at the first, as though the sight of her was repulsive to him.

By the time they retired to the wagon, her nerves and emotions were stretched to the breaking point. Clancey had almost raped her—she knew the meaning of the word now. She had watched her friend die. Wasn't there any sympathy due her?

Ross's indifference infuriated her. Didn't her feelings warrant his consideration? After getting Lee settled, she turned toward Ross, ready to force him to tell her what he was sulking about. He was rolling up a pallet.

"What are you doing?" It had been weeks since he had slept away from her.

"Sleeping outside."

She wet her lips. "I wish you'd stay in here with me . . . and Lee." He went about his business, not glancing at her. She wouldn't admit to him how much she would miss the comfort of his arms. She used another argument. "That man could still be roaming around. I'll feel safer if you're in here."

His back was to her and he was making his way to the end of the wagon. He stopped, turned, and ran his eyes up and down her body with undisguised dislike. He snorted a contemptuous laugh. "Lydia, even a fool can see that you're perfectly capable of taking care of yourself."

He turned away from her again. That disregard, that smug expression on his face, fired her temper as nothing else could. She launched herself at him.

Chapter Nineteen

She flew toward his departing back, grabbed his arm, and spun him around. Had she not totally surprised him, she would never have been able to accomplish that feat. But he was taken unawares by her attack, as he was by the fiery heat in her amber eyes.

"What do you mean by that, Ross Coleman? Tell me why you've not looked at me, not touched me since yesterday. I dare you to tell me."

Ross flung down the bedroll as though throwing down a gauntlet. He braced his hands on his hips. "All right. I'll tell you," he said. Because of a sleeping Lee and their close neighbors, he kept his voice low. That made it no less violent. It shook with rage.

"I didn't like finding my wife out in the woods alone with another man, her dress ripped open, her breasts exposed for all the whole damn world to see. I'm sorry Hill got shot, dreadfully sorry. But goddammit, what were you doing out there with him in the first place?"

"I *wasn't*," she flared. "I was alone. Just walking. Cooling off." She hated lying to him, but she couldn't let him think she and Winston had been meeting for a secret romantic tryst. "Winston came by just in time. Don't you realize what would have happened to me if he hadn't stopped that man?"

The muscles in Ross's jaw knotted. "Well, it wouldn't surprise me. You have that effect on men and you damn well know it. Hill was in love with you himself, and if he hadn't been such a Southern gentleman, he'd have had you long ago. Hal Grayson looks at you with calf's eyes. Every man on this train stops what he's doing to gawk when you walk by. Even Bubba Langston gets a bulge in his breeches when you smile at him. They're all just dying to have a go at you. Don't look so shocked." He sneered when she recoiled in dismay. "You know it's true." He took her shoulders under his hands and lifted her to within an inch of his face as he said with the sibilant deadliness of a rapier, "You invite it."

Lydia stared up into his hard, accusing face until the full impact of what he had said hit her. Then furious tears filled her eyes. She threw off his hands and backed away from him like a she-cat spitting her anger.

"How do you know anything about it, Mr. Coleman? Mr. self-righteous Coleman married to your lily-pure Victoria. How do you know anything about me, what I feel, what I am? You know nothing!" she said in a loud whisper.

Ross was entranced by this transformation. Her hair surrounded her head like a wreath, burnished by the lantern light. Her eyes glowed with the hypnotizing quality of a flame in the dark.

"Did I invite it when my stepbrother raped me?"

"Your—"

"Yes, my stepbrother. Not by blood. His pa was married to my mama. And when the old man died and there was no one threatening him to leave me alone, he took me. The first time it happened in the lean-to where we kept what sorry farm animals there were on that stinking place. And it was appropriate, because that's what I felt like, an animal. He surprised me and threw me down in the muck. He hurt me. I had blood on my legs when he was done and teeth marks on my breasts. The same breasts that offended you so much yesterday. And . . . Oh, God . . . what do you care?"

She covered her face with her hands and sank to the floor of the wagon, abysmally wretched as the memories came rushing back. "I was dirty, so dirty. I washed and washed, scrubbed inside and out, but I still felt unclean."

Ross, his eyes never leaving her, caught a stool leg with the toe of his boot and pulled it toward him. His anger, full-blown only moments ago, deflated like a sail caught in a sudden calm. He sat down, clasping his hands together and pressing the knuckles of his thumbs to his lips as he witnessed her misery. "It was this stepbrother who got you pregnant?"

Lydia nodded dispiritedly, the fight having gone out of her too. She stared vacantly into space. "When I wasn't quick enough to avoid him, or strong enough to fight him off, he would do it again."

"You could have run away," Ross suggested quietly.

She scoffed, sweeping back her curtain of hair with her hand as she glared up at him. "My mama was sick. The old man had worked her like a mistreated and underfed slave for years. When he died, she just lay down and never got back up. If I had run away, or killed myself, which I wanted to do many times, my stepbrother would have left her to die of starvation or smothered her in her sleep. He wouldn't have taken care of her. I had to stay."

Lydia plucked at the fabric of her skirt. "When Mama realized I was going to have a baby, she cried for days and days. She got up from her bed and threatened to kill him for what he had done to me. He laughed and slapped her down. She cried more, blaming herself for what had happened. In a few weeks she died. She just went to sleep one night and never woke up." Unheeded tears traced crystal paths down her cheeks.

"I left the next morning and wandered for weeks, living off what I could find. A farm family was kind to me. They fed me and I stayed with them for a time, but then . . . I had to move on. I walked until I fell down to have my baby. You know the rest."

Lydia fell silent, thinking that her dream for a better life had just come to an end. Ross would never want her now that he knew about her past.

She had left out the part about Clancey finding her the first time. She had told the kind farmer and his wife that her husband was dead and that she was trying to make it back to her folks' place before her baby was born. Clancey had come along behind her and told them she was a wayward wife. She had fled, but he caught up with her before she had covered a mile. She had fought him. During their struggle he had fallen and hit his temple on a rock. She had thought he was dead. What would Ross say if she told him this detestable stepbrother was still stalking her?

They sat in strained silence. Finally he shifted his weight and sighed deeply. "I was an outlaw, Lydia."

That was the last thing she had expected him to say. Her head came up and she looked at him, her expression having gone from desolation to awe. "An outlaw?" she repeated. It wasn't anything she didn't know. She had seen that poster. What she couldn't believe was his confessing it to her. Wasn't that a sign of trust?

"I rode with the James brothers. Held up trains. Shot people. Killed a few." His words were clipped, but she sensed the floodgate opening up inside him. He had kept this secret for years and now he wanted to talk about it.

"Tell me," she said softly.

"My mother was a whore," he said bluntly, and whipped his eyes toward her to test her reaction. He had visualized telling Victoria that, had imagined the horror he would see on her face, a paling of the skin, a tremor of the lips, a shuttering of her eyes. On Lydia's face he read none of that. She only looked back at him expectantly. He wanted to brutalize her understanding, perhaps to test it. "Understand me. She was a fat, lazy, dirty whore." If anything, her features softened compassionately.

"Did you love her?"

The question brought him embarrassingly close to tears. He answered introspectively. "I wanted to. God, I wanted to. Maybe I did. When I was a little kid. I wanted her to love me, but . . ." He shrugged in a defensive gesture and straightened his back. "I was an inconvenient accident and she never let me forget it."

"Your pa?"

"I never knew who he was." He laughed mirthlessly. "She didn't either. I don't even know my exact birthday. The madam of the house let me stay in a back room with the bartender, who would clout me every time I opened my mouth. Daisy, that was her name, she wouldn't let me call her ma, worked all night and slept during the day. Mostly I was on my own, roaming the streets of town, getting into mischief, stealing, breaking windows, anything I could get away with. And I was good at getting away with pranks. I became bored with them. So I got a job in the livery stable.

That's where I learned horses. When I was about fourteen, Daisy died."

"How?"

"She woke up one morning with a bellyache. It didn't get better. The old doc said she had stomach fever and there was nothing he could do. She was dead by the next afternoon.

"The madam booted me out. By this time I'd gotten bored with working at the livery too. I figured, no matter what I did, in the eyes of everybody in town I was always going to be Daisy the whore's son. What was the use of trying to better myself? By then I had spent hours in the gambling hall of the whorehouse, learning to drink, cuss, play poker. I learned a lot about taking care of myself.

"I stole a horse from the man I had worked for and lit out on my own. I went all over, raising hell for the most part. The first man I killed had accused me of cheating at poker. He drew on me when I called him a goddamn liar. I drew faster."

"Were you cheating?"

He smiled sadly. "Of course. I think it was a five-dollar stake. I killed a man over five lousy dollars." He looked at her solemnly for a moment before continuing. "I was about twenty when the war broke out. I joined a guerrilla band. It was like a party. I could steal and kill, and I had the sanction of the Confederate Army. For all that, I was a good soldier. Men who don't care whether they die or not take daring chances and usually live. It's the noble men who die," he said reflectively.

"But the war came to an end and there was nothing for a gunman to do except go on doing that until someone beats him at it. One night in a saloon I drew on a man who eventually backed down. Cole Younger was there, saw how I had handled my gun, and invited me out to meet Jesse and Frank. That's when I started riding with them."

She didn't know about these men he named, but she assumed they were notorious outlaws. "I was with them for about two years. Then we hit a bank that was supposed to be easy pickings. An overzealous deputy got himself killed in the gunfight. I had gone back to pick up one of the

Youngers whose horse had been shot out from under him. Someone, the sheriff I think, shot me up bad. I was the only one seriously wounded. They had to leave me in the woods in order to outride the posse after us."

"They left you?"

"They had to." He shrugged. "If it had been one of them, I'd have ridden off too."

"But you could have died!"

He laughed at her naïveté. "That was the general idea. I was supposed to. Lydia, my real name is Sonny Clark. Sonny Clark died that afternoon somewhere in the hills of Tennessee."

Comprehension dawned on her face. "That's when John Sachs found you."

"I don't remember it. I woke up days later in his cabin. Somehow, God knows how, with all those potions he forced me to drink and the rank-smelling poultices he put on my wounds, somehow I lived and in a few months was moving around again. That scar on my chest?" She nodded. "A bullet went straight through. How it missed my heart and lungs I'll never know."

Her mind was working, piecing together the rest. "You changed your name."

"Sachs suggested it. While I was unconscious he had cut my hair to treat a scalp wound." Lydia trembled at the thought of him bleeding. Before either of them noticed the motion, she was sitting between his knees, her hands on his thighs. "My moustache and beard grew. I shaved the beard, but the moustache made me look older, different. I worked on his place for almost a year, spent the winter there. When I left it, I wasn't the same man."

His hands were in her hair now, idly sifting. Her cheek was resting on his thigh. "I changed on the inside too. I wanted to live and make my life count for something. I guess I have Sachs to thank for that. He was the first human being who'd ever given a tinker's damn about me in my whole goddamn life. I felt I owed him something for having gone to the trouble of saving me.

"The only thing I knew, besides killing, was horses. Sachs suggested looking for work around the Gentry stables. I put the past behind me, Lydia. But underneath the new name and face I'm still Sonny Clark, a killer, still an outlaw, probably still wanted in some states."

He was, but she wasn't going to tell him that. She lifted her head and looked up at him. "You *are* changed and you're not Sonny Clark. You said yourself that he died years ago." She touched his moustache. "You're Ross Coleman."

His eyes took on a rare tenderness. Ross wouldn't have recognized himself. "I'm sorry about what I said earlier. Having been what I was and coming from where I did, who am I to judge you?" His fingers tangled in her hair. "God, Lydia, what hell you must have lived through."

She encircled his waist with her arms and laid her head on his chest. "Until I met you. You've made me feel like a proper lady. But . . . but yesterday, when you looked at me like—"

He whispered apologies into her hair. "I was wrong. I was crazy with jealousy, Lydia."

"Jealousy? Because you thought I had sneaked away to meet Winston? He was my friend. That's all. And those others you named, I've never—"

"I know you haven't done anything intentional. I wasn't being straight in my mind. But, dammit, I went livid when all those men were standing there ogling your breasts."

"I don't want another man, Ross. I didn't think I would ever want one." Her hands came up and she ran her fingers through his thick hair. "But you kissed me and touched me . . ." Her voice dwindled to nothingness as she ducked her head shyly. "And now I love what you do to me."

He spoke one of those profanities that in context wasn't profane at all. Tilting her face back up, his thumb glided lightly over her lips. "I love what we do together."

He kissed her ravenously but tenderly, his tongue probing the cushiony recess of her mouth. His hand slid from her shoulder to her breast and covered it. At her soft moan, he pulled away instantly.

"I know you were frightened and hurt yesterday. God, when I think of what almost happened—" He squeezed his eyes shut and gnashed his teeth, which shone straight and white beneath the moustache. "We don't have to do anything now. I'll understand."

Lydia stood up and offered him her back, lifting her hair off her neck. "Would you help me with these buttons, please?"

Ross's whole chest swelled with an emotion unnamed, but more potent than any he had felt in his life. He sat on the edge of the stool. Lydia was standing between his outstretched legs. At first his fingers were clumsy as he began to unbutton the row of buttons on her shirtwaist.

When they were undone, he unfastened the waistband of her skirt, untied the bands of her petticoat, and pulled them down her legs. Reaching under her chemise, he undid the waist of her bloomers. When he lowered them to her ankles, she gracefully stepped out of the garments and pushed them out of the way with her foot.

There was something incredibly arousing about her wearing only her blouse and chemise now. When she shrugged out of the blouse and began to unbutton her chemise, he reached around her and caught her hands with his.

"Let me."

With only his sense of touch to guide him, he felt for each button and slowly released it. His hands fumbled between her breasts, taking lengthy intermissions to caress her through the sheer cotton. They moved past her waist to unbutton all the buttons on the chemise.

Gently, with no objection from her, he peeled the chemise down her shoulders and arms until the material was encircling her hips like a cloud. Her back was a flawless expanse of warm, glowing skin. From her shoulders to her hips, her spine tunneled a shallow groove. He placed his fingertip in it and drew it down, past the small of her back to the very base.

Alluring twin dimples were on both sides of her spine at the first gradual swell of her hips. He kissed them in turn, then nibbled his way up her delicately ridged backbone to her shoulder blades.

Lydia shivered with delight when she felt the wet warmth of his tongue dragging down the center of her back.

At her waist, he planted his mouth firmly on her skin and kissed her ardently, his hands coming around to find her breasts and knead them lovingly. His tongue caressed as his mouth applied a sweet sucking pressure to the erogenous spot.

"Turn around," he commanded softly.

As he knew they would be, her nipples were large and dark at his fingers' urging. Placing his hands over the cheeks of her buttocks, he brought her closer and kissed the taut coral peaks. He nudged her breasts with his nose, affectionately butting his head against them.

The softly glowing lantern cast flickering light on her, making shadows dance across the golden, fragrant skin. He wanted to devour it. Instead, he curbed the cannibal instinct and curved his hands under her breasts, his thumbs meeting in the valley between her ribs.

Leaning forward, he let his lips skim her stomach lightly. Then his tongue etched a pattern of erotic sensations down her midriff. His thumbs continued to caress the undersides of her breasts, frequently venturing high enough to sweep across her nipples that were flushed and aching to be appeased. His mouth reached her navel. He circled the dainty rim with the pointed tip of his tongue. Then, with a gentle probing, he deflowered it.

Her hands dug through his hair to close around his head. She had never known such levels of pleasure could exist. Was what they were doing wicked? Was it something everyone else knew, but that she was just now learning?

Ross's body was in chaos. Blood pumped erratically yet irrevocably to his loins. He could feel her hands moving in his hair, smell the scent of her skin, taste her loveliness. He was drowning in her, but it wasn't enough. Not nearly enough. He wanted more. Everything.

He pulled back and in the dim light saw the wedge of flesh revealed between the opening of the chemise where it still rested on her hips. Below her navel it was shadowy, but he could see the curling nest of tawny hair barely catching the light.

His pulse pounded, his rampant sex tested the buttons of his pants. He wavered, wondering if he dared. Then he leaned forward again and put his lips between the edges of fabric. She didn't move. He rubbed his moustache lightly, so lightly, against her belly, then down, down, until it teased the top edge of that sweet triangle. His lips opened. His breath fanned the soft hair.

She reacted with a sudden jolt of her entire body. Her breath was sucked in sharply, and she gasped loudly in the stillness, her hands automatically clenched in his hair.

He was instantly ashamed of the advantage he had taken and pulled back quickly. Clumsily he stood up, almost banging his head against the canvas. Quite naturally she shimmied out of her chemise and stood before him wearing only shoes and stockings.

She still didn't realize how seductive she was and her inadvertent naïveté temporarily restored his sanity. "Take off your shoes, but leave your stockings on."

"Why?" she asked breathlessly.

He pulled off his boots and pants. The ridge of flesh pressing against the front of his underwear was more than a little obvious. "I like the way you look in them."

She did as he bid, catching her bottom lip with her upper teeth as she smiled up at him impishly. Ross groaned and began tearing at the buttons of his shirt. "Here, let me do that before I end up having to sew all those buttons back on."

She batted his hands out of the way and began undoing the buttons. Off came his shirt. First her eyes, then her fingertips found the puckered scar. Lovingly she touched it and whispered, "You almost died." She raised herself to tiptoes until her mouth was level with the scar. When her lips moved, they lightly caressed the pinkish skin. "I'm very glad you didn't."

Shedding her last vestiges of modesty, she kissed him there, dipped her tongue into the misshapen hollow. A soft moan issued out of his throat and his arms came around her. Gaining confidence, she let her lips trail over his chest. The crinkly hair tickled her lips and nose, but she liked the feel of it against her face. Her breasts grazed his stomach and the silky column of dark hair that bisected it. His nipple contracted when her fingers ghosted over it and she found that so worthy of attention that she touched the nodule with her tongue. Daintily she licked it.

Ross was amazed by the hot sensation that raced through him. "Goddammit," he cursed through his teeth and began fumbling with his underwear. "You're teaching me things I didn't know."

Lydia fell back onto the sleeping pallet, but then she began to giggle at his frantic efforts to get rid of his underwear. He glared at her threateningly through slitted green eyes.

"You think it's funny?"

She tried to stifle her laughter, but couldn't. It came out rich and full and spontaneous. As she rolled from side to side in her hilarity, Ross couldn't help but smile himself. Naked, he lay down beside her and smothered her in a bear hug. "You think it's funny?" he repeated, tickling her ribs.

"No, no. Stop, please," she gasped, fighting off his hands.

"That laughter at my expense will cost you," he said, nuzzling her neck roughly.

"What?"

"You have to leave your stockings on." He was lying between her legs now, sprawled above her, his hardness cushioned between them.

Their breath mingled as the laughter subsided. They gazed hotly into each other's eyes. He saw the fluttering heartbeat in her throat. When she felt his masculinity pulsing against her mound, her eyes dilated glassily.

"I guess I can leave my stockings on. If you like them."

"I like you." She was surprised no less than he by his unhesitating declaration. Their eyes flew together and stilled, boring into the soul and mind of the other.

"Do you?" Her voice was so low he could barely hear her.

"Yes."

If he hadn't realized it before, he was convinced now. He had fought it every step of the way, but she had come to mean more to him than he ever could have imagined. The jealousy that had consumed him the night before was only a mild harbinger for the emotion that now seized him. It shook him to the very foundations of his being.

He couldn't ignore it. He thrilled to it. He was terrified of it. He no longer wanted to combat it.

He didn't know what to say. Demonstrations of affection would have to be his language. His finger wandered idly over her breasts, circling the nipples that pouted for him prettily. "I've never had such closeness to a woman's body before," he said self-consciously.

Knowing the pride it had cost him to say even that much, she caught him behind the neck with her hand and drew his head down to her breast, lifting it to him with her other hand. "It feels wonderful when you touch me with your tongue."

A hungry sound rumbled in his throat as he sponged her nipples with his tongue, sliding the matching textures together until she was whimpering with escalating passion.

"Ross, nothing else could feel that good," she panted.

Only the tip of his shaft had been introduced into her moist cleft. He was savoring the growing anticipation of total possession. "Yes," he mouthed against her breast. "Some things could."

"What?" she asked in a soft moan as he pressed a fraction of an inch deeper into the smooth, wet confines. "Show me."

His breathing came in rasping shudders as he raised his head and stared into her eyes. He read only an honest curiosity in them. There was no fear, no self-sacrifice. Certainly no previous knowledge.

He levered himself up so that he was kneeling between her thighs. Still watching her face for signs of revulsion or fear, he ran his palm down her shin, still encased in the black cotton stocking. Then he turned his head and kissed the inside of her thigh just above the garter, rubbing the sensitized skin with his whole mouth.

"Ross." She sighed.

"You have beautiful legs, Lydia," he whispered. His hands ran up and down the supple skin and slipped beneath the garter to tease the back of her knee. He rolled the stocking down far enough to kiss her knee, to touch the back of it with his tongue.

He practiced the same erotic rite on the other leg. A prisoner of carnal pleasure, she turned her head to one side and watched as he walked his hands up her thighs, massaging, caressing. When his eyes met hers, their intensity burned into her soul and she, whispering his name, closed her eyes against it.

"You're so pretty here." His fingers combed through the russet tuft. "A beautiful color." His voice had changed pitch and resonance. It was gruff, thick with passion, laden with desire.

Lydia thrilled to the sound of it and to his touch. His finger outlined her mound, traced the gullies at the tops of her thighs to where they flowed together. He touched her then in that most intimate of places, stroking lightly, taking up her creaminess on his fingertips, and praising her in whispered adoration for the quantity of it.

Her lassitude vanished and her eyes flew open wide when she felt the damp caress high on the inside of her thigh. His hair tickled her skin silkily, his beard stubble scratched deliciously, but she couldn't believe what he was doing until her eyes verified it.

"Ross!" she cried in shock and closed her fingers around strands of his hair to lift his head. But it was too late. He was kissing her, and rather than bringing him away, her hands pressed him closer. Her head fell back on the pillow with a spasm of ecstasy.

He kissed her with the same finesse as he kissed her mouth.

And it was wonderful and he couldn't stop.

His thumbs tenderly parted the protective folds that housed the center of her womanhood. Deftly he applied his tongue. Each lavish stroke was his tribute to her sweetness, her youth, her innocence despite the abuse she had suffered. His caressing mouth healed her of the emotional wounds left behind; he kissed them away. His suppliant lips expressed his gratitude for the generous way she shared her body with him. For never had he been granted the privilege of such loving.

The waves of bliss washed over her in ebbing currents until she was gasping for breath. What was happening was beyond anything she could have conjured in her mind. And while it shocked her, she knew it to be a rare gift from Ross to her and that the pleasure was in accepting it with equal unrestraint.

The overwhelming pleasure continued with each agile movement of his tongue, with each loving caress of his mouth, until she quickened and her womb contracted. Just when she lost control, he positioned himself over her and held her shuddering body close. His manhood was a thrumming pressure that filled her completely. He drove deep in one swift thrust before his seed rushed into her in a scalding torrent.

Long moments later, when she had regained her senses, she realized that they were lying perfectly still and that her hands were gripping the backs of his thighs. He was still hard and full inside her.

"Ross?" she queried softly.

"I'm sorry. It wasn't enough."

He began to move, slowly at first and then with the thorough, mind-stealing, gradually accelerating thrusts that robbed her of thought and brought her again to the brink of that unfathomable sphere. This time they were hurled into it together, swallowed into its black satin oblivion, swathed in its warm velvet embrace.

He joyfully sobbed her name as they sank into that golden, languorous aftermath, his face buried in her neck.

"I'm tired, but I don't want to go to sleep. I'm afraid I'll wake up and this will all have been a dream." Lydia was tweaking clumps of his chest hair between her fingers.

Ross sighed with contentment. "I know. I don't want to sleep either. It feels so damn good to hold you." His arms tightened around her and he touched a soft kiss to her temple. "Lydia, living as you did, how did you come to speak so well? As Ma pointed out to me one night in a blistering lecture about how foolish and pigheaded I was being, your manners are refined. I imitated Victoria and her father. Who taught you?"

"I didn't always live there. We, my real papa and Mama and I, lived in a town. I don't remember much about that town, but I do remember our house. Mama grew flowers in pots on the front porch. I had a room upstairs with a window. I remember in the summertime sitting in that window at night and letting the curtains blow against my face. They were white and ruffled and you could see through them."

Ross's hand lazily fondled the curve of her buttocks. "When we build our house, I'll get you some white ruffled curtains." She snuggled closer. "What happened to your papa?"

"He died. His name was Joseph Bryant." She sat up suddenly and announced proudly, "That's my name, Lydia Bryant."

He pulled her back down and kissed her soundly on the mouth. "Not anymore. It's Coleman now."

"You know what I meant," she murmured, settling drowsily against him again. "Papa wrote stories for the newspaper. Sometimes he was angry because people didn't like what he'd written. I think it was about the slaves. He told Mama he was going to the North to find us a new place to live. We were excited. But he got sick up there and died. We never saw him again. I barely remember him."

"Imagine never even knowing who your father was. Not that any of my mother's clientele was prime father material."

She looked into his embittered face and soothed away the tautness with her finger. "To have sired you, he must have been extremely handsome and strong. But it doesn't matter to me who he was."

His features softened and he kissed her hand. "Go on. When did your mother remarry?"

"I'm not sure. I was about ten, I guess. We had had to move out of our house and leave everything in it. I don't think folks treated Mama nice because of the things Papa had written."

Ross filled in the missing pieces. Bryant had been an abolitionist. He went North, probably couldn't take the change in climate, and died of some bronchial ailment. Lydia's mother, a widow, had lost everything.

"I remember a dark room at the top of an old house.

That's where we lived. Mama sewed, doing embroidery on other ladies' handkerchiefs and things. One day she came in and told me she had met a man who lived on a farm in the hills."

She sighed. "They got married and he said he was taking us to his house. His house wasn't a house at all, but a shack that was cold in winter and hot in summer. I had to sleep in a loft and the only way to get up there was by climbing a ladder. The place was filthy and Mama had to work hard every day just to get meals and keep the shack livable. I know now she must have been desperate, to marry him. She thought there would be plenty to eat on a farm, that it would be a healthier place for me to grow up in than an attic. He had boasted and Mama had been ready to believe his exaggerations. He got himself a free slave."

"And the stepbrother?"

"He was older than me. He was grown when Mama and I moved there. He and the old man were always fighting with each other and with their neighbors, whom they hated. And everyone hated us, too. When we would go in to town for supplies, people would call us names. Mama cried and soon refused to go in to town anymore, so I didn't get to go either. I was afraid to be with the men by myself."

Ross hugged her close. "That life is over, Lydia. I'm glad you told me. It explains a lot of things. And it was a relief to tell you about me. You're the only living soul who knows the truth. My secret died with John Sachs. I never told anyone else."

She wasn't the only one who knew about him. Clancey knew. There were others looking for Sonny Clark too. But they would never find him if she could help it. Her arms tightened around him. "You never told Victoria?"

His hands stilled their caressing. "No," he replied softly. "I never told her."

Lydia smiled privately. Victoria might have had his love. Had it still. But she had something Victoria hadn't had. His faith.

"Ross?"

"Hmmm?" He was marveling over how soft her

stomach was. The backs of his fingers were strumming the skin lightly.

"What you did a while ago . . ."

He became still. "Yes?"

"Nothing, never mind."

"What? Tell me."

"It's . . . I don't know . . . You'll probably think . . ."

"I won't know what to think if you don't tell me."

"Well, I was wondering if . . ." She rolled over to prop herself against his chest and peer down into his eyes. "If that could be done to you."

Chapter Twenty

Jefferson was teeming with activity. Second only to Galveston as the largest city in Texas in 1872, it was a hub of commerce and travel. Multileveled paddlewheelers were lined up at its docks, disgorging passengers who would continue their trek west in wagons, unloading merchandise, taking on vast quantities of cotton bales to be shipped down to the markets in New Orleans.

The streets were thronged with people, mostly transients, who were buying, selling, trading, bartering, loading, or unloading. Money and goods exchanged hands. Freed Negroes kept a low profile. Aristocrats who had lost everything during the war kept up the pretense that the conflict hadn't changed their lives, particularly their place in society. Carpetbaggers were spat upon or graciously received, depending upon the amount and color of their money and how ebulliently they were spreading it around. Respectable family men rubbed shoulders with the most feckless adventurers who roamed the wharf area at night. It was a good place to meet and be met . . . or be lost in.

Vance Gentry, surveying from horseback the sea of

campers that surrounded the city for miles on all sides, sighed his discouragement. "How in the hell do you expect to find them amid all *that*?" he asked Howard Majors with an emphatic jerk of his head.

"We'll find them," Majors said quietly.

"Well, let's get started," Gentry said, nudging his horse with the heel of his boot.

"No," Majors said. "Tonight we start asking around without being conspicuous. If we barge in, peering into every wagon, we could alert him. If he wanted to hide, he could easily in this mass of people."

Gentry cursed in flowery language. Since Madam LaRue had put them onto Ross's trail, he had spent days of travel on dusty, smoky trains, with endless delays in schedules, improperly cooked meals, hard beds—if any at all. He and Majors had caught a paddlewheeler in Shreveport, but that had been overcrowded and sluggish. His temper was wearing thin and Majors's constant insistence on caution was irritating him, especially since they were this close.

They knew the wagon train was going to break up here. Victoria could be in any of the wagons surrounding the town. He wanted to relieve her from whatever humiliation and hard work she was suffering as soon as possible and before Coleman had a chance to move on. He had almost forgotten how relieved he had been to hear from Madam LaRue that she had seen Mr. Coleman's wife and that she appeared in good health.

"All right," he conceded grudgingly. "Tonight we ask questions. Tomorrow I start looking for my daughter whether you like it or not." He yanked on the reins of his mount and headed back toward the center of the city, where they had been lucky enough to acquire rooms.

Majors followed close behind. He was sick to death of Gentry's threats. If he weren't so determined to capture Sonny Clark before retiring and go out in a blaze of glory, he would have thrown this over weeks ago and told Gentry to hire someone else. Gentry would have hired gunfighters, no doubt. He didn't want word to get out that his son-in-law was the notorious Sonny Clark. What better way to prevent that than to kill the man?

Majors spurred his horse into a faster trot. He wasn't going to let Gentry out of his sight. As many times as he had told him he wanted to take Clark alive, he didn't think the man had listened. In any event he didn't trust him.

Twin teardrops as large as peas spilled over Priscilla Watkins's lower lids and rolled down her cheeks. "You're hateful, that's what you are, Bubba Langston. I thought after what you did to me, you'd do the proper thing and ask my pa if you could marry me."

Bubba admired the sunset as he gnawed on a sweet-tasting stem of grass. "Is that what you thought?"

He had changed. Priscilla had seen him changing more every day. He no longer had the gawky gait of a youth, but the assured stride of a man who knew who he was. His eyes weren't full of wonder and puzzlement about what the world was going to offer up next, they were the steady, assessing eyes of a man who took nothing for granted. And they revealed all those new traits now as he gazed at the sunset through slitted eyelids. Priscilla was vexed that he hadn't even noticed she had worn her best dress in celebration of their reaching Jefferson. Recently, whenever they met, he rarely noticed anything. He only went about his business, taking her quickly and methodically. She had been glad when he had finally gotten out of his doldrums after Luke's murder. But he had never been as sweet, had never whispered lovely things to her, since that first time.

"Why do you think I let you do that to me?" she asked, casting an anxious glance toward the wagon and hoping that her ma couldn't hear. "I planned on marrying you or I never—"

"And what were you planning to do with Scout?" Bubba demanded, swinging his eyes away from the flaming sky to stare down on her.

She licked her lips and blinked. If he had slapped her, she couldn't have been more stunned. "Scout?" she asked in a high squeak.

"Yeah, Scout. Did you reckon on marryin' up with him too? Or was you just hankerin' on gettin' away from your ma and didn't much care who you suckered into helpin' you?"

On the inside she was boiling with fury. Who did this stupid *boy* think he was talking to? But she managed to manufacture another set of perfect, heavy tears to slide down her cheeks. "Bubba, Bubba, who told you these lies about me? You know I only love you. Always. Whoever told you that was jealous, that's all. Because I love you and nobody else."

Bubba stretched his long body, which had filled out considerably in the past three months. He no longer looked all arms and legs. "Way I hear it, you been lovin' just about everybody who weren't otherwise attached."

Desperation seized her. Scout had already bid her a derisive farewell. He had completed the job he had been hired to do and was off to another adventure, leaving her fuming in indignation at the easy way he dismissed her.

Bubba was her last chance. She wasn't about to get stuck on some dreary farm with only her henpecked pa and her overbearing ma for company. She would never have a chance at any kind of life except one of pure drudgery. Glancing worriedly toward the wagon, she took his hand and placed it on her breast, letting her eyes close in feigned passion.

"Bubba, feel my heart. It's beating with love for only you. I swear it. Feel how much I love you, Bubba."

A shiver of breath threaded through her lips when she felt his hand begin to move over her. A smile of triumph tugged at the rapturous pout. He fondled her with new-found expertise. She groaned softly when her nipple peaked beneath his revolving thumb.

Her eyes came wide when he dropped his hand. "You're pretty, Priscilla, and you got the goods that'd attract any man. But I don't cotton to havin' a wife what spread it around for everybody to sample first."

"You bastard," she hissed, backing away from him.

He didn't realize until then how ugly she could be. Her face twisted into a ferociously cruel mask. She was spoiled rotten and would always demand her way. Bubba felt nothing but relief that Ross had cautioned him about this bitch.

"You weren't a man until I showed you how to be one.

And being with you was like rutting with a pig. Do you hear me?" she screamed. "A rutting pig!"

Bubba grinned good-naturedly. "Well, I couldn't have asked for a better teacher. Thanks for the lessons and the practice."

He turned on his heel and walked away with the loose, relaxed saunter of a man who had disposed of a grievous burden.

With impotent fury, Priscilla spun around to find her mother standing just behind her. Her narrow face was flushed with hot color. The nostrils of the skinny nose were pinched almost closed. With a clawlike hand, she reached out and slapped her daughter as hard as she could, leaving a red stain on Priscilla's cheek.

The girl didn't flinch. She simply stared at her mother, and as she did, a slow smile parted her voluptuous lips. Without a word she entered the wagon, took down a wicker suitcase, shoved her speechless father aside, and began tossing her belongings inside.

"What do you think you're doing, missy?" Leona demanded.

"Getting away from you. I'm going in to Jefferson and get me a job."

Leona's colorless eyes blinked fast and furiously. "You aren't going anywhere."

"Watch me." Priscilla turned on her mother. "I'm not going to end my life an unhappy, dried-up old woman like you, stuck on some godforsaken plot of ground with an old fart like him." She jabbed a finger toward her father. "I'm going to live my life different from you."

"How? You'll starve."

Priscilla continued her packing, laughing contemptuously. "I'll have a job before nightfall."

"Doing what?"

Priscilla snapped the fastenings on the suitcase closed and faced her mother again. "Doing what I love to do," she said, her eyes flashing. "And what I've been doing for a long time for free. They'll have to pay me for it from now on."

"Whoring?" Leona whispered, aghast. "You're going to be a whore?"

Priscilla smiled confidently. "The highest-paid one in history. You see, Ma, when you aren't loved, you crave to be loved. I've had years to dream of ways for someone to love me. I intend to cash in on all that love you didn't give me. Every time I hug a man between my legs, I'll be thinking of all the times you didn't hug me. Live with that."

She threw her suitcase out the end of the wagon and dropped down beside it. Picking it up, she headed in the direction of Jefferson, never looking back.

Leona whirled on her husband. "Well, you spineless idiot, are you just going to sit there and do nothing?"

He looked at his wife with rheumy, tired eyes that showed more animation than they had in years. "Yep. I'm gonna do nothing to bring her back. Whatever unhappiness she brings to herself, it'll be a better life than she would have had with you. Wish I'd had her kind of gumption years ago."

"We can write letters," Lydia said tearfully.

"Can't read or write, but when one of the young'uns learns . . ." Ma's voice gave out on her as she strangled on emotion. "I'm gonna miss you. I've thought of you as one of my own."

"I wouldn't even be here if it weren't for you."

Lydia and Ma embraced each other again, Lydia taking the strength of this woman into herself. The girls were weeping openly, clinging to Lydia's skirts. Micah and Samuel were standing solemnly beside their father. All looked sad.

Lydia had already bid farewell to the other families on the train. One by one they had been absorbed into the pandemonium of Jefferson, going on to their next destinations. The Langstons were leaving early the following day. As soon as fresh supplies were loaded into their wagon, they were going to move it to the outer western borders of the campsite. Since they wouldn't see Lydia again, they were saying their good-byes now.

"We'll come see you. Ross has already said we could. Maybe in a year or two when the house is built. Did I tell you Moses is coming with us? He's going to be such a help.

Ross was planning to ask him even before Moses offered his services." She was talking too much and too quickly, but if she stopped, she knew she would cry.

"You love him, don't you, girl?" Ma asked quietly when Lydia paused for breath.

"Yes, I love him. He makes me feel . . ." She searched for the right words, but there were none that described how she felt about herself since Ross had come to care for her. And she knew he cared. He didn't love her as he had loved Victoria, but he cared. "He makes me feel clean and new inside. Respected and honored. It doesn't matter what I've been before."

"He loves you too," Ma said, patting Lydia's hand.

She shook her head in denial. "He still loves Victoria."

Ma dismissed that with a flick of her hand. "He might think he does, but you're the one in his bed. It'll occur to him one of these days that you're the one he loves. And the way he's been flashin' those white teeth of his around lately, I don't think that day's too far off. He never looked like that when she was alive. He looked like he was worried about somethin' all the time, like he was tryin' real hard to keep her happy. The two of you will have a good life together. I know it."

"I think so, too, Ma."

The older woman studied Lydia. "You know, there was a time there a week or so back when I thought you were mad at me over somethin'."

Lydia avoided Ma's perceptive eyes. It was true that she had been unable to confide in Ma after she found out Clancey had killed Luke. Her guilt over the boy's murder wouldn't permit her to maintain the close relationship she had once shared with the other woman. She hadn't realized Ma had noticed her avoidance of them. "I wasn't mad at you. I guess I was already dreading this time when I'd have to say good-bye and was trying to get used to living without having you around." Tears dammed up behind her lids. "I love you, Ma. All of you."

Ma embraced her hard. "We love you, too, Lydia."

When they pulled apart, Lydia hugged all the girls in turn. She even hugged Zeke, who blushed like a boy. "Take care, Lydia girl," he said bashfully.

"Bubba said he would come to your wagon and say good-bye later," Ma said, dabbing at her eyes with a corner of her apron. "He wanted to wait for Ross to get back. That boy's plumb tore up about leavin' his hero."

"Ross should be back from town soon. I need to hurry so his supper will be ready." Taking Lee from Anabeth's reluctant arms, she looked at them, memorized their kind, loving faces, and missed seeing Luke standing among them. Forever she would have his death on her conscience. If it hadn't been for her . . .

"Good-bye," she said and turned away before she collapsed in tears.

Thinking about Clancey, Lydia stepped hurriedly as she wended her way through the campsite toward her own wagon. She had to get the bag of jewelry from its hiding place. Clancey would come for it, she knew it. He had probably been following the train since the night he had shot Winston. When had he realized that he didn't have the jewelry with him? He would be furious and capable of violence. Lydia wanted to be prepared when he appeared again. He would come, and when he did, she intended to hand the jewelry over to him immediately.

She was convinced now that Ross knew nothing of the jewelry. Victoria had hidden it in their wagon. Lydia knew he took pride in having lifted himself out of a criminal life into one of respectability. He depended on nothing but his own determination and hard work. He would never have let Victoria bring her family's wealth with them. She had done it on her own. So if Lydia turned the jewelry over to Clancey, bought him off with it, Ross would be none the wiser.

She rushed to get supper started, but Lee seemed determined to distract her. First he soiled his diaper and had to be changed, then he started crying when she was trying to build up the fire. He refused to be quieted until she had fed him half a bottle of milk. Ross had purchased a cow upon their arrival in Jefferson so they would no longer have to depend on the Norwoods.

The delays prevented her from retrieving the velvet bag from its hiding place. When supper was finally beginning to simmer, she climbed into the wagon. She had just pushed the chest an inch or two when she heard Ross shout, "Lydia!"

Sighing her consternation, she smoothed her hair and went toward the back of the wagon. "I'm in here." She stuck her head through the canvas opening in time to see Ross vaulting from the seat of a flatbed wagon. The man sitting next to him removed his battered hat but remained seated.

Ross grinned up at her. "You'll never believe our luck," he said, smiling broadly. "This is Mr. Pritchard. My wife, Lydia." The man nodded his head in Lydia's direction. She stared at him, a sense of foreboding worming its way through her. Ross went on enthusiastically. "He and I met in town. He's been waiting for weeks to buy a wagon. I sold him ours and he wants to take possession right now. Says he wants to cover as many miles as possible before early winter. Thought that if they got started right now, his family could make it to El Paso and spend the winter there before going on toward California."

"He wants to take the wagon? Now?"

"As soon as we unload everything he's not going to buy," Ross said, laughing. "He's offered to help, so let's get busy. I bought this flatbed with the money Mr. Pritchard paid me because we'll need it later on. You and Lee can sleep in Moses's wagon while we're still traveling. We'll hang on to it for the time being in case we don't get the cabin up as soon as I'd like."

"Why don't you just sell him Moses's wagon?" she asked frantically.

"Because it's not as large as this one and he's got five children." Ross turned his head to Mr. Pritchard, who smiled back at him. "Everything you need handy, start transferring to the flatbed."

She stood transfixed as Mr. Pritchard climbed down from the flatbed and he and Ross began to dismantle the home she had known for the past two months.

When he paused long enough to notice her standing dismayed and idle, Ross came to her and, placing his hands on her shoulders, squeezed lightly. "Lydia? What's wrong?"

"Nothing," she stammered. With Moses's help, Mr. Pritchard was unloading the chest from Ross's wagon and carrying it to the one Moses had inherited from Winston. It wouldn't take her but a few seconds to retrieve the velvet bag, but there was no opportunity. Ross was looking at her strangely. "I . . . I had to say good-bye to the Langstons."

He drew her to him and kissed her firmly on the mouth. "I know you're sad about it, but I promised we could go see them and I meant it. Maybe next year." He kissed her again. "Now please help me sort through this stuff and tell me what you think you'll need and what we can sell."

They worked past dark to complete the job. The Pritchards, who had come to Jefferson from Mississippi, were anxious to be on their way after a six-week delay due to the demand for goods and the drain on the ready supply. Mrs. Pritchard and the children—five boys, the man had proudly boasted as he admired Lee—were in town buying up what they could to supplement the items Ross was selling them.

At last, after two hours of hard work, he was waving them good-bye. Ross had advised him on how to team the horses and had personally said good-bye to each of them. They almost seemed reluctant to go, but obeyed Mr. Pritchard's commands as he drove them away. He waved and wished them good luck as he drove off with the wagon, with the team, the spare wheel, two water barrels, trail equipment . . . and the Gentry jewels.

There hadn't been a single chance for Lydia to get them out of the wagon. She would have been glad to see them go were it not for Clancey. What was she going to do when he showed up? *What?*

Tired as they were, Ross insisted that they move the Hill wagon and the new flatbed to the south edge of town and away from the crowd of other transients. Lydia performed each task desultorily, the weariness in her mind taxing her body's strength. Her face must have shown her worry because as soon as they were settled for the night, Ross came up to her and pulled her close.

"You'd better join Lee in Moses's wagon and get some sleep."

She clung to him, worrying that even now Clancey might have alerted the law to his whereabouts. "No. Sleep with me tonight, Ross. Come to bed with me now and hold me. Please," she begged, her fingers latching onto his leather vest.

He smiled into her hair. "I want to. But Moses and I have a lot of work to do tonight. You rest. Day after tomorrow we strike out for home."

Her head came up with mention of the word. "Home," she repeated, like a term of endearment. "Ross, will it happen? To me? To us?" She hugged him hard, wishing they were already in their home, safe from all that threatened.

"It will happen," he reassured her in a soft whisper. He kissed her, pressing his tongue deep into her mouth. Through their clothes he felt the familiar contours of her body molding to fit his. He responded by growing solid against her. "Lydia," he chided, "see what you do to me?" His lips tracked her hairline before he sacrificially pushed her away. "I have work to do, woman." He swatted her on the fanny as he pointed her in the direction of the Hill wagon.

Lydia wished she could have lost herself in the warmth of Ross's embrace, used his loving as a potion that would keep her from thinking about Clancey. Should she tell him everything? About Clancey? About the jewels? She stopped in the dark night and turned around. He was already working side by side with Moses, arranging things on the flatbed and talking animatedly about plans he had made that afternoon.

Dare she go to him now when, if Ma were right, he was close to loving her, and tell him that neither of them was free of the stepbrother who had defiled her?

Beside the threat Clancey himself posed was the question of what Ross would do. Suppose he took her vengeance upon himself and killed Clancey? That would no doubt bring the law down on him. Or, rather than despising Clancey, would he turn his disgust onto her? Learning that

Clancey was still a factor in her life, would he regret ever having taken her for his wife, ever having made love to her? No, she wouldn't tell him. She could only hope that Clancey wouldn't follow them.

Thinking that, she turned around and found the very nemesis of her thoughts blocking her way into the wagon. "Evenin', little sister," he drawled. Lydia's blood ran cold at the tone of his voice.

She cast a hasty glance toward Ross and Moses. Moses was building a fire to make coffee while Ross was arranging things in the flatbed. They were chatting as they worked. "Are you insane?" she asked Clancey, swiveling her head back to him. "If Ross sees you—"

"We'd have a lot to talk about, wouldn't we? Like the way you was gonna steal jewelry from him and hand it over to your dear stepbrother."

She swallowed hard and stepped around the wagon, blocking herself from Ross's sight should he happen to glance up and see her talking to the man she had once claimed not to know. Clancey followed her and closed his fingers around her upper arm like a vise. "Where's the jewelry? I want it now! Somehow you managed to get it back when that pretty boy attacked me."

"I did not!" she answered heatedly and struggled to wrest her arm free. "I wanted you to have it so we'd be free of you. Winston grabbed it as he fell. I put it back under the floorboards in the wagon and—"

"Git it."

She bit her lower lip till she tasted blood. Drawing in a deep breath she said, "I can't." He flung her against the wagon so hard her ears began to ring and the breath was knocked out of her.

"I said, git it," he snarled close to her face.

"Ross sold the wagon this afternoon. It's gone. I didn't know he was going to get rid of it so soon. I swear it, Clancey. It was sold and gone before I had time to get the jewelry out."

He stared down at her with baleful eyes and then darted his eyes around the campsite, verifying what she had said. "Shit!" he cursed and the word struck her in the face like a slap. "Well, that's just too bad for you, ain't it?" he asked, releasing her so abruptly she almost fell to the ground.

"What do you mean?" Her lips felt rubbery and wouldn't work correctly. Her mouth had gone dry. Her head was spinning.

"I mean there's still five thousand dollars waitin' for the man who sics the law on your husband, that's what I mean."

"No, Clancey—" She reached for his sleeve, but he shook her off.

"You had your chance to buy my silence. The price was them jewels you cheated me out of."

"I told you—"

"Shut up." He drew back his hand as though to strike her. Instead he laid it against her neck caressingly. "Maybe my price has changed. Maybe I want you instead. Are you willin' to leave that strong, fine husband of yours right now and come with me if it'd save his hide?"

Revulsion swamped her. His touch was cold and chilling as though he were smearing slime over her skin wherever he touched. Her stomach rebelled and sent its contents gushing to the back of her throat. She shivered uncontrollably. She couldn't bear it. Never again. Not for anything.

For Ross? To save Ross's life?

But how could she let this animal touch her after having known Ross's love? God help her, how? But she would submit to anything, even Clancey, if that's what it took to save Ross and Lee.

She opened her eyes, which had closed because she couldn't bear to look at his ugliness, and stared back at him coldly. "All right. I'll go with you."

He laughed, softly, but no less deadly. He ran his hand roughly over her breasts. "I could have you anyway, little sister." He stepped away from her. "Good as you look, five thousand dollars looks a sight better this here minute. Tight and juicy as you are, you ain't got the bargainin' power right now."

He had humiliated her, but she was beyond caring. She would beg if necessary. "Clancey, please, no. Don't do this to us."

"I worked hard for that money, sugar pie," he said silkily. "Remember that boy I had to kill? What'd you call him?"

"Luke Langston."

"Yeah, Langston. Tough little bastard, that one. Nearly got away from me, he did. Fought like a wildcat. And that fancy fellow."

"Winston Hill. You killed them. And they were both my friends."

"*I* was your friend, 'fore you turned on me. Remember that. You left me for dead, missy. You were my woman. You ran off with your belly swole with my young'un. I aim to see that you pay for the way you done me. I got things to do in town."

"What are you going to do?"

"Look for that wagon for one thing. If you're tellin' me the truth, it couldn't have gone too far."

Lydia thought of Mr. and Mrs. Pritchard and their five sons. More innocent people on her conscience. "You won't be able to find it," she said, making it sound futile even to try.

He clutched her jaw in his hand and whispered lethally. "You better hope I do or else I'll see you in the morning with the law right behind me."

With that he swung away. Lydia stared at his retreating figure. Repeating his list of crimes against her had only made her realize just how much she hated him, how she wished him dead. She took two running steps after him, but then stopped. How would she kill him? She had no weapon. He would only overpower her, maybe kill her, and then come back for Lee and Ross.

God, what am I going to do? she asked herself as she climbed into the wagon where Lee slept peacefully. She couldn't just sit here and let that animal ruin her life again. There had to be something she could do. But what? *What?*

Outside, a shadow separated itself from those surrounding the wagon. It materialized and took the form of a man. He peeked into the wagon, where he could see Lydia bending over the baby. She was wringing her hands and weeping. He looked after the lumbering man who was determinedly striding toward town. His lips thinned and he balled his hands into fists.

Then, soundlessly, he followed the man.

Clancey couldn't believe his good luck. Of all the goddamn luck!

He had spotted the Coleman wagon on the main street of town parked outside the dry-goods store. The dumb sod buster and his stringy wife and five boys were hauling supplies outside the store and onto the boardwalk, arguing good-naturedly on how to best load them into the wagon.

Covertly he had watched them from across the street. When all went inside for another load, he scuttled across the street and climbed into the wagon before anyone noticed him. It took him only moments to locate the floorboards scarred from Lydia's having pried them apart. Before the Pritchards returned with their arms full, Clancey had the velvet bag in his shirtfront and was strolling down the sidewalk, glad that he hadn't had to kill anybody and attract attention.

He had been trying to decide the best way to approach the law. Should he just go barging into the sherriff's office, loudly declaring he knew where Sonny Clark was? Clancey didn't credit the law with having much intelligence. The sheriff might not even know who Clark was. After all, Texas hadn't been the outlaw's territory. It might take days for the law to gather enough information to make an arrest. In the meantime, Clark and Lydia could get away. No, he would kill them before he would let that happen. And how could he keep an eye on both of them and a dumbass sheriff?

Supposing Lydia went shooting off her mouth about the killings? Of course it would be her word against his, and who would believe the woman of a criminal like Clark? But then several witnesses could say they had seen Clancey around the wagon train. They couldn't pin anything on him, but they could sure as hell stall him from getting his reward money.

Now that he had the jewelry, he wanted to get on with turning Clark in for the reward and be on his way. But what was the best way to go about it?

He was puzzling through that when he pushed his way into the hotel lobby on his way to the saloon. He scanned the room, looking for the bar. The first thing his mind registered was the two men sitting alone in armchairs with a small table between them. One was expounding on something, leaning over the table, thumping it with his fists, talking earnestly. The other was listening, a bored expression on his unremarkable face, but his eyes busy surveying the crowd in the adjoining saloon in a professional fashion.

Clancey stared, letting other carousers entering the busy building eddy around him as he stared at the two men. He had still been woozy from his wound and not a little drunk that night in Knoxville, but not so drunk that his memory didn't serve him now. The same two men. The men who had first put him onto the idea that Lydia could have taken refuge with the wagon train. The men who were after Clark.

He all but crowed. Goddamned if he weren't a lucky bastard.

He reached for the tattered poster he always carried in his shirt and pressed the bag of jewelry flatter against his stomach as he made his way across the carpeted floor of the lobby and approached them. Without speaking a word, he tossed the poster, face side up, on the table between them.

The man with the crest of white hair stopped his long-winded speech and looked up in annoyance. "What the hell—"

The other man clamped silencing fingers over his wrist when he realized what it was Clancey had thrown down on the table.

"You buyin' whiskey for a man with a powerful thirst and a lot to talk about?" Clancey pushed his greasy hat back and looked at them cockily, feeling his importance.

Majors pulled a vacant chair up to the table and took another glass from a tray on a nearby sideboard. Clancey grinned at them like he knew a secret they would love to be let in on, and they looked at him with disgust but undeniable interest. They couldn't afford fastidiousness now.

When Clancey had swilled down several tumblers of whiskey, he wiped his mouth with his sleeve and said, "Name's Russell. Clancey Russell."

"I'm Howard Majors of the Pinkerton Detective Agency. This is Mr. Vance Gentry."

Clancey leaned back in his chair, gazing around the room nonchalantly before pouring himself another generous shot of whiskey. "I got me a place in Tennessee near the North Carolina border," he boasted expansively. "For months been chasin' after my wife, what run away with my baby in her belly."

"For godsakes, man—" Gentry began, only to be interrupted by Majors's calm, professional voice.

"This is all very interesting, Mr. Russell, but would you mind telling me how you came to possess this piece of paper and what you know about it?"

Clancey's rotted teeth were revealed when he said, leering, "Nothin' 'cept I know where he is right this very minute."

Gentry bolted out of his chair, grabbing Clancey by the collar and all but pulling him out of his chair. Whiskey sloshed over Clancey's hand. "Where?" Gentry demanded.

Majors was so angered by Gentry's outburst, he almost pulled his concealed pistol on him. He stood, shoved the man hard, and commanded him to sit down and be quiet. The group was already drawing attention from other patrons of the hotel and attention was something Majors didn't want. At least not yet. Gentry, reluctant, and casting a threatening glance at Clancey, obeyed.

Majors turned back to Clancey, who was slurping the spilled whiskey from his hand. "I'm sorry, Mr. Russell. Mr. Gentry is overwrought. His daughter is married to Clark. They ran away from her home in Tennessee months ago and haven't been heard of since. He's very concerned about her."

Clancey knew all that, but he didn't want to let on like he did. His plans for a quick grab at the reward money and a hasty disappearance afterward didn't include getting involved with the law or Gentry. Let Lydia and Clark break the news of his daughter's death to him.

It would behoove him to play dumb about the jewelry too. He would bury it tonight. Then tomorrow Lydia could only implicate herself if she told them she knew about it. While he was at it, he would cook Lydia's goose with that husband she admired so much. To Clancey's mind, she hadn't paid near enough for the wrongs she had done him. Now he would see to it that that little missy met with her comeuppance.

Clancey could be a good actor when he wanted to be. His reaction was one neither of the other men expected. He burst into guffaws of laughter. "Married to your daughter, huh? Well, I don't know how to break this to ya, Gentry"—he sneered the name—"but I been trackin' the man 'cause he took my woman. Claims she's married to him 'stead of me, and that the young'un they got is his, not mine. I ain't heard of no other woman 'round him."

"This is a waste of time," Gentry snapped, not deigning to look at Clancey. He addressed Majors. "He obviously doesn't know what he's talking about. He's drunk."

This time it was Clancey's turn to lunge across the table. "You're lookin' for Sonny Clark, right? Alias Ross Coleman? Well, he's here, camped just a mile from town. I had a little discussion with my woman when I caught up with them today. She's come back to her senses." He winked with lewd implication. "Fine-lookin' little piece, she is. She's keepin' him good and busy tonight till I can get back there with the law."

An hour later the three men parted company. When Clancey was out of earshot Gentry turned to Majors.

"You can't mean what you said about waiting until morning for him to guide us out there?" Gentry exclaimed as Majors headed toward the stairs.

"I meant exactly what I said. I don't want to go in at night. He could use the dark as a cover to escape."

"It would be a total surprise."

"It will be a surprise in the morning. From what Russell told us, Clark doesn't suspect a thing."

"He's done something to Victoria," Gentry whispered

harshly, though the lobby was now deserted, save for a sleepy clerk behind the desk. "Russell didn't know anything about her. Are you going to chance Clark's getting away, with my daughter's whereabouts still unknown?" His voice had risen and with it his temper. "Well, by God, I'm tired of putting up with your caution. I'm not waiting until morning. I'm going after him now and—"

Gentry found himself whipped around and slammed into the wall. Majors wasn't as tall, nor as strong, but despite his retirement age, he was wiry and had the element of surprise on his side. He cannily subdued the other man.

"You listen to me, Gentry. I've had it with you and your temper and your tirades. You're paying the agency, so all right, I've had to put up with you. But you're not going to dictate to me how to do my job. We do it my way. *My* way." For emphasis, he dug his fists deeper into the man's chest where he had gripped him by the lapels.

"Now, if it means chaining you to your bedpost or calling the sheriff and having you hauled off to jail for some trumped-up charge, I'll do it to keep you from storming in tonight and ruining everything. What's it going to be?"

Gentry, hating the position he found himself in, stared down into the detective's eyes and saw a resolution even a Gentry would be hard-pressed to shake. "I'll wait 'til morning," he said tersely.

Majors released the fine fabric of Gentry's summer-weight coat slowly. He didn't speak a warning. His sharp, incisive eyes said it all.

Clancey weaved his way down the boardwalk, humming tunelessly, a stupid grin on his face. He would teach her, the bitch. He planned to be there with Majors and Gentry first thing in the morning when they surprised her and her husband. He hoped they caught them in bed.

He laughed licentiously and thought of her breast filling his hand. Hellfire, there were tits all over the country. He would buy himself the best. He would have that reward money tomorrow after they arrested Clark. He already had the jewelry.

Clancey Russell would be sitting pretty. Yes, sirree. He was on his way up in the world. There was nothing to keep Clancey down now.

"Hey, mister?" a voice whispered from the dark shadows of the alley.

"Huh?" Clancey asked, swaying drunkenly and trying to get his eyes to focus. "Who wants me?"

"I do." The voice stepped out of the shadows. "Do I look familiar?"

Clancey blinked until the two images bled into one and then his jaw went slack and his eyes nearly popped out of his head. He was seein' a goddamn ghost!

"This is for Luke. My brother."

Bubba plunged the knife to the hilt between Clancey's ribs and ripped it upward. He watched the ugly face contort first with surprise, then with horror and pain, and finally collapse into the sagging expression of death.

Bubba pulled the knife free and let the body fall with a sickening thud to the garbage-littered alley. He knelt over it for only a second before slipping back into the shadows unseen and silent.

Chapter Twenty-one

*R*oss lay on his bedroll, his hands clasped behind his head, staring up at the black velvet sky studded with stars and a crescent-shaped moon. He was happy; he was at peace. Contentment rivered through his body like rich, heavy cream.

When he had watched Victoria die, he'd thought his life was over. It was far from over. He was learning that life offered as much joy as it did heartache. It didn't have to be a constant struggle to prove one's worth. When someone cared for you, it automatically made you feel worthy.

Lydia cared for him.

Not that Victoria hadn't. She had. She wouldn't have defied her father and married him had she not loved him. Convention and class had been scorned. But would she have married him, knowing everything of his past? Would she have loved him just as well?

Ross didn't think so. Maybe, but he didn't think so. He had never had the courage to test the strength of her love. To him she had been a treasure, something to cherish and protect, to shelter from all that was ugly, to hold on to at all costs. He didn't think she could have tolerated the truth about him. Lydia, on the other hand, seemed to love him more because of it.

Love? Why had that word come to his mind? Did she love him? There were a hundred ways she had shown her love, in the small favors she did for him, the expectancy in her eyes when she looked at him, the breathless catch in her voice when they spoke. He hadn't taken those testimonies of affection into account until now. His heart and mind had been too full of Victoria. But now . . .

He groaned and rested one forearm across his closed eyes as he remembered the night she had demonstrated her love so freely. God, had any woman ever created been more adept at loving a man? The memory of that night came back to stroke him, the way her fingers had stroked him to full hardness in her dainty hand.

His nakedness had never repelled her. The very thought of a naked man would be repugnant to most "decent" women. Without shame or timidity, Lydia had studied his body with an honest admiration. Her hands had glossed over his flesh, sensitizing it.

She had lain against him, slowly and tantalizingly inching down his form. She trailed swift, light kisses down his chest, flicking his nipples with her tongue, plucking at the skin with her lips, dusting the hair with her fingertips. She kissed his navel with wanton thoroughness.

"Lydia, you don't have to," he had grated out. Belying his words, he had wound her hair around his fingers.

"I want to," she had whispered back, disturbing the hair on his abdomen with her soft breath.

The first touch of her lips was tentative, demure, shy. Ross had held his breath. His shaft throbbed against the entrapment of her hand. He felt more of a man than ever before, and yet weak and helpless because this woman's sweet loving had subjugated not only his body but his heart.

He had cursed and prayed and repeated her name like one deranged when her tongue began to acquaint itself with every texture and taste of him. He was separated from logical thought and responded only to the magic she wove. Emboldened by his reaction, no longer bashful, her lips adored all of him.

When he felt the first tremor of climax, he pulled her up to straddle him, and her warmth sheathed him. She fell atop his chest, draping them both with her glorious hair. He cupped her face between his hands and brought her mouth to his for a kiss as plundering and intimate as the fusion of their bodies. He tasted himself on her lips and poured love words into her mouth as she took his seed inside her.

Ross's body was covered with a fine sheen of sweat now as he thought back on that last time they had made love. The pressure in his loins was pounding as hard as it had then and he cursed himself for insisting that she sleep alone with Lee tonight.

He suddenly felt compelled to go to her. What would she say if he asked her now how she felt about him? She had alway been honest with him. He couldn't fault her on that score. She had never lied. Even though she hadn't professed to love him, he thought that, with the least encouragement, she would. He wanted to hear her say the words. He wanted that damn bad. It was suddenly vital that he hear her say she loved him.

He glanced toward the wagon and sighed with regret. She would be sound asleep and it would be cruel to wake her. But tomorrow night . . .

Tomorrow night and the one after that, and all the other nights for the rest of their lives. He looked forward to every one.

* * *

Bubba crept to the end of the Hill wagon and softly called her name.

Afraid Clancey had come back, Lydia flew across the wagon floor and parted the canvas.

"It's me. Bubba."

Her shoulders slumped in relief. "What are you doing walking around at this time of night?" She was whispering. Bubba was too.

"I brought you this."

Her free hand clapped over her mouth to stifle a loud gasp. The familiar bag of jewelry felt unaccountably heavy. "Where did you get this?" Her throat all but closed around the words and she found she had very little breath.

Bubba didn't specifically answer her question. "He won't be killin' no more innocent people like Luke. I made goddamn sure of that."

Bubba had killed Clancey! "The people who bought the wagon—"

"I followed him, saw him get the bag out. He didn't hurt nobody and they never knew any better."

She was suddenly struck by how changed Bubba was. He wasn't the boy he had been weeks ago. This straight young man barely resembled that boy. There was a new hardness around his jaw, a trace of mistrust in his once guileless eyes. When had that naïveté been replaced by so much knowledge? He met her stare levelly, where once a glance from her would have made him blush and look away.

Tears blurred her eyes. That lovely boy had become a man and now knew all the hateful things that men have to face and act on. His revenge had been for his brother, but the act had been a gift to her too. She didn't know how he had found out about Clancey and wouldn't ask. Thanks to Bubba he was dead, and with his death, Ross was free again.

She touched Bubba's cheek with her fingertips. Gratitude for his killing a man would be unthinkable, but she wanted him to know what it meant to her. "You know about Ross?"

He nodded. "Enough. No one will ever hear it from me, Lydia. And he'll never know about you and . . ." He let the rest of the sentence dwindle.

"You gave both of us our lives back. First when I was lying there in the woods waiting and wanting to die. And now this. We owe you, Bubba."

He shook his head in adamant denial, his white-blond hair shining in the moonlight. "I owed this to Luke."

She looked at the bag of jewelry. "I don't want this."

"Reckon you don't."

"It doesn't belong to either Ross or me."

"What about the young'un? What about Lee?"

Of course! Lee would one day be told about his mother. Ross would want to give him something of hers. Lydia decided to hide the bag of jewelry in one of their packing boxes and let Ross "discover" it for himself. He could save it for Lee.

"Yes. I guess it does belong to Lee."

Lydia smiled at Bubba and it was a smile he knew he would remember for the rest of his life. Just as he would remember Clancey Russell's expression in death. Bubba knew that would stay with him for a long time. He didn't feel guilty about killing him. Russell had deserved to die. He had murdered Luke and Mr. Hill. The law of the hills, an eye for an eye, was too deeply ingrained in Bubba's young mind for him to feel guilty about settling the account.

He only regretted that he had had to do it. He hadn't enjoyed it. It had made him sick to his stomach. He would never boast about it. He would even keep the secret from his parents, never telling them that Luke's death had been avenged. He could never pay back the debt he owed his brother, but he had helped Ross and Lydia. That in itself was reason enough to have done what he had.

"Good-bye, Lydia."

She swallowed a knot of emotion. "Good-bye, Bubba. I'll think of you often."

He stared at her moon-bathed face for a long moment, wishing he had been a few years older when their destinies had brought them together. Then he hated himself for the thought. She belonged to Ross and their being together was right. He only hoped one day he would find a woman as fine as Lydia.

Lest his emotions reveal themselves, he doffed his hat and, turning on the heels of his boots, disappeared into the darkness.

Feeling her way in the darkness, Lydia opened a crate of extra bedding and crammed the velvet bag deep between two quilts. Then she crawled to her pallet and lay down. It had been a long time since she had prayed. Long before Mama had died, she had given it up as futile. Now she tried to remember the right words, but couldn't, so she fashioned her own. Her prayer wasn't lyrical or poetic. It was awkward, but from the heart. She hoped God understood how grateful she was.

She wrapped her arms around herself and let all the worry and fear drain out of her. She and Ross were free. Tomorrow they would start toward their new home. No one would know about their pasts. They would be Mr. and Mrs. Ross Coleman, envied for their happiness.

Maybe tomorrow she would find the courage to tell Ross how much she loved him.

A twig snapped beneath Bubba's boot and, before he took another step, Ross's pistol was pointing at his chest. "Damn, Ross, it's me, Bubba."

"Sorry," Ross said, letting down the hammer of his Colt and tucking it back under his saddle which served as his pillow. Old habits were hard to break. He looked toward Moses, who was snoring softly nearby. His eyes came back to the young man, who had hunkered down beside the fire. "What are you doing sneaking around in the middle of the night?"

"Couldn't sleep."

Ross sighed, still aggravated with his rampant desire that wouldn't be quelled. He missed like hell not having Lydia lying beside him. "Neither could I."

"Besides, I wanted to come say good-bye."

Ross looked at Bubba's silhouette against the red glow of the campfire. Where was the eager boy he had first met in McMinn County, Tennessee? He had filled out. His chest was no longer concave. There was a trace of beard fuzzing his chin and upper lip. His voice was different. His attitude had made a complete conversion from that of boy to man.

"So you're not taking me up on my offer," Ross said quietly, sensing the struggle going on inside the boy.

Bubba muttered a foul expletive and flicked the pebble he had been toying with into the fire. He searched out Ross's eyes in the dim light. "Ross, you know I'd love nothin' better than to go with you and Lydia and Moses, to work for you, but I can't."

"I know, Bubba. I want you, make no mistake, but I knew when I asked that you'd have to go with your family. I just wanted you to know how much you'll be missed."

"Thanks for that, Ross." He stared glumly into the fire. "My pa's gettin' old. He took Luke's killin' hard. I don't think he's as enthusiastic about homesteadin' as he was when we left."

"Once he finds a piece of land, he will be."

"Maybe," Bubba replied without conviction. "But he's gonna need help and I'm the oldest son. He and Ma are dependin' on me. I can't let 'em down even if it means givin' up goin' on with you."

Ross left his bedroll to squat down beside the boy and clamp him tightly on the shoulder. "That's a man's decision. I'm proud of you for making it." Their eyes met briefly, emotionally, then both looked away, embarrassed. Ross dropped his hand.

They stared into the coals for a long while before Ross broke the silence. "Lydia's set on coming to see all of you. I was thinking that maybe by a year or two from now your farm would be well enough established for you to handle a few horses of your own. What if I were to bring you a good mare and stud, help you get started?"

Bubba's eyes took on that bright, childlike delight no one had seen in weeks. "Do ya mean it?" he asked excitedly. But immediately his enthusiasm deflated, as did his smile. "We won't have much money, Ross."

Ross shrugged. "We'll work something out. You be sure and have a corral ready for them."

"I will. But, damn, *two years!*"

Ross chuckled. "It'll go quicker than you think."

Unnecessarily, Ross stirred the fire. He cast a surreptitious glance at Bubba before he asked casually, "Have you said your farewells to Priscilla?"

Bubba snorted unflatteringly. "Yeah. You were right, Ross. She's a slut. I got with Scout before he left and we started comparin' notes, so to speak. I ain't never gonna git involved with another woman like her."

Ross laughed softly again. "Maybe not like her, but you'll get involved all right. We can't leave them alone, you know. They get to us before we know what hit us."

"Yeah?" Bubba asked, indicating that he had been giving the subject some thought. "What are we supposed to do, Ross? I mean, I want to marry someday and all, but hell, I walk around strainin' the buttons on my fly every hour of the day."

Ross smiled self-derisively. "Then we've got that in common."

"You mean—"

"I mean that when you've got it good at night, you miss it even more in the daytime."

Bubba stared at his idol and then both men laughed until Moses stirred in his sleep and rolled to his other side.

"We had best be quiet or we're going to wake everyone up."

"I gotta git back anyhow. My ma still don't sleep until all her chicks are in the roost, and our wagon's almost a mile from here."

Ross stood and extended his hand. "Take care, Bubba. And don't worry about the ladies. If you can survive a summer with Priscilla, you'll know how to handle the next one."

Bubba took Ross's hand and shook it solemnly. "I like you better than any man I ever met, Ross, 'cept maybe Luke."

He gripped Bubba's hand tighter. "That's a high compliment, Bubba. Thanks. Lydia's been teaching Anabeth to read and write. See that she writes us letters to keep us informed."

Bubba came near to making a fool of himself again as tears stung his eyes. He let go Ross's hand and took several steps away. "You take good care of Lydia and Lee."

"I will."

"I reckon I've earned the right to be called by my name, don't you?"

Surprised, Ross considered this a moment. "Reckon you have." Then he barked a soft laugh. "What is it?"

"Jacob," Bubba muttered self-consciously. "Don't cotton much to that." After a short silence he said, "How 'bout Jake?" Jake Langston. That had a good sound to it. He straightened and tilted his head to one side. "Yeah, Jake."

Ross nodded his head. "Take care, Jake."

"See ya, Ross."

"In a year or so, Bubba."

Ross lay back on his pallet, indefinably sad over Bubba. Something about him was different. More than maturity. Ross recognized a tenseness about the young man. Almost like the stress Ross had felt when at sixteen he had killed . . .

But that was impossible. Bubba had been a good boy. He would be a better man. Ross had every confidence in that.

As he drifted to sleep, he was feeling confident about the entire future. It would begin tomorrow. He could hardly wait for sunrise.

"Don't move, you sonofabitch."

Ross knew reaching for the Colt now would be foolhardy. Every trained nerve told him so. And they were proved right when he opened his eyes and stared into the barrel of a pistol, not as long and intimidating as the one he owned, but one just as deadly if fired at a range no greater than the end of his nose.

The sky was dove gray, just becoming tinged with pink. He hadn't been asleep that long. It was early. The surrounding countryside was still.

He looked at the hand holding the pistol, then tracked the stout arm up to an impressive set of shoulders and into the granite face of his father-in-law. His eyes glared down on Ross from beneath a wide-brimmed hat.

Ross's surprise was controlled as strictly as he governed his muscles not to move. "Mr. Gentry?" he croaked, wondering what in hell the man was doing hundreds of miles away from home pointing a gun in his face. They had had their differences. Gentry hadn't wanted Victoria to marry him, but why now was hate emanating from him like cheap perfume from a whore? "What—"

"Where is she? Where is Victoria?"

Ross did react then. He came up on his elbows and blinked up into the man's florid face. "Victoria?" he asked incredulously. Didn't the man know? Hadn't the letter he sent ever been delivered? "Victoria is dead, Mr. Gentry," Ross said softly.

He saw a shudder pass through the older man, but only Gentry's eyes flickered. And his grip on the gun tightened. Otherwise he remained perfectly still. "Dead?"

"I wrote to you months ago. She died before we left Tennessee. During childbirth."

"You lying bastard," the man hissed and kicked Ross viciously in the ribs.

Ross heard his ribs crack at the same time he heard Moses awaken and sit up. "Keep still, nigger, unless you want me to kill your friend here," Gentry threatened.

"Ross?" Moses asked uncertainly.

"Do as he says," Ross gasped, tears of pain coming to his eyes. He lay on his side with one protective arm across his broken ribs. "Tell him about Victoria."

Moses looked at the white man and recognized his cruel prejudice immediately. But he had no choice but to speak up and help Ross. "Mr. Coleman's wife died giving birth to their baby son just before we reached Memphis," Moses said quietly. "We buried her."

Gentry barked a short laugh. "You think I'd take his word for anything? My daughter wasn't carrying a child. She would have told me. Or didn't you give her time before you kidnapped her and stole the jewelry? Where did you dump her? I believe she's dead all right. And I think you killed her."

Jewelry? Ross shook his head, hoping he would wake up soon and bring an end to this ridiculous nightmare. Waves of agony were washing over him, causing his vision to be riddled with bright flashes of yellow light. He needed to vomit.

"Mr. Gentry, I don't know what you're talking about,"

he said on short puffs of air. "Sachs gave me the deed to some land here in Texas."

"Sachs is dead," Gentry snapped.

That didn't surprise Ross. He had known the old man was close to dying the last time he saw him before they left. Still, hearing of his passing saddened him. Sachs had been the first human being on earth to give a damn about Sonny Clark. "He gave me the deed because he knew he would never claim it. Victoria and I decided to take my own horses and move here, to start our own ranch. We'd heard about the formation of a wagon train and joined up so we could travel in safety."

"You expect me to believe that my daughter deserted her home, everything she loved and held dear, to follow you on some wild-goose chase?"

His face was growing redder by the minute. He was bristling with fury, and Ross didn't like the way his finger restlessly fiddled with the trigger of that pistol. He couldn't reach for his own gun, especially with broken ribs to slow him down. Besides, he had no desire to draw on his father-in-law.

"It was Victoria's decision, not mine," he said with a calmness he didn't feel. "I wanted to wait until you got back from Virginia before we left. I wanted to tell you about the baby—"

Gentry swung his arm down and slammed his fist into Ross's jaw. He fell back. "Shut up your lying mouth about a baby. Isn't it enough you killed her?"

"Ross? What is it?"

Ross heard Lydia's voice through a fog of pain and anger. He was going to take Gentry's insane accusations only so long and then he was going to have to put a stop to them. But what could he do with blurred vision from the stunning blow from Gentry's fist and cracked ribs digging into his gut?

"Lydia," he gasped, calling as loudly as his whistling breath would allow. "Bring Lee."

She was puzzling over that gravelly sound in Ross's voice and his crouching posture when she realized he was hurt and that the man standing over him had a gun. Lydia jumped off the tailgate, holding Lee firmly to her chest, and came running. She hadn't taken time to dress and the tops of her breasts over her chemise shone as gold and pink as the eastern horizon.

That was what Gentry focused on, keeping his pistol still inches beyond Ross's nose. The girl was trash. Lewdness was stamped all over her. Clark had disposed of the beautiful, graceful, lovely Victoria, and taken up with this whore. Russell's runaway wife. Gentry felt a new wrath brewing inside him. That Clark would prefer this trollop to his beloved daughter was an insult that added another dimension to his hatred.

"Stand back," he ordered Lydia as she drew closer to Ross.

She came to an abrupt standstill, clutching Lee to her breasts. "Who are you? What do you want?"

"Lydia, this is Victoria's father. Show him Lee. That's your grandson, Gentry."

"Liar."

"That baby is your grandson. I swear it. Victoria died birthing him."

"It's true," Lydia contributed urgently. "My baby was stillborn. I wet-nursed Lee. Ross didn't marry me until weeks after Victoria had died."

"I figured the two of you would try to foist this baby off as Victoria's to get money from me," Gentry said. He spat into the dirt near Ross's face. "To think you ever touched my daughter makes me sick," he said softly.

"I know that, dammit," Ross ground out. "That no longer bothers me. But for the sake of pride are you going to deny Victoria's son? Your own blood?"

The man didn't so much as glance at the infant. "What kind of fool do you take me for . . . *Clark*?" When Ross's head snapped to attention, Gentry laughed, gloating. "Oh, yes, I know all about you, you goddamn outlaw. I know about this white trash girl too. Quite a touching scene she's playing out here. But I met her husband in town last night. Had a nice chat with Mr. Russell. You, big shot Sonny Clark, are being made a fool of by a couple of hillbillies."

Ross stared blankly at his father-in-law. "Russell?"

"Husband?" Lydia repeated.

"Clancey Russell. He said he had met you a week or so

back. Said you interrupted him and his woman when they were making plans to turn you in so he pretended to want a job."

That his father-in-law had gone stark raving mad was Ross's first thought. Then his eyes found Lydia's and her face revealed the truth. It was colorless, guilt-ridden, fearful. "He was your *husband*?" he asked in disbelief, wanting her to deny it.

"No. Clancey Russell was not my husband," she averred, slowly shaking her head from side to side. Even in death, Clancey was inflicting torment on her. "My stepbrother."

"Godamighty, they are related too," Gentry said scathingly.

"*The* stepbrother?" Ross roared.

Her eyes pleaded for understanding. "Yes."

"Goddammit to hell," Ross cursed. "You knew about me, didn't you? Before I ever told you."

"Yes, but—"

"And you and this stepbrother you claim to hate—"

"I did . . . *do* hate him." She couldn't give away her knowledge of Clancey's death and incriminate Bubba.

"The two of you were plotting to turn me in for a reward."

"No," she protested frantically. "Ross, no. He threatened to tell if I didn't give him the jewelry."

"Jewelry, jewelry? What jewelry?" he asked.

"The jewelry you took from me," Gentry supplied. "Heirlooms of the Gentry family. No doubt you forced Victoria to open the safe behind the painting in the dining room and take it. We had effectively hidden it from the Yankees only to have a thief like you take it from us. I didn't realize Russell knew about it. Probably this woman you claim is your wife told him."

"If it's the jewelry you want, I'll give it to you," Lydia said, taking a step toward Gentry. She would gladly give it to him so he would take that gun off Ross. "Lee . . . ? She lifted the baby up to his grandfather.

He backed away, as though the baby were the devil's child. "Give him to the nigger and go get the jewelry."

Moses took Lee, who was now whimpering with

hunger and the tension that crackled around him. Lydia lifted the hem of her chemise and raced to the wagon, pulled herself inside and took the jewelry from where she had hidden it only hours before. She avoided Ross's accusing eyes as she ran back to Gentry and extended the bag to him.

"Drop it." She tossed the bag onto the ground. "Look at it, Clark. I've caught you with the evidence. That's enough to kill you for."

"I've never seen it before," Ross exclaimed.

"He didn't steal this," Lydia cried. "Victoria brought it with her when they left Tennessee."

"Shut up!" Gentry shouted. "You're not good enough to even speak her name." He grabbed Lydia's arm with his free hand and crammed it against her back, shoving her hand up between her shoulder blades. He spun her around to face Ross.

"Look at her, Clark. This is the kind of woman more suited to you than my Victoria. Look at her, running around in her underclothes without any trace of shame. Did she keep you busy last night as Russell said she would so he could notify us of your whereabouts?"

"No!" Lydia moaned then, both from pain and shame. Clancey was extracting his own brand of revenge. She could ignore Gentry's insults. It was Ross's look of disillusionment that was killing her in the most agonizing way.

"How did you know about that jewelry, Lydia?" His voice was without inflection.

She swallowed, blinking back the wrenching pain of Gentry's hold on her. "Clancey told me. I don't know how he found out. He showed up with wanted posters of you and threatened—"

"When?"

"Right after Luke was killed."

Ross cursed and began to laugh. First it was only deep rumbles in his chest, then he bellowed with it. He knew the pain in his side was making him delirious, but he gave in to the hysteria. "Weeks ago." Had everything she had done been a lie?

His razor-sharp eyes sliced small bleeding incisions across her face. She wet her lips in appeal. "He killed Luke,

Ross, because Luke saw him snooping around in the woods near the train. He was the man who attacked me and shot Winston."

"And you didn't see fit to tell anyone? To tell me?"

"I was afraid he would hurt you and Lee."

"Or you were protecting him," he snapped furiously. He was looking at her breasts as they spilled over the edge of her chemise. She was partially bent, trying to alleviate the pain of Gentry's grip, and that only served to enhance the wanton fullness of her bosom. Her hair was a wild mane encircling her head and flowing around her shoulders. "You've been sneaking around behind my back, meeting him in secret."

"Yes, but—"

"And last night? Was he here last night?"

"No. I mean yes, but—"

"When you begged me to sleep with you, was that to keep me busy? You were his whore, weren't you? He could command you to do anything and you'd do it?"

The words hit her like a cannonball in her chest. The air rushed out of her body at the impact. She stared into cold green eyes she barely recognized. After all they had been to each other in the past few weeks, he could still believe the worst of her.

"Yes," she hissed through her teeth. "Yes, I was his whore. And yes, he was here last night. I offered to go with him. I offered him unrestricted use of me, of my body. I had been his whore to save my mama's life. I would have been his whore for the rest of my life if it would have saved you and Lee. How could being his whore be any worse than being yours? Because that's how you still think of me, isn't it?"

Her face was glowing in the sunlight. The new rays burnished her hair, making it look li¹ flame. Her eyes were radiating a fiery light as she glared down at him. She had never looked more beautiful. All heat and fire and sexuality and pride and courage. God, what courage to confess what she just had. And Ross loved her for all of it.

But before he could say anything, Gentry slung her to the ground. Lydia reached for his gun, but he deflected her hand. Their tussle distracted Gentry for a fraction of a second, time enough for Ross to roll to his side, at the same time yanking his Colt from under the saddle and pulling back the hammer.

Gentry spun around and fired at Ross's moving figure. Lydia screamed, but the bullet plowed into the dust an inch beyond Ross's head. Years of knee-jerk reaction had taught him but one response. He fired the Colt.

Gentry stared stupidly at the flesh wound through the torn and blackened sleeve of his coat. He raised his pistol again.

"I wouldn't." All Ross's conditioned reflexes came into play. He no longer felt the pain in his side from the broken ribs. His vision was no longer blurred. His voice had the brittle ring of ice chips falling onto a mirrored surface. He had missed on purpose the first time. Now his gun was aimed directly at Gentry's forehead. "Drop the gun, Mr. Gentry."

"You killed her. Whether in cold-blooded murder or otherwise, you're responsible for her death. I'm going to kill you for it, even if it costs me my life."

"I don't want to kill you, Mr. Gentry."

The older man laughed nastily. "You'd love to kill me. Because you know I always hated you. I saw right through those polite manners you tried to copy from your betters. You're trash. Always were. Always will be." His bleeding, numbing arm aimed waveringly at Ross. "The world will thank me for eliminating you."

"I don't want to kill you, you sonofabitch!" Ross yelled. "Drop the goddamn gun."

Gentry smiled and his finger tightened on the trigger.

Ross flung his Colt aside to plop with a thud into the dust. "I won't kill you, Gentry. I refuse to. You'll be killing an unarmed man." His green eyes didn't veer from the other man's. If one watched the eyes . . . And Ross knew he was about to be shot.

"Have it your way," Gentry said softly as he squeezed closed his index finger.

"No!" Lydia screamed and catapulted herself in front of Ross.

"Drop the gun!" The order shouted at Gentry came

from the man rearing up on horseback. He had a rifle on his shoulder and was staring down its steely length.

The guns went off simultaneously. Gentry's heart was pierced by a bullet that killed him instantly.

The man who had shot him cursed blasphemously and swung down from his horse before it had come to a complete standstill.

Moses drew the squalling Lee to his chest and muttered, "Lord, Lord," under his breath.

The bullet from Gentry's gun struck Lydia. She felt the searing pain and clutched Ross's shirtfront. She tried to raise her head, to look into his eyes. She longed to see forgiveness, understanding. But she hadn't the strength to lift her head. A black curtain was drawn across her eyes and she saw nothing.

Ross cried her name as she collapsed on him. He felt the warm flow of her blood soaking his chest. "Lydia, Lydia," he called hoarsely, oblivious to everything around him and aware only of her soft weight sprawled lifelessly across him.

He eased her gently onto her back and looked down into her face. It was deathly pale. "No, God, no!" Ross mouthed, though no sound came from his lips.

Was this to be his hell for all the sins he had committed? Loving two women. Losing them both. He had loved Victoria for what she had represented, for what she had taught him. But Lydia, Lydia. She had taught him what it meant to love. To love without qualification. To love not because of, but in spite of.

"Don't die," he pleaded, laying his head on her breasts and listening prayerfully for a heartbeat. "I need you. Don't die." He felt the slightest vapor of breath against his cheek and sobbed thankfully.

A rifle barrel nudged his shoulder. He raised his head. A man he had never seen before was staring down at him. Ross knew the man recognized him as Sonny Clark.

"My name is Majors. I'm a Pinkerton man."

Ross stared back at him, his eyes as steely now as his nerves. The day he had always dreaded had come. He had expected it. One always had to pay. Always. Happiness, even brief snatches of it, demanded a high price.

He looked down at the softly parted lips struggling for each precious breath. Her eyelids were a delicate violet in the morning light. Their translucent frailty touched him with a soul-shattering emotion.

"I'll sign a confession to everything," Ross said softly, still looking down at Lydia. Then the Pinkerton detective was speared by green eyes that had struck terror in the hearts of better men than he. "If you'll save my wife's life."

Chapter Twenty-two

Ross stared at his boots and the grimy floor beneath them. He was as filthy as it was. Unshaved, unwashed, sweat stained. Blood stained. Her blood had left a stiff brownish stain on his shirtfront.

Four days, he thought, swinging his clasped hands down between his knees. Four godforsaken days he had sat in this cell and wondered if she were alive or dead. Where was she, where was Lee? He figured Moses must be taking care of the baby, but he couldn't be sure.

Apparently his ribs had only been cracked and not completely broken. For the first two days he had lain motionless and hoped they would reset themselves. Now they ached occasionally, but the pain they gave him was secondary to his mental anguish.

He had seen no one except the other prisoners, who were usually brought in on drunk and disorderly charges. After they had puked and pissed in the corner, and noisily slept off cheap whiskey, they were released. The fat deputy who brought the meals he couldn't force himself to eat wouldn't tell him anything.

He knew nothing except that a Pinkerton detective and Vance Gentry had discovered who Ross Coleman really was and they had come after him. He would be tried, but the verdict was frightfully predictable. He would be hanged.

He came off the dingy cot and prowled the square room, avoiding the puddles of slime he chose not to identify. Why couldn't he have died three years ago from wounds that should have killed him? Lydia had probably given her life trying to save his. How much more love could a man demand of anyone? And she had died thinking he hated her.

"Coleman."

He spun around. It was the deputy. The man was a pig, both in his lack of cleanliness and behavior. Ross didn't answer him.

He pitched a pair of handcuffs between the bars. Ross caught them midair. "Put 'em on," the deputy directed around a wad of tobacco that eked a brownish drool from either side of his fleshy mouth.

Ross did as he was told. Was that detective finally coming to see him, question him, take his confession? He wouldn't utter a goddamn word until they told him about Lydia. And if she had . . . died, he wouldn't say anything until he was allowed to see her body.

The jailer unlocked the barred door and jerked his head in a silent command that Ross come out. They walked down the narrow hall, the deputy keeping only a few steps behind his prisoner. The air in the outer office, despite its closeness and the summer heat, was considerably better than that in the cell, and Ross drew great quantities of it into his lungs to clear the stench out of his nostrils.

"Come on," the deputy said, clamping Ross's hat on his head. "No funny business," he warned.

He led Ross down the boardwalks of the town. Folks rushing about their business hardly gave the handcuffed man a glance. Apparently Majors hadn't announced who they had in their jail. His name might not be too well-known this far west, but everybody had heard of Frank and Jesse James. The lack of curiosity about him was puzzling.

They walked for several blocks before the fat man said, "Here," and waddled up the stone sidewalk that led to a neat one-story house.

Ross let the man push him through a front door into a hallway with a grandfather clock ticking cozily. "Doc?" the deputy called.

A man came out of a room at the back of the house, closing the door behind him. He tugged his vest over his paunch and came forward, glaring balefully at the deputy from beneath a wild pair of eyebrows. "Thank you, Ernie," the doctor said, brushing past Ross to open the front door in a subtle hint for the deputy to leave. The fat man doffed his hat begrudgingly and left.

The short, balding man stared up into Ross's bearded face. "I'm Doc Hanson." He pointed at the door he had just come through. "Your wife is in there."

Ross's heart dropped to the bottom of his soul like lead. She must be dead. Otherwise they wouldn't have taken him out of jail. If she were alive, they would have eventually let her come to see him.

He drew in a deep, shuddering breath and went toward the door. It was difficult, but he managed to turn the knob even with his hands still shackled in the heavy metal cuffs. He passed through the door and closed it behind him, keeping his back to the room. Slowly he turned and gazed around the breeze-cooled room until he found the bed.

He had expected to find Lydia laid out in her best dress, hands folded across her still chest. Instead there was only a brightly patterned quilt spread over the narrow iron bed and a knitted comforter over the end railing.

His eyes went on a darting search of the unfamiliar room until he saw her sitting in a rocking chair near an open window, staring at him with wide, unblinking eyes. She sat perfectly still. She was neatly dressed in a shirtwaist and skirt. Nothing moved save the hair around her face that the breeze whimsically lifted and let fall on cheeks that were no longer deathly pale, but still pallid.

The Pinkerton man was standing beside her.

He spotted the handcuffs. "That damn fool deputy," he grumbled. Taking a small key from his pocket, he briskly walked across the floor and unlocked the cuffs, letting them fall from Ross's wrists. He caught them and tucked them in his pocket.

"I'm sorry, Mrs. Coleman, for having your husband delivered to you like a common criminal," he said in an almost jovial manner.

Ross thought he had either lost his hearing or was still in the throes of some bizarre dream. Had the man called her Mrs. *Coleman*?

Lydia smiled benignly at the detective. Ross wanted simply to drink up the sight of her, but Majors was speaking to him.

"Of course all of Mr. Gentry's ridiculous charges against you have been dropped."

Ross stared at the man in stunned disbelief. His eyes flashed a million questions as rapidly as Morse code.

Majors cleared his throat gruffly and turned away from those piercing eyes. He didn't want to be reminded that the thing he was about to do was unheard of. It went against every principle he had held dear throughout his career. Things were either black or white, wrong or right. Up until recently he hadn't believed in that gray area, where duty and responsibility were squelched by emotions and gut instinct.

But he had virtually lived with Vance Gentry for the last two months. He hadn't liked the man's dogmatic, unshakable commitment to an idea, whether that idea was true or false. He had seen the man folks knew as Ross Coleman bent over his wife pleading with her not to die. He had spent hours with the girl, probing into her past, asking her about the man she had married under unorthodox circumstances.

He had argued with himself for days, but in the early morning hours of this day, he knew what he was going to do. The rightness of it was dubious and depended entirely on one's point of view, but he was going to do it anyway.

He went to the other window in the room and pulled the curtain aside, ostensibly to enjoy Mrs. Hanson's late summer roses. Actually, it was to keep his back to them.

"The way I see it, Mr. Coleman, was that Gentry felt his daughter had deserted him. He was angry over the two of you sneaking away from him. As a father I can't blame him for feeling the way he did. But it's not a crime for a wife to go off with her husband without notifying her parents."

From over his shoulder, he glanced at them. The man hadn't budged, but was staring at him in wordless suspicion. The woman was looking at her husband. He faced the window again. "I've spent these last few days checking around. Victoria Gentry Coleman died in childbirth. You could have saved yourself a heap of trouble, young man, if you had had her death duly recorded."

Ross's mouth worked uselessly. Was this some kind of trap? For what purpose? The man knew damn good and well who he was. He hazarded an inquiring glance at Lydia. Imperceptibly she shook her head, letting him know she was as much in the dark as he. "The parson who came out to officiate at Victoria's burial assured me he would see to the records."

Majors shook his head. "He didn't, but everyone on that wagon train I've tracked down and talked to confirmed the story your wife, your *current* wife, told me." He turned to face Ross again. "By the way, I'm sorry you had to stay in jail until I could check these things out."

Ross said nothing. Nor did Lydia. She hadn't spoken since he had entered the room. Was she in pain? In shock? Why was she looking at him with that same wariness he had seen in her eyes the first night she had been brought to his wagon to nurse Lee?

Majors took something out of his pocket and tossed it onto the bed. It was the black velvet bag. "Gentry accused you of stealing these pieces of jewelry."

"They belonged to Victoria. I don't want them," Ross said tersely.

If Majors had harbored any doubts up to that point, he was assured then that he was doing the right thing. Sonny Clark wouldn't have openly wept over a wounded woman. Sonny Clark would have been shooting his way out of a sticky situation. Sonny Clark was reputed to have almost destroyed any jail cell unfortunate enough to have him as a guest. Ross Coleman had spent the last few days staring at the walls, silent and seemingly absorbed in grief.

Ross Coleman was a man admired and respected by all those he had traveled with. Justifiably, he could have killed Gentry in self-defense. Yet he hadn't. He had gone docilely, if a bit hostilely, when he was arrested. His main concern had been for his wife. He had asked not one favor for himself, but had pleaded that she be taken to a doctor immediately. He had made no attempts to escape.

Now he was turning down a small fortune in jewelry. No, this man was no longer Sonny Clark. He was Ross Coleman, and Majors was going to let him live in peace. He must be getting sentimental in his old age. But somehow retirement with these two ruined lives on his conscience didn't sound attractive in the least.

"You may not want them, but they rightfully belong to your son, Mr. Coleman. Don't you think you should keep them for him until he's of age?"

Ross nodded slowly. Majors handed the bag to Ross, who awkwardly in turn passed it on to Lydia.

"Mr. Gentry's remains are already on their way back to Tennessee. I wired his lawyer, who telegraphed me back that he would see to the funeral arrangements." Majors coughed behind his hand and paced the area in front of the window before he spoke again. "I've questioned your wife about her deceased stepbrother and—"

"Deceased?"

"Ah, yes, that's right. You couldn't have known about that. I found him dead that morning as I was running to catch up with Gentry. I had told Gentry not to confront you with allegations of theft and kidnapping without my being there. When I woke up and checked his room, I discovered him gone."

Majors pursed his lips when he remembered how angry he had been at that point. He had raced out of the hotel and was headed for the livery stable when he noticed Clancey's body lying in the alley at the side of the hotel. He had asssumed Gentry had killed Russell to prevent the story of his daughter's marriage to Sonny Clark being spread around.

"Russell's murder remains unsolved," he said reflectively. Coleman couldn't have done it. When questioned, Moses had said Coleman had been with him from late afternoon until Gentry woke them the next morning. And the girl? Majors looked at her now. If she had sneaked off and murdered her stepbrother, which he doubted, she would have been justified in doing it.

Lydia sat silently, hoping Majors couldn't read her thoughts. She would never name Clancey's killer. Not even to Ross. Bubba had been willing to keep her secret. She would keep his.

"You ever hear of a gunman named Sonny Clark?" Majors asked suddenly.

Lydia's eyes clashed with Ross's before they both refocused on the detective. Ross let his head bob sharply in affirmation. He would speak nothing aloud until he knew what game Majors was playing.

Lydia's heart was in her throat, pounding.

"I heard he was dead," the detective said slowly, watching Ross's face. "Heard he died a few years back from gunshot wounds he got in a bank robbery. What do you have to say on that theory?"

"He's dead," Ross said unequivocally.

"You're sure of that?"

"Yes."

Still eyeing Ross shrewdly, Majors nodded his head. "If he is, I don't guess he could shed any light on where the James brothers might be holed up right now."

"I swear to God, I don't know anything about that," Ross answered evasively, but truthfully.

All Major's instincts told him the man wasn't lying. "No," he said, coming out of his pensive state. "I don't think you do." He scratched his ear as though what they had been discussing was a topic of minor consequence. "My last official duty as a Pinkerton detective will be to circulate the word that Sonny Clark is dead." He laughed lightly. "I'm sure there will be many lawmen and bounty hunters disappointed to hear that. They won't be collecting a reward off him."

Difficult as it was, both Ross and Lydia remained stoic. Only Ross's Adam's apple slid up and down his throat as he swallowed hard.

Majors went to the door and opened it. "I see no reason to detain you further." He made a broad sweep with his hand to indicate they could leave.

The only other souls who knew of Ross Coleman's real name were dead. Vance Gentry and Clancey Russell.

Madam LaRue would get a letter from Majors telling her that the outlaw had died of gunshot wounds. He would fail to specify a date.

Majors had drilled Moses at length, asking him if he had ever known Mr. Coleman to show signs of violence. The freed slave had vowed that Mr. Coleman was one of the finest men he had ever had the pleasure of knowing. He knew nothing of Coleman's past.

Of course the man was lying. Moses had heard every word Gentry had said that morning. But Majors knew that Moses would go to his grave with the secret intact. Lydia Coleman would never speak of her husband's turbulent past. One only had to see the way she looked at him to know that her love for him went beyond the bounds of normalcy.

She had been helped to her feet by her husband, though no word passed between them. Majors saw the tears of gratitude sparkling in her unusual eyes as she approached him. She chose her words carefully. "You have been very kind. Thank you."

She exited the room, leaving Ross alone with the detective. Ross's eyes bored into those of the Pinkerton man and held them. He opened his mouth, but Majors reached for his hand and halted his words.

"It's best if you don't thank me." A thank-you would be tantamount to a confession. Neither could risk admitting that an unprecedented favor was being granted.

Ross squeezed the man's hand hard in acknowledgment. Then he turned away quickly to join his wife. Howard Majors watched them leave. He smiled wistfully to himself and wondered if he were a demigod or merely an old, soft-hearted fool.

Doctor Hanson drove them to where Moses was camped with their two wagons on the edge of town. They were enthusiastically greeted by him and reunited with Lee, who had been well tended. Lucky and the mares were faring as well as they did under Ross's care. The new milk cow looked none the worse for wear either. After Lydia and

Ross had each thanked the doctor, he returned to town. Ross hitched up the wagons.

They traveled only a few miles that day, following the river which eventually flowed into Ross's land. He had filed his claim in the land office the day he sold his wagon to the Pritchards. Everything was in order for them to assume immediate possession.

Soon after they made camp for the night, Moses tactfully made himself scarce. "I think I'll go downstream a ways and see if I can't catch some fat catfish for our supper." He sensed the unsettled tension between Ross and Lydia, who hadn't spoken a word to each other. Ross had driven the flatbed wagon, Moses the covered one. Lydia had lain in the back of it.

"Thank you, Moses," Ross said as he unhitched the teams. "That sounds good."

"I'll take Lee with me. He can snooze in the shade, and, if he wakes up, I can start teaching him the finer points of fishing."

"If you're sure he won't bother you."

"He won't. We're great friends by now." His dark eyes met Ross's with full understanding. "We'll probably be gone a long time."

Ross finished his chores around the camp, got the fire going, and then treated himself to a bath in the river. He scrubbed relentlessly, washing the stink of the jail off. After wading ashore and pulling on a fresh pair of pants, he shaved off the four days' growth of beard and began to feel truly human again.

He was making his way back to the camp when Lydia stepped onto the tailgate of the Hill wagon. She retreated slightly when she saw him, then determinedly took the steps to the ground. "It's hot in the wagon. I think I'll sit by the water for a spell." She had taken off her shirtwaist, but had left her skirt on. Her feet were bare. Seeing the white gauze bandage wrapped around her shoulder was a heart-twisting reminder of their near tragedy. It left Ross speechless.

She went past him, not meeting his eyes. When he caught up with her, she was sitting on the sloping grassy bank of the river, staring into the gently flowing water. Light from the setting sun poured over her like molten gold. She looked almost too beautiful, too ethereal, to touch. Almost.

Ross sank down beside her. After a long, silent moment, he turned to her and gently touched the bandage with his finger. "Why did you do it, Lydia?"

"Do what?" she asked huskily. When he had come into the room at the doctor's house looking gaunt, underfed, haunted, and dirty, she had longed to jump from her chair and fling herself into his arms. But she had remembered the disgusted look on his face when Gentry had forced him to see her as she truly was. Was he even now going to make her repeat her motivations for being involved with Clancey?

"Why did you step between me and that bullet?"

She raised her head. Their eyes melted together. Her lips barely moved as she whispered. "Because I love you. And I would have done anything to save you."

"Even if it meant going back with Russell?"

A spasm of revulsion altered her face momentarily, but there was no hesitation in her eyes as she softly declared, "Even that."

"Lydia." Her name was a broken cry across his lips as he enfolded her in his arms and dropped his head into the curve of her neck. "I thought you were dead. They told me nothing. God, the agony I went through, thinking that you had sacrificed your life for mine."

Her hands were on his hair, still damp from his bath. She smoothed it with gentling hands, afraid to believe what she was hearing.

He took her face between his hands and tilted it back. His thumbs lightly raked her lips. "I thought I had lost you before you knew how much I loved you."

"Ross!" she exclaimed. "I thought you despised me. I saw your eyes. Your face—"

"I'm sorry, I'm sorry," he said as he rained hot, urgent kisses over her face. "For a moment I did, but then I realized what it had cost you to say that you would go back with Russell. I knew how much you loathed him. That's when I knew how much you must love me."

He kissed her then. His hand wrapped around the back of her neck and pulled her toward him. He slanted his mouth over hers, nuzzling with his lips and moustache before his tongue plunged recklessly into her mouth and wandered at will.

When at last they pulled apart, breathless, she cradled his head between her hands and peered into his eyes. "I'm sorry you had to find out about Victoria taking the jewelry. I was trying to keep Mr. Gentry from shooting you or I never would have said that."

He gently rubbed her earlobes between his thumbs and index fingers while her hair teased the backs of his hands. "She didn't have faith in me, Lydia. She didn't trust me to take care of her."

"I'm certain she did. She was just accustomed to having nice things." He didn't think so, but he nodded sadly. "I know you loved her, Ross, and it's all right."

He studied her mouth and wondered if he was ever going to tire of tasting it. No, he thought. "I loved Victoria for what she did for me. I'll always love her because of Lee. But," he added significantly, brushing his lips over hers, "you are my love. My dearest love that I'll go on loving and needing every day of my life."

She barely had time to whisper his name before his lips claimed hers once again. As the kiss itensified, they gradually reclined onto the cool, green grass beneath them. When his lips finally left hers, they lay facing each other. His index finger followed the lacy border of her chemise and elicited pangs of desire that trilled through her.

"Why do you think he did it, Lydia?" His hand stilled.

Her fingers, which had been adoring the hard planes of his face, rested as well. "I don't know."

"For four days I didn't know if you were dead or alive. I kept thinking about how you looked lying there bleeding as they dragged me away from you. God." He pressed his face into the valley between her breasts. "If Majors put me through the hell of not knowing what had happened to you, why did he let me go?"

She threaded her fingers through the midnight hair. "I think he saw that you weren't the man you used to be, that you were completely changed. But he had to make sure. He came to the conclusion that it wasn't fair to make Ross Coleman pay for the sins of Sonny Clark."

"And what of the sins of Ross Coleman? Can you ever forgive me for doubting you?"

Her smile was a shade mischievous. "If you'll love me now."

His eyes sparked with suppressed passion given vent. "We can't. I'll hurt you." He kissed the bandage.

"It's only a flesh wound. The doctor said I fainted more from shock than from the gunshot." She saw the pain in his eyes and misinterpreted it. "It's ugly. I'll be scarred," she said self-consciously.

He groaned and kissed the upper curves of her breasts. "That beautiful scar will always remind me of your love."

"Even when we're fighting, as we're known to do?"

"Even then. Hell, I've enjoyed every one of our fights. You excite me." He raised his head and grinned down into her face. "And if we start comparing scars, you've got a few to go to catch up with me."

His hands went to the ribbon on her chemise and pulled free the bow. "You're sure you feel well enough?"

"Yes," she said dreamily as she helped him with the tiny buttons and eased the garment off her shoulders.

When she was once again lying relaxed, he looked down at her breasts. "From one time to the next I forget how gorgeous you are. Each time is like discovering a treasure."

He filled his hands with her, caressed, kneaded. The pads of his fingers played her nipples into tight response. Ducking his head, he took one in his mouth and suckled gently.

"You still taste milky. That first night you were brought to me, I remember seeing this"—his finger outlined the areola—"pearly with your milk. I wanted you even then. God forgive me, but I did."

"Ross, please."

He answered the entreaty in her voice and stood to take off his pants. She surprised him by rising to her knees in front of him. She had no compunction about making love in the open. She had heard Moses say that he and Lee would be gone for a long while.

Looking up at Ross with smoldering amber eyes, she placed her hands on his stomach. "I'll take them off for you."

Her mouth swept over his hair-whorled navel. His fingers closed around her head as her name trembled on his lips. She undid the buttons of his pants one by one, her lips delicately greeting what was slowly revealed. It was that elusive touch of her breath, her lips, her tongue, that drove him mad with mounting passion.

Her palms rubbed up and down the backs of his thighs, then over his hips. She lowered the pants with one sustained stroke downward over the taut muscles of his buttocks. His hard perfection was both a bold statement of his love and a beautiful representation of masculinity. She kissed him with tender reverence.

"Ah, my love." He groaned loudly as he freed himself of the breeches. He eased her away and back onto the grass. Kneeling beside her, he unfastened her skirt, untied her petticoat, and peeled them and her other clothing down her legs.

He smiled down on her. Her hair was spread out behind her. A rainbow of sunset colors painted her body with vermilion, gold, and lavender. The natural glow of her flesh gave the spectrum a special radiance. The starkly white bandage did not diminish the excellence. Rather, it embellished it. He lay down beside her and took her in his arms, turning her to face him with her injured shoulder uppermost.

"You are so very beautiful," he said. "You love me well, Lydia. It now has meaning." He touched her breasts, kissed them, licked her nipples until they shone wetly. Then his fingers drifted through the russet nest of hair and lingered. Tenderly his hand prized her thighs apart.

He lowered himself and kissed her stomach, then whisked his mouth over that precious mound of femininity.

His lips honored the very threshold of her womanhood with a fervent kiss. Then he loved her thoroughly with an imperious tongue determined to give her pleasure and demonstrate his love.

"Ross, Ross," she gasped brokenly and reached for him.

He climbed his way back up to face her and lifted her thigh over his hip. "Don't hurt yourself," he instructed softly. "Let me do it." With one smooth projection he imbedded himself inside her. He lovingly hugged her to his chest and delved deeper with each stroke. She rocked her hips against his belly and when he murmured his supreme pleasure, she repeated the evocative movement.

The tumult came to her as it always did, though each time was unique. First upon her was that sensation of being stroked with a velvet glove inside and out, all over at once. Then she was plunged headlong into a state of mindlessness where only her senses ruled. Next came that shower of light with the burst of liquid heat from Ross's loins. It rushed into her, flooding her womb, her whole body, with love. Most sublime of all was that weightless glide back into his embrace where she felt the security of his love.

"I love you," she whispered against his chest, where the hair was now curled and damp. She kissed the puckered scar above his left breast.

"I love you too. You freed me from the past."

She sighed. "And me, Ross. And me. We have only the future now."

They lay, his body still nestled in hers, for a long time. Fireflies darted like tiny shooting stars in the gathering dusk. The red disk of the sun hung suspended on the western horizon as though reluctant to leave the day behind. The sky overhead darkened to a vivid indigo. Sunset closed around them and they welcomed it.

And from this day, dawn would be just as sweet.